'I loved *The Authenticity Project*. It has such an intriguing premise, wonderful characters and is utterly truthful about the lies that we all tell. It's a clever, uplifting book that entertains and makes you think.'
Sophie Kinsella

'One of the best books I've read in a long time. Original, engaging and unforgettable.'
Sarah Morgan

'A quirky cast of characters you can't help but root for.'
Woman & Home

'Beautifully written, thought provoking and uplifting, *The Authenticity Project* is a warm and endearing tale about truth, friendship and the power of connection. Pooley's characters will stay with you long after you turn the final page. It was a joy to read.'
Mike Gayle

'It's full of life's truths, funny, poignant and ultimately uplifting. I thoroughly enjoyed it.'
Fanny Blake

'*The Authenticity Project* cracks the facades that people present to the world and shows what happens when you're willing to share your true self. This is a story of love, of community, of found family, and of forgiveness. A beautiful book with a poignant message, perfect for our time.'
Jill Santopolo

www.penguin.co.uk

The Authenticity Project

Clare Pooley

BANTAM PRESS

TRANSWORLD PUBLISHERS
61–63 Uxbridge Road, London W5 5SA
www.penguin.co.uk

Transworld is part of the Penguin Random House group of companies
whose addresses can be found at global.penguinrandomhouse.com

Penguin
Random House
UK

First published in Great Britain in 2020 by Bantam Press
an imprint of Transworld Publishers

A CIP catalogue record for this book
is available from the British Library.

ISBNS 9781787631793 (cased)
9781787631786 (tpb)

Typeset in 11.25/15.75 pt Sabon LT Std by Jouve (UK), Milton Keynes
Printed and bound in Great Britain by Clays Ltd, Elcograf S.p.A.

Penguin Random House is committed to a sustainable
future for our business, our readers and our planet. This book
is made from Forest Stewardship Council® certified paper.

MIX
Paper from
responsible sources
FSC
www.fsc.org   FSC® C018179

1 3 5 7 9 10 8 6 4 2

For my father, Peter Pooley,
who taught me to love words

Ring the bells that still can ring
Forget your perfect offering
There is a crack in everything
That's how the light gets in.

LEONARD COHEN

Monica

She had tried to return the book. As soon as she realized it had been left behind, she'd picked it up and rushed after its extraordinary owner. But he'd gone. He moved surprisingly swiftly for someone so old. Maybe he really didn't want to be found.

It was a plain, pale-green exercise book, like the one Monica had carried around with her at school, filled with details of homework assignments. Her friends had covered their books with graffiti of hearts, flowers and the names of their latest crushes, but Monica was not a doodler. She had too much respect for good stationery.

On the front cover were three words, beautifully etched in copperplate script:

The Authenticity Project

In smaller writing, in the bottom corner, was the date: *October 2018.* Perhaps, thought Monica, there would be an address, or at least a name, on the inside so she could return it. Although it was physically unassuming, it had an air of significance about it.

She turned over the front cover. There were only a few paragraphs on the first page.

How well do you know the people who live near you? How well do they know you? Do you even know the names of your neighbours? Would you realize if they were in trouble, or hadn't left their house for days?

Everyone lies about their lives. What would happen if you shared the truth instead? The one thing that defines you, that makes everything else about you fall into place? Not on the internet, but with those real people around you?

Perhaps nothing. Or maybe telling that story would change your life, or the life of someone you've not yet met. That's what I want to find out.

There was more on the next page, and Monica was dying to read on, but it was one of the busiest times of the day in the café, and she knew it was crucial not to fall behind schedule. That way madness lay. She tucked the book into the space alongside the till with the spare menus and flyers from various suppliers. She'd read it later, when she could concentrate properly.

Monica stretched out on the sofa in her flat above the café, a large glass of Sauvignon Blanc in one hand and the abandoned exercise book in the other. The questions she'd read that morning had been niggling away at her, demanding answers. She'd spent all day talking to people, serving them coffees and cakes, chatting about the weather and the latest celebrity gossip. But when had she last told anyone anything about herself that *really mattered*? And what did she actually know about them, with the exception of whether they liked milk in their coffee, or sugar with their tea? She opened the book to the second page.

My name is Julian Jessop. I am seventy-nine years old, and I am an artist. For the past fifty-seven years I've lived in Chelsea Studios, on the Fulham Road.

Those are the basic facts, but here is the truth: I AM LONELY.

I often go for days without talking to anyone. Sometimes, when I do have to speak (because someone's called me up about payment protection insurance, for example), I find that my voice comes out in a croak because it's curled up and died in my throat from neglect.

Age has made me invisible. I find this especially hard, because I was always looked at. Everyone knew who I was. I didn't have to introduce myself, I would just stand in a doorway while my name worked its way around the room in a chain of whispers, pursued by a number of surreptitious glances.

I used to love lingering at mirrors, and would walk slowly past shop windows, checking the cut of my jacket or the wave in my hair. Now, if my reflection sneaks up on me, I barely recognize myself. It's ironic that Mary, who would have happily accepted the

*inevitability of ageing, died at the relatively young age
of sixty, and yet I'm still here, forced to watch myself
gradually crumble away.*

   *As an artist, I watched people. I analysed their
relationships, and I noticed there is always a balance of
power. One partner is more loved, and the other more
loving. I had to be the most loved. I realize now that I
took Mary for granted, with her ordinary, wholesome,
pink-cheeked prettiness and her constant thoughtfulness
and dependability. I only learned to appreciate her after
she was gone.*

Monica paused to turn the page and take a mouthful of
wine. She wasn't sure that she liked Julian very much,
although she felt rather sorry for him. She suspected he'd
choose dislike over pity. She read on.

   *When Mary lived here, our little cottage was always
filled with people. The local children ran in and out,
as Mary plied them with stories, advice, fizzy pop
and Monster Munch. My less successful artist friends
constantly turned up unannounced for dinner, along
with the latest of my artist's models. Mary put on a
good show of welcoming the other women, so perhaps
only I noticed they were never offered chocolates with
their coffee.*

   *We were always busy. Our social life revolved
around the Chelsea Arts Club, and the bistros and
boutiques of the King's Road and Sloane Square. Mary
worked long hours as a midwife, and I crossed the*

country, painting the portraits of people who thought themselves worth recording for posterity.

Every Friday evening since the late sixties, at 5 p.m. we'd walk into the nearby Brompton Cemetery which, since its four corners connected Fulham, Chelsea, South Kensington and Earl's Court, was a convenient meeting point for all our friends. We'd plan our weekend on the grave of Admiral Angus Whitewater. We didn't know the Admiral, he just happened to have an impressive horizontal slab of black marble over his last resting place which made a great table for drinks.

In many ways, I died alongside Mary. I ignored all the telephone calls and the letters. I let the paint dry solid on the palette and, one unbearably long night, destroyed all my unfinished canvases; ripped them into multi-coloured streamers, then diced them into confetti with Mary's dressmaking scissors. When I did finally emerge from my cocoon, about five years later, neighbours had moved, friends had given up, my agent had written me off, and that's when I realized I had become unnoticeable. I had reverse metamorphosed from a butterfly into a caterpillar.

I still raise a glass of Mary's favourite Baileys Irish Cream at the Admiral's grave every Friday evening, but now it's just me and the ghosts of times past.

That's my story. Please feel free to chuck it in the recycling. Or you might decide to tell your own truth in these pages, and pass my little book on. Maybe you'll find it cathartic, as I did.

What happens next is up to you.

Monica

She Googled him, obviously. Julian Jessop was described by Wikipedia as a portrait painter who had enjoyed a flurry of notoriety in the sixties and seventies. He'd been a student of Lucian Freud at the Slade. The two of them had, so the rumours went, traded insults (and, the implication was, women) over the years. Lucian had the advantage of much greater fame, but Julian was younger by seventeen years. Monica thought of Mary, exhausted after a long shift delivering other women's babies, wondering where her husband had gone. She sounded like a bit of a doormat, to be honest. Why hadn't she just left him? There were, she reminded herself, as she tried to do often, worse things than being single.

One of Julian's self-portraits had hung for a brief period in the National Portrait Gallery, in an exhibition titled *The London School of Lucian Freud*. Monica clicked on the image to enlarge it, and there he was, the man she'd seen in her café yesterday morning, but all smoothed out, like a raisin turned back into a grape. Julian Jessop, about thirty years old, slicked-back blond hair, razor-sharp cheekbones, slightly sneering mouth and those penetrating blue eyes. When he'd looked at her yesterday it had felt like he was rummaging around in her soul. A little disconcerting when you're trying to discuss the various merits of a blueberry muffin versus millionaire's shortbread.

Monica checked her watch. 4.50 p.m.

'Benji, can you hold the shop for half an hour or so?' she asked her barista. Barely pausing to wait for his nod in response, she pulled on her coat. Monica scanned the tables as she walked through the café, pausing to pick up a large crumb of red velvet cake from table twelve. How had that been overlooked? As she walked out on to the Fulham Road, she flicked it towards a pigeon.

Monica rarely sat on the top deck of the bus. She prided herself on her adherence to health and safety regulations, and climbing the stairs of a moving vehicle seemed an unnecessary risk to take. But in this instance, she needed the vantage point.

Monica watched the blue dot on Google Maps move slowly along the Fulham Road towards Chelsea Studios. The bus stopped at Fulham Broadway, then carried on towards Stamford Bridge. The huge, modern mecca of the Chelsea Football Club loomed ahead and there, in its shadow and sandwiched improbably between the two separate entrances for the home and away fans, was a tiny, perfectly formed village of studio houses and cottages, behind an innocuous wall that Monica must have walked past hundreds of times.

Grateful for once for the slow-moving traffic, Monica

tried to work out which of the houses was Julian's. One stood slightly alone and looked a little worse for wear, rather like Julian himself. She'd bet the day's takings, not something to do lightly given her economic circumstances, on that being the one.

Monica jumped off at the next stop and turned almost immediately left, into Brompton Cemetery. The light was low, casting long shadows, and there was an autumnal chill to the air. The cemetery was one of Monica's favourite places – a timeless oasis of calm in the city. She loved the ornate gravestones – a last show of one-upmanship. *I'll see your marble slab with its fancy biblical quotation and raise you a life-sized Jesus on the cross.* She loved the stone angels, many now missing vital body parts, and the old-fashioned names on the Victorian gravestones – Ethel, Mildred, Alan. When did people stop being called Alan? Come to think of it, did anyone call their baby Monica any more? Even back in 1981 her parents had been outliers in eschewing names like Emily, Sophie and Olivia. Monica: a dying moniker. She could picture the credits on the cinema screen: *The Last of the Monicas.*

As she walked briskly past the graves of the fallen soldiers and the White Russian émigrés, she could sense the sheltering wildlife – the grey squirrels, urban foxes and the jet-black ravens – guarding the graves like the souls of the dead.

Where was the Admiral? Monica headed towards the left, looking out for an old man clutching a bottle of Baileys Irish Cream. She wasn't, she realized, sure why. She didn't want to speak to Julian, at least not yet. She suspected that approaching him directly would run the risk of embarrassing him. She didn't want to start off on the wrong foot.

Monica headed towards the north end of the cemetery, pausing only briefly, as she always did, at the grave of Emmeline Pankhurst, to give a silent nod of thanks. She looped round at the top and was halfway back down the other side, walking along a less-used path, when she noticed a movement to her right. There, sitting (somewhat sacrilegiously) on an engraved marble tombstone, was Julian, glass in hand.

Monica walked on past, keeping her head down so as not to catch his eye. Then, as soon as he was gone, about ten minutes later, she doubled back so that she could read the words on the gravestone.

ADMIRAL ANGUS WHITEWATER
OF PONT STREET
DIED 5 JUNE 1963, AGED 74
RESPECTED LEADER, BELOVED HUSBAND
AND FATHER, AND LOYAL FRIEND

ALSO, BEATRICE WHITEWATER
DIED 7 AUGUST 1964, AGED 69

She bristled at the fact that the Admiral got several glowing adjectives after his name, whereas his wife just got a date and a space for eternity under her husband's tombstone.

Monica stood for a while, enveloped in the silence of the cemetery, imagining a group of beautiful young people, with Beatles haircuts, mini-skirts and bell-bottom trousers, arguing and joking with each other, and suddenly felt rather alone.

Julian

Julian wore his solitude and loneliness like old, ill-fitting shoes. He was used to them, in many ways they had grown comfortable, but over time they were bending him out of shape, causing calluses and bunions that would never go away.

It was 10 a.m., so Julian was walking down the Fulham Road. For five years or so after Mary, he often didn't get out of bed and day morphed seamlessly into night, the weeks losing their pattern. Then he'd discovered that routines were crucial. They created buoys he could cling to to keep himself afloat. At the same time every morning, he went out and walked the local streets for an hour, picking up any supplies he needed on the way. His list today read:

Eggs
Milk (1 pint)
Butterscotch-flavoured Angel Delight, if poss

(he was finding Angel Delight more and more difficult to track down)

And since today was a Saturday, he would buy a fashion magazine. This week was *Vogue*'s turn. His favourite.

Sometimes, if the newsagent wasn't too busy, they would discuss the latest headlines, or the weather. On those days, Julian felt almost like a fully functioning member of society, one with acquaintances who knew his name, and opinions that mattered. Once, he'd even booked an appointment at the dentist, just so he could pass the time of day with someone. After spending the whole appointment with his mouth open, unable to speak as Mr Patel was doing goodness knows what with a selection of metal instruments and a tube that made a ghastly sucking noise, he realized this was not a clever tactic. He'd left with a lecture on gum hygiene ringing in his ears, and the resolution not to return for as long as possible. If he lost his teeth, so be it. He'd lost everything else.

Julian paused to look in through the window of Monica's Café, which was already filled with customers. He'd walked this road for so many years that in his mind, he could picture the various reincarnations of this particular shop, like peeling back layers of old wallpaper when you're redecorating a room. Back in the sixties it was the Eel and Pie Shop until eel fell out of favour and it became a record shop. In the eighties it was a video rental store and then, until a few years ago, a sweet shop. Eels, vinyl records and VHS tapes – all consigned to the dustbin of history. Even sweets were now being demonized, blamed for the fact that children were getting larger and larger. Surely it wasn't the fault of the sweets? It was the children to blame, or their mothers.

He'd definitely chosen the right place to leave The

Authenticity Project. He liked the fact that he'd ordered tea with milk and not been asked all sorts of complicated questions about what specific type of leaf he wanted and what sort of milk. It came in a proper china cup, and no one demanded to know his name. Julian's name was accustomed to being signed at the bottom of canvases. It did not sit comfortably scrawled on a takeaway cup, like they'd done in Starbucks. He shuddered at the memory.

He'd sat in a soft, scarred leather armchair in the far corner of Monica's, in an area lined with bookshelves that he'd heard her call The Library. In a world where everything seemed to be electronic and paper was a rapidly disappearing medium, Julian had found The Library, where the smell of old books mingled with the aroma of freshly ground coffee, wonderfully nostalgic.

Julian wondered what had happened to the little notebook he'd left there. He often felt like he was slowly disappearing without trace. One day, in the not too distant future, his head would finally slip under the water and he'd leave barely a ripple behind. Through that book, at least one person would see him – properly. And writing it had been a comfort, like loosening the laces on those uncomfortable shoes, letting his feet breathe a bit more easily.

He walked on.

Hazard

It was a Monday evening, and getting late, but Timothy Hazard Ford, known to everyone as Hazard, was avoiding going home. He knew from experience that the only way to escape the comedown after a weekend was to just keep on going. He'd begun pushing the start of the week further and further back, and bringing the weekend further forward until they almost met in the middle. There was a brief interlude of horror at around Wednesday, and then he was off again.

Hazard had been unable to persuade any of his work colleagues to hit the City bars that evening, so instead he'd headed back to Fulham, and stopped off in his local wine bar. He scanned the sparse crowd for anyone he knew. He spotted a reed-thin blonde, her legs entwined round a high stool and her torso leaning over the bar, looking like a glamorous bendy straw. He was pretty sure that she was the gym buddy of a girl his mate Jake used to go out with. He had no idea what her name was, but she was the only person available to have a drink with, and that made her, at this moment, his very best friend.

Hazard walked over, wearing the smile he reserved for exactly this sort of occasion. Some sixth sense caused her to turn towards him and she grinned and waved. Bingo. It worked every time.

Her name, it turned out, was Blanche. Stupid name, thought Hazard, and he should know. He poured himself lazily on to the stool next to hers and grinned and nodded as she introduced him to her group of friends whose names floated into the air around him like bubbles, then popped, leaving no impression at all. Hazard was not interested in what they called themselves, only their staying power and, possibly, their morals. The fewer the better.

Hazard slipped easily into his usual routine. He took a roll of banknotes out of his pocket and bought a showy round, upgrading requests of glasses to bottles, and wine to champagne. He reeled out a few of his well-tested anecdotes. He plundered the long list of his acquaintances for mutual ones, and then spread, possibly even invented, a flurry of salacious gossip.

The group coalesced around Hazard in the way it always did, but gradually, as the large station clock on the wall behind the bar ticked past the hour, the crowd thinned out. *Gotta go, it's only Monday*, they said, or *Big day tomorrow*, or *Need to recover from the weekend, you know how it is*. Eventually, only Hazard and Blanche were left and it was just 9 p.m. Hazard could sense Blanche getting ready to leave and felt a rising sense of panic.

'Hey, Blanche, it's still early. Why don't you come back to

mine?' he said, resting his hand on her forearm in a way that suggested everything yet, crucially, promised nothing.

'Sure. Why not?' she replied, as he knew she would.

The revolving door of the bar spat them out on to the street. Hazard put his arm around Blanche, crossed the road and strode down the pavement, not noticing or caring that they were occupying its whole width.

He didn't see the small brunette standing in front of him like a traffic obstruction until it was too late. He barrelled into her, then realized that she'd been holding a glass of red wine which was now dripping rather comically off her face and, more importantly, was spreading like a knife wound over his Savile Row shirt.

'Oh, for fuck's sake,' he said, glaring at the culprit.

'Hey, you walked into me!' she replied in a voice cracking with indignation. A drop of wine trembled at the end of her nose like a reluctant skydiver, then fell.

'Well, what on earth do you think you were doing just standing in the middle of a pavement with a glass of wine?' he yelled back at her. 'Can't you drink in a bar like a normal person?'

'Come on, leave it, let's go,' said Blanche, giggling in a way that made his nerve ends jangle.

'Stupid bitch,' said Hazard to Blanche, keeping his voice low so the stupid bitch in question wouldn't hear. Blanche giggled again.

Several thoughts collided when Hazard was woken by his strident alarm. One: *I can't have had more than three hours' sleep.* Two: *I feel even worse today than I did yesterday, what on earth was I thinking?* And three: *there's a blonde in my bed who I do not want to deal with and whose name I can't remember.*

Luckily, Hazard had been in this position before. He slammed off the alarm while the girl was still asleep, mouth open like a Japanese sex doll, and carefully picked up her arm by the wrist, removing it from his chest. Her hand dangled down like a dead fish. He placed it carefully on the rumpled, sweaty sheets. She appeared to have left so much of her face on his pillow – the red of her lips, black of her eyes and ivory of her skin – that he was surprised she had any left. He eased himself out of bed, wincing as his brain clattered against his skull like a ball in a game of bagatelle. He walked over to the chest of drawers in the corner of the room and there, just as he'd hoped, was a scrap of paper with a message scribbled on it: HER NAME IS BLANCHE. God, he was good at this.

Hazard showered and dressed as quickly and as quietly as he could, found a clean piece of paper and wrote a note:

Dear Blanche, you looked too peaceful and beautiful to wake. Thanks for last night. You were awesome. Make sure you close the front door properly when you leave. Call me.

Had she been awesome? Since he had virtually no memory of events after around 10 p.m. when his dealer had shown up (even quicker than usual on account of it being a Monday), it hardly mattered. He wrote his mobile number at the bottom, carefully transposing two of the digits, in order to avoid it being at all useful, and left the note on the pillow next to his unwelcome guest. He hoped there'd be no trace of her when he returned.

He walked to the tube station on autopilot. He was, despite the fact that it was October, wearing sunglasses to protect his eyes from the weak glare of the new day. He paused as he reached the spot of his collision last night. He was pretty sure he could see a few splatters of blood-red wine still on the pavement, like the remnants of a mugging. An unwelcome vision floored him: a feisty, pretty brunette, glaring at him as if she really, really hated him. Women never looked at him like that. Hazard didn't like being hated.

Then a thought struck him with the vicious sideswipe of an inconvenient truth: *he hated himself too. Right down to the smallest molecule, the tiniest atom, the most microscopic subatomic particle.*

Something had to change. Actually, *everything* had to change.

Monica

Monica had always loved numbers. She loved their logic, their predictability. She found making one side of an equation balance with the other immensely satisfying, solving x and proving y. But the numbers on the paper in front of her now would not behave. No matter how many times she added up the figures in the left-hand column (income), they wouldn't stretch to cover the total in the right (outgoings).

Monica thought back to her days as a corporate lawyer, when adding up the numbers was a chore, but never something to keep her awake at night. Every hour she spent poring over the small print on some contract, or leafing through endless statutes, she'd bill the client two hundred and fifty pounds. She'd have to sell *one hundred* medium-sized cappuccinos to make the same.

Why had she allowed herself to make such a monumental life change with such alacrity, and for such emotional reasons? She who found it difficult to choose a sandwich filling without running through a mental list of pros and cons, comparing price, nutritional values and calorie counts.

Monica had tried every café on the commute between her flat and her office. There were the soulless ones, the tired and grubby ones and the identikit, mass-produced chain ones. Every time she handed over money for an overpriced, mediocre takeaway coffee she'd picture her ideal café. There would be no brushed concrete, moulded plastic, exposed pipework or industrial-style lamps and tables; rather it would feel like being invited into someone's home. There would be comfy, mismatched armchairs, eclectic art on the walls, newspapers and books. Books everywhere, not just for show, but ones you could pick up, read and take home with you, so long as you left another one in its place. The barista wouldn't ask your name in order to misspell it on your cup, he (or she, Monica added quickly) would know it already. They'd ask after your kids and remember the name of your cat.

Then, she'd been walking down the Fulham Road and noticed that the dusty old sweet shop, which had been there for ever, had finally closed. A large board on its front announced TO LET. Some local wag had painted a large I in between the letters O and L.

Every time Monica walked past the vacant shop she could hear her mother's voice. In those last few weeks, the ones that smelled of disease and decay and were punctuated by the constant electronic beeps of medical machinery, she'd urgently tried to impart decades' worth of wisdom to her daughter, before it was too late. *Listen to me, Monica. Write it down, Monica. Don't forget, Monica. Emmeline*

Pankhurst didn't chain herself to those railings so we could spend our lives as a tiny cog in someone else's wheel. Be your own boss. Create something. Employ people. Be fearless. Do something you really love. Make it all worthwhile. So, she had done it.

Monica wished she'd been able to name the café after her mother, but she was called Charity, and it seemed like a really bad business decision to give a café a name that implied no need to pay. Things, as it turned out, were hard enough.

Just because this café was her dream didn't mean anyone else would necessarily share it. Or, at least, not enough of them to cover her costs, and she couldn't keep making up the shortfall for ever; the bank wouldn't let her. Her head was throbbing. She walked over to the bar and poured the remainder of a bottle of red wine into a large glass.

Being the boss was all very well, she told her mother, inside her head, and she loved her café, the essence of which had seeped into her bones, but it was lonely. She missed the office gossip around the water cooler, she missed the camaraderie forged over pizza during late-night working sessions, she even found herself remembering fondly those ridiculous team bonding days, the office jargon and impenetrable three-letter acronyms. She loved her team at the café, but there was always a slight distance between them, because she was responsible for their livelihoods, and right now she couldn't even manage her own.

She was reminded of the questions that man – Julian – had asked in the notebook he'd left on this very table. She'd approved of his choice. Monica couldn't help herself judging people by where in her café they decided to sit. *How well do you know the people who live near you? How well do they know you?*

She thought of all the people who'd come in and out today, the bell ringing jauntily with each arrival and departure. They were all connected, more than ever before, to thousands of people, friends on social media, friends of friends. Yet did they, like her, feel like they had no one they could actually talk to? Not about the latest celebrity eviction from some house, or island, or jungle, but about the important things – the things that keep you awake at night. Like numbers that wouldn't obey your command.

Monica shuffled her papers back into their file and pulled out her phone, loading up Facebook and scrolling through. There was still no sign of Duncan, the man she'd been dating until a few weeks ago, on her social media. She'd been ghosted. Duncan, the vegan who'd refused to eat *avocados* because the farmers exploited bees in their pollination, but who thought it perfectly acceptable to have sex with her and then just *disappear*. He cared more about the sensitivities of a *bee* than he did her.

She kept scrolling, despite knowing this would not be a comfort, more a form of mild self-harm. Hayley had changed her relationship status to 'engaged'. Whoop whoop. Pam had posted a status about her life with three kids, a boast thinly and inexpertly disguised as self-deprecation, and Sally had shared her baby scan picture – twelve weeks.

Baby scans. What was the point in sharing those? They all looked the same, and none of them resembled an actual child, more like a weather map predicting an area of high pressure over northern Spain. And yet, every time Monica saw a new one it stopped her breath and floored her with a wave of yearning and a humiliating stab of envy. She felt, sometimes, like an old Ford Fiesta, broken down on the hard shoulder, while everyone sailed past her in the fast lane.

Someone had left a copy of *HELLO!* on a table today; it screamed a headline about a Hollywood actress's 'baby joy' at forty-three. Monica had scanned the pages during her coffee break, looking for clues as to how she'd done it. IVF? Egg donation? Had she frozen her eggs years ago? Or had it happened easily? How much time did her ovaries have left? Were they already packing their suitcases for a relaxing retirement on the Costa Brava?

Monica picked up her glass of wine and walked around the café turning off all the lights and straightening any errant chairs or tables. She went out on to the street – keys in one hand, glass in the other, locked the café door and turned to unlock the door to her flat above.

Then, out of nowhere, a large bloke, towing a blonde like a motorbike's sidecar, careered into her so hard that she was momentarily winded, and the glass of wine she was holding erupted, all over her face and his shirt. She could feel rivulets of Rioja coursing down her nose and dripping off her chin. She waited for his abject apology.

'Oh, for fuck's sake,' he said. Monica felt a heat rising from her chest, making her face flush and her jaw clench.

'Hey, you walked into me!' she protested.

'Well, what on earth do you think you were doing just standing in the middle of a pavement with a glass of wine?' he said. 'Can't you drink in a bar like a normal person?' His face, with its perfectly symmetrical planes, would have been classically handsome, but it was split by the ugly gash of a sneer. The blonde pulled him away, giggling inanely.

'Stupid bitch,' she heard him say, deliberately pitching his voice just loud enough for her to hear.

Monica let herself into her flat. *Honey, I'm home,* she said, as she always did, silently and to no one, and thought for a minute she was going to cry. She put the empty glass down on the draining board of her kitchenette, and wiped the wine off her face with a tea towel. She was desperate to speak to someone, but she couldn't think who to call. Her friends were all caught up in their own busy lives, and wouldn't want her inflicting her misery on their evenings. There was no point calling her dad, since Bernadette, her stepmother, who saw her as an inconvenient backstory to her new husband's life, acted as gatekeeper, and would no doubt announce that her father was busy writing and couldn't be disturbed.

Then Monica saw, sitting on the coffee table where she'd left it a few days ago, the pale-green notebook labelled *The Authenticity Project*. She picked it up and turned again to the first page. *Everyone lies about their lives. What would happen if you shared the truth instead? The one thing that defines you, that makes everything else about you fall into place?*

Why not? she thought, feeling the thrill of being uncharacteristically reckless. It took her a while to find a decent pen. It seemed a bit disrespectful to follow Julian's careful calligraphy with a scrawl in manky old biro. She turned to the next clean page, and began to write.

Hazard

Hazard wondered how much of his life he'd spent bent over toilet cisterns. Probably whole days, if you added it all up. How many potentially lethal bacteria was he hoovering up along with a roughly chopped line of Colombia's finest nose candy? And how much of it was actually cocaine and not talcum powder, rat poison or laxative? These were all questions that wouldn't be bothering him for very much longer as this was the last line in the last gram of coke that he was ever going to buy.

Hazard searched in his pockets for a banknote, before remembering that he'd used his only twenty on the bottle of wine that he was halfway through drinking. In this fancy, overpriced wine bar, a twenty bought a bottle that was closer on the spectrum to methylated spirits than fine wine. But it did the job. He checked all his pockets, pulling out a folded-up sheet of A4 from inside his jacket. A copy of his resignation letter. Well, that had a nice symbolism to it, he thought, as he ripped off a corner and rolled it into a tight tube.

After a hefty sniff, the familiar chemical taste hit the back of Hazard's throat and, within minutes, the edginess he'd been feeling was replaced by a sense of, if not euphoria (the days of that were long gone), then at least wellbeing. He crumpled the rolled paper, along with the tiny plastic bag that the powder had been in, and threw them into the toilet bowl, watching as they were sucked into the depths of London's sewers.

Carefully, Hazard lifted up the heavy, porcelain lid of the toilet cistern and leaned it against the wall. He took his iPhone – the latest model, obviously – out of his pocket and dropped it into the water filling the cistern. It made a satisfying plop as it sank to the bottom. Hazard replaced the lid, trapping the phone inside, alone in the dark. Now he couldn't call his dealer. Or anyone who knew his dealer. The only number on that phone he knew by heart was his parents', and that was the only number he needed, although he'd have a fair bit of making up to do when he next called it.

Hazard checked his reflection in the mirror, wiping away any tell-tale signs of white powder from under his inflamed nostrils, then walked back to his table, with more of a strut in his step than he'd had when he left. His positivity was partly chemical, but he also felt a tinge of something he hadn't felt for a long while – pride.

He looked quizzically at the table. Something was different. The bottle of wine was still there, along with two glasses (so it looked like he was waiting for someone, rather than drinking alone) and the dog-eared copy of the *Evening Standard* he'd been pretending to read. But there was something else too. A notebook. He'd had one like it when he was a rookie trader, filled with snippets of information he'd gleaned from the *FT* and hot tips thrown at him, like treats to an enthusiastic puppy, by the veterans on the trading floor. But this one had *The Authenticity Project* written on the cover. It sounded like a load of new-age nonsense. He looked around for anyone suitably 'spiritual' who might have mislaid it, but there was just the usual crowd of midweek drinkers, busily shrugging off the stresses of the working day.

Hazard pushed the book to the edge of his table, so that its owner might spot it, while he got down to the important business of finishing the wine in front of him. His last bottle of wine. Because cocaine and wine went together, like fish and chips, eggs and bacon, MDMA and sex. If he was going to give up one, he had to give up the other. Along with his job, because after years of surfing the markets on a wave of chemical high, he didn't think he could do it, or wanted to do it, sober.

Sober. What a horrible word. Serious, sensible, solemn, staid, steady – nothing like Hazard himself, who was a case of nominative determinism in action. Hazard put his hand firmly on his right thigh, which was jiggling up and down under the table. He realized that he was also grinding his teeth. He hadn't slept properly for thirty-six hours, since the night he'd spent with Blanche. His head was wired and desperate for more stimulation, fighting against his body, which was bone-deep tired and yearning for oblivion. Hazard was, he realized, finally exhausted with it all, with his life and the constant merry-go-round of uppers and downers, the sleaziness of the desperate calls to his dealer, the constant sniffing and the increasingly dramatic nosebleeds. How had the occasional line at a party that made him feel like he could fly turned into something he had to do just to get out of bed in the morning?

Since nobody seemed to be interested in the abandoned notebook, Hazard opened it. Densely packed handwriting covered the page. He tried to read it, but the letters danced around on the page. Hazard closed one eye and looked again. The words settled down into more orderly lines. He flicked forward a few pages and found that there were two different types of handwriting – the first a delicate calligraphy, the second a simpler, rounder, more ordinary hand. Hazard was intrigued, but reading through one eye was tiring, and made him look like a nutter, so he closed the book and pushed it into his jacket pocket.

Twenty-four hours later, Hazard was looking for a pen in his jacket and found the book again. It took him a while to remember how it had got there. His brain was a fog. He had a crashing headache, and although he was more tired than he could ever remember, sleep was elusive. He lay down on his bed, a tangle of musty, sweaty bedsheets and duvet, clutching the book and started to read.

How well do you know the people who live near you? How well do they know you? Do you even know the names of your neighbours? Would you realize if they were in trouble, or hadn't left their house for days?

Hazard smiled to himself. He was a coke-head. The only person he was interested in was himself.

What would happen if you shared the truth instead?

Ha! He'd probably be arrested. Certainly fired. Although it was a bit too late to fire him now.

Hazard read on. He rather liked Julian. If he'd been born forty years or so earlier, or Julian forty years later, he could imagine they'd have been friends – out on the town together, pulling the birds and raising merry hell. But he wasn't at all sure about the idea of telling his story (he didn't want to tell it to himself, let alone anyone else). Authenticity was something he could do without. He'd been hiding from it for years. He turned the page. Who, he wondered, had picked up the book before him?

My name is Monica, and I found this book in my café.

Having read Julian's story about feeling invisible, you're probably imagining a stereotypical pensioner, all dressed in beige, with elasticated waists and orthopaedic shoes. Well, I have to tell you, that's not Julian. I saw him writing in this book before he abandoned it, and he's the least invisible septuagenarian I've ever come across. He looks like Gandalf (but without the beard) and dresses like Rupert the Bear, in a mustard yellow, velvet smoking jacket and checked trousers. He's right about having been gorgeous though. Check out his self-portrait. It was in the National Portrait Gallery for a while.

Hazard reached over for his mobile, so that he could Google Julian's portrait, before remembering that it was still submerged in the flush mechanism of the local wine bar's loo. Why had he thought that was a good idea?

I'm afraid I am far less interesting than Julian.

Hazard didn't doubt it. He could tell just from her cautious, precise handwriting that she was an uptight nightmare. Still, at least she wasn't the sort of woman who drew smiley faces inside all her 'o's.

Here is my truth, horribly predictable, and boringly biological: I really want a baby. And a husband. Perhaps a dog and a Volvo too. The whole, stereotypical nuclear family thing, in actual fact.

Hazard noted Monica's use of a colon. It looked a little incongruous. He didn't think people did grammar any more. They barely did writing. Just texts, and emojis.

Oh God, that looks so terrible written down. After all, I'm a feminist. I totally reject the notion that I need a man to complete me, support me, or to do the DIY even. I'm a businesswoman and, between us, a bit of a control freak. I'd probably be a terrible mother. But however hard I try to think rationally about the whole thing, I still feel like there's an ever-expanding vacuum inside me, that one day is going to totally swallow me up.

Hazard stopped reading while he knocked back another two paracetamol. He wasn't sure that he could handle all this hormonal angst right now. One of the pills caught in the back of his throat, making him gag. He spotted a single strand of long, blonde hair resting on the pillow next to him, the reminder of another lifetime. He flicked it on to the floor.

I used to be a solicitor, in a big, prestigious City firm. They paid me a small fortune, in exchange for making their gender equality numbers look good, and swapping my life for billable hours. I worked every moment I could, including much of the weekend. If I had any spare time, I'd head to the gym to run off the stress. The only social life I had revolved around work parties and client entertaining. I felt like I was still in touch with my school and university friends because I saw their status updates on Facebook, but I hadn't actually seen many of them in real life for years.

My life might have carried on like this for ever, nose to the grindstone, doing what was expected, achieving promotions and meaningless accolades, had it not been for something my mum said, and a girl called Tanya.

I never met Tanya, or at least I don't think I did, but her life was much like mine – another high-achieving City solicitor, but ten years older than me. One Sunday she went into the office, as usual. Her boss was there. He told her that she shouldn't be at work every weekend, that she should have a life outside. He meant it kindly, but that conversation must have triggered something, made Tanya realize how empty it all was, because the next Sunday she

*came into the office, as usual, took the elevator to the top
floor, and jumped off the roof. The papers ran a photo of
her on her graduation day, standing between her proud
parents, eyes filled with hope and expectation.*

*I didn't want to be Tanya, but I could see that was
where my life was heading. I was thirty-five years old,
single and had nothing in my life except for work. So,
when my great-aunt Lettice died and left me a small
legacy, I added it to the fairly large pot of money I'd
managed to save up over the years, and did the first, and
only, surprising thing in my life: I quit. I took over the
lease on a derelict sweet shop on the Fulham Road,
turned it into a café, and called it Monica's.*

Monica's Café. Hazard knew it. It was just opposite the bar
where he'd found the book. He'd never been in there himself. He preferred the more anonymous coffee shops, where
the ever-changing gang of baristas were unlikely to notice
how many mornings he staggered in, hungover, or that he
often had to unroll a bank note before he handed it to them.
Monica's always appeared terribly *cosy. Wholesome.* All
organic and granny's favourite recipe. Places like that made
Hazard feel a bit grubby. The name put him off too. *Monica's.* It was the sort of name you'd expect a teacher to have.
Or a fortune teller. Even a brothel-keeper. *Madame Monica*, massage with happy endings. Not a good name for a
café. He carried on reading.

*Being my own boss, instead of a name in a box of a
complicated organizational hierarchy, is still a thrill (as*

well as a huge learning curve; let's just say that Benji is not my first barista). But there's a huge void. I know how old-fashioned it sounds, but I really do want the fairy-tale. I want the handsome prince, and to live happily ever after.

I've done Tinder. I've been on endless dates. I try not to be too fussy, to ignore the fact that they haven't read any Dickens, have dirty fingernails or talk with their mouth full. I've had a number of relationships, and one or two that I honestly thought were going somewhere. But, eventually, I end up hearing the same old excuses, the 'It's not you, it's me. I'm not ready to settle down . . .' yada, yada, yada. Then, six months later I get a Facebook notification saying their relationship status has changed to 'engaged', and I know that it WAS just me, but I don't know why.

Hazard could hazard a guess.

All my life I've had plans. I've been in control. I write lists, I set objectives and milestones, I make things happen. But I'm thirty-seven years old and running out of time.

Thirty-seven. Hazard mulled the number over in his addled brain. He'd definitely swipe left at that one, despite the fact that he himself was thirty-eight. He remembered explaining to a mate on his desk at the bank that when you were buying fruit at the supermarket (not that he ever did buy fruit, or go to a supermarket), you didn't pick the peaches that were the closest to turning rotten. In his experience, older women were trouble. They had expectations. Agendas. You knew that, within a matter of weeks, you'd be having *the conversation*. You'd have to discuss where your relationship was going, as if you were on the number 22 bus, trundling down Piccadilly. He shuddered.

Whenever a friend posts a picture of their baby scan on Facebook, I click on 'like' and call them up and gush down the phone about how excited I am for them, but, honestly, I just want to howl and say why not me?
Then I have to go and shop in the haberdashery depart-ment of Peter Jones, because no one can feel stressed in a haberdashery, surrounded by skeins of wool, crochet hooks and assorted buttons, can they?

Skein? Was that even a word? And a haberdashery? Did they still exist? Surely people just bought everything ready made in Primark? And what a strange way to de-stress. Much less efficient than simply downing a double vodka. Oh God, why did he have to start thinking about vodka?

My biological clock is ticking so loudly that it's keeping me awake at night. I lie there cursing the fact that my hormones are turning me into a cliché.
So, there it is. I've done what Julian asked. I do hope I don't live to regret it.
As for Julian, well I have a plan.

Of course she has a plan, thought Hazard. He knew her type. It was probably divided into sub-sections, each with an allocated key performance indicator. She reminded him of an ex-girlfriend of his who had, one memorable evening, presented him with a PowerPoint presentation on their relationship – strengths, weaknesses, opportunities and threats. He'd wrapped that one up pretty smartish.

I know exactly how to get him out and about again. I've designed an advertisement, for a local artist to teach a weekly evening class at the café. I've posted it in the window, so now all I have to do is to wait for him to apply. And I'm going to leave this book on a table in the wine bar over the road. If you're the person who picked it up, then what happens next is in your hands.

Hazard looked down at his hands, the antithesis of a 'safe pair'. They hadn't stopped trembling since the end of his last big bender twenty-four hours ago, the day he'd found the book. Bugger. Why him? Apart from anything else, he was leaving the country tomorrow. He'd have to pass Monica's on his way to the tube station. He could pop in for a coffee, check her out and give her the book back so she could hand it over to someone more suitable.

Just as Hazard was closing the book, he noticed that Monica had written something else on the next page.

P.S. I've covered this book in clear sticky-backed plastic to give it a bit of protection, but please try not to leave it in the rain, in any case.

Somewhat to his surprise, Hazard found he was smiling.

Julian

Julian peeled the handwritten note off his front door as he went in. He didn't stop to read it. He knew what it said and, besides, it was all written in capital letters which he thought a bit rude and shouty, undeserving of attention.

Julian made himself a cup of tea, sat down in an armchair, untied his shoelaces, slipped off his shoes and rested his feet in the foot-shaped dents in the threadbare, tapestry-covered ottoman in front of him. He picked up his latest glossy magazine – *Bazaar* – which he'd been carefully rationing so it would last until the end of the week, and was just starting to lose himself in its pages when he was rudely interrupted by a knocking on the window. He sank lower into the armchair, so his head wouldn't be visible from behind. He'd become rather adept over the last fifteen years at ignoring visitors. He was aided by the fact that his windows hadn't been washed in much of that time, their opacity a happy unintended consequence of his slovenliness.

Julian's neighbours were becoming increasingly intrusive

in their attempts to attract his attention. With a sigh, he put the magazine down and picked up the note he'd been left. He read it, wincing at the exclamation point following his name.

MR JESSOP!
WE NEED TO TALK!
WE (YOUR NEIGHBOURS) WISH TO ACCEPT
THE FREEHOLDER'S OFFER.
WE NEED YOUR APPROVAL,
WITHOUT WHICH WE CAN'T PROCEED.
PLEASE CONTACT PATRICIA ARBUCKLE, NO. 4
WITH THE UTMOST URGENCY!

Julian had bought his cottage in 1961 when the leasehold had sixty-seven years left to run. That had felt like an eternity, from the vantage point of his twenties, and certainly nothing to be concerned about. Now there were only ten years left on the lease, and the freeholder was refusing to extend, as he wanted to use the land on which the studios stood to build a 'corporate entertaining complex', whatever that might be, for the Stamford Bridge stadium. The stadium had grown and modernized around Julian over the years he'd lived in its shadow, while Julian himself had become smaller and increasingly unmodern. Now it was threatening to explode, like a monstrous carbuncle, sweeping them all away in a river of pus.

Julian knew that the logical thing to do was say yes. If they let the lease run out, their properties would be worthless. The freeholder was prepared to buy them out now at close to the market rate. But he wasn't interested in buying out all Julian's neighbours if he was still left with the problem of Julian's little cottage squatting in the middle of his proposed building site.

Julian knew that his neighbours were becoming increasingly desperate at the prospect of their life's savings, which were – like most Londoners' – bound up in bricks and mortar, disappearing, but, however hard he tried, he simply couldn't picture living anywhere else. Surely it wasn't too much to ask, to be allowed to see out his final years in the home he'd lived in for most of his life? A decade should easily suffice. And what use would the cash offer from the freeholder be to him? He had a decent enough income from his investments, he hardly lived an extravagant lifestyle and what little family he had left he hadn't seen for years. He had no qualms about their inheritance disappearing in a puff of legal paperwork and expired deadlines.

He knew, however, that refusing the offer was selfish. Julian had spent many years being unutterably selfish, and he'd been paying for that behaviour for some time. He really wanted to think that he was a changed man – repentant, humble even. So, he hadn't said 'no'. But he couldn't say 'yes' either; instead, he was sticking his metaphorical fingers in his metaphorical ears and ignoring the problem, despite knowing that it wasn't going away.

After five minutes or so of increasingly frantic knocking, and a final exasperated exclamation of *I know you're in there, old man*, Julian's neighbour finally gave up. Old man? Really.

Julian's cottage was more than a home, and certainly

more than a financial investment. It was everything. All that he had. It housed all his memories of the past and the only vision he could imagine of the future. Every time Julian looked towards his front door, he could picture himself carrying his new bride over the threshold, heart bursting, convinced that the woman he held in his arms would be all he'd ever need. When he stood at his stove he could see Mary in a pinny, hair tied back, stirring a giant pot of her renowned boeuf bourguignon with a ladle. When he sat by the fire, Mary sat on the rug in front of him, knees pulled up to her chest, the sharp bob of her hair falling forwards as she read the latest of her romances, borrowed from the local library.

There were the uncomfortable memories too. Mary, crying silent tears, clutching a love letter she'd found pinned to his easel by one of his models. Mary standing at the top of the spiral staircase leading to their bedroom, hurling another woman's stilettos at his head. Often, when he looked in a mirror, Mary looked back at him, her eyes filled with sadness and disappointment.

Julian didn't avoid the bad memories. If anything, he encouraged them. They were his penance. And, in a strange way, he found them rather comforting. At least they meant he could still feel. The pain they caused gave him momentary relief, rather like drawing one of his artist's scalpels across his skin and watching it bleed, which he only did on very bad days. Apart from anything else, his skin took so much longer to heal now.

Julian looked round the walls of his home, almost every inch covered by a jigsaw of framed paintings and sketches.

Each one told a story. He could lose himself for hours, just staring at them. He'd think back to conversations he had had with the artist, advice and inspiration shared over carafes of wine. He'd remember how each had come to be here – a birthday gift, as payment for Mary's endless hospitality, or purchased from a private viewing because he'd particularly admired it. Even their positions on the wall had meaning. Sometimes chronological, while others were thematic – beautiful women, London landmarks, peculiar perspectives, or a particular use of light and shade. How could he possibly move them all? Where else could they go?

It was nearly 5 p.m. Julian took a bottle of Baileys out of his drinks cupboard and decanted some into a silver hip flask, shrugged on his overcoat and, once he'd ascertained that the coast was clear of irate neighbours, left for the cemetery.

He spotted that something was different about the Admiral's grave from some distance away, but it took a while for it to sharpen into focus. It was another letter – black writing on white paper. Were his neighbours leaving notes for him *everywhere*? Had they been following him? He could feel his irritation building. This was persecution.

As he got closer, he realized that it wasn't a message from his neighbours at all. It was an advertisement, and he'd seen it before, just that morning. He hadn't thought much of it then, but now it became clear that it was designed specifically for him.

Monica

By Saturday, Monica was starting to lose faith in her brilliant plan. It had been several days since she'd put the poster up in the café window, but there'd been no sign of Julian. In the meantime, she'd had to politely turn down a whole slew of applicants for the position of art teacher, with ever more ridiculous excuses. Who knew there were so many local artists looking for work? She was also, as an ex-lawyer, painfully aware that she was breaking every employment law going, although part of her rather enjoyed the idea that, for the first time in her life, she was doing something not entirely by the book.

The other problem was that every time someone new walked into the café, Monica found herself wondering if they'd been the one who'd picked up the book she'd left on the empty table in the wine bar, and read the horribly embarrassing ramblings of a desperate spinster. Argh. What had she been thinking? If only she could delete those pages, like a badly judged Facebook post. Authenticity, she decided, was totally overrated.

A woman came up to the counter, holding a tiny baby, not more than three months old, dressed in the most adorable, old-fashioned smocked dress and cardigan. The baby fixed Monica with her big blue eyes, that looked as if they'd only recently learned how to focus. Monica felt her stomach lurch. She recited her mantra silently: *I am a strong, independent woman. I do not need you* . . . As if the baby could sense her thoughts, she let out a piercing wail, and her face went tight and red, like a human version of the angry-face emoji. *Thank you*, Monica mouthed at the baby, and turned to make the peppermint tea. As she handed over the mug, the door opened, and in walked Julian.

The last time she'd seen him, he'd resembled an eccentric Edwardian gentleman. Monica had assumed that his entire wardrobe was inspired by that era. It appeared not, because today he was dressed in New Romantic style, circa mid-1980s. He wore drainpipe black trousers, suede ankle boots and a white shirt, with *frills*. Lots of them. It was the sort of look that would usually be finished off with a generous helping of eyeliner. Monica was relieved to discover that Julian hadn't taken it that far.

He sat down at the same table in The Library he'd occupied last time. Monica walked over, rather nervously, to take his order. Had he seen her advertisement? Was that why he was here? She glanced over at the café window where she'd posted it. It was gone. She looked again, as if it might have magically reappeared, but no, just a few sticky patches left behind by the Sellotape she'd placed in each corner. She made a mental note to remove the marks with a bit of vinegar.

Well, so much for that plan. Her irritation quite quickly

morphed into relief. It had all been a stupid idea anyway. She approached Julian a little more confidently, now that it appeared he'd only dropped in for a coffee.

'What can I get you?' she asked, brightly.

'I'd like a strong, black coffee, please,' he replied (no fancy flat whites for him, she noted) as he unfolded a piece of paper he was holding, smoothed out the creases and placed it on the table in front of him. It was her advertisement. But not the original, a photocopy. Monica felt herself blushing.

'Am I right in thinking that this was meant for me?' Julian asked.

'Why, are you an artist?' she stammered, like a panellist on *Question Time*, scrabbling around for the correct answer, not sure whether to tell the truth or to obfuscate.

He held her gaze for a while, a snake hypnotizing a small vole. 'I am,' he replied, 'which is why I think your advertisement was posted on the wall of the Chelsea Studios where I live. Not one single copy, but three.' He jabbed at the paper on the table, three times in emphasis. 'Now, that might have been a coincidence, but yesterday, I went to visit the Admiral in Brompton Cemetery, at my usual time, and there, *on his headstone*, another copy of your advertisement. So, I figured that you must have found my little notebook, and be talking to me. By the way, I'm not sure about the typeface you used. I'd have stuck with Times New Roman. You can't go very far wrong with Times New Roman, I find.'

By this point, Monica, still standing beside Julian's table, felt very much like a naughty schoolgirl being told off by the headmaster. Or rather, she felt how she imagined that would feel, as she had, obviously, never been in that position herself.

'May I?' she asked, gesturing at the chair opposite Julian. He tilted his head slightly, in a half-nod. Monica sat down and took a moment to gather herself. She was not going to be intimidated. She pictured her mother.

If you feel anxious, Monica, imagine you are Boudicca, Queen of the Celts! Or Elizabeth I, or Madonna!

'Mother of Jesus?' she'd asked.

No, silly! Far too meek and mild! I meant the pop star. And her mum had laughed so hard the neighbours had banged on the wall.

So, Monica channelled Madonna and turned an unwavering stare on the rather imposing and slightly cross man opposite her.

'You're right, I did pick up your book, and it was written for you, but I didn't post it on your wall, or on the Admiral.' Julian raised one eyebrow in an impressive display of scepticism. 'I only made one copy, and put it in the window.' She nodded over at the empty space where the poster had once been. 'This is a photocopy. I didn't make that. I wonder who did.' The question gnawed at her. Why on earth would someone steal her poster?

'Well, if it wasn't you, it must be someone else who's read my story,' Julian said, 'otherwise how would they know where I live? Or about the Admiral? It surely can't be a coincidence that the only gravestone sporting a copy of your poster was the one I've been visiting for forty years?'

Monica's unease increased as she realized that if someone else had read Julian's story, they must also have read hers.

43

She mentally filed that thought in 'too uncomfortable to consider for the time being'. She'd no doubt revisit it later.

'So, are you interested?' she asked Julian. 'Will you teach an evening art class for me? In the café?'

Her question hung in the air for so long that Monica wondered if she should repeat it. Then, Julian's face wrinkled like a concertina, and he smiled.

'Well, since you and, it seems, someone else have gone to so much trouble, it would be rude not to, don't you think? I'm Julian, by the way,' he said, proffering his hand.

'I know,' she replied, shaking it. 'And I am Monica.'

'I look forward to working with you, Monica. I have a hunch that you and I might just become friends.' Monica went to make his coffee, feeling like she'd just been awarded ten points for Gryffindor.

Hazard

Hazard looked out at the crescent-shaped beach, fringed with palm trees. The South China Sea was a perfect, Tiffany blue, the sky cloudless. If he'd seen this on Instagram he'd assume it'd been photo-shopped and filtered. But, after three weeks here, all this *perfection* was starting to get on his nerves. During his morning walk along the beach (before the sand became too hot to walk barefoot), he'd found himself longing to find a dog turd lying on the white, powdery sand. Anything to break up the monotonous beauty. Hazard often felt the urge to shout for help, but he knew that this beach was like deep space; no one could hear you scream.

Hazard had been to this island before, five years ago. He'd been staying on Koh Samui with some friends, and they'd taken the boat over for a couple of days. It was too far off-grid for him, and he'd been keen to get back to the bars, clubs and full-moon parties of Samui, not to mention reliable electricity, hot water and Wi-Fi. But, hidden amongst the endless grubby and sordid flashbacks of one-night

45

stands, drunken inappropriate texting and rendezvous with dodgy dealers in dark alleyways, the memory of this place shimmered, like an oasis of tranquillity in the inhospitable desert of his recent history. So, when he'd finally made the decision to clean up his act and sort his life out, he'd booked a one-way ticket out here. Surely, this island was too far away from anything for him to get into any trouble, and cheap enough for him to be able to survive for months, if necessary, on his last City bonus?

At one end of the small beach was a café – Lucky Mother – and at the other end, a bar called Monkey Nuts (after their only bar snack). Strung between the two, like a row of pearls, but without the sheen, were twenty-five huts, erected amongst the palm trees overlooking the sea. Number eight belonged to Hazard. It was a simple, wooden structure, not much bigger than his father's garden shed.

There was a bedroom, almost entirely filled with a double bed, draped in a large mosquito net riddled with holes large enough to admit whole coach parties of hungry insects. A small bathroom with a loo and a cold-water shower was tacked on to one side, like an escape pod clutching on to the mothership. The windows were little more than hatches, lined with more mosquito netting. The only other furniture was a bedside table made from an old Tiger beer crate, a single bookshelf, housing a motley and eclectic collection of books bequeathed to Hazard by travellers who were moving on, and a few hooks on which Hazard hung the assortment of sarongs he'd picked up in town. He wondered what his old mates would think of him parading around all day in nothing but a *skirt*.

Hazard was swaying gently in a hammock, hanging between two supports at either end of the wooden deck which ran the length of his hut. He watched a small motor boat moor up on the beach, collecting the fifteen or so day trippers from Samui, leaving only the residents behind. The sky was turning stunning shades of red and orange as the sun dipped to the horizon. Hazard knew that in a matter of minutes it would be dark. Out here, so close to the equator, the sun made a hasty exit. There were none of the drawn-out, showy and teasing goodbyes he was used to back home – it was more like lights out in the dorm at boarding school.

He could hear the Lucky Mother generator crank up, and caught the faintest whiff of petrol along with the sound of Andy and Barbara (a westernized approximation of their Thai names, Hazard assumed) getting ready to produce the evening meal.

It had been twenty-three days since Hazard had last had a drink or a drug. He was certain about this, because he'd been carving a tally on the wooden base of his bed, like a prisoner of Alcatraz rather than a tourist in one of the most beautiful corners of the earth. That morning, he'd counted four little batches of five, and three extras. They had been long days, punctuated by waves of headaches, sweating and shivering, and nights of the most vivid dreams, during which he relived his wildest excesses. Just last night he'd dreamed he was snorting a line of coke off Barbara's taut, tanned belly. He could barely look at her at breakfast.

Hazard was, however, starting to feel better, at least physically. The fog and tiredness had begun to recede, but they had been replaced by a tsunami of *emotions*. Those pesky feelings of guilt, regret, fear, boredom and dread that he'd always magicked away with a shot of vodka, or line of coke. He was haunted by memories of secrets spilled for the sake of a good anecdote, of girlfriends betrayed for a quickie in a nightclub toilet cubicle, of disastrous trades made off the back of a chemical sense of invulnerability. And oddly, in the middle of all of this horrible introspection he'd often find himself thinking about the stories in that green notebook. He had visions of Mary trying to ignore Julian's models, Julian slashing away at his canvases in the middle of the night, Tanya splattered over the pavement and Monica handing out muffins and dreaming of love.

When he'd turned up at Monica's Café to return the notebook, Hazard had realized, to his horror, that Monica was the same woman he'd collided with the night before he'd resigned from his job and turned his back on all remnants of his previous life. He'd exited quickly, before she spotted him. So, he still had the notebook, and the longer he held on to it, the more the secrets it held lodged in his brain and refused to budge. He wondered if Monica had managed to persuade Julian to teach her art class, and what sort of bloke would make her happy.

The sound of a bell ringing travelled along the beach. 7 p.m. Time for supper. Lucky Mother served just one evening meal. It was the only place in walking distance to eat, and you ate what you were given. After decades of endless choice, of every decision having sub-sections – tea or coffee? Cappuccino, Americano, latte? Regular milk, skimmed or soya? – he found the lack of options curiously refreshing.

The open-sided restaurant, with its wooden floor and thatched roof, was laid out with one large table stretching its whole length. There were a few smaller tables dotted around too, but new visitors worked out pretty quickly that the accepted thing to do was to join the group at the communal table, unless you wanted everyone to look at you suspiciously, wondering what you had to hide.

As Hazard watched the other residents of his beach walking towards Lucky Mother, he had an idea. So many of the people he'd met here were from London, or had a visit planned on their itinerary. He could check them all out, and find a boyfriend for Monica. He did know a fair bit about her, after all. More than he'd ever bothered to find out about most of his girlfriends. He could be like her fairy godmother, her secret matchmaker. It'd be fun. Or, at least, it'd be something to *do*.

Hazard took a seat and, feeling re-energized by his new mission, surreptitiously checked out the other guests. As far as he could tell, he was now about the fourth longest standing resident. Most people stayed no longer than five days or so.

Neil, Hazard's neighbour at number nine, had been here the longest. Nearly a year. He had invented some sort of app, which he'd sold to a big tech company, and ever since then, he'd been indulging his inner hippy. He'd tried to teach Hazard to meditate, perhaps sensing his inner turmoil, but Hazard had been unable to clear his mind from thinking about Neil's feet, which were covered in yellowing, dead skin, his toenails thick and crusty, like hooves. This put Neil out of the running in Hazard's new game. However desperate Monica was, those feet wouldn't wash. Actually, he thought, a wash was exactly what Neil needed. Monica struck him as someone rather hot on personal hygiene.

Rita and Daphne were the two other relatively long timers; both retired, one widowed, one never married, both ferocious sticklers for good manners. Hazard watched Rita glare at one of the guests, who'd reached rudely across her for the water jug. They each had their own hut. Daphne, in theory, lived in number seven, but Hazard, who had become an early riser, had only ever seen her entering her hut in the morning, rather than leaving it, leading him to suspect they were enjoying a sapphic fling in the autumn of their years. And why the hell not?

Andy laid a dish containing a large baked fish, big enough to share amongst three or four of them, in front of Hazard with a flourish.

Hazard's practised eye scanned down the long table, discounting all the couples, in various stages of loved-upness, and any men under the age of thirty. Even if one of them were open-minded enough to cop off with an older woman, they weren't likely to be ready for that whole *procreation* thing, which was, for Monica, a bit of a deal-breaker.

Hazard's glance snagged momentarily on two Californian girls. They were, he guessed, no older than twenty-five, and had that peachy, innocent, box-fresh glow about them. Hazard wondered, idly, if he should make a play for one of them. Maybe both. But he didn't think he was ready to try to pull without the false confidence of a drink, or a line, to chivvy him along.

Hazard hadn't, now he thought about it, had sex since

Blanche. Actually, he hadn't had sex *sober* since ... He rewound his memory back further and further before settling on *for ever*. The idea was terrifying. How was it possible to be so present during something so intimate and revealing? Surely all that squelching and thrusting and groaning, and sometimes even farting, would just be deeply embarrassing without the numbing effect of narcotics? Perhaps he'd never have sex again. The thought was, strangely, almost less terrifying than the thought of never having a drink or a drug again, and that one he'd already been contemplating for weeks.

Hazard turned to the Swede on his left, offering his hand. He looked like a good place to start.

'Hi, you must be new here. I'm Hazard.'

'Gunther,' he replied, with a smile that displayed some impressive Scandinavian dentistry.

'Where are you from, and where are you going?' Hazard employed the standard opening gambit on the island, a bit like discussing the weather back home. No point in discussing the weather here, since it was invariably the same.

'I'm from Stockholm, on my way to Bangkok, Hong Kong then London. You?'

Hazard gave himself a mental high five at the mention of London. This could work.

'I'm from London, just out here for a few weeks while I'm between jobs,' he replied.

Hazard chatted to Gunther on autopilot as he ate his fish. He was finding it difficult to concentrate on the conversation as he was mesmerized by Gunther's ice-cold beer. Condensation dripped down the side of the glass bottle. Hazard worried that if he didn't find some other distraction, he might just wrestle the beer from him and down it.

'Do you play backgammon?' he asked as soon as they'd finished eating.

'Sure,' replied Gunther.

Hazard walked over to one of the tables in the corner, which was inlaid with a chess board on one side, and backgammon board on the other.

'So, what do you do back home, Gunther?' asked Hazard as they set up the pieces.

'I'm a teacher,' he replied. 'What about you?'

This, thought Hazard, was extremely good news. An easily transferable skill, good with children and, he noted, looking at Gunther's large hands with their clean, nicely trimmed fingernails, acceptable levels of grooming.

'I was a banker,' Hazard replied. 'Equity trader. But I'll be looking for a new career when I get home.'

Gunther threw a six and a one. Hazard waited for him to make the classic blocking move. He missed it. What an amateur. This would, for Hazard, be a red line. He quickly reminded himself that he was not looking at Gunther as a life partner for himself, and that Monica was, presumably, less fussy when it came to the ability to play a good game of backgammon.

'Do you have a wife back home, Gunther?' asked Hazard, cutting to the chase. He'd not noticed a wedding ring, but it was always sensible to double-check.

'Not wife. Girlfriend. But, how do you say in English? What goes on tour stays on tour, right?' He nodded conspiratorially over at the two Californian girls.

Hazard felt his mood deflate like a popped balloon. Impressive use of English idiom, perhaps, but terribly loose morals. Gunther, he concluded, with a sense of paternalistic protectionism which surprised him, just wasn't going to make the grade. Monica deserved better. Now, how quickly could he wipe this board clear of all Gunther's pieces and go to bed?

When Hazard got back to number eight, clutching an oil-fired hurricane lamp, since the generator was now off for the night, he found he wasn't tired. He didn't, however, want to join the crowd at Monkey Nuts; the idea of watching other people drink alcohol while he sipped a Diet Coke was just too exhausting. He looked at the books on his bookshelf. He'd read them all at least once, apart from the Barbara Cartland that Daphne had given him. He'd tried the first chapter in desperation yesterday, but it had made his eyeballs bleed. Then he spotted Julian's little notebook poking out, as if begging to be picked up. Hazard took it off the shelf, picked up a biro, turned to the first clean page and began to write.

Julian

Julian woke up with a sense that something was different. It took him a while to work out what it was. These days he felt like his mind and his body were running at different speeds. First thing in the morning, his body would wake up, but his mind would take a little while to catch up, to work out where he was, and what was going on. This was odd, as he was always in the same place, and there was never anything going on. There would be a brief moment of intersection, of synchronicity, then – for the rest of the day – his body lagged several steps behind his mind, struggling to keep step.

While he thought, Julian stared at the lines of green on the wall next to his bed; different shades, like blades of grass dappled in the sunlight. Mary had painted these when she was trying to decide how to redecorate their bedroom. In the end, none of those colours had been chosen, and the room remained the same grubby ivory. Perhaps Mary had known by then, that there would be no point.

Eventually, Julian realized what was new about this morning: a sense of *purpose*. Today he had things to do. An appointment. People were expecting him. Relying on him. He threw back the covers with more gusto than usual, hauled himself out of bed and walked carefully down the spiral staircase which led from the mezzanine floor, where his bedroom and bathroom were, to the open-plan sitting room and kitchenette. There, pinned to the fridge door was his list.

1. Choose outfit
2. Collect materials
3. Art shop
4. Props
5. Be at Monica's 7 p.m. prompt

He'd underlined *prompt* twice. Not because he was likely to forget, but because he hadn't had to be anywhere, with the possible exception of his dentist, *prompt* for years, and it was giving him a curious thrill.

Having drunk his first strong coffee of the day, Julian walked into his dressing room. It had, in the days when he and Mary had had overnight visitors, been the guest room, but now it was filled with rows and rows of Julian's clothes, all hanging on metal rails, with boots and shoes lined up underneath. Julian loved his outfits. Each one held a memory – of an era, an event, a love affair. If you closed your eyes and inhaled extravagantly, some still held the scent of a bygone age – Mary's homemade marmalade, the cordite from a firework display at a masked ball in Venice, or the rose petal confetti from a wedding at Claridge's.

The chaise longue in the corner was draped with a variety of potential outfits for today, which Julian had decided to sleep on (not literally; that would just lead to more ironing). Getting dressed took so long these days that it was crucial to get the wardrobe selection absolutely right before he started, or he could be there all day, doing up and undoing buttons with increasingly uncooperative and arthritic hands. He cast a critical eye over the various options, before deciding to go with the understated one. Professional. Workmanlike. He didn't want his clothing to distract from the matter in hand – the art lesson.

Next, Julian went into his studio, double height and flooded with light from the glass roof and the floor-to-ceiling windows, and opened the drawer marked PENCILS. Julian was not, by nature, a tidy person. His cottage was, by anybody's standards, rather a mess. But the two areas of his life that were beautifully maintained and arranged were his clothes and his art materials. He carefully selected a range of pencils, graphite sticks and erasers, some fairly new, some dating back to the Beatles era, and everything in between. Julian's favourite pencils had been sharpened so many times that they were barely long enough to hold, but he couldn't throw them away. They were old friends.

Julian was rather chuffed that he could still pull a crowd. That nice lady, Monica, had told him there were ten people coming to that evening's class. She'd even had to turn people away! There was, it appeared, life in the old dog yet.

Julian moved around the studio, collecting things that might be useful for his new students. He found a selection of boards for them to pin their sketches to. He pulled an assortment of fabrics from the mannequins they were draped over, for use as a backdrop. He rifled through his lovingly curated reference books to find the ones that might be most inspirational for the *ingénue*. He tried not to get distracted by his chronologically arranged collection of exhibition catalogues, which could so easily transport him back to the London art world of the sixties, seventies and eighties.

Monica was charging fifteen pounds per head for the two-hour lesson. He'd thought that was rather a lot, but she'd pooh-poohed him, saying, *This is Fulham. People pay their dog walkers more than that.* He was being paid seventy-five pounds for the session (a small fortune!), and Monica had given him what she'd described as 'petty cash' to spend on any extra supplies he needed from the art shop.

Julian checked his pocket watch. It was 10 a.m. The art shop would just be opening.

As Julian walked past the café, he could see Monica negotiating her way around the queue at the counter, carrying a tray of drinks. Monica, he had noticed, was never still. Even when she was sitting she was animated, her jaunty dark ponytail swinging from side to side. When she was concentrating on something, she'd twist a strand of hair round and round her index finger, and when she was listening to someone, she cocked her head to one side, just like his old Jack Russell had done.

Julian still missed his dog, Keith. He'd gone just a few months after Mary. He blamed himself for being so wrapped up in his grief about Mary that he didn't pay enough attention to his pet. Keith had just pined away, gradually becoming less energetic and less animated, until one day he'd stopped moving at all. Julian had tried to emulate this slow, determined manner of checking out, but in that, as in so many things, he'd failed. He'd carried Keith's body into the cemetery in a Waitrose Bag for Life (ironically), and, when no one was looking, had buried him next to the Admiral.

Monica always appeared to know what she was doing and where she was going. Whereas most people seemed to be swept along by the vicissitudes of life, Monica looked like she was directing, or even fighting, it every step of the way. He'd only known her a week or so, yet already she seemed to have picked him up, rearranged everything around him, and put him down in a strangely, wonderfully, altered reality.

Yet, while Monica had already had a huge impact on his life, Julian was aware that he barely knew her. He really wanted to paint her, as if his brushes might be able to uncover the truths beneath the protective barrier she seemed to have erected around herself. Julian hadn't wanted to paint anyone for nearly fifteen years.

How many times in the last few years had Julian walked down this road marvelling at all the people rushing past him, wondering where they were going and what they were doing, while he was just putting one foot in front of the other for no particular reason at all, apart from the fear that if he didn't he would completely seize up? But today, he was one of them; someone with somewhere to be.

Julian started humming to himself, causing a couple of people to turn and smile at him as he passed by. Unaccustomed to eliciting this reaction, Julian glared at them suspiciously, at which point they picked up their pace and hurried on. At the art shop, he picked up twenty large sheets of cartridge paper and took them to the till. There was, he mused, nothing more exhilarating, nor as terrifying, as a blank sheet of paper.

'I'm buying supplies for the art class I teach,' he told the cashier.

'Uh huh,' he replied. He was not what you'd describe as a conversationalist.

'I wonder if there'll be any budding Picassos in the class this evening,' he said.

'Cash or card?' replied the cashier. A badge on his lapel displayed five stars for customer services. Julian wondered what the one-star cashiers were like.

Next stop: props.

Julian paused at the corner shop, where large baskets of fruit and vegetables spilled out on to the street. A bowl of fruit perhaps? No. Dull and clichéd. Even a beginners' class could be more adventurous than that, surely? Then, much like being slapped in the face by a wet kipper, he was hit by the smell of the fishmonger. He looked in the window and there it was: just the thing.

Monica

Monica looked at the large station clock on the wall of the café. Two minutes to seven. Most of the art class were here already, firing up their creative juices with glasses of red wine. Monica had offered the first glass for free as an extra incentive to get people to sign up. Finding students had been a bit of a nightmare. She'd had to pull in a few favours. She'd cajoled a couple of her suppliers into joining up, as well as Benji's boyfriend, Baz. She'd even stooped to flirting with her window cleaner in order to fill the last place, apologizing as she did so to the memory of Emmeline Pankhurst. Needs must. Now, if she included herself, there were ten participants. A respectable number. If Benji managed to flog enough additional glasses of wine and other refreshments, she might just (after paying Julian and Benji, and buying the materials) break even, despite reducing the price of the first lesson to ten pounds. She glanced at the clock again. She did hope Julian hadn't lost his nerve.

There was a buzz in the room, as the students competed

to tell each other quite how artistically untalented they were. Then, the door opened and everyone fell silent. Monica had told them all that Julian was a little *eccentric*. She'd also bigged up his CV just a bit. She was pretty sure that he hadn't actually painted the Queen's portrait. But nothing could quite prepare the class for Julian's entrance. He stood in the doorway, in a billowing artist's smock, a burgundy red fedora, an extravagantly patterned cravat and *clogs*.

Julian paused, as if to let the class drink him in. Then, he reached under his smock, and, with a flourish, pulled out a large lobster. Baz choked, spraying red wine all over table ten and Benji's brand-new Superdry t-shirt.

'Class!' said Julian, with a small, but theatrical bow. 'Meet today's subject.'

'Christ!' spluttered Baz, under his breath. 'Is it still *alive*?'

'He's pretty old, but not dead yet,' retorted Benji.

'I meant the lobster, obviously,' said Baz, rolling his eyes.

'Don't be a pillock. It's red, which means it's been cooked.'

'What's a pillock? Some kind of fish?' asked Baz.

'No, that's a pollock,' said Benji.

'I thought Pollock was an artist,' Baz replied, now totally confused.

Benji and Baz were both sitting on the same armchair, as there hadn't been enough smaller chairs to go around. Baz was on the cushion, and Benji was perched on one of the arms. They were both in their mid-twenties, had names that fitted together in a pleasingly lyrical, alliterative fashion, but physically they were complete opposites. Benji was a redheaded Scot who, on a bad hair day and facing into the wind, looked like you'd imagine Tintin would if he'd grown up and reached six foot tall. Baz, of Chinese heritage, was short, dark and wiry. Baz's parents ran the Chinese restaurant, which had been opened by his grandparents, opposite the Broadway, and all three generations lived in the apartment above the shop. Baz's grandmother was constantly on the look-out for a nice girl for her only grandson, who would, eventually, take over the busy kitchen.

Monica had arranged the smaller café tables into a circle, with a larger table in the middle. Julian placed the lobster ceremoniously on a hastily produced platter on the central table, then handed round the sketching paper, boards and a selection of pencils and erasers.

'My name,' said Julian, 'is Julian Jessop. And this handsome crustacean is called Larry. He gave his life so that you could be inspired. Don't let him have died in vain.' His hard stare swept round the open-mouthed class. 'We are going to sketch him. It doesn't matter whether you have any experience or not, just give it a go. I'll wander around and help. We're sticking to pencil this week. Drawing, you see, is to art what grammar is to literature.' Monica felt a little more comfortable. She loved grammar. 'Next week we can move on to charcoal or pastel, then eventually watercolours.' Julian waved his arm extravagantly, causing the sleeve of his smock to billow like the wing of a giant albatross. Monica's sheet of paper was blown off her table by the resulting draught. 'Off you go! Be bold! Be brave! But, above all, be yourselves!'

Monica couldn't remember the last time two hours had passed so quickly. Julian had glided, silently, around the outside of the circle, swooping in from time to time to encourage, to praise, to adjust the tone in a shadow, as his students tried valiantly to commit the prehistoric-looking creature to paper. Monica felt relatively happy with the proportions of her Larry; she'd measured him as precisely as she could using the technique Julian had taught them of holding up a pencil and closing one eye. She couldn't help thinking that a ruler would be more accurate and efficient. But she was aware how terribly two-dimensional her lobster looked, as if he'd been squashed by a heavy object landing from a great height. She sensed Julian behind her. He reached around her, pencil in hand, and deftly sketched a lobster claw in the corner of her page. In just a few strokes he'd created something that seemed to leap out from the paper.

'There. Do you see?' he asked her. Yes, she could see the difference, but could she recreate it? Not a hope in hell.

A few times the silence had been broken by the ringing of mobiles and the pinging of voicemail, Twitter and Snapchat. Julian had swept around the room, collecting everyone's phones into his fedora, ignoring the groans and protestations, and they'd promptly been banished behind the bar. Monica realized that it was the first time for years that she'd gone for two hours without checking her phone, except when she had actually been asleep or out of signal. It was strangely liberating.

At 9 p.m. on the dot, Julian clapped, causing half the class – lost in concentration – to jump. 'That's it for this week, ladies and gentlemen! A jolly good start. Well done to you all! Don't forget to sign and date your drawings, then bring them up to the front, here, so we can all look at them.'

The class shuffled forward, rather reluctantly, clutching

their sketches, which – despite the fact that they'd all been drawing the exact same lobster – were hugely varied. Julian managed to find something positive to say about each of them, pointing out unusual compositions, arresting observations of light, and pleasing shapes. While Monica admired his somewhat unexpected sensitivity, she really just wanted to know one thing: *had she won?*

'Now,' Julian said, turning to Monica, 'what are we going to do with Larry?'

'Er, eat him?' replied Monica.

'My thoughts precisely! Right, we'll need plates, napkins. Any bread going spare? Cheese? A bit of salad, perhaps?'

Monica hardly dared point out that she hadn't meant *right now*. Good grief, this was turning into a *dinner party*. Without an iota of planning or preparation. Surely this could not end well?

Benji and Baz dashed backwards and forwards from the small kitchen with plates, a couple of baguettes left over from lunch time, half a very ripe Brie, a few random salad items and a huge jar of mayonnaise. Julian seemed to have produced a bottle of champagne from somewhere. Had it been hiding alongside Larry under his smock? What else might he have stashed up there? Monica shuddered.

Before long, and despite herself, Monica found she was getting into the swing of things. Trying to not think about her rapidly diminishing profit margin, she brought some candles down from her flat above the café. Soon, a party was under way.

Monica looked over at Julian who was leaning back in his chair, telling anecdotes about the swinging sixties.

'Marianne Faithfull? Such fun! Face like an angel, obviously, but she had a better range of dirty jokes than a sex-starved schoolboy,' she heard him say. In the mellow candlelight, and with his face animated, he looked, for a moment, just like his portrait in the National Gallery.

'What was Fulham like back then, Julian?' she asked him.

'Dear girl, it was like the Wild West! I was just on the border with Chelsea, and many of my friends would refuse to venture any further in. It was very grubby and industrial and poor. My parents were horrified and never came to visit. They were only happy in Mayfair, Kensington and the Home Counties. But we loved it. We all looked out for each other. To Larry!' he cried, raising his glass of champagne. 'And, of course, to Monica!' he added, as he looked over at her and smiled. 'Talking of which, everyone stick a tenner in my hat for the dinner. We don't want her out of pocket!'

And, at that, Monica smiled too.

Hazard

Andy placed a large platter of fish down on the table.

'Gosh, how yummy!' said the new arrival, in an accent that Hazard guessed had been kicked off by a Norland nanny, moulded in an English country prep school and finessed in the officers' mess. He was looking rather uncomfortable and out of place in chinos and a tailored, buttoned-up shirt. At least it was short-sleeved. Hazard set himself the challenge of getting him into a sarong before the week was out.

Hazard had already done some groundwork. He knew that the floppy-haired, braying, but very jolly and well-meaning, newbie was called Roderick and he was the son of Daphne. So far as Hazard could tell, he was totally oblivious to his mother's grand love affair with Rita. He'd told Hazard that he'd given up waiting for Daphne to come back to the UK, and had decided to visit her for a couple of weeks instead. He couldn't quite understand why she insisted on staying so long, but if it helped with her grieving for his dear departed father, then that had to be a good thing. Hazard had nodded gravely, not mentioning that he hadn't seen the slightest evidence of mourning from the merry widow.

'Where do you live, Roderick?' asked Hazard as he helped himself to rice and fish.

'Battersea!' he replied. 'I'm an estate agent!' Roderick barked out every word with such energy and enthusiasm that Hazard couldn't imagine him ever being negative or depressed. He would cheer Monica up no end, surely? Hazard was rather fond of estate agents, who languished alongside bankers as the nation's most loathed people. Monica didn't strike him as so narrow-minded that she'd rule out an entire profession, and at least it meant that he was likely to be comfortably off, and a home owner. Battersea was another bonus. Only just over the river from Fulham.

'Your wife not with you?' asked Hazard, trying to sound casual.

'I'm divorced,' replied Roderick as he picked little fish bones out of the side of his mouth, revealing, as he did so, acceptable levels of oral hygiene. He placed them neatly on the side of his plate. 'All jolly amicable though. Lovely girl. Childhood sweethearts. Just grew apart. You know how it is.' Hazard nodded, empathetically, despite the fact that he couldn't empathise at all, having never had a relationship longer than a few months.

'Has it put you off marriage, though? Do you think you'd ever do it again?'

'Crikey, yes, like a shot. Best institution in the world.' His expression softened as he looked over at Daphne, not appearing to notice her hand resting on Rita's knee as she whispered in her ear. 'My parents were terrifically happy, you know. Married for more than forty years. I do hope Mummy isn't too lonely.' He looked rather wistful for a moment, then pulled himself together. 'I don't manage very well on my own, to be honest. Need someone to keep me in line, not to mention do the cooking. Ha ha! Just need to find someone foolish enough to take me on!'

Hazard thought back to Monica's story in the book: *I try not to be too fussy, to ignore the fact that they haven't read any Dickens, have dirty fingernails or talk with their mouth full.*

'I don't suppose you brought any books with you, did you? I'm running out. I'd love a Dickens to read,' said Hazard, crossing his fingers under the table.

'Only on Kindle, I'm afraid, and I haven't read any Dickens since school.'

That would do. Hazard smiled to himself. After several weeks of grilling every single man of roughly the right age to no avail, it looked as if he might finally have cracked the brief.

Hazard realized, as he exchanged banter with his newly appointed Romeo, that he felt a little sad. Bereft. His quest to fix up a girl he'd barely even spoken to might have been a little odd, but at least it had taken his mind off his own issues. What was he going to do now?

Monica and Roderick. Roderick and Monica. Hazard pictured Monica looking at him again, but this time with an expression of the deepest gratitude, where before there'd been disgust. Now, how was he going to arrange a meeting of his two star-crossed lovers when he was on the other side of the world? The book – that was the answer. He needed to find a way to plant it in Roderick's luggage. The book would lead him to her.

Hazard was about to go back to his hut to retrieve the notebook when he remembered the final, and most important, test of all.

'Did you and your wife have children?' he asked Roderick.

'One. Cecily,' he replied, with a goofy smile on his face, fishing around in his wallet for a photo. As if Hazard cared what she looked like. All he cared about was the answer to the next question.

'Would you like to have more, one day? If you found the right woman?'

'No chance of that, old boy. I had the snip. The wife insisted, said she wasn't going through all that again. You know – pregnancy, nappies, sleepless nights.' Hazard didn't know. Nor did he want to, at least not right now. 'That was one of things we argued about. Beginning of the end, and I just wanted her to be happy. Plus, it was either that or no bedroom action. Ha ha!'

'Ha ha,' echoed Hazard, groaning inwardly, because with that, all his well-laid plans, like Roderick's sperm count, had been dashed. The reproduction thing was a non-negotiable for Monica. He had to cross Roderick off the list and start again.

Many times over the following weeks, Hazard considered giving up on his matchmaking game. It seemed so improbable that the right man would just show up on this tiny beach on this tiny island. But, as is so often the case, as soon as he'd decided to stop trying, as if the universe was flirting with serendipity, the perfect solution just dropped into his lap.

Julian

Julian couldn't quite believe how much his life had changed since he'd left his notebook in Monica's Café five weeks ago. He wasn't sure what he'd imagined would happen when he'd started The Authenticity Project, but he certainly wasn't expecting to end up with a job and a group of people who were well on the way to becoming his friends.

He'd walked round to the Admiral's gravestone last Friday, as usual, with his bottle of Baileys, and as he'd approached he'd thought his mind was playing tricks on him. It wasn't unusual for the past and present to collide in his head, so he wasn't entirely surprised to see two of his old friends waiting for him, glasses and bottle of wine in hand. But this time it wasn't a memory, it was Benji and Baz (such nice boys). Monica must have told them where to find him.

He realized that he had a slight spring in his step, where until recently there'd only been a shuffle. Where was it now, he wondered, that little book that had caused such a transformation? Had his project ground to a halt so soon, or was it out in the world somewhere weaving more magic?

Tonight was the third week of his art class. It had grown to fifteen students, as word had spread, aided by the fact that Monica had pinned up a few of the best sketches of Larry on the café pinboard. The casual, but rowdy, suppers (still charged at ten pounds in the hat) following the class had proved as much a draw as the class itself. This evening he'd brought some velvet slippers, a leather-bound book and an old pipe from home, which he'd arranged on a swathe of patterned fabric in a tableau on the central table. Having covered the importance of tone, using pencil and charcoal, he'd brought boxes of pastels along for their first foray into colour, and was showing the class some simple techniques.

Julian was just passing round some examples of Degas pastels for inspiration, when there was a rattle behind him, and he turned to see someone trying the door handle. Monica pushed back her chair and went over to open the door.

'I'm afraid we're closed,' he heard her say. 'It's a private art class. It's not too late to join in though, if you have fifteen pounds and you're game enough.'

As Monica rejoined the group with a young man in tow, it was obvious to Julian why he hadn't been sent away. He was not the sort of man who was often turned down, Julian imagined. Even with his critical eye for facial symmetry and underlying bone structure, he had to admit the newcomer was gorgeous. Dark-skinned, and even darker brown eyes, but a mop of unruly, improbably blond curls. And as if that wasn't enchanting enough, he turned to greet the group with 'All right guys? I'm Riley,' in an Australian accent that brought the beach with it.

Monica collected an extra sheet of paper and placed it on the same table as hers, pulling up an additional chair, and moving her things along to make room.

'Just give it your best shot, Riley,' he heard her explain. 'Apart from Julian here, we're all amateurs, so don't be embarrassed. I'm Monica, by the way.' Everyone else around the circle took turns introducing themselves, ending with Julian, who announced his name with a theatrical bow and a flourish of the panama hat he'd chosen that morning to go with his cream linen suit, causing three mobile phones to fall out. With one swoop of the arm he'd morphed from looking like a plantation owner to a pickpocket.

Julian had noticed how each new entrant to the class changed the dynamic and the mood of the whole group, like mixing a new colour on to a palette. Riley added yellow. Not a pale-primrose yellow, a deep-cadmium yellow or a dark ochre, but the bright, hot yellow of sunshine. Everyone seemed a bit warmer, more animated. Sophie and Caroline, the two middle-aged mums who always sat together, exchanging gossip from the school gates as they worked, turned towards him like daffodils seeking the light. Baz looked totally smitten, and Benji a little jealous. Riley himself seemed utterly unaware of the effect he was having, in the same way a pebble doesn't see the ripples it forms in a pond. He frowned in concentration at the blank black cartridge paper in front of him.

Sophie whispered something to Caroline as she nodded over towards Riley. Caroline burst out laughing.

'Stop!' she said. 'Please don't make me laugh. After three children, my pelvic floor can't take it.'

'I have no idea what this *pelvic floor* is,' said Julian, 'but next time please leave it at home and don't let it disrupt my art class.' That told them, he thought, and was a bit miffed when Sophie and Caroline laughed even harder.

Julian began his customary circuit of the room, adding a word of encouragement here, a smudge of colour there, a quick correction to proportion or perspective. When he reached Monica, he smiled. Monica was one of his most diligent students. She listened intently, and was really keen to get it right. But today, for the first time, she was drawing with her heart, not just her head. Her strokes had loosened up, become more instinctive. As he watched her laughing and joking with Riley, he knew what had made the difference: she'd stopped trying so hard.

Julian wondered, for a moment, whether he might just be witnessing the start of a romance. A grand love affair perhaps, or just a brief interlude. But no. One of the benefits of being *an artist* is that you spend so much time watching people, looking not just at all the shades and contours of their faces, but into their souls. It gives you an almost uncanny insight. You gained, particularly when you got to Julian's age, the ability to read people and know how they were going to react. Monica, Julian could tell, was far too independent, too driven and focused to be distracted by a pretty face. She had loftier ambitions than marriage and babies. That was one of the things he admired so much about her. Even back in his heyday, he wouldn't have made a play for Monica. She would have terrified him. Riley, he surmised, would be wasting his time.

Monica

The rattling of the door had irritated Monica. She'd been deep in concentration, trying to recreate the right shade of burgundy for her slippers. She'd got up to send the unwanted visitor away, but then she'd opened the door and been met by a man with a smile so bewitching that she'd found herself ushering him in and making a space in their circle. Next to her.

Monica was not terribly good with strangers. She was usually far too concerned about making the right impression to be able to relax. She'd never forgotten being told before her first big job interview that 90 per cent of the opinion people have of you is formed in the first two minutes. But Riley wasn't the type of man who could ever feel like a stranger. He seemed to just slot into their group, like the final ingredient in a recipe. Did he fit in like that everywhere he went? What an extraordinary skill. She always had to muscle her way into a circle, using her elbows, or stand on the outside, craning her neck to look in.

'How long have you been in London, Riley?' she asked him.

'I got off the plane the day before yesterday. I left Perth ten days ago, and did a couple of stops on the way. I'm staying with some friends of friends, in Earl's Court.'

Riley's whole demeanour was easy-going and relaxed, such a contrast to the rigidity of most Londoners. He'd slipped his shoes off, and was swinging one of his bare, tanned feet back and forth. Monica wondered if there were still grains of sand between his toes. She fought the urge to drop a pencil just so she'd have an excuse to scrabble around under the table and have a look. *Stop it, Monica*, she chided herself, remembering one of her mother's favourite sayings: *A woman needs a man like a fish needs a bicycle*. But it was all so bloody contradictory at times. How on earth did that fit in with *Don't leave it too late to have a family, Monica. Nothing brings more joy than family*? Even Emmeline Pankhurst had a husband, and children – five of them. Doing life properly wasn't easy.

'Have you been to London before?' she asked Riley.

'No. This is my first time in Europe, actually,' he replied.

'I'm going to Borough Market tomorrow, for supplies. You want to come? It's one of my favourite parts of London,' she said, almost before she knew what she was doing. Where had that come from?

'I'd love that,' he replied with a grin that looked totally genuine. 'When are you leaving? I have no plans at all.' How could anyone have no plans? And he hadn't even asked what, or where, Borough Market was. Monica would never have agreed to an arrangement without the necessary due diligence. But she was very glad he had.

'Why don't you meet me here at ten-ish? After the early-morning rush.'

Monica had added a bright-red sweater, low-heeled boots, some large hoop earrings and a dash of red lipstick to her work outfit of crisp white shirt and black trousers. She kept reminding herself that this was a *work trip* and not a date. Riley wanted to get to know London better; she needed some help carrying the bags. If it *had* been a date, she'd have agonized for days about what to wear, planned a few witty anecdotes to be tossed casually into the conversation should it flag, and looked up potential venues for any impromptu change in plans. Preparation is the key to effective spontaneity. Not that any of that had worked so far, thought Monica, remembering Duncan, the bee-loving vegan. She prodded that thought, like checking a sore tooth, to see if it still hurt. Nothing but a dull ache. Well done, Monica.

Riley had turned up late. She knew she'd said ten-*ish* (she'd been trying to sound relaxed and casual), but she'd meant ten, obviously. Not ten thirty-two. But being cross with Riley felt like kicking a puppy. He was so bouncy and enthusiastic about everything, and so different from herself that she found him intriguing, if a little exhausting. He was also drop-dead gorgeous, she thought, then ticked herself off for being so shallow. Sexual objectification was not OK, under any circumstances.

'I wish my brothers and sisters could see all this,' Riley said as they wove their way around all the stalls. The various cultures and influences that made up the melting pot of London butted up against each other, assaulting the senses and competing for custom.

'I wish I *had* brothers and sisters,' said Monica. 'I was a much longed-for only child.'

'Did you invent an imaginary friend?' asked Riley.

'No, I didn't actually. Does that mean I have a terrible lack of imagination? But I did give all my teddy bears names, and ticked them off on a register every evening.' Oh God, was she sharing too much? She was *definitely* sharing too much.

'I spent all my spare time at Trigg Beach surfing with my older brothers. They took me out when I was so small I couldn't even carry my own board,' said Riley. They joined the queue for pulled pork rolls. 'I just love street food, and eating with my fingers, don't you?' said Riley. 'I mean, who invented knives and forks? What a killjoy!'

'Actually, if I'm honest, street food makes me a bit nervous,' said Monica. 'I'm pretty sure they don't get regular food safety inspections, and *none* of them are displaying a food hygiene certificate.'

'I'm sure it's all perfectly safe,' said Riley. Monica loved his optimism, but thought him dangerously, if sweetly, naive.

'Is it though? Look at the lady serving. She's not wearing gloves, despite doing the cooking *and* handling all that money, which is a *hotbed* of bacteria.' Monica knew that she was probably coming across as a little obsessive. It was likely, actually probable, that Riley had much less interest in food safety than she did. She also found herself flushing at the use of the words 'hot' and 'bed' next to each other. Get a grip, Monica.

After a bit, though, Monica realized that, despite herself, she was enjoying being the sort of girl who ate with her fingers on the street, with a gorgeous man she barely knew. She was being positively reckless. The world suddenly seemed much bigger and more laden with possibility than it had just a few moments ago. They moved on to a stall selling Mexican churros, still warm, covered in sugar and dipped in molten chocolate.

Riley took his thumb and dabbed it gently at the corner of her mouth. 'You missed a bit of chocolate,' he said. Monica felt a yearning much stronger than the one for sugar. She quickly ran through her mental list of all the reasons why the positively steamy but totally unwelcome visions that had forced their way into her head were never going to be a reality:

1. Riley was just passing through. There really was no point in getting involved

2. Riley was only just thirty, seven years younger than her. And he seemed even younger; a lost boy in Neverland

3. He'd never be interested in her anyhow. She knew roughly where she sat in the pecking order of attractiveness. Riley, with his exotic beauty (Australian father, Balinese mother, she'd discovered) was *way* out of her league

'We should be heading back,' she said, aware that if a spell had been woven, she was breaking it.

'Are your parents foodies too, Monica? Is that where you

get it from?' asked Riley, as they wound their way past a stall groaning with baskets of olives in every shade of green and black.

'Actually, my mother's dead,' replied Monica. Why had she said that? You'd think she'd know by now how quickly that could put a downer on a conversation. She carried on, in a gushing stream of words, to avoid a pause that Riley would feel the need to fill. 'Our home was filled with convenience foods – instant mashed potato, Findus pancakes and, for special occasions, M&S Chicken Kievs. Mum was an ardent feminist, you see. She thought that cooking from scratch would be surrendering to the patriarchy. When my school announced that the girls were going to do home economics while the boys did woodwork, she threatened to handcuff herself to the school gate unless I was allowed a free choice. I was so envious of my friends, carrying home beautifully decorated fairy cakes while I slaved over a wonky birdbox.'

Monica could remember so vividly shouting at her mother: *You are not Emmeline Pankhurst! You are just my mother!*

Her mother had replied, in a voice that was pure steel, *We are all Emmeline Pankhurst, Monica. Otherwise what was it all for?*

'I bet your mum would be really proud of you now, Monica. Owning your own business,' said Riley.

It was so precisely the right thing to say that Monica felt a lump forming in her throat. Oh God, please don't cry. She channelled Madonna again. Madge would never, ever, let herself weep in public.

'Yes, I think she would. That's one of the main reasons I started the café, actually,' she said, managing to keep the wobble out of her voice. 'Because I knew how much she'd have loved it.'

'I'm really sorry about your mum,' said Riley, putting his arm around her shoulder, a little awkwardly as he was carrying so much of her shopping.

'Thanks,' she replied. 'It was a long time ago. I just never understood *why her*. She was such a firebrand, so vivid and alive. You'd think cancer would have picked on an easier target. She used to hate it when people talked about "fighting" or "battling" the disease. She'd say, *How am I expected to fight something I can't even see? It's not a level playing ground, Monica.*'

They walked in step, in a slightly strained silence, then Monica brought the conversation back round to pricing structures, which made her feel much more comfortable.

'I'm not sure I could cope with this climate for long. What was I thinking coming to England in *November*? I've never been anywhere so cold,' Riley told her as they walked over London Bridge, back to the north side of the river. 'I only had room for light stuff in my rucksack, so I had to buy myself this overcoat before I froze to death.' His Australian accent turned every statement into a question. The wind picked up, whipping Monica's long, dark hair across her face.

They stopped for a minute, in the middle of the bridge, so Monica could point out some of the landmarks lining the Thames – St Paul's Cathedral, HMS *Belfast* and the Tower of London. As she was talking, something extraordinary happened. Riley, still clutching an armful of boxes and bags, leaned towards her and *kissed her*. Just like that. Mid-sentence.

Surely, you couldn't do that? In this day and age, it was entirely inappropriate. You had to ask *permission*. Or, at least, wait for a signal. She'd been saying *if the Tower of London ravens fly away, superstition says the Crown and country will fall*, and she was pretty damn sure that that sentence couldn't be seen as a come-on. She waited for her sense of outrage to gather. Instead, she found herself kissing him back.

Frailty, thy name is woman! she thought, quickly followed by *oh, sod it*. She grasped, desperately, for her mental list of reasons why this was *absolutely not a good idea*. Then, as he kissed her again she tore it in half, ripped it into shreds, scattered those pieces over the side of the bridge and watched them float like snowflakes into the river below.

Riley was never going to be a sensible long-term proposition, obviously, he was too different from her, too young, too transitory, and she'd like to bet he'd never read any Dickens. But maybe she could just have a fling? See what happened. Be spontaneous. Maybe she should try on that persona, like she would a fancy dress outfit, just for a while.

Riley

Riley had been several hours into his journey to Heathrow, fascinated by the flight tracker on the screen in front of him, which showed a little aeroplane travelling across the northern hemisphere. Until last week, he'd never crossed the equator. Was it true that the water in England swirled in the opposite direction down a plughole? He didn't suppose he'd be able to find out, since he'd never noticed which way it circled back home. I mean, why would you ever pay attention to that?

He reached into the backpack by his feet to find the Lee Child he'd been reading, and pulled out a pale-green notebook. It didn't belong to him, although it reminded him of the book he used back home to jot down customer briefs for his gardening business. For a moment, he wondered if he'd got the wrong bag, but everything else in it was his; his passport, wallet, guidebooks, and a chicken sandwich, lovingly packed by Barbara. He turned to the friendly-looking, middle-aged woman in the seat next to him.

'Does this belong to you?' he asked, thinking that she might have mistaken his bag for her own, but she shook her head.

Riley flipped the book over to look at the front cover. On it were the words *The Authenticity Project*. Authenticity. Great word. There was something really *British* about it. He rolled it over in his mouth, trying it out loud. It tied his tongue into knots and made him sound like he had a speech impediment. Riley turned to the first page. He had eight hours left to go, he might as well see what was in it, since it appeared to have hitched a lift in his luggage.

Riley read Julian's story, and Monica's. Julian sounded like a proper character, exactly as he'd imagined the English to be. Monica needed to chill out a bit. She should come and live in Australia! She'd soon relax and have a brood of half-Australian kids running around her feet and driving her crazy. He looked up Fulham in the London A to Z he'd been given as a leaving present from a client. It was just around the corner from Earl's Court where he was headed. What a coincidence. How strange to think that these were people he'd never met but whose deepest secrets he now knew.

He turned to the next page where the handwriting changed from Monica's neat and rounded script to a more haphazard scrawl, as if an insect had walked through a pool of ink and then died.

My name is Timothy Hazard Ford, although when you have a middle name like Hazard, no one is going to call you Timothy, so for most of my life I've been known as Hazard Ford. Yes, I have heard all the jokes about sounding like a road sign. Hazard was the surname of my maternal grandfather, and using it as one of my names was probably the most unconventional thing my parents ever did. Since then, their whole lives have been dominated by the question 'What would the neighbours think?'

Hazard. Riley knew exactly who he was. The ex-banker he'd met on his last stop in Thailand, the one who'd been so interested in Riley's life and his plans. How had Hazard's book ended up in his bag? How on earth was he going to return it?

You'll have read Julian and Monica's stories. I've never met Julian, so I can't tell you any more about him, but I can fill you in a little about Monica. I live just a few minutes' walk from her café (which is at 783 Fulham Road, by the way, next to Nomad Bookshop. You will need that information!), so I dropped in there after I read her story.

You will need that information? Who, Riley wondered, was Hazard talking to? Hopefully he'd find out.

I only went there to give her the book back, but I never did. Instead, I took it with me to Thailand, to a tiny island called Koh Panam.
   I was at a boys' school that took girls in the sixth form. When the new girls first walked into the dining room we would each hold up a score card giving them

*marks out of ten. I'm not kidding. I feel terrible about
it now, obviously. Anyhow, had Monica walked into
that room I'd have given her an eight. Actually, I was
such a raging mass of hormones and unrequited desires
that I'd probably have upped it to a nine.*

*She's quite fit, Monica. She's slim, with neat little
features, a turned-up nose and hair like a show pony.
But she has an intensity to her that I find off-putting to
the point of terrifying. She makes me feel that I must be
doing something wrong (which I probably am, to be
honest). She's the sort of person who arranges all the
tins in her cupboards so they're facing outwards, and
puts all the books on her shelves in alphabetical order.
And she has an air of desperation that I might be
exaggerating in my imagination because I've read her
story, but it makes me want to run for the hills. She
also has an annoying habit of obstructing pavements,
but that's another story.*

*In short, Monica's not my type. But I'm hoping that
she might be yours, because, as you can see, the girl
really needs a good man, and I expect that you are a
better man than I am.*

*I don't know if Monica's plan to help Julian by
advertising for an art teacher worked, but I know it
wouldn't have done if I'd left it up to her. She'd put one,
rather inadequate, poster up in the café window, which
there was no way he'd notice. So, I gave her a bit of a
helping hand. I took the poster down, went to the
nearest printing shop and made about ten copies which
I posted all around Chelsea Studios. I even found the*

Admiral's gravestone, the one Julian mentioned, and stuck one on there. I nearly missed my flight, wandering around that bloody cemetery. Looking back, I see that I wasn't being altruistic. It was displacement activity. Concentrating on Monica's advertising campaign stopped me heading for the off-licence to buy vodka for the journey. I do hope all that effort paid off.

I suppose I should answer Julian's question: what's the one thing that defines you, that makes everything else about you fall into place? Well, I don't have to think about that for very long: I AM AN ADDICT.

For the last ten years or so, pretty much every decision I've made – big or small – has been driven by my addiction. It's led to my choice of friends, how I spend my spare time, even my career. Trading is, let's be honest, just a legitimized form of gambling. If you'd met me back home, you'd have assumed I had it all together – the insanely well-paid job, beautiful apartment and gorgeous women, but the reality was I spent a huge proportion of every day just planning my next high. I would be floored by even the tiniest flicker of anxiety, stress or boredom and would escape to the toilet with a hip flask of vodka or a wrap of coke to take the edge off.

Riley wondered for a moment whether he could be reading about a different Hazard. The guy he'd met was a health nut. He didn't drink, he didn't party – he was in bed by about 9 p.m. most nights and up really early *meditating*. Riley had assumed he was completely vegan (perhaps because of the hipster-style beard and the way he wore sarongs all the time) until he'd seen him eating fish. But, he reasoned, what was the likelihood of anyone else being called Hazard whose book could have found its way into his bag? Zero.

Riley frowned. How could he have misjudged Hazard so badly? Was everyone so complicated? He certainly wasn't. Did he really know anyone at all? He read on, slightly warily.

I'd long passed the point where it was any fun. The highs weren't high any more, they were just what I needed to get through the day. My life got smaller and smaller, stuck on this miserable treadmill.

Recently I found a photo of me, aged about twenty, and realized that I'd lost myself. Back then, I was kind and optimistic and brave. I used to travel, seek out adventures. I learned how to play the saxophone, to speak Spanish, to dance the salsa and to paraglide. I don't know if it's possible to be that man again, or if it's just too late.

There was one moment, just yesterday, when I found myself awestruck by the phosphorescence in the South China Sea at night, and it made me think that perhaps I could rediscover that sense of wonder and joy. I hope so. I don't think I can bear the idea of living the rest of my life with no highs.

So, what now? I can't go back to my old job. Even if I could manage to mix with the old crowd and work the markets while staying sober, I rather burnt my bridges. When I resigned to my old boss (while high, obviously; last hurrah, and all that), I let slip that at the last office party I'd shared a gram of coke with his wife and shagged her on the very desk he was sitting behind. I'd then made a joke about going out with a bang. He's unlikely to give me a glowing reference.

By this stage, Riley's eyes were on stalks. He didn't think people like Hazard actually existed in Perth.

Anyhow, working in the City eats away at your soul. You never actually make anything, other than more money. You don't leave a legacy. You don't change the world in any meaningful way. Even if I could go back there, I wouldn't.
So, Riley. What are you going to do now?

Riley gasped out loud at seeing his name written on the page, causing the middle-aged woman sitting next to him to look at him curiously. He smiled at her, apologetically, and carried on reading.

The Authenticity Project didn't land in your bag by chance. I've spent the last few weeks looking for the right person to take it on. You're carrying Julian's book back to the same part of the world I took it away from. I wonder whether you might be the right sort of person to be a friend to Julian, or a lover for Monica. Or both. Will you go and find the café? Will you change some-one's life? Will you write your story?
I hope one day I'll find out what happened next, because I'll miss this notebook. At a time when I was

floating aimlessly in space, it kept me tethered to the space station.

Bon voyage, Riley, and good luck.

Hazard

It'd been two days since Riley had arrived in London, and it still felt surreal, like he was living in a travel show. His flat in Earl's Court appeared to be in the middle of a gigantic building site. Everything around him was either being torn down or rebuilt. It gave him an unsettled feeling, as if standing still would put him at risk of being demolished and remodelled.

Sometimes, Riley wished he'd never found The Authenticity Project. He didn't like knowing other people's secrets – it felt like prying. Yet, once he'd read their stories, he hadn't been able to forget about Julian, Monica and Hazard. It was like being partway through a novel, becoming invested in the characters, then leaving it on a train before you reached the end.

He'd not been able to resist checking out the café. He'd thought he could have a look at Monica, maybe Julian too, see if the reality matched the images he couldn't shake from his head. That couldn't do any harm. What he wouldn't do, he'd promised himself, was to *get involved*. But, as he'd walked towards Monica's Café, his sense of anticipation had increased, to the point that, when he reached the door, he'd quite forgotten about remaining a spectator, and, having seen all the people inside, he'd pushed on the door handle.

Before he knew what had happened, he'd found himself

joining an art class taught by *Julian*. And now he was wandering around this awesome market with *Monica*.

Monica was so different from the jolly, fun and uncomplicated girls Riley hung out with back home. One minute she was opening up to him about her mother's death, the next minute she'd clammed up and started talking about profit margins on the items she was buying. That was a bit of an eye-opener. With his gardening business, he'd worked out prices by having a rough guess at costs, then adding on however much he thought his customer could afford. He always made a loss on the work he did for Mrs Firth (recently widowed), but charged the hedge-funder down the road double. That seemed the fairest way to work.

He decided not to suggest this to Monica, as she was really *scientific* about her pricing. She muttered about percentages, overheads and volume discounts, and worked it all out without a calculator, jotting down notes in a tiny book she kept in her pocket.

Trying to get close to Monica was like playing the children's game of Grandmother's Footsteps – slowly edging forward whenever she wasn't looking, and constantly being sent back to the beginning whenever she turned around and caught him moving. But, instead of being off-putting, it only made him want to know her more.

The only thing taking the edge off Riley's enjoyment, apart from Monica's strange obsession with bacteria, was the knowledge that he had to tell her about The Authenticity Project. It felt deceitful knowing more about her than she did about him, and he was, by nature, a very honest person. What you saw was what you got with him.

He hadn't been able to mention the book when he first met Monica, in the middle of that art class. It didn't seem fair to say 'By the way, I know all about your desperation for a husband and a baby' in front of a crowd. But the longer he left it, the more difficult it became. And now, somewhat selfishly, he didn't want to ruin the mood of the day by embarrassing her and making her feel uncomfortable, which confessing to knowing her deepest secrets was bound to do. He felt like he was walking around carrying an unexploded bomb amongst all the artisan cheeses, hams and chorizo. In the end, he decided not to say anything. It was quite possible that he wouldn't see Monica again after today, in which case, what she didn't know wouldn't hurt her.

And then, he'd ended up kissing her.

She'd been talking about London landmarks, or something. He'd rather lost track, as he'd become mesmerized by the fact that, with her dark hair, red lips, pale skin and cheeks rosy from the biting wind, she looked just like Snow White in the Disney cartoon. She was so strong and fearless. Usually a girl like her would scare the pants off him. Yet he'd read her story. He knew that, underneath the tough exterior, she just wanted rescuing. Feeling, for a fleeting moment, like the handsome prince in the fairy-tale, he'd kissed her, and she'd kissed him back. Quite enthusiastically, actually.

He'd happily have stayed like that for ever, nose to nose, on a bridge over the Thames, were it not for the secret that slid between them, like a barrier. How on earth could he tell her now?

He wasn't sure whether to curse Hazard, or thank him.

Julian

Julian was having guests for tea.

He couldn't remember the last time he'd had proper visitors, not just political canvassers, or Jehovah's Witnesses. He was trying to do something he believed would be described as 'decluttering'. But, after two or three hours of hard work, he'd barely made a dent in the decades' worth of acquisitions that were crowded into his sitting room.

He at least needed to make enough space for everyone to sit down. Why had he let it get like this? What would Mary, who had always kept the place so spic and span, say? Perhaps the compulsion to fill every inch of space was because it made him feel less alone, or because every single object was imbued with memories of happier times, and the objects had proven more reliable than the people.

He'd filled up both dustbins outside his cottage with rubbish, then he opened the door to the understairs cupboard and squeezed as much as he could into it: books, magazines, a stack of vinyl records, three pairs of wellington boots, a tennis racket, two lamps which no longer worked, and a bee-keeping outfit left over from a short-lived hobby two decades ago. He leant his back against the door afterwards to close it. He'd deal with it all properly later. At least he'd cleared the sofa and a few chairs.

The buzzer sounded. They were on time! Julian wasn't expecting that. He had always turned up to social events at least thirty minutes late. He'd liked to make an entrance. Perhaps prompt timekeeping was the latest fashion. He had so much to learn.

Julian walked out of the cottage and over to the black gate which led out to the Fulham Road. He opened the gate with his customary flourish and ushered in his three guests: Monica, that pretty Australian boy Riley, and Baz. Benji, they'd told him, was minding the café.

'Come in, come in!' he said as the three of them stood, open-mouthed, staring at the paved courtyard, with a bubbling fountain in its centre, the neatly mowed lawns, ancient fruit trees and the little village of studio buildings.

'Wow,' said Riley, 'this place is awesome.'

Julian winced at the use of American slang, accentuated by the Australian uplift, but decided to let it go. Now was not the time for a lecture on the beauty and versatility of the English language.

'I feel like the little girl in *The Secret Garden* who's followed the robin and discovered the magical place hidden behind the wall,' said Monica. She was far more lyrical than Riley, Julian noted with approval. 'It's like being in a different time, in another country.'

'It was founded in 1925,' Julian told them, encouraged by

CLARE POOLEY

their enthusiastic response, 'by a sculptor called Mario Manenti. Italian, obviously. He modelled it on his estate near Florence, so that he'd feel at home when he was in London, and only let the studios to other like-minded artists and sculptors. Now, of course, they've all been converted into flats. I'm the only artist left, and even I haven't painted since Mary . . .' His voice tailed off. Why had he not realized that Mary was his muse until she was no longer there? He'd assumed a muse must be ethereal and fleeting, not the one always around being taken for granted. Perhaps if he'd understood that, things would have been different. He rallied himself. Now was not the time for introspection and regrets. He was busy.

Julian ushered them over to the bright-blue painted door which led into his cottage.

'Look at the floor!' Monica said to Riley, gesturing at the wooden boards running the length of the ground floor; they were almost completely covered in paint splashes, as if a rainbow on the ceiling had exploded, occasionally broken up by bright, Moroccan-style kilim rugs. 'It's almost an artwork in itself.'

'Don't just stand around gawking. Sit, sit!' said Julian, as he led them over to the newly cleared chairs and sofa around a coffee table fashioned from a large piece of bevelled glass, balanced on four stacks of antique books. In front of them, laughing in the face of the local council's clean-air policy, a roaring fire burned in the grate.

'Tea! English breakfast, Earl Grey or Darjeeling? I might even have peppermint. Mary used to like it,' said Julian.

As Julian pottered around the little kitchen area, putting

94

tea bags into a pot, Monica searched the shelf he'd pointed out to her for the peppermint tea. Finally, she found a metal tin with an old, yellowing label marked PEPPERMINT. She opened the lid to take out a tea bag. Inside the tin was a folded-up piece of paper. She unfolded it carefully and read the words on it out loud: 'ALWAYS REMEMBER TO OFFER YOUR GUESTS A BISCUIT.'

Julian put the kettle down and covered his face with his hands. 'Oh, my goodness. That's one of Mary's notes. I used to find them all the time, but that's the first new one for a while. She was obviously worried about how I'd cope on my own, because when she knew she was going, she started hiding notes all over the cottage, giving me helpful tips. Damn, I forgot the biscuits. But don't panic. I have crumpets!'

'How long ago did she die, Julian?' asked Monica.

'On March fourth it will be fifteen years,' he replied.

'And you haven't opened this tin since then? Perhaps I'll have the English Breakfast.'

Monica stopped in front of a pencil sketch, pinned to the shelf above the stove, of a woman stirring a large casserole pot, and smiling over her shoulder.

'Is that Mary, Julian?' she asked.

'Oh yes. That's one of my favourite memories. You'll see them pinned up everywhere. There's one in the bathroom of her brushing her teeth, one in there' – he gestured back towards the living room – 'of her curled up in her armchair with a book. I don't believe in photographs. They have no soul.'

They sat around the fire, in varying degrees of comfort, depending on which of Julian's various items of decaying furniture they'd landed on, toasting crumpets over the fire.

'I feel like I've been transported into an Enid Blyton novel,' said Baz. 'Julian's just like Uncle Quentin. Monica, are you going to suggest a trip out to Kirrin Island with a tin of sardines and lashings of ginger beer?'

Julian wasn't sure he liked the idea of being Uncle Quentin. Wasn't he a paedophile?

'I'm wondering if you lot could help me with something,' he said.

'Of course,' said Baz, automatically, without even waiting to hear what Julian was going to ask.

'I've been thinking that I might need a mobile telephone. So you could get in touch with me if there's some problem with the art class, or something.' Having blurted that out, he rather wished he could take it back. He didn't want to sound needy, or make anyone feel obliged to telephone him.

'Do you really not have a mobile already?' asked Baz, with the total incomprehension of one born after the invention of the internet.

'Well, I haven't been terribly mobile for a while, and nobody tends to telephone me, so what would be the point? I use that,' he said, gesturing at a dark-green Bakelite telephone in the corner with a *dial*, and a heavy receiver attached to a coiled cord. Monica went over to look more closely. The disc in the centre of the dial read *Fulham 3276*. 'Besides,' continued Julian, 'you can slam down a phone like that. You can't slam down a mobile. Imagine, a whole generation who'll never know the joy of slamming down a phone.'

'My parents had a phone like this in the hall, when I was little,' said Monica.

'I did have a mobile phone in the past. In fact, I was an

early adopter,' Julian told them. 'I was given one of the first models to try out, since I was rather fashionable back then, and one of the magazines wanted to interview me on whether I thought they would catch on. I've probably still got it somewhere.'

He tried to pull himself out of his chair, but it was much deeper than the one he usually sat in. Baz held out his hand and helped him to his feet. 'Thank you, Baz,' he said. 'These days, if I sit for terribly long, everything seems to seize up.'

'You should take up tai chi, like my granny,' he said. 'She swears by it. Only way to start the day. Keeps the old body moving and the mind alert, she says.'

'So, did you say that they'd catch on? Mobile phones?' asked Monica.

'No!' laughed Julian. 'I said no sane person would want to be tracked down all the time, I certainly didn't, and that it was an invasion of privacy!'

Julian reached up to a high shelf in the corner of the room and brought down a large, dusty cardboard box. Inside it was a phone which could hardly be described as mobile. It was shaped like a brick, with a long, solid aerial protruding from the top, and was larger than Monica's handbag. You'd need a small suitcase to carry it around.

'Julian, that is the exact model that Gordon Gekko owned in *Wall Street*,' said Riley. 'You could sell that on eBay for a fortune. It's a proper collector's item.'

'I did have a much more up-to-date Nokia, too,' said Julian, 'back in the nineties, but when it gave up the ghost, after Mary went, I didn't bother replacing it. I've never had one of those clever phones.'

'Smart phones,' corrected Riley.

'But you do have access to the internet, right?' asked Baz, in shock. 'You've got a laptop or something?'

'I'm not a total Luddite, young man. I have a computer. I keep up to date. I read the newspapers, all the fashion magazines and watch television. I suspect I know much more about the influences on the Spring/Summer 2019 looks than even you do! After all, one thing I have plenty of is spare time.'

Baz picked up a viola, leaning against the bookcase, covered in a film of dust. 'Do you play, Julian?' he asked.

'It's not mine, it's Mary's. Please put it down. Mary doesn't like anyone touching her viola.' As he said it, Julian realized that he'd spoken in an unnecessarily curt voice and could easily be accused of overreacting. Poor Baz was looking a little taken aback.

'Can I use your dunny?' asked Riley, causing a welcome distraction. A *dunny*? This was central London, not the outback. Julian decided to let it go, and pointed Riley back towards the front door.

A huge crash caused Monica to spill some of the tea she was drinking on to her lap. They all turned around to see Riley, rooted to the spot in shock, surrounded by a mountain of objects that had erupted out of the cupboard like Jack from his box. A mound of records, which had fallen out of their sleeves, wellington boots and magazines and, balanced on the top, a bee-keeper's hood.

'I think I got the wrong door,' he shouted back to them, trying to push everything back into the cupboard. This was an impossible task, as the pile of contents seemed to take up twice as much room as the cupboard they'd escaped from.

'Do leave it, dear boy,' said Julian. 'I'll sort it out later. I need to do a trip to the dump.'

'Don't you dare, Julian!' said Riley, looking horrified. 'I'm sure there are some real treasures in here. I'll help you sell them online.'

'I couldn't possibly ask you to do that,' protested Julian. 'You have far better things to occupy your time, I'm sure. Or, at least, I'd have to pay you a fair wage.'

'Tell you what, if you give me 10 per cent of everything I make, then we're both happy. You get rid of some of the clutter, and I get some funds for my trip. I'm dying to see Paris.'

'And I can help with the phone,' interjected Monica. 'I upgraded my iPhone recently, so you can have my old one. We'll get you a pay-as-you-go SIM card.'

Julian looked at Riley and Monica, now sitting side by side on his sofa. If he wasn't mistaken, Riley was a little smitten. He'd noticed, with his artist's eye for postural detail, how he mimicked her gestures and sat just a little closer than one would expect (although that might be the result of the exposed springs and stuffing bursting out of the sofa to his left).

Oh, the optimism of youth.

Monica

Monica wiped down the counter in preparation for opening. She squirted the bottle of cleaning fluid she was holding, breathing in the satisfying scent of mountain pine. She realized that she was humming. Monica was not a hummer by nature, but recently, and surprisingly, she had quite a lot to hum about.

Since she'd started the weekly art class, she'd been approached by a knitting circle and a pregnancy yoga class, both looking for local evening venues. Monica's Café seemed to be turning into a hub of the local community, just as she'd dreamed of ever since she first saw the boarded-up sweet shop. And, even better, when she'd sat down to corral her numbers last night, they had very nearly added up. For the first time, she could see a chink of liquidity at the end of the dark tunnel of her overdraft.

Then there was Julian. She genuinely loved his company and his art lessons, but she also had the warm, self-satisfied glow of someone who's done something *good*, changed someone's life for the better. You didn't get *that* feeling often when working for a corporate law firm.

It struck Monica that she'd started the art class as a way of helping someone else, but now it seemed to be helping her even more. She'd never believed in karma until now.

And the icing on the cake was Riley. Of course, she knew he wasn't the whole cake. If she delved too deeply into their relationship, or looked too far ahead, she knew it didn't meet her criteria. So, she wasn't delving. Monica was staying in the moment. She was taking each day as it came and just enjoying herself. Who knew what lay around the next corner or how long Riley would stay in London?

This obviously did not come naturally. It took a lot of planning and hard work for Monica to be this relaxed. She was getting up half an hour earlier than usual to do her sun salutations and repeat her mantras.

'Yesterday is history, tomorrow is a mystery, today is a gift,' she'd chant to herself as she brushed her teeth. 'It's not happy people who are grateful, it's grateful people who are happy,' she'd say as she brushed her hair.

Monica was rather proud of her new, almost-on-the-verge-of-being-chill attitude. Usually by this stage, she would have fast-forwarded the movie of her life in her head to the point where she'd have worked out where and when she and Riley would get married, what their children's names would be and the colour of the towels in the guest bathroom (white).

Monica thought of all the self-help books she'd bought, the mindfulness course she'd attended and the meditation apps cluttering up her iPhone. All that effort spent trying to stop worrying about the future, when all she'd really needed was someone like Riley, because she was sure her attitude change was down to him.

Most of the men Monica knew had *hang-ups*. They felt inadequate about the school they'd been to, the house they'd grown up in, their lack of sculpted abdominal muscles or the number of notches on their bedpost. Riley, however, seemed totally comfortable in his own skin. He was so straightforward, easy-going and uncomplicated. He was not a man of mystery or hidden depths, but – on the upside – he was completely honest and transparent. Riley never stressed himself out by thinking too far ahead. Actually, he didn't seem to spend much time thinking at all, but nobody was perfect. And his attitude seemed to be infectious. For once, Monica didn't feel she needed to play games or to build any protective walls around herself.

Yesterday, they'd gone to Julian's extraordinary time warp of a house for tea. Monica had loved it, despite it being an obvious health hazard. She'd not been able to stop herself screaming when she first went into the kitchen and practically walked into a gruesome strip of yellow, hanging from the ceiling covered in the tiny desiccated corpses of hundreds of insects. Julian had been completely unperturbed by her horror, telling her it 'was only fly paper'. *Fly paper?* Was that really a thing? Surely even Julian realized that dead bodies were not generally advised in food preparation areas?

They'd actually toasted crumpets over a real fire (she'd tried not to think of the impact on climate change and all those poor baby polar bears, separated from their mothers by the melting ice floes) with proper toasting forks. She'd sat next to Riley on the sofa, and when no one was looking, he'd squeezed her hand.

After tea, Riley had come back to her flat. They hadn't discussed it, she hadn't invited him and he hadn't asked. It had just happened. Spontaneously. She'd made them supper with whatever she could find in her fridge and cupboards – pasta with pesto and a tomato, mozzarella and basil salad. He'd said it was the best meal he'd had in weeks. She smiled at the memory of the elaborately planned and executed meals she'd provided for men in the past – the soufflés, flambés and reductions, most of which had got nothing like as enthusiastic a reception.

There had been a tense moment when she noticed Riley examining her bookcase. Had she anticipated this romantic dinner à deux, she'd have removed some of the books in advance. She cringed particularly at the idea of him noticing *He's Just Not That into You, Ignore the Guy, Get the Guy, The Rules* and *Men are From Mars, Women are From Venus.* Monica saw all this reading as sensible groundwork. She approached dating in the same way as she would any project: do your background research, make a plan, set your goals. Riley, however, would probably see it as obsessive. Neither of them had mentioned the self-help books, and the awkward moment had passed quickly.

He hadn't stayed the night. They'd watched a movie on Netflix, curled up on the sofa together, sharing a bowl of tortilla chips. They spent much of the time kissing and joking about having missed most of the overly complicated plotlines. She'd been trying to work out how to let him down gently if he tried to push it too far, and then had been rather disappointed when he didn't.

Julian

Julian was not at all used to his intercom buzzing at 7.30 a.m. But then, many strange, new things had happened since he launched The Authenticity Project. He was still dressed in his pyjamas, so he threw on the nearest jacket he could find (Alexander McQueen circa 1995, wonderful epaulettes and gold frogging) and a pair of the wellingtons which had sprung from the understairs cupboard, and walked out to the gate.

Julian had to look down a couple of feet from his six-foot vantage point to see his visitor. She was a tiny, bird-like Chinese lady, face like a walnut, eyes like raisins and a wild thatch of short grey hair. She was, quite possibly, even older than himself. He was so busy staring at her that he quite forgot to speak.

'I am Betty Wu,' she said, in a voice much bigger than she was, seemingly undaunted by the appearance of a man dressed in a combination of haute couture, threadbare night-wear and wet weather gear. 'I come for tai chi.'

'Tai chi?' echoed Julian, aware he was sounding rather gormless.

'My grandson, Biming, he says you want to learn tai chi,' she replied slowly, in a tone one might use if talking to an idiot, or very young child.

'Biming?' echoed Julian, sounding like an idiot, or a very young child. 'Oh, do you mean Baz?'

'I do not know why he does not like Chinese name. Is he ashamed?' huffed the lady called Betty. 'He says you want me to teach you tai chi.'

Julian had said nothing of the sort, but realized that there was no point in arguing with this force of nature.

'Er, I wasn't expecting you, so I'm not exactly dressed for the occasion,' protested Julian who knew, far better than most, how important it was to wear the right outfit. 'Perhaps we should start another time?'

'No time like present,' said Mrs Wu, narrowing her narrow eyes at him. 'Take off the coat and big boots.' She glared at his wellies as if they'd badly offended her. 'You have big socks?' Julian, who was wearing his warmest woollen bed socks, nodded silently.

Mrs Wu walked into the centre of the paved courtyard, shrugging off her black wool coat, which she placed on the wrought-iron bench, to reveal loose black trousers, tied with a drawstring, and a pale-grey smock top. Although it was cold, the sheltered courtyard was lit by the pale winter sunshine. A light frost glittered like fairy dust.

'I talk, you copy,' instructed Mrs Wu as she planted her feet some distance apart, bent her knees and raised her arms in an extravagant swooping motion above her head, like a giant heron, breathing in through her nose in an exaggerated fashion.

'Tai chi is good for posture, circulation and flexibility. Makes you live longer. I have one hundred and five years old.' Julian stared at her, not sure how to respond politely, then she grinned broadly, revealing small, spaced-out teeth, not big enough for her mouth. 'It is only joke! Tai chi good, but not that good.'

Mrs Wu bent her knees again, then turned sideways, bending one arm behind her and pushing the other forwards, palm first, as if to ward off an intruder. 'Tai chi is about the balance of yin and yang. If you use hardness to resist force then both sides will break. Tai chi meets hardness with softness, so incoming force exhausts itself. It is philosophy for life also. You understand?'

Julian nodded, although he was finding it very hard to take in everything Mrs Wu was telling him, while simultaneously following her movements. Multi-tasking had never been his forte. That's why he'd never mastered the piano. He couldn't get his two hands to do different things concurrently. Right now, he was trying to balance on one foot with his right elbow touching his right knee.

'When we first come here in 1973, two men came to restaurant and say, "Go back to China and take your filthy, foreign food with you." I say, "You are angry. Anger comes from stomach. Sit. I bring you soup. For free. It will make you feel better." They ate my wonton soup. Recipe from my grandmother. They have been customers of restaurant for forty years. Meet force with softness. Recipe for life. Now you understand.' And, strangely, he did.

As Julian continued to mimic Mrs Wu's wide, sweeping movements, a robin flew down, reminding him of Monica's description of his Secret Garden. He perched on the edge of the stone fountain, cocked his head and looked at Julian, as if wondering what he was doing. *You may well ask*, thought Julian, wobbling on one foot.

After about half an hour, Mrs Wu put her hands together in prayer position and bowed towards Julian, who, still copying her, lowered his head towards hers.

'It is good for first lesson,' she said. 'In China, we say *one meal won't make a fat man*. You need to do little and often. I see you tomorrow. Same time.' She picked up her coat and shrugged it on, in one fluid motion.

'How much do I owe you for the lesson?' Julian asked.

Betty inhaled through her nose so sharply that her nostrils went white. 'No pay! You are friend of Biming. You are artist, yes? You teach me to paint.'

'OK,' Julian called after her as she bustled out of the gate. 'I'll see you at my art class on Monday. Come with Baz. I mean Biming.'

Without turning around, Mrs Wu raised her hand in acknowledgement and was gone, leaving the courtyard feeling emptier than before she'd arrived, as if she'd sucked up some of its energy and taken it with her.

Julian picked up his jacket and his wellingtons and walked back into the cottage, with more of a spring in his step than he'd had for a long time.

Fridays seemed to be coming around faster, thought Julian, as he walked towards the Admiral. It seemed like no time at all since he was last here. This time he was less surprised to see some figures already resting against the marble tombstone, bundled up in coats and scarves. As he got closer he could make out Riley, Baz and Mrs Wu.

'I told Granny I was coming here,' said Baz, 'and she insisted on bringing some of her wonton soup.'

'It's cold today. My soup warms the body, warms the soul,' said Mrs Wu, pouring soup from a huge Thermos into four mugs which Baz had been carrying in a wicker basket.

'Do sit down, Mrs Wu!' said Julian, gesturing at the marble slab over the Admiral. He wasn't actually worried about her comfort, but she was standing on Keith.

'To Mary!' said Riley, raising his mug. Mrs Wu raised her eyebrows into two curious caterpillars.

'His wife. Dead,' mouthed Baz to his grandmother.

'To Mary!' they all replied.

Riley

Riley was sorting through Julian's understairs cupboard. It was like the TARDIS from *Doctor Who* – far bigger on the inside than you could possibly imagine from the outside. He wondered whether, when he finally reached the back of it, he'd find himself in another universe. Or Narnia perhaps. He certainly wouldn't be surprised if it was snowing back there. It was freezing in here without a fire in the grate.

He'd spent one day last week photographing some of his discoveries and uploading them to eBay, and he'd already made more than seventy-five pounds in commission. If Julian would only let him have a rummage around in that dressing room, they could make a fortune. He'd suggested as much to Julian. 'You are not selling one single sock,' Julian had growled at him. Just to make sure he'd been clear enough, he'd stood in the doorway, spreading out his gangly arms to bar entry, like a giant mutant stick insect.

CLARE POOLEY

Riley was surrounded by three large piles. One pile was for items he thought would sell well, one was things to throw away, and one was things to keep.

Today, he'd arrived just before 10 a.m., knowing that Julian would be going out for his walk. Julian slowed the process down significantly. He would hover over Riley like a hawk, then swoop down, pulling a broken vase from the 'dustbin' pile, exclaiming, 'Charlie gave that to me after my 1975 exhibition on New Bond Street. Sold out in two days! Princess Margaret came, you know. I think she rather fancied me.' Theatrical gaze into the distance. 'Mary did not like her. Not one little bit. Filled with pink peonies, if I remember correctly! Can't possibly let go of that one, young Riley. No, no, no. That wouldn't do at all.'

This morning, after an hour to himself, he'd made significant progress. As soon as Julian was back, they'd start the long and torturous negotiation process, made bearable by being interspersed with Julian's wonderfully colourful and ribald anecdotes from the sixties, seventies and eighties.

He would pick up one of the vinyl albums from the pile, dust it off and place it on the old record player, regaling Riley with stories of how he'd partied with Sid Vicious and Nancy, or who he'd seduced to the soundtrack of Blondie's 'Heart Of Glass'. Riley wasn't sure how much he believed. Julian seemed to have been present at every significant social event in recent history, from dinners with Christine Keeler and Mandy Rice-Davies to the party where Mick Jagger and Marianne Faithfull were arrested for possession of marijuana.

Yesterday, Julian had introduced Riley to the Sex Pistols,

110

Talking Heads and Frankie Goes to Hollywood. When he'd sat on the beach in Perth, imagining his trip to London, he had not thought that he'd spend his time playing air guitar while a geriatric belted out the lyrics of 'Anarchy In The UK' into an empty beer bottle, masquerading as a microphone. He'd realized with some alarm, as the song (if you could call it that) came to an end, that Julian's eyes had welled up.

'Are you OK, Julian?' he'd asked.

'I'm fine,' he'd replied, flapping a hand in front of his face like a dying moth. 'It's just that when I listen to songs like this, it comes rushing back so vividly. I'm surrounded again by all those extraordinary people, my friends, in that incredible era. Then the track ends, and I remember I'm just an old man left with a dusty stylus bobbing up and down on smooth vinyl and too many regrets.' Riley hadn't known what to say to that. What was a stylus?

Riley's trip to London was proving to be the best of times and the worst of times. He loved the city, despite the tooth-numbing cold. He'd made some wonderful friends. The only problem was Monica. The more time Riley spent with her, the more he admired her. He loved her determination, her feistiness and her fierce intellect. He loved the way she'd picked up Julian and so elegantly pulled him into her circle, making him feel wanted and useful, not pitied. He loved her passion for her café and its customers. Just being with Monica made him feel more brave, energetic and adventurous.

But Riley hated the fact that their whole relationship was founded on a lie. Or, at least, a lack of truth. And the longer he left it, the harder it was to come clean. How was she going to react when she discovered that she was an ex-coke-head's pity project? She'd be furious. Or devastated. Or humiliated. Or all three.

Riley kept trying to forget about The Authenticity Project, but the information he'd read couldn't be unread. Usually, he'd just relax and enjoy the time he had with a potential lover, going with the flow and seeing where it led. But with Monica, he was too conscious of what she'd written in the book. He knew she wanted a long-term relationship, marriage, babies, the works, but he was just looking to have fun on his way through Europe. Wasn't he?

The spirit of Hazard had even haunted the lovely evening he'd spent in her flat. Remembering Hazard's hypothesis about Monica alphabetizing her bookcase, he hadn't been able to resist checking it out. It turned out she didn't sort her books by alphabet; she colour-coded them. More visually satisfying, she'd said.

The truth was, he had too much information, and Monica had not enough, and it was complicating everything. He couldn't even work out how much he genuinely liked Monica, and to what extent his feelings were a result of Hazard's matchmaking. If he'd been left to his own devices, would he have liked her less? Or perhaps more? In all likelihood, they'd never have met.

Until Riley had come across The Authenticity Project, he'd been totally authentic. Now he was a sham.

The only solution he could see was to make sure he didn't get any more deeply involved. Then, when he moved on in a few months, Monica wouldn't be too hurt and – crucially – she'd never find out how it'd all started. That meant no more kissing. Actually, scrap that – that (rather enjoyable) ship had already sailed – but definitely, categorically, *no sex*. Riley was good at treating sex casually, but he rather suspected Monica wouldn't be.

Hazard

Hazard felt like he was trapped in Groundhog Day. Every day the sun shone. Every day he'd follow the same routine: meditation with Neil, walk on the beach, swim, read in hammock, lunch, siesta, swim, dinner, bed. He realized he was 'living the dream'. He was in the picture on the screensaver that illuminated thousands of offices. He should be horribly grateful. But he was bored. Bored rigid. Bored stupid. Bored to death.

It struck Hazard that he had no idea what day of the week it was. His whole life had been run by the tyranny of the calendar – the sinking feeling of Sunday night, the rude awakening of Monday morning, the neither-here-nor-there hump of Wednesday and the euphoria of Friday evening. Yet now, not a clue. He was adrift.

Every day there'd be at least one departure from the beach, and at least one new arrival, usually several, so there were always new people to meet. But, after a while, those conversations all blurred into one. *Where are you from?*

Where are you going next? What do you do back home?
They'd just skate over the surface of the getting-to-know-each-other thing, and then they'd be gone. All these constant new beginnings, without any middles or satisfactory endings, were exhausting.

Just a few more weeks, Hazard told himself, and I'll be strong enough to move on, to resist temptation, to go home.

Hazard was spending more and more time thinking about home. Strangely, he wasn't thinking about his family and friends – there was too much regret bound up in those memories. He knew all about 'making amends'. One evening, about a year ago, he'd had a phone call from a girl called Wendy. She was, she'd told him, doing 'the steps'. The conversation had been derailed for a while as Hazard thought she was referring to an exercise class. Wendy had explained that step nine of the Alcoholics Anonymous twelve-step programme was 'making amends', so she was calling to apologize for having two-timed him a few years earlier. She'd not told him she was married. Hazard was a little nonplussed, as it had taken a great deal of scrolling back through old photos on his iPhone before he remembered her at all. But now he thought back to Wendy, and her insistence that 'making amends with those you have wronged' was crucial to recovery. All those bridges burned had to be rebuilt, but not yet. He was too far away, and it was too difficult, so he filed it under 'deal with when I get home'.

In the meantime, because it was so much simpler and less entangled with self-hatred, he was thinking about Julian, Monica and Riley.

Had Monica managed to persuade Julian to teach her art

class? Was Julian less lonely? And, the question that taunted him most of all: had Riley found Monica, and was he the man of her dreams? Hazard felt like a writer, who'd started a story, then, partway through, his characters had just wandered off the page and started doing their own thing. How dare they? Didn't they realize they owed everything to him? He knew how unlikely a happy ending was, but sitting in his hammock, in this improbably beautiful setting, totally removed from reality, anything seemed possible.

Hazard basked in the unfamiliar warmth of having done something *good*. Something selfless. Kind. He had, so long as Riley cooperated, changed someone's life. Monica was going to be so grateful! Not that he needed thanks, obviously.

He threw a tanned leg out of his hammock and pushed his toes against the wooden slats of his deck to swing gently from side to side. He cursed himself for not getting Riley's mobile number, or the address where he was staying. He didn't even know his surname. He wished he could just send a text saying 'Hi. It's Hazard. How's it going in London?' Although, he reminded himself, he didn't have a phone to text from anyway. He knew where Julian was, and Monica, but they hadn't read his story, and Riley might not have told them about him yet. But he couldn't bear feeling so *left out*. Hazard always liked being in the centre of the action – that's probably what got him into this mess in the first place.

Then, he had an idea. It wasn't perfect, but it was just a small way to insert himself back into the story, to let them know that he was still part of The Authenticity Project.

There were two minibuses on the island which did circuits of the beaches, picking up tourists and dropping them into the only town, with its post office, bank and shops. The next time it stopped at Lucky Mother, Barbara gave him a shout, and Hazard jumped on.

The bus bumped along the dusty, potholed track. There were no doors, just a canvas roof to keep off the sun, and an open back. The air was sticky and smelled of sweat and sun lotion. Two benches faced each other, five or six tourists on each one, some clutching rucksacks, some just beach bags. Hazard looked down the row of legs alongside his – all various shades of white, brown and red, often covered in the raised red bulges of mosquito bites and grazes from the coral reef. They exchanged the usual: *where are you staying? Where have you been? What do you recommend seeing?* Hazard had had this conversation enough times to know all the tourist sites, restaurants and bars to recommend, both on the island and further afield, and didn't confess to not having been to any of them himself, other than his little beach and, from time to time, the town. He didn't want to explain why: *I can't trust myself.*

The bus stopped at the tiny ferry dock, where a boat was waiting to take passengers to Koh Samui. There, a bigger boat could take them on to Surat Thani on the mainland. For a few minutes, Hazard wondered if he should just get on that boat. He had his passport and cash in the money belt he was wearing under his t-shirt. And perhaps he might have done, he didn't mind the thought of leaving all his belongings behind in his hut, but he owed a week's rent to Andy and Barbara, and, after all their kindness, he didn't want them thinking he'd deliberately done a bunk.

Hazard went into the general store. This is where he'd

bought his sarongs, his sun cream, shampoo and tooth-paste. Just inside the doorway was a carousel of postcards. Hazard spun it round, until he found one which showed his beach. An aerial view. You could even just about make out his hut.

Hazard sat at a table outside the café, drinking coconut water through a straw inserted into a large coconut, and watched the ferry from Koh Samui belch some new tourists on to the wooden dock. They chattered excitedly about the beauty of their destination, ignoring the boatman who was struggling with their rucksacks. Using a biro borrowed from the waiter, he started to write.

Monica, Monica's Café, 783 Fulham Road, Fulham, London, UK.

To the lady who sells the best coffee in town.
See you soon.
Hazard.

Before he could change his mind, Hazard went into the post office, bought a stamp and posted it.

Monica

Monica was setting up the café for the evening's art class. Her mobile rang for the fifth time. She didn't even need to check who it was. It was Julian pocket-calling her again. He hadn't quite got to grips with his new mobile phone. He had, however, managed to call her on it earlier today to say that he'd decided the class were ready to move on to 'the human form', and could she please find someone to model for them.

That had not been as easy as it sounded. There wasn't enough time to run an advertisement, so she'd approached Benji. She explained that it wasn't gratuitous nudity, it was art. No one would be looking at him as Benji naked, but as a *subject*, much like Larry the lobster, only he wouldn't end up as dinner. She was sure that the pose Julian chose would be tasteful and discreet. No one would see his ... (she'd tailed off at this point). Finally, she'd resorted to offering him double overtime and an extra day off, and the deal had been done.

Julian arrived, wearing leather this evening, like a geriatric version of Danny in *Grease*, and the class started to fill up. 'I got chills, they're multiplying,' hummed Baz quietly to Benji. Benji didn't smile, he just lurked behind the counter managing to look both nervous and mutinous. Once everyone had taken a seat behind a table, Julian handed out paper and pencils.

'We're reverting back to pencil today, ladies and gentlemen, because we're moving on from still life to figure drawing. Before we start, please may I introduce you all to Mrs Wu.'

Everyone called out greetings to the diminutive Chinese lady, who stood and bowed. She wasn't a great deal taller standing up than she had been sitting down.

'Call me Betty!' she said, somewhat ferociously.

'Dear Benji has kindly agreed to model for us today,' said Julian, once all the introductions had been done. 'Can you come over here, Benji?'

Benji sidled up to the group. 'Er, where should I take my clothes off?' he asked.

'Clothes? Don't be silly, old chap. We only need to see your hands! No point running before you can walk. Here, sit on this chair and clasp this mug, interlocking your fingers. That's it. The hands are one of the most difficult parts of the body to draw, so for today, that's all we're focusing on.'

Benji glared darkly at Monica, wondering if he'd been set up. Monica glowered back, aware that she'd massively overpaid him for sitting in a chair, fully clothed, for two hours. Sophie and Caroline looked rather crestfallen. Sophie whispered something to Caroline who snorted with laughter.

Julian continued, seemingly oblivious to the undercurrents around him. 'Even the most experienced artists find hands difficult.' Julian paused and raised an eyebrow, as if to convey that this obviously didn't apply to him. 'Try not to think about what you *know* hands and fingers look like. Instead, look at them as a combination of shapes, edges and contours. Think about how you can use your pencil marks to describe the difference between the flesh and bone of the hand and the hard object it's holding. And do, please, try not to make Benji's elegant fingers look like a bunch of bananas.'

Gradually, a peace settled over the class, only broken by the scratching of pencils and the occasional murmured aside, or instruction from Julian.

As the class drew to a close, Riley put his hand up.

'What is it, young man? We're not at *school*, you know! You don't have to raise your hand!' Julian said, looking very much like a stern headmaster.

'Erm, I'm planning a trip to Paris and was wondering if you could recommend some good art galleries to visit,' said Riley as he lowered his arm awkwardly, and ran his hand through the blond frizz of his hair.

Monica felt the treacherous knot in her stomach that appeared whenever Riley mentioned leaving London. She wiped it out, like a smudge on one of her café windows. She was living in the moment, she reminded herself sternly.

'Ah, Paris. I haven't been for at least twenty years,' said Julian. 'So much to choose from – the Louvre is a must, obviously. The Musée d'Orsay and the Pompidou. Those would be a good place to start.' He stopped, frowning in thought. 'You know what? We should all go! Class field trip! What do you say?'

Monica, who loved nothing more than a new *project*, chipped in. 'What a great idea! I could do a group booking on the Eurostar. If we book now for January, we should be able to get a good deal. I'll work out some costs and report back next week. In the meantime, the ten-pound supper tonight, for anyone who's staying, is courtesy of the wonderful Betty Wu.'

'Crabmeat and sweetcorn soup, prawn and chive dumpling and vegetable spring rolls,' announced Betty. 'Biming! Hand round chopsticks, bowls and soup spoons, please.'

'Biming?' whispered Monica to Benji.

'I know. Don't say a word,' Benji replied. 'He's in denial.'

Riley hung back as everyone left the café, clutching their drawings of Benji's hands with varying degrees of pride and embarrassment, the warm glow of Betty's soup providing insulation against the cold night air.

'Would you like me to help you shut up shop?' he asked Monica, running his hands down her spine. He hooked his hands over the belt of her jeans and pulled her closer towards him. The feel of his surfer's thighs against hers made her breath catch in her throat.

'Thank you,' she replied, wondering whether she should let him stay tonight, if he asked. She imagined his face in sleep, his long, dark eyelashes resting against his cheeks. She pictured his dark limbs, tangled in her crisp, white bed linen. Her face felt so hot she was quite certain she was blushing. She wasn't sure she'd have the strength to send him home. She walked over to lock up the till. Riley followed her, carrying a couple of stray glasses back to the bar.

'What are these?' asked Riley, pointing at her array of colour-coded Post-it notes behind the counter.

'Those are my customer notes,' Monica replied. Riley picked one up and peered at the neat handwriting he recognized from the notebook.

'*Mrs Skinner. Dairy allergy. Baby called Olly. Ask after new puppy,*' he read aloud. 'And there was me thinking you just had an extraordinary memory.'

'I *do* have an extraordinary memory,' Monica replied. 'I wrote all those notes for Benji. Hey, I'm so excited about this trip to Paris!' she said, distracting Riley before he moved on to her less charitable notes, like *Watch out for Bert, the Fulham Football Club fanatic. Uses hand to wipe nose. Need anti-bacterial wipes.*

'Do you think everyone will come? I'm going to look up the best places to eat. There are just too many to choose from. You're going to love it, Riley. It really is one of the most beautiful cities in the world,' she said, having swiftly substituted 'beautiful' for 'romantic' mid-flow. This was a cultural expedition, not a dirty weekend. Having said that, perhaps she could book a charming boutique hotel, so that the two of them could stay on for an additional night. They could do a sunset walk along the Seine and eat warm pains au chocolat in bed for breakfast, with strong coffee and freshly squeezed orange juice.

She shook herself out of her reverie, and noticed that Riley was distracted, looking over her shoulder. She turned around to see what had caught his attention. It was a post-card she'd pinned on the noticeboard.

'Beautiful beach, isn't it? Somewhere in Thailand.' She squinted at the inscription in the bottom right corner. 'Koh Panam, apparently. Really strange though, I have no idea who it's from, although they obviously know me. Look.' She unpinned the postcard and flipped it over, handing it to Riley. 'It's addressed to Monica. *See you soon.* Do you think he's some kind of stalker? And it's signed *Hazard*. I mean what sort of a name is that? Sounds like a road sign!'

Then, with hardly a goodbye, Riley announced that he had to go. And Monica was left holding the strange post-card and wondering what on earth she had done wrong.

Julian

Monica hadn't told Julian she was coming. Julian suspected she'd deliberately caught him unawares, so he couldn't protest. She was standing on his doorstep, clutching a bucket filled with cleaning products in various garish colours, bright-yellow rubber gloves on her hands. Had she worn those in public? Surely not.

'It's a quiet day at the café today,' she said, 'so I thought I'd come round and give you a bit of a spring clean.' He must have looked as alarmed as he felt, because she quickly added, 'Not you. Your cottage. Don't worry – it's really not a chore. Cleaning is one of my all-time favourite activities, honestly. And this place is just an amazing . . .' She paused for a few seconds before pulling out the word 'challenge', like a rabbit from a hat. 'This, my friend, is the Rolls-Royce of cleaning projects.'

'Well, that's jolly kind of you, old girl,' he said, although he wasn't entirely sure that it was. She bustled past him into the hall. 'But it's really not necessary. I like it just the way it is. Honestly. Apart from anything else, it smells of Mary. If you start attacking the place with all that . . . *stuff*, you'll wash her right away.' She couldn't exactly argue with that, could she?

Monica stopped and turned to stare at him.

'Julian, no offence, but' – Julian resisted the urge to put his fingers in his ears; people always used that expression right before saying something really, really offensive – 'are you telling me that Mary smelled of mildew, dust and something unidentifiable that must have died under your kitchen cabinets?'

'Well, no, of course not!' he replied, horrified and a bit cross, actually. Maybe Monica sensed this because she took his hand in hers, thankfully having removed the ridiculous, ugly gloves first.

'Tell me what your cottage smelled like when Mary was here, Julian,' she said.

Julian closed his eyes and thought hard for several minutes, as he layered one scent on top of the other in his mind.

'I remember rose blossom, homemade strawberry jam and fresh lemons. That hairspray that came in big, gold cans. Oh, and paint, obviously,' he said.

'OK. Give me half an hour. I'll be back,' said Monica, and disappeared, as abruptly as she'd arrived.

When she returned, twenty-nine minutes later, she was carrying even more stuff. She piled her bags in a corner and stood in front of them so he couldn't see what was inside.

'Julian, I think it's probably best if you go out and leave me to it,' she said. 'Go and sit in the café. I've told Benji to put whatever you want to eat or drink on the staff tab. Stay away as long as you can. I'm going to need a while.'

Julian, who was beginning to learn that arguing with his new friend was a waste of time and energy, left, and spent a very pleasant afternoon chatting to the people coming and going in Monica's Café.

Benji taught him how to make a proper cappuccino, using the coffee machine that was the size of a small car, and just as complicated. Then he and Benji spent ages giggling like naughty schoolboys over Monica's 'customer notes', and adding a few made-up ones of their own.

He was trying very hard not to think about the devastation being wrought in his cottage.

For the first time in as long as he could remember, perhaps for ever, Julian knocked on his own front door. He was rather nervous about going in, and feeling like a visitor rather than the owner. After a minute or two, Monica appeared, her hair wrapped in a scarf, from which several damp tendrils had broken free. Her face was flushed and her eyes sparkled, as if she'd spring-cleaned them too. She was wearing one of Mary's pinnies. Where on earth had she found that?

'I'm afraid I've only done the sitting room and the kitchen,' she said. 'I'll come back and do the rest another day. Come in!'

'Monica!' he said. 'It's been *transformed*.' And it had. Light streamed through the windows, hitting surfaces which were cleared and polished. The rugs had gone from being a collection of sludgy colours to bright and vibrant, and there wasn't a cobweb in sight. It looked like a *home* again, as if Monica had washed away fifteen years, along with all the grime.

'What can you smell?' she asked. He closed his eyes and inhaled.

'Lemons, definitely,' he said.

'Yup. I used lemon-scented cleaning products. What else?'

'Strawberry jam!'

'Right again. Simmering on the clean and shiny hob in the kitchen. We'll need to find some jam jars. Take a seat while I finish up.'

Monica disappeared outside and came back carrying three large bunches of roses, which she must have hidden in the courtyard. She bustled around finding vases and arranging them on various surfaces.

'And now,' she said theatrically, 'for the finishing touch!' and she produced a can of Elnett hairspray – exactly the brand Mary had used – and spritzed it around his sitting room. 'Close your eyes, Julian. Now does it smell like it used to when Mary was here?'

He leant back in his favourite armchair (which didn't feel greasy any longer) and inhaled. And it did. He wanted to keep his eyes closed for ever, and to stay in 2003. But it needed one last thing.

'Monica,' he said. 'We have to do some painting. I'll give you a private lesson. It's the least I can do.'

Julian threw open the double doors from the sitting room into his studio. He pulled out a roll of canvas, spread it out on to the floor and started to mix paint with some linseed oil.

'This evening, Monica, we are going to do Jackson Pollock. I've watched you draw. It's all very neat and precise. You try to copy exactly what you see. But Pollock said, *Painting is self-discovery. Every good painter paints what he is.* He said it's about expressing your feelings, not just illustrating. Here, take this brush.' He handed Monica a brush almost the size of her hand. 'Pollock used household paints, but I don't have any, so we're using oils mixed with linseed and turpentine. He laid his canvas on the ground and painted in the air over it, using his whole body to do so, like a ballerina. Are you ready?'

He suspected she wasn't, and could see that she was worried about messing up his newly restored cottage, but she nodded anyway. He went back into the sitting room, selected a vinyl album and placed it on the turntable. There was only one man up for a task this theatrical: Freddie Mercury.

Julian took off his shoes, and slid across the now polished and shiny wood floor, back into the studio, singing 'Bohemian Rhapsody' with all the gusto, if not the talent, of Freddie. He picked up a brush, dunked it in a pot of burnt sienna and flicked it across the canvas, scattering paint into a wide arc.

'Go, Monica, go!' he cried. 'Use your whole arm. Feel it from your stomach. Let it out!'

She started off small at first, but he watched her as she started to laugh, to loosen up, hurling paint over her head, like a tennis player serving from the baseline, scattering drops of cadmium red in her hair as she did so.

Julian slid the whole length of the canvas in a wide plié, showering paint as he went with sharp flicks of the wrist. 'Will you, Monica? Will you do the fandango? What is a fandango, anyhow? And who the hell is Scaramouche?' And they both collapsed, exhausted and laughing, on the floor next to their wonderful riot of colour. The smell of fresh paint hung in the air above them, mingling with the scent of roses, lemons, jam and Elnett.

'Did Mary die at home, Julian?' Monica asked when they'd calmed down and were breathing normally again. 'I do know how it feels, you know . . .'

'I don't want to talk about it, if you don't mind,' Julian said, cutting her off abruptly. Then he felt awful. It had sounded like she wanted to tell *him* something. Thankfully, she changed the subject.

'Didn't you and Mary ever have children?' Monica asked. Christ, this topic was hardly any better.

'We tried,' replied Julian. 'But after a series of ghastly miscarriages we decided it wasn't meant to be. It wasn't an easy time.' This was a bit of an understatement.

'And you didn't want to adopt?' asked Monica, like his dog Keith, refusing to give up a bone.

'No,' he said, which wasn't really the truth. Mary had been desperate to adopt, but he'd vetoed the idea. He hadn't seen the point of children if he couldn't pass on his own genes. Imagine scrutinizing your own child's face for ever, wondering where it had come from. He suspected that this explanation wouldn't make him sound very sympathetic. People were strangely sentimental about babies.

'Do you have any other family? Siblings? Nephews and nieces?' Monica asked.

'My brother died in his forties – multiple sclerosis, horrible disease,' Julian replied. 'I wasn't as much help as I should have been. I'm not at all good with physical imperfections. One of my many failings. He didn't have children.

My sister, Grace, emigrated to Canada in the seventies. She hasn't been back for more than a decade. Too old to do the journey, she says. She has two children, but I haven't seen them since they were babies, except on Facebook. Marvellous invention, that. Although I'm glad it wasn't around when I was still beautiful. I may have become obsessed.' He realized he was gabbling.

'So who are you planning to spend Christmas with?' asked Monica. Julian pretended to think very hard.

'Gosh, I've so many options, I haven't been able to decide yet,' he said. Was she going to invite him to something? He tried not to get over-excited in case she was simply being curious.

'Well,' Monica ploughed on through the awkward silence, 'my dad and Bernadette are going on a cruise. To the Caribbean. It's their fifth wedding anniversary, which means that I'm on my own. So is Riley, since his family are on the other side of the world. So, we thought we might do Christmas lunch in the café. Would you like to join us?'

'I can't think of anything I'd like more,' replied Julian, feeling positively giddy. 'I don't think I've ever told you how pleased I am that it was you who found my little book, Monica.'

'I'm very happy I found it too,' she replied, putting her hand over his. He realized how unaccustomed he'd become to physical contact. The only person who touched him regularly was his barber.

'Julian, you should paint Riley!' said Monica. 'He'd be a wonderful model.'

'Mmm,' said Julian, thinking that he wouldn't need many

layers. He chided himself. That was not a charitable thought, and he was not that mean-spirited person any longer.

'Talking of Riley,' said Julian, trying hard to sound casual, 'I suspect he might be the teensiest little bit in love with you.'

'Do you think so?' asked Monica, looking ever so slightly sad. 'I'm not at all sure.'

'Did you write in the book too?' he asked, moving on in case he'd made Monica feel uncomfortable. He imagined that this was how a father would feel – wanting to show interest, but wary of over-stepping the line. If that Riley upset her, he'd have Julian to deal with.

'Yes, but I'm rather embarrassed about what I wrote now. Although, remember you said *maybe telling that story will change your life*? Well, I think just writing it down created some sort of magic, because my life has really changed since then. Everything seems to be coming together. At least, I'd thought it was. I left the book in a wine bar, weeks ago.'

'I wonder who found it. Remember what I wrote next? *Or the life of someone you've not yet met.*'

'Well,' said Monica, 'it's achieved quite a lot already, don't you think?' And she smiled at him, the friend he'd known for a short time that somehow felt like for ever.

Riley

Riley was sitting on his narrow, single bed, with a laptop – borrowed from Brett, one of his flatmates – on his knees. He could feel one of the mattress springs, hard and lumpy, under his right thigh, so he shifted slightly to the left, readjusting the keyboard on his lap. He was drinking tea without milk, since someone had finished the pint he'd bought only yesterday. His six-pack of lagers was now a four-pack, and his Cheddar cheese was missing a sizeable corner and had gained a set of tooth marks. He'd resorted to putting labels on all his remaining stuff, but resented his flatmates turning him into that kind of guy. He was not a territorial labeller.

The room was lit by the tepid December sun, trying valiantly to penetrate the grime coating Riley's windows, accumulated from the exhausts of thousands of cars thundering up the Warwick Road, twenty-four hours a day. Riley was feeling like an etiolated plant – weak, yellow and spindly through lack of sunshine and fresh air. His naturally dark skin had taken on a jaundiced hue and his white-blond hair was getting darker. Soon, he thought, his hair and skin would end up the same shade.

For the first time since he'd arrived in London, Riley felt an almost unbearable longing for Perth, for his days spent in the sunshine, feeding, watering, weeding and pruning other people's gardens. He looked at the pinboard by his bed, at his montage of photos from home. Him as a teenager with his dad and two brothers, all surfing the same wave. They were grinning at his mum, who was taking the photograph. As always, she'd messed up the framing so there was far too much sky. His mum holding him as a baby on a trip back to see her family in Bali. A group of his friends, raising bottles of beer to the camera, at the barbecue party they'd thrown to see him off on his grand tour. Why had he swapped a life surrounded by gloriously verdant nature for one hemmed in by concrete, inhaling pollution with every breath?

Riley was checking the progress of his various lots on eBay. Julian's (barely worn) bee-keeping outfit had gone for a small song. Who knew there were so many amateur bee-keepers around? And the Tiffany lamp, which he'd described honestly as 'not functioning' and 'needing some restoration', was attracting new bids every few minutes. Best of all, Julian's ancient mobile phone was looking to sell at a higher price than the latest iPhone. Riley blew a corkscrew curl of hair out of his eyes as he scrolled down.

The only furniture in Riley's room was a chest of drawers, a clothes rail with a few wire hangers dangling from it, and a slightly lopsided bookcase which looked as if someone had had a few too many drinks when following the IKEA instruction sheet. Out of the corner of his eye, Riley could see Julian's notebook poking out from between his dog-eared novels and travel guides, goading him.

Riley felt like he was sinking ever deeper into quicksand. He remembered the sick feeling in his stomach when he'd seen the postcard of that beach on Monica's pinboard, and how he'd hoped it was just a coincidence. The minute Monica had mentioned the name *Hazard*, he should have come clean. He could have said, *Oh yes, that's the guy I met in Thailand, just before coming here. He gave me a notebook, which is how I found you.* Would that have been so very hard? But he'd flunked it. Even worse, he'd done a runner, leaving Monica just standing there holding the postcard looking bemused. And now he was drowning in deceit. He'd never be able to claim that the right moment hadn't come up, that he hadn't had the opportunity to confess. Nor could he argue that he thought it was from a different Hazard. If only he'd been called something normal, like James or Sam or Riley. You couldn't go wrong with a name like Riley.

Riley did a deal with himself. He would tell Monica the whole story and face the consequences. If she never wanted to see him again, then so be it. Perhaps it was time for him to be moving on anyway. But she might take it on the chin – find it an amusing anecdote she could repeat to her friends as the story of how they'd met. Surely, she'd see that although Hazard had engineered their meeting, what had happened after that was because he genuinely liked her? More than liked her, he realized, surprising himself.

It was only a week before Christmas, and Riley didn't want to risk ruining Monica's carefully laid plans. He knew how excited she was about catering Christmas lunch in the café. He'd seen all the lists on the coffee table in her flat: the shopping list, the minute-by-minute plan for the cooking, the present list (she'd hidden that one before he could see what she was giving him). She'd tried to engage him in a conversation about Jamie Oliver versus Nigella, but had obviously clocked his blank expression and had given up.

Monica had invited the whole art class to drop in for pre-lunch drinks, before going on to their own family celebrations. Most of them were going to be out of town, but Betty and Baz were planning to drop in. Benji was coming for lunch as he'd decided to join his family in Scotland for Hogmanay instead of Christmas.

He would, he decided, tell her after Christmas, but defin-itely before New Year.

Having made that promise to himself, the weight of Riley's deception felt a little lighter. He looked over at the exercise book. He wanted to get rid of it. Now he'd decided what to do, he wanted to forget about The Authenticity Project for the next week or so – but that was impossible to do with the book sitting there.

He thought about just throwing it away, but he didn't want to be the one to break the chain. It felt like terribly bad karma, destroying people's carefully written, heartfelt stor-ies. Perhaps he should pass it on, as Monica and Hazard had done. Maybe it would bring someone luck – it had, after all, introduced him to Monica and a whole group of friends. It had even found him employment, if you could describe Julian's eBay project as such. He was sure the next recipient wouldn't be as stupid as he'd been, would remem-ber that the whole idea was about *authenticity*, not lies.

A rhythmic banging noise, interspersed with some overly theatrical moaning, started up from the room next door. The walls of this badly converted flat were so thin that Riley could hear a subtly delivered fart two rooms away, and he was way more acquainted than he'd like to be with Brett's rather active love life. Brett's current girlfriend was, he'd concluded, faking it. No one could be having that much fun with his Neanderthal flatmate.

Riley took the book off the bookcase, searched through the side pocket of his rucksack for a pen, and started to write.

By the time Riley had finished, it was dark outside. He felt like a weight had lifted from his shoulders and been transferred on to the page. It was all going to be OK. He walked over to the window, and as he went to close the rather inadequate curtains he spotted something extraordinary. He had to tell Monica.

Monica

Monica was just turning the sign on the door from OPEN to CLOSED when Riley appeared, looking as if he'd run all the way from Earl's Court. If she hadn't opened the door, he would have barrelled right into it.

'Monica, look!' he shouted. 'It's SNOWING!' He shook his head, scattering droplets of water everywhere, like an enthusiastic retriever after a swim.

'I know,' she replied, 'although I doubt it will stick. It hardly ever does.' She could tell that this was not the response Riley had been hoping for. 'Riley, have you never seen snow before?'

'Well of course I have, in movies and on YouTube and stuff, but not actually falling from the sky, like that,' he replied, pointing at some rather desultory flakes. Monica looked at him with amazement, bordering on alarm. 'Well,' he said, sounding slightly indignant, 'have you ever seen a desert storm or a wildfire in the outback?' She shook her head. 'I thought not. Anyhow, we have to go out! There's a skating rink down by the National History Museum. Let's go!'

'*Natural* History Museum,' corrected Monica. 'And I can't go out just like that. I have to clear up here, do the till, prepare everything for tomorrow. Sorry.' Had he forgotten that the last time she'd seen him, he'd just walked out on her mid-sentence?

'Monica,' said Riley, 'you have to live a little. All of that stuff can wait. Seize the moment. Stop worrying about the future and have some fun. You're only young once.' Monica winced at the clichés he was churning out like the script of a bad Hollywood movie.

'You're going to tell me next that no one said on their deathbed that they wished they'd spent more time at work, aren't you?' she said. Then she looked at his face, all glowing and expectant, and thought *why the hell not?*

Monica had had skating lessons as a child, along with lessons in ballet, piano, flute, gymnastics and drama. Until she was sixteen, when everything stopped. But within a few minutes her muscles had dredged up those long-forgotten memories, and she was gliding and spinning with confidence, even panache. Why, she wondered, had she never started skating again? All those passions she'd had when she was younger, the things that had made her heart race and filled her dreams, all abandoned in favour of working hard, being sensible, planning for the future.

Talking of dreams, not in her wildest ones had she imagined being with anyone as utterly gorgeous as Riley. She had to keep pinching herself. Wherever they went, people stared at them. Riley must have been stared at his whole life, because he seemed totally oblivious to it. Were they all wondering *what is he doing with her?*

Riley was completely unselfconscious about his appearance. Right now, he looked like Bambi on his first excursion on to the frozen lake – a tangle of uncooperative limbs which spent more time sprawled on the ice than upright. He lay on his back with his blond curls spread around his head like the halo of an angel cast out of heaven. She held her hand out to pull him up. He grabbed it, lurching to his feet, which then flew out from beneath him, and he crashed to the ground again, taking Monica with him.

Monica lay in a jumbled heap on top of Riley. She could feel the whole journey of his laugh, from where it began, deep in his stomach, to where it bubbled up in his chest, and then exploded right next to her ear. She trapped it in her mouth with a kiss. And with the sound of that laugh along with the feel of that kiss, so natural and uncomplicated, she realized that all the clichés were true. Sure, Riley didn't meet all her criteria, but perhaps the criteria were to blame, not him.

Riley grinned up at her. 'How do you do that, Monica? Twirling around the ice so gracefully, like an Arctic Tinkerbell. I am in awe.' Monica thought she might explode with happiness; she was, it appeared, a woman who inspired *awe*.

Riley stood up and helped a small child, who'd also fallen over, back on to her feet. She gaped at him as if he were Santa Claus. Even the under-tens weren't immune to his charm, it seemed.

By the time Monica and Riley got back to the café it was

nearly 10 p.m. Monica knew that she should finish the chores she'd abandoned earlier, but she was still being carried along on a wave of spontaneity which felt almost like temporary insanity.

As Monica turned the café lights on, she saw the postcard again, behind the bar, and rallied herself to confront Riley.

'Riley, why did you run off so quickly the other night?' she asked, trying not to sound confrontational. 'Did I upset you somehow?'

'God, no. Please don't think that,' said Riley. And she believed him. Riley was too straightforward to lie convincingly. 'I was just a bit, y'know, *freaked out* suddenly.' He looked down at his feet and shuffled around awkwardly.

Monica totally got it. After all, she freaked out about their relationship – all her relationships – on a regular basis. She could hardly blame him! In fact, she was rather relieved to discover that Riley wrestled with complex emotions, too. Perhaps they were more alike than she'd thought.

'Why don't we have some mulled wine?' she suggested, thinking that the alcohol might help to restore the previous relaxed atmosphere. She went into the small kitchen at the back of the café, turned on the gas ring and poured a bottle of wine into a large pan, along with a selection of spices, oranges and cloves. She could hear Riley putting the music on next door. Ella Fitzgerald. Good choice. She stirred the wine for ten minutes, which wasn't nearly long enough, but she was flying by the seat of her pants today.

Monica carried two glasses of the partly mulled wine back into the café. Riley took both of them from her, placed them carefully down on a table, took one of her hands in his and started dancing with her, expertly avoiding all the chairs and tables as he spun her away, just keeping her tethered by the tips of her fingers, and then pulled her in close. The arms and legs that had been so inept earlier were suddenly so beautifully coordinated and in control that it was hard to believe they belonged to the same person.

As Monica danced, she realized that the knot of anxiety that she usually carried around with her was no longer there. She wasn't, for this moment at least, worried about *what next? What if? Where is this going?* Or her most recent worry: *who on earth is reading that stupid book I wrote in?* The only thing that mattered was the beat of the music and the feeling of being held in Riley's arms.

A bus went past, lighting up the pavement outside for a moment, and there, right in front of her window, stood a young woman, holding the most gorgeous, plump baby like a modern Madonna and Child. The baby had his (her?) mother's hair wrapped in his fist as if he wanted to be sure that she'd never let him go.

For a second, her eyes met those of the young mother, who seemed to say, *Look at your life, so frivolous and empty. This is what really matters; what I have.*

As the bus carried on towards Putney, the pavement outside was plunged into darkness again, and the vision disappeared. Perhaps it had never been there at all. Maybe it was a figment of her imagination, her subconscious reminding her not to forget her unfulfilled dreams and ambitions. But, whether the vision was real or not, that moment of carefree euphoria had gone.

Alice

It was nearly 11 p.m., and Alice was pounding the streets with Bunty in her buggy, trying to get her to go to sleep. It seemed to have worked, as the yells had morphed into snuffles and, for the last fifteen minutes, blessed silence. Alice turned back towards home, desperate for some sleep herself. Who would have thought that there would come a day when the thing she wanted most in the world – more than money, sex, fame or a pair of the latest Manolo Blahniks – was eight hours of uninterrupted sleep?

As Alice passed one of her favourite cafés – what was it called? Daphne's? Belinda's? Something old-fashioned – she stopped. The lights were on inside and she could see two people, dancing around the tables like an improbably perfect scene from the latest feel-good Hollywood romance.

Alice knew she should move on, but her feet were welded to the ground. She watched, from the comfortable anonymity of the dark pavement, as the man looked down at the

143

woman in his arms with such love and tenderness that she wanted to cry.

At the beginning, Max had gazed at her as if she were a fairy-tale princess and he couldn't quite believe his luck. But he'd not looked at her that way for a long time. She suspected that watching the love of your life go through labour, with all the yelling, sweating, tearing and bodily fluids involved, rather changed the view you had of them for ever. She had asked him to stay at the 'head end', but he'd insisted on seeing his firstborn appear into the world which had been, she was sure, a ghastly mistake. Apart from anything else, they'd needed to bring in an extra midwife to deal with Max when he'd keeled over and split his head open on the trolley. Just yesterday Max had mistaken her haemorrhoid cream for his toothpaste. It was hardly any wonder there was little romance left in their relationship.

Alice was certain that the woman in the movie playing in front of her did not have a young baby, stretch marks or piles. She was free, unencumbered, independent. The world was her oyster. Then, as if to remind Alice that she herself was none of those things, Bunty started yelling, woken by the sudden cessation of movement from the buggy.

Alice picked Bunty up, wrapped in her Brora cashmere blanket, wishing that she could feel something other than annoyance. To add injury to insult, Bunty wound her fists in Alice's hair and pulled them towards her mouth, yanking the hair at its roots. Then a bus went past, lighting up the pavement, and, just at that moment, the woman in the café turned and looked at Alice with pity in her eyes. *You poor thing*, she seemed to say, *don't you wish you were me?*

And she did.

Alice's broken night had been interspersed with dreams about the couple in the café. Although, in her dream, she was the woman dancing, and someone else – she didn't know who – was watching. Alice shook her head, trying to dislodge the vision so she could concentrate on the task in hand. All she managed to dislodge was her stupid festive headgear.

Alice and Bunty were both wearing reindeer antlers. Alice angled Bunty so that their noses were almost touching. Bunty's full face, with its beaming, gummy smile was in the picture, but you could only see Alice's honey-gold highlights (courtesy of @danieldoeshair) and a small amount of profile. Alice took a few shots, to be on the safe side.

Bunty's real name was Amelie, but they'd nicknamed her Baby Bunty in the few days after her birth when they were still arguing about what to call her (still arguing about pretty much everything, if truth be told), and the nickname had stuck. Now @babybunty had almost as many followers as @aliceinwonderland.

Alice pulled up the best of the shots on Facetune and whitened the small amount of her eye in shot, removed the dark shadow underneath it and erased all her fine lines. Bunty, who you'd never know from her Instagram feed suffered from milk rash and cradle cap, got the same treatment. Then Alice added a filter, typed in 'Christmas-is-a-coming!' and added some festive emojis and all the usual mummy and fashion blogger hashtags, tagged @babydressesup, who'd sent her the antlers, and pressed DONE. She put her phone face down on the table for five minutes, then turned it over to check the number of likes. 547 already. That one would perform well. Matching mum and baby shots always did.

Bunty began to howl, causing Alice's left boob to start leaking milk all over her t-shirt. She'd only just got dressed, and this was her last clean item of clothing. Sleep deprivation was making her feel disassociated, as if she were watching her life rather than being in it. She wanted to cry. She spent a lot of time wanting to cry.

Alice winced as Bunty clamped her hard gums around her sore, cracked nipple. She remembered the idyllic, arty breast-feeding shot she'd posted yesterday on @babybunty, the lighting, camera angle and filter masking the blisters, pain and tears. How could something as natural as feeding your own child be so *ghastly*? Why had no one warned her?

Sometimes she wanted to strangle the community midwife with the lanyard she wore round her neck, which shouted BREAST IS BEST BREAST IS BEST on repeat, a finger-wagging admonishment to any mother who dared even consider mixing up a bottle of formula. Surely, wanting to kill a *midwife* was not a healthy thought for a new mother?

She pushed aside the mashed avocado on toast that she'd photographed at breakfast time and reached into the cupboard, Bunty still docked on lefty, for the emergency Jaffa Cakes. She ate the whole packet. She waited for the usual feeling of self-hatred to emerge. Oh yes, there it was, bang on time.

Once Bunty had finished, and burped up a mouthful of regurgitated milk over the other side of Alice's t-shirt, Alice started rooting through the pile of baby clothes from her sponsor @babyandme. She needed to post another baby fashion shot before it was too late for Christmas delivery. She found the cutest double-breasted tweed coat with matching hat and booties. That would do.

Now Alice had to go outside. It would show off the coat better, and Alice's small terraced house was so crammed with cardboard boxes, baby toys, piles of washing and a sink full of washing-up, that it really wouldn't do for a backdrop. @aliceinwonderland lived in a tasteful, pristine, aspirational home. Anyhow, walks in the fresh air with your baby were what new mums did, weren't they? They were *on brand*.

She really couldn't face trying to track down another clean top, so she just threw a coat over the baby sick and milk stain. Hopefully no one would get close enough to smell her. She took her antlers off and added a woollen hat with a jaunty pom-pom on top (@ilovepompoms) to cover the greasy hair. She looked at herself in the hall mirror. At least, looking this awful, no one would recognize her. She made a mental note to sort herself out before Max got home. Appearances were important to a man like Max. Before she'd had a baby, he'd never seen her less than perfectly made-up, blow-dried and waxed. It had all gone a little downhill since then.

Alice then spent what felt like hours packing the bare necessities into her vast shoulder bag – muslin, wet wipes, Sudocrem, nipple pads, nappies, teething gel, rattle and Dudu (the favourite stuffed rabbit). Since Bunty's arrival, four months ago, leaving the house felt like preparing for an expedition to Everest. She thought back to the days when all she needed were her keys, money and a mobile phone stuffed into a jeans pocket. It felt like a different life, belonging to a very different person.

With Bunty all dressed up and strapped into the Bugaboo, Alice backed down the steps to the pavement. Bunty started to cry. Surely, she couldn't be hungry again already?

Alice had thought that she'd be totally attuned to her baby's cries. She'd be able to differentiate hungry from tired, and uncomfortable from bored. But the reality was, all Bunty's cries seemed to mean the same thing: disappointment. *This is not what I expected*, she appeared to say. Alice understood, because she felt very much the same. She picked up her pace, hoping that the rocking motion of the pushchair might appease Bunty, without making her go to sleep before she'd had her photo taken.

Alice headed towards the little playground in the local park. She could put Bunty in the baby swing – that would show off her outfit nicely, and Bunty loved the swing, so hopefully she'd smile. When she frowned she looked uncannily like Winston Churchill. That look would lose her a whole host of followers.

Alice wished that some of her old school or university friends had had babies too. At least then she might have someone to talk to about how she really felt about all this. She could find out if it was normal to find motherhood so hard, so exhausting. But her friends thought that twenty-six was far too young to be having children. Why on earth hadn't Alice felt the same? She'd been in such a rush to complete the perfect picture: handsome, wealthy husband, terraced Victorian house in the right part of Fulham and beautiful, happy baby. She was living the dream, wasn't she? Her followers certainly thought she was, which made her feel horribly ungrateful.

The playground was empty, but the baby swing wasn't. There was a notebook in it. Alice looked around to see who it might belong to. There was nobody about. She picked up the book – it looked very like the one she had used to note down Bunty's feeds. *5.40 a.m. ten minutes left breast, three minutes right breast.* She'd been trying to establish some sort of routine, like the experts had suggested. That hadn't lasted long. She'd eventually thrown the book into the nappy bin in a fit of pique, as it was only serving as a testament to her total failure.

Her book had had three words on the front: *Bunty's Feeding Diary.* She'd drawn a heart around the word Bunty. This one had three words too, but in much more beautiful handwriting: *The Authenticity Project.* Alice liked the sound of that. Her brand (*brands*, she reminded herself, since Bunty had joined in) was, after all, all about authenticity. *Real life fashion for real life mums and their babies. Smiley face.*

Alice opened the book, and was about to start reading, when it started to rain. Argh. Even the bloody *sky* was crying. Big fat drops were already blurring some of the ink. She blotted the rain off the page with her sleeve and popped the book in her bag, between a nappy and the baby wipes, to keep it dry. She'd figure out what to do with it later. Right now, she had to get home before they both got drenched.

Julian

Julian was rather pleased with his tai chi outfit. He'd bought it online. These were, he realized, the first new clothes he'd bought since Mary. Now he knew how easy internet shopping was, he'd ordered a large number of new underpants and socks. It was about time. Perhaps he'd ask Riley to sell his old ones on eBay. He'd love to hear his response to that suggestion. It would serve him right for trying to raid Julian's dressing room.

Julian had gone for the geriatric ninja look. All black. Loose trousers and a wide-armed shirt with braid fastenings down the front. Mrs Wu (he did find it hard to think of her as Betty) was very impressed, he could tell. She'd raised her eyebrows so high that, for a moment, they'd stopped meeting in the middle.

Julian and Mrs Wu were going through the now-familiar warm-up routine. He was, he thought, far less wobbly and a little more flexible than he had been when Mrs Wu had first turned up at his gate, two weeks ago. She'd started bringing a bag of seed with her, which she'd scatter at the beginning of the session, so that before long they'd be surrounded by birds.

'Is good to be surrounded by nature,' she'd explained. 'And is good karma. The birds are cold, hungry. We feed them, they are happy, we are happy.' Sometimes, as he bent forward, arms behind him, following Mrs Wu, he'd see the birds swoop down on some seed and had the strangest sense that they were joining in. 'Can you feel your ancestors, Julian?'

'No, should I?' he asked. Where were they, and where was he expected to feel them? What an uncomfortable thought. He looked around, half expecting to see Papa sitting on the bench and looking at him disapprovingly over his reading glasses.

'They are around us always,' said Mrs Wu, obviously at peace with this concept. 'You feel it here,' she said as she banged her fist hard against her chest. 'In your soul.'

'How did we get so old?' asked Julian, moving on to more comfortable territory. He heard his knees creak in disapproval at the exercise. 'I still feel twenty-one on the inside, then I catch sight of my hands, all wrinkled and mottled, and they don't feel like they belong to me. I used the hand drier in Monica's Café yesterday, and the skin on the back of my hands actually *rippled*.'

'Growing old is not good in this country,' said Mrs Wu. Julian had already discovered that this was her favourite conversational topic. 'In China, elders are respected for their wisdom. They have lived long life, learned much. In England, old people are nuisance. Families send them away, put them in homes. Like prisons for elders. My family would not do that to me. Would not dare.'

Julian could well believe it. However, he wasn't at all sure that he was wise, or had learned very much. He didn't feel very different from the man he was in his twenties, which is why it was always such a terrible shock when he looked in the mirror.

'You have a lovely family, Mrs Wu,' he said, raising his right leg to the front, arms stretched to the side.

'Betty!' she replied, looking fierce.

'Baz, I mean Biming, is such a lovely boy. And super boy-friend too, that Benji.'

Mrs Wu stopped, mid-pose. 'Boyfriend?' she asked, look-ing puzzled.

Julian realized that he must have just made a terrible mis-take. He'd assumed she knew that her openly affectionate grandson was that way inclined. 'Yes, I mean, friend who is a boy. They get on very well. As friends. You know.'

Mrs Wu gave Julian a hard stare and said nothing, as she moved elegantly into the next pose.

Julian exhaled with relief. Luckily, he had a higher emo-tional intelligence than the average person. It looked as if he'd salvaged the situation.

Monica

Monica had gone to town with the Christmas decorations in the café this year. Julian's art classes must have unleashed some long-buried creative instinct. She'd put up a tree in The Library, decked with traditional glass decorations and plain white LED lights. Each of the tables had centrepieces of holly and ivy, and a large bunch of mistletoe hung above the bar. Benji was happily doling out kisses to men and women alike.

'Tart!' yelled Baz from table six.

'Bakewell or lemon?' retorted Benji, with a grin.

A Christmas compilation had been playing on a loop all day. If Monica heard Bono ask whether they knew it was Christmas one more time she'd merrily chuck Benji's iPad in the sink with the washing-up.

The rich, complex aroma of mulled wine filled the café. As it was Christmas Eve, Monica had told Benji that the wine was complimentary for all her regulars. Benji had deliberately misunderstood, and handed over every glass with a compliment: *Looking HOT this evening, Mrs Corsellis!* The children were all getting free chocolate coins, resulting in lots of smiles and chocolatey fingerprints. She was desperately fighting the urge to follow them all around with a damp cloth. This, she reminded herself, was very good practice for motherhood. She looked at her watch. It was nearly 5 p.m.

'Benji, I'm just going to run a flask of this down to the cemetery, if that's OK?' she said.

'I'm not sure the folks in there will be needing your mulled wine, love,' quipped one of the women in the queue.

Monica hopped on the bus, grinning at the driver who was wearing a Santa hat. She couldn't remember the last time she'd been so excited about Christmas. It was like the Christmases before *that one*, when they'd been a happy family of three.

As Monica approached the Admiral from the Fulham Road end of the cemetery, she could see Riley walking towards her from the Earl's Court side. He waved at her.

' "God rest ye merry gentlemen," ' he sang as they sat simultaneously on the marble tombstone. Then he kissed her. The heat of the kiss, its depth and the way it made her feel dizzy mirrored the effect of the mulled wine she'd been drinking. She wasn't sure how much time had passed with them entwined, like the ivy covering the nearby gravestones, before they heard Julian's voice.

'Um, should I perhaps go somewhere else?' They jumped apart, Monica feeling like she'd been caught snogging outside the school disco by her dad.

'No, no, no,' said Riley. 'After all, you were here first. By at least forty years.'

'We brought you mulled wine,' said Monica, waving the Thermos at him.

'Well, I can't say I'm surprised to see you two *getting on so well*. I had predicted as much, from the moment Riley walked into my art class. We artists see things other people don't. It is both our blessing and our curse,' he said with the theatrical delivery of a Shakespearean actor. 'Well, isn't everything coming up roses? Just when I thought Christmas couldn't get any better.'

Monica poured them each a cup of mulled wine, thankful for the excuse not to share Julian's Baileys. It may have been Mary's favourite, but it was so sweet she could almost feel her teeth dissolving when she sipped it. 'Merry Christmas, Mary,' she said, feeling guilty about her uncharitable thought.

'Merry Christmas, Mary!' echoed the others.

'Good news on the eBay front, Julian,' said Riley. 'We've netted nearly a thousand pounds. Your understairs cupboard is a proper gold mine.'

'Excellent work, young Riley,' replied Julian. 'I can go shopping in the online sales. I've found this wonderful website – it's called Mr Porter. It has everything a fashion-conscious gentleman requires. You should check it out.'

'I'll stick with Primark, thanks, Julian. More in my budget.'

'Julian, I have to get back to the café, to help Benji close up,' said Monica. 'But I'll see you at 11 a.m. tomorrow.'

'I'll walk you back, Monica,' said Riley, eliciting a knowing wink from Julian that would have looked incongruous on any other pensioner.

They walked along the Fulham Road, Riley's arm slung over Monica's shoulder. London had emptied out for the holiday, and the roads were eerily quiet. Every passer-by told a story – the man doing some emergency last-minute present buying, the mum ushering her children home so she could wrap their stocking presents, the group of lads returning from their office Christmas lunch that had stretched into the late afternoon.

Monica couldn't remember the last time she'd felt this relaxed. She realized, much to her surprise, that she didn't really care whether Riley would be leaving London soon. She didn't mind what his intentions were. For the time being, she was able to mentally file all her worries about being a barren spinster, abandoned on a dusty shelf, under 'pending'. All she cared about was the perfection of this moment, her head resting on his shoulder and the soft synchronized tread of their feet on the pavement, marking the beat of the Christmas carol playing from the pub. She congratulated herself on becoming a veritable guru of mindfulness.

'Monica,' said Riley, an uncharacteristic note of hesitation in his voice, 'I hope you know how much I like you.' Monica's stomach lurched as if she were on a roller coaster – pleasure and fear so bound together that she didn't know where one ended and the other began.

'Riley, this sounds like the point in the novel where the hero says he has a wife and family back home,' she said, trying to sound jocular. He didn't have, did he?

'Ha, ha! No, of course I don't. I just wanted to make sure you knew, that's all.'

'Well, I like you a lot, too.' This felt like as good a moment as any to utter the words that had been on standby for a while. She'd spent some time crafting the perfect level of nonchalance. She'd even recorded her delivery on her iPhone and played it back. God, had she remembered to delete it? 'Would you like to stay tonight, since you're coming around tomorrow anyway? So long as you don't mind me running around stuffing the turkey and peeling the sprouts.'

Riley hesitated, just a beat too long. Long enough to semaphore what was coming. 'I'd love to, but I promised my flatmates I'd celebrate with them this evening, since I won't be there tomorrow. I'm really sorry.'

Monica heard the familiar voice in her head chanting *he's just not that into you* and crushed it like a bothersome gnat. She refused to let anything spoil her mood. Tomorrow was going to be a perfect day.

Alice

What Alice wanted most in the world for Christmas was a lie-in. Just until 7 a.m. But Bunty had other ideas. She'd woken up demanding food and attention at five. Alice had had to use formula, which Bunty hated, in case her milk was still boozy from the night before. She wasn't even responsible enough to feed her own baby properly. The kitchen looked as if there'd been a riot in a toy shop. She'd meant to tidy everything up and prepare all the vegetables for Christmas lunch before she'd gone to bed, but the terrible row she'd had with Max had rather put paid to that. She reached into the cupboard for the Nurofen, as if she could medicate away the memory, along with her hangover.

Max had come home rather late, and obviously a bit worse for wear, after taking his team out for a festive lunch, which had turned into a rowdy afternoon. By the time he got back, she was exhausted and was sure she had the beginnings of mastitis: horribly painful boobs, hard as rocks, and a slight fever. She'd Googled the symptoms and read that chilled cabbage leaves placed inside your maternity bra would help. She'd not been able to get out to the shops without waking Bunty who was, finally and thankfully, fast asleep. So, when Max eventually appeared, she asked him to go and buy a cabbage.

He was gone for what seemed an age, while Alice simmered slowly with resentment that he'd been having fun all day, while she'd been up to her armpits in nappies and wet wipes. Eventually he came back with a bag of *Brussels sprouts*! He'd explained that, as it was Christmas Eve, most of the shops were closed, or their shelves bare.

'What am I supposed to do with *Brussels sprouts* with their stupid little ineffectual leaves?!' she'd yelled at him.

'I thought you wanted to *eat them*. Doesn't everyone eat Brussels sprouts at Christmas? It's practically the law,' he'd replied, not unreasonably, she now realized, ducking as she threw the offending vegetables at his head. They missed, but hit the wall, like shrapnel, knocking a framed collage of Bunty's baby pictures, taken from her Instagram page, off centre.

Alice had pulled a bottle of wine from the fridge along with a box of After Eight mints (both earmarked for Christmas Day), and had finished them both in record time, while scrolling through all her social media and thinking, darkly, *that'll show him*.

Now she realized that it hadn't shown him at all, or at least not what she'd intended to show him. All it had done was make her wake up at 3 a.m., dehydrated and sweating Sauvignon Blanc. Then she'd tossed and turned, yelling silently at herself for two hours, at which point Bunty had joined in, yelling at her very loudly indeed.

Max walked into the kitchen, kissed the top of her head (which was still in her hands) and said 'Merry Christmas, darling.'

'Merry Christmas, Max,' she replied, as merrily as she could muster. 'I don't suppose you could take over with Bunty for a while, while I grab some more sleep?'

Max looked at her, goggle-eyed, as if she'd suggested inviting the elderly neighbours round for a swinging session. 'You know I would usually, darling' – she knew no such thing – 'but my parents are going to be here in a few hours and we have *a lot to do*.' That statement came loaded with blame, and accompanied by significant looks at the piles of toys, overflowing sink and rubbish bins and unpeeled potatoes.

'When you say *we*, Max, does that mean you're going to help?' Alice asked, trying to keep her tone as neutral as possible. She didn't want another argument on Christmas Day.

'Of course I am, sweetie-pie! I just need to finish up a couple of annoying admin things first, and I'll be right with you. By the way, you are going to change into something more appropriate before my parents arrive, aren't you?' he asked.

'Of course I am,' said Alice, who hadn't been planning to. As Max disappeared back into his office, she wished she could change her life as easily as she could her clothes.

Alice put Bunty into a papoose so that she'd be happy and safe while she rushed around tidying the house and getting lunch ready for the in-laws. Alice didn't dislike Max's mother (at least she *tried* not to), but Valerie had *standards*. She was rarely overtly critical, but inside Alice knew she was a seething mass of judgements, all the more virulent for being contained. She'd never quite got over the fact that Alice had been brought up on a council estate on the outskirts of Birmingham by a single mother who was a dinner lady. Alice's father had left them all when her youngest brother was a tiny baby.

Valerie had sat ramrod straight in her lavender skirt suit and matching hat throughout their wedding, casting sidelong looks across the aisle at Alice's family, with a face like a disappointed prune. She'd expected better for her only son. She set the bar so high that Alice, despite all her immaculate grooming, careful manners and practised pronunciation, could never hope to reach it, so she generally ended up drinking at it instead.

Max, of course, was blind to all of this. In his eyes, Mother could do no wrong.

After two hours of frenetic activity, the kitchen was looking presentable and lunch was in hand. It might not be ready at lunch time, but they should be able to eat by 3 p.m. Alice, however, was still far from ready or presentable. Her hair was unwashed and piled on top of her head in a messy bun, her face was ravaged after all the wine, chocolate and lack of sleep, and her post-baby belly, augmented by her Jaffa Cake addiction, was pouring over the top of her yoga pants.

She walked into Max's study without knocking. She noticed him quickly close the lid of his laptop. What hadn't he wanted her to see? She dumped Bunty unceremoniously in his lap, and went to have a shower.

Alice had presumed that having a baby would bring Max

and her closer. They'd have a new purpose and shared adventure. Yet in reality, Bunty's arrival seemed to be driving them further apart.

She thought back to the closed laptop, the late night meetings and the ever growing silences between them. Was he having an affair? Would it really be so awful if he *were* having an affair? At least then she wouldn't need to feel guilty about how often she feigned sleep, or a migraine, to avoid having sex. But the mere idea of such a betrayal made her feel breathless with anxiety. She already felt inadequate, unsexy and unlovable. Max's confirmation of those suspicions might just finish her off. And what if he wanted a divorce? She couldn't bear to give up her perfect life, the one she'd worked so hard for, that had thousands of less lucky women double-tapping on her Instagram shots.

Stop it, Alice. It's just the hormones. It's all going to be OK, she told herself as the power shower pelted water at her tired skin.

It was only later that Alice realized, in all her worry about Max leaving her, she hadn't once thought that she might miss him. Which, of course, she would.

Julian

Julian was taking extra care dressing, since it was a *special day*. He'd selected an outfit by his old friend Vivienne Westwood (perhaps he should look her up again; she probably thought he was dead) – a fine kilt and jacket in contrasting tartans with asymmetric hems. If you couldn't wear Westwood on Christmas Day, then when could you? He had his radio tuned to a music station that was playing 'Fairytale Of New York', and he was singing along about how he could have been someone.

Julian *had* been someone, and then no one. Today, he felt like someone again. Someone with an invitation to Christmas lunch, at least. With *friends*. They were friends, weren't they, proper ones? Monica hadn't just asked him out of pity, or a sense of duty, he was sure she hadn't.

He remembered the first Christmas after Mary, when he hadn't even realized the significance of the day until he'd turned the TV on in the mid-afternoon. All the festive televisual jollity had driven him back to bed with a cold tin of baked beans, a fork and a bowlful of regrets.

He tried out one of his tai chi moves in his full-length dressing-room mirror. He realized he looked like a crazed highlander. He walked into his sitting room where his presents for Monica, Riley, Benji, Baz and Mrs Wu were sitting on the coffee table waiting to be wrapped. It took him a little longer than he'd anticipated as his clumsy fingers got in rather a mess with the Sellotape. He tried to untangle them by grabbing the tape with his teeth, and got his mouth stuck to his hands.

As Julian walked out on to the Fulham Road, he spotted Riley walking towards him. He must have cut through the cemetery from Earl's Court. He hadn't stayed at Monica's then. How old-fashioned. Julian had never been that old-fashioned, even in the days when one was supposed to be. Riley looked a little stunned by his outfit. He was obviously impressed.

Monica opened the door of the café looking adorable. She was wearing a red dress, covered by a plain white chef's apron. She looked like she'd been working at a hot stove, because her cheeks were flushed, and the tendrils of hair that had escaped from her customary ponytail were damp. She was also holding a wooden spoon, which she waved in a sweeping motion as she said, 'Come in!'

A long table had been laid for lunch in the centre of the café. It was covered in a white linen tablecloth scattered with rose petals which had been spray-painted gold. Each place setting was marked by a gold pine cone which held a small card with a name on it. There were red crackers, red

THE AUTHENTICITY PROJECT

and gold candles and a centrepiece of holly and ivy. Even to Julian's critical eye, it looked stunning.

'Have you been up all night, Monica?' he asked. 'It looks gorgeous. As do you. And that's a professional opinion.' Monica's cheeks reddened even more.

'I did get up rather early. You two go and join Benji in The Library, and put those presents under the tree.'

A bottle of champagne lounged in an ice bucket on one of the coffee tables, alongside a large platter of smoked salmon blinis. The air was filled with the smell of roasting turkey and the sound of the King's College choir singing carols. It was one of those days when all plans came together.

Monica came over, taking off her apron as she sat down. 'Right, we've got an hour before I need to put the last vegetables on. Shall we open some presents? We could do some now, and some after lunch.'

Julian, who, unlike Monica, was not a fan of delayed gratification, said, 'Please can we do mine first?' Not giving them any time to object, he pulled his pile of presents, wrapped in matching paper, from under the tree and handed them round.

'I'm afraid I didn't actually *buy* anything,' he explained. 'I just had a rummage around my cottage.'

Benji, who had been first to rip the paper off his parcel, was looking at the present on his lap open-mouthed. 'A *Sergeant Pepper* album. In vinyl. You can't give this away, Julian. It'll be worth a fortune,' protested Benji, although he was clinging on to the record as if he couldn't bear to be parted from it.

'I'd rather give it to someone who'll appreciate it properly, dear boy, and I know how much you love the Beatles.

165

They were never really my thing. Too goody-goody. The Sex Pistols. They were right up my alley.'

He turned to Riley who was holding up an original Rolling Stones t-shirt in awe. 'Well, you've been wanting to get your hands on my clothes for ages, young Riley. You can sell it if you like, but I think it'd look rather good on you.'

The present Julian really wanted to see opened was Monica's. He watched her carefully peel off the Sellotape, taking an age.

'Just rip it, dear child!' he told her. She looked slightly shocked.

'You can't reuse it if it's ripped,' she said, as if admonishing an over-excited toddler.

Finally, she peeled back the paper and gasped. That was the reaction he'd been waiting for. The others gathered around to peer at the present lying in her lap.

'Julian, it's beautiful. Far more beautiful than I am,' she said. He'd painted her in oils, partly from memory, and partly from the sketches he'd managed to do surreptitiously during their art classes. It was only a small canvas, showing Monica, chin resting on her hand, with a strand of her hair entwined around her index finger. Like all Julian's portraits, the brushstrokes were bold and sweeping, almost abstract, and the painting conveyed as much in the details left out as in the ones he'd included. He looked at the real Monica. She seemed as if she were about to cry. In a good way, he assumed.

'It's the first thing, apart from our recent Pollock collaboration, I've painted for fifteen years,' he said, 'so I'm afraid I'm a bit rusty.'

They were interrupted by a banging on the door. Benji,

realizing that it must be Baz and his granny coming round for drinks, went to unlock it. Julian put Baz and Mrs Wu's gifts on the table next to him in preparation. He had his back to the door, so didn't see Baz's face until he joined them. The others had gone quiet.

'Is something the matter, Baz?' asked Monica. 'Where's Betty?'

Julian had a terrible feeling that he knew what was coming next. He could feel Baz's eyes boring into him as he spoke, but he dared not look at him. Instead, he focused on his shoes. Classic, black brogues, beautifully polished. So few people polished their shoes properly these days.

'Granny hasn't come out of her room since last night,' he said, in a voice tight with controlled rage.

'Why not?' asked Benji. 'Is she ill?'

'Maybe you should ask Julian,' Baz replied.

Julian had a mouth full of blini, but he couldn't swallow it as his throat seemed to have dried up. He picked up his glass of champagne and took a big gulp.

'I'm really, really sorry, Baz. I thought she *knew*. Surely it's no big deal these days who you fall in love with? It's not like the sixties when my friend Andy Warhol was the only openly homosexual man I knew. The closet, meanwhile, was bursting with them.'

Everyone had gone silent, having put two and two together and made four.

'Granny hasn't quite caught up with the modern trend. She's not exactly *woke*. She's been wailing for hours about how her life will have been in vain. What's the point in having worked her fingers to the bone setting up a business for her descendants to inherit if she wasn't going to have any? She's beside herself.' Baz sat down and put his head in his hands. Julian thought he preferred him angry to desolate.

'What about your parents, Baz? Are they OK?' asked Benji, reaching for his hand. Baz snatched it away, as if his grandmother might be watching.

'They're surprisingly sanguine about it. I think they've known all along.'

'I'm not trying to excuse my letting the proverbial cat out of the bag, dear boy, but isn't it better to have these things out in the open? Isn't it a relief? Secrets can make you sick. I should know,' said Julian.

'*It was not your secret to tell, Julian!* I would have told her in my own way, in my own time. Or not at all. Honesty is not always the best policy. Sometimes we have secrets for a reason – to protect the people we love. Would it have been so very terrible if Granny had gone to her grave believing that my Chinese wife and I would take over the restaurant and fill it with little baby Wus?'

'But, I—' said Julian, before Baz interrupted.

'I don't want to hear it, Julian. And, by the way, I don't believe for one minute that you were a friend of Andy Warhol. Or Marianne Faithfull. Or Princess bloody Margaret. You're one big fake, sitting there in your ridiculous checked skirt. Why don't you go back to your rubbish dump and stay out of my business?' And, with that, he stood up and walked out.

In the stunned silence he left behind him, you could have heard a pine needle drop on to the polished oak floor.

Riley

Riley could never have imagined that the tiny, warm-hearted and good-natured Baz could get so angry. He'd turned the full force of his rage on Julian, who'd seemed to shrink back into his seat, like a desiccated fly trapped in a web. Since Riley had known Julian, he'd grown in stature, becoming more and more confident and exuberant. In the space of a few minutes, all that had gone.

Riley looked at Benji, a clear case of collateral damage. He looked horrified and terrified in equal measure. The sound of the door banging behind Baz reverberated through the café for several seconds. Then Benji spoke, in an uncharacteristically small voice.

'Do you think I should go after him? What do I do?'

'I think you need to leave him for a while, to work things out and to talk to his family,' said Monica.

'What if his family hate me? What if they won't let him see me any more?'

'You know, it doesn't sound like they have a problem

with *you*. It doesn't even sound as if his parents have a problem with Baz being gay. This is 2018, for God's sake. His granny just needs to get to grips with the whole dynastical thing,' said Riley. 'Anyhow, they can't not let him see you. You're both grown-ups. This isn't *Romeo and Juliet*.'

'I should leave,' said Julian who sounded every year of his age. 'Before I cause any more trouble.'

'Julian,' said Monica as she turned to him, looking fierce, palm forward, like a traffic officer halting oncoming cars, 'stay right there. Baz didn't mean what he said. He was just lashing out. This is not your fault. You weren't to know. I know you didn't mean for this to happen.'

'I really didn't,' said Julian. 'As soon as I realized I'd said the wrong thing, I backtracked. I thought I'd gotten away with it.'

'Things may all work out for the best in the end. Benji, wouldn't it be nice if you didn't have to worry about Baz's family finding out all the time? If you could walk past the restaurant hand in hand? Move in together, even. You may decide, one day, that Julian's done you both an enormous favour. Oh, Christ. The roast potatoes!'

Monica dashed off to the kitchen, and Julian reached into his bag, pulling out a dusty bottle of port.

'I bought this for after lunch, but perhaps a good glug of it now would be classed as medicinal,' he said, pouring a large slug into Benji's and Riley's glasses, followed by his own.

Riley didn't like conflict; he wasn't used to it. Was everything always so complicated over here, or was it just the circle he'd landed in?

The three of them sat in silence, drinking the viscous,

blood-coloured port, too stunned by recent events to talk. After fifteen minutes or so, which felt like hours, Monica called out that lunch was ready.

Luckily, the change of location from The Library to lunch table effected a change in mood. They pulled their crackers and each donned a paper hat, and gradually some of the bonhomie from earlier in the day seeped back into the proceedings. All four of them seemed determined to forget, at least for the time being, the *incident*.

'Monica, this food is amazing. You are amazing,' said Riley, squeezing her knee under the table. Then, unable to resist the urge, he ran his fingers up her thigh. Monica flushed, and choked on a Brussels sprout; he wasn't sure if that was the result of the compliment or the physical contact. He moved his hand a little higher.

'Arrgghh!' he yelled, as Monica stabbed him in the hand with her fork.

'What's the matter, Riley?' Benji asked.

'Cramp,' he replied.

Riley watched his friends eat. Monica cut up each portion of food precisely, and chewed each mouthful for ages before swallowing. Julian had arranged his plate like an abstract artwork. Every now and again he would, mid-mouthful, close his eyes and smile as if savouring every flavour. Benji, meanwhile, pushed his food around in a rather melancholy way, barely eating a thing.

They took turns reading out the terrible jokes from the crackers, drank more wine, more quickly than was wise, and the day seemed to be getting back on track. They would deal with the whole Baz situation later.

Riley helped Monica clear all the plates away from the table. They loaded them into the dishwasher. Or, rather, Riley loaded things into the dishwasher, then Monica took them out and put them somewhere different. She had, she said, a system. Then Riley picked Monica up, sat her on the kitchen counter and kissed her, wrapping his arms around her and squeezing her tight. She smelled of blackcurrants and cloves. The kiss, the wine and the heady emotion of the day made him feel dizzy.

He pulled Monica's hair out of her ponytail and combed his fingers through it. He curled her hair around his fingers, gently tugging her head back, then kissed the damp, salty hollow at the base of her neck. Monica wound her legs around his back, pulling him closer. He loved travelling. He loved London. He loved Christmas. And he was starting to think that he loved Monica.

'Get a room!' shouted Benji, and Riley turned to see Benji and Julian standing in the doorway, grinning. Julian was holding a gravy boat, and Benji a bowl of leftover sprouts.

'But not until we've had pudding!' added Julian.

Monica placed the Christmas pudding in the centre of the table and they all stood around it. Julian poured brandy over the top and Riley struck a match and set it alight, but not before burning his fingers.

'That's what happens when you play with fire, Riley,' said Monica, raising an eyebrow suggestively. He wondered how long it would be before Julian and Benji left.

'Oh, bring us some figgy pudding!' sang Benji. Riley put his arm round Monica's waist, and she rested her head on his shoulder.

Then the door opened. Riley realized that none of them had locked it again after Baz had left. He turned around expecting to see Baz or Mrs Wu. But it was neither of them.

'Merry Christmas, everyone!' A tall, dark-haired man said in a voice that seemed to fill the space and reverberate off the walls. 'I just love it when a plan comes together!'

It was Hazard.

Hazard

It was three days before Christmas. The beach was awash with newcomers, including at least three honeymooning couples who peppered every sentence with the words 'my husband' and 'my wife', and tried to outdo each other with their public displays of affection. Hazard was having tea at Lucky Mother with Daphne, Rita and Neil. They'd started this peculiarly English ritual a couple of weeks previously, and found it a comforting reminder of home, although Hazard couldn't remember the last time he'd had afternoon tea in London. He'd been more likely to tuck into Lucozade and ketamine in the afternoon than tea and cake. Rita had even taught Barbara how to make scones, which they ate warm with coconut jam. If only they had clotted cream it would be perfect.

Neil was showing them the tattoo he'd had done during his last trip to Koh Samui. It was some writing in Thai, winding around his left ankle bone.

'What does it say?' asked Hazard.

'It says *stillness and peace*,' replied Neil. Judging by

Barbara's rather shocked face as she looked to see what they were admiring, Hazard suspected it didn't say that at all. He winked at Barbara and put his finger to his lips. What Neil didn't know wouldn't hurt him.

'What are we doing for Christmas lunch, Barbara?' asked Daphne. 'Are we having turkey?'

'Chicken,' replied Barbara. 'Not the skinny chickens from here. I have fat, fat chickens coming from Samui. Everything fatter in Samui. Even tourists fatter in Samui.' She blew out her cheeks and mimed fatness with her arms, while her guests basked in the unintended compliment.

Hazard felt a sudden yearning for London. For turkey with chestnut stuffing, roast potatoes and sprouts. For cold weather and Christmas carols. For double-decker buses, traffic pollution and overcrowded tube trains. For the BBC, the speaking clock and Kebab Kid on the New King's Road. And that's when he knew.

He was going home.

The only flight Hazard could get a seat on was the one no one else wanted: flying overnight on Christmas Eve and arriving in Heathrow on Christmas morning. The plane was terribly festive, with the cabin staff doling out free champagne and twice as many drinks as usual. Everyone was getting merrily drunk. Except for Hazard, who tried to keep his eyes straight ahead, glued to the film playing on his screen, ignoring the snap of metal caps on bottles being unscrewed and the pop of champagne corks. Would he ever be able to hear the sound of a cork being released without feeling a visceral yearning, he wondered.

The airport and the streets were spookily deserted. It felt a bit like being in a zombie apocalypse film, but a lot merrier and without hosts of shabbily dressed undead. The people who were around were filled with love for their fellow man and tended to be wearing comedy hats and festive jumpers.

Hazard had managed to share one of the few available taxis as far as Fulham Broadway, where he jumped out, greeting the cold air like an old friend and heaving his rucksack on to his back. It felt like a lifetime since he was last here, when he was a completely different person. He hadn't told his parents he was back yet. He didn't want to disrupt all their plans and, anyhow, he could do with a few days to acclimatize before he started the long slog of building bridges.

He walked down the Fulham Road towards his flat. He could see Monica's Café ahead of him. He was dying to know what had happened since he sent Riley off with The Authenticity Project. He realized it'd become rather an unhealthy obsession – something to take his mind off his desperate desire to get out of his head. He knew that it was highly unlikely that Monica would have met Julian, let alone Riley; it was just a story that had been playing in his fevered imagination.

As he reached the café, he couldn't resist looking inside. It looked like a tableau from a Christmas card – all candles, holly and ivy and a table groaning with the remains of a Christmas feast. For a moment, he thought his mind was playing tricks, because there, just as he'd imagined it, were Monica and Riley, *hugging*. And an old man in an extraordinary two-tone tartan ensemble who couldn't be anyone other than Julian Jessop.

He was a genius! What an amazing bit of social engineering, a fabulous random act of kindness come good. He couldn't wait to meet Monica and Julian properly, to introduce himself as a key player in the drama and to discuss how this had all come about. He pushed on the door and walked in, feeling like a conquering hero.

The reaction wasn't quite what he'd been expecting. Monica, Julian and the fourth chap, a tall redhead, just looked at him blankly. Riley, meanwhile, looked a bit rabbit-caught-in-headlights. Horrified, even.

'I'm Hazard!' he clarified. 'You obviously found the book then, Riley!'

'You're the man who sent the postcard,' said Monica, after a few more seconds of stunned silence. She was looking at him, not with gratitude, as he'd imagined she would, but with suspicion and distaste. 'You'd better explain what's going on.'

Something told Hazard, just a little too late, that this wasn't such a great idea after all.

Monica

Monica was shattered after all the running around, the emotional roller coaster and too much alcohol, but she couldn't remember being happier. She was high on goodwill, friendship and – thanks to her steamy snogging session in the kitchen with Riley – pheromones. She'd even managed not to think about the health and safety ramifications of making out on a professional kitchen work surface.

Then a man walked into the café. He had dark, wavy hair that looked as if it hadn't seen a pair of scissors for some time, the strong jawline of a comic book hero covered in a short beard, and a deep tan. He was carrying a large rucksack and looked like he'd literally just got off a plane from somewhere exotic. He looked vaguely familiar, and had the air of someone who expected to be recognized. Was he some sort of B-list celebrity? If so, what on earth was he doing in her café on Christmas Day? He was, he'd announced, called Hazard.

It took Monica a few seconds to remember where she'd

heard that name. The postcard! She also remembered where she'd seen that face. He was the arrogant arsehole who'd barged into her on the pavement a few months ago. A thinner, browner and hairier version. What had he called her? *Stupid cow? Silly bitch?* Something like that.

Monica was so distracted that she missed what he'd said next, but he obviously knew Riley. Something felt not quite right. She'd shown Riley the postcard, and he hadn't said he knew Hazard. A snake of anxiety coiled and uncoiled in her stomach as her mind grappled with all the facts, trying to fit them together.

Monica refused to offer him a chair. She was damned if she was going to be hospitable. He could explain what on earth was going on while standing up. *Stupid bitch*, that was it.

'Er,' Hazard said, looking rather nervously at Monica. 'I found the notebook, The Authenticity Project, on a table in the bar, just over there.' He waved at the wine bar opposite. 'I read Julian's story' – he nodded at Julian – 'and thought you could do with a bit of a hand with your rather inadequate advertising campaign.' Monica gave him one of her steeliest glares. He cleared his throat, and carried on.

'So, I copied your poster and stuck it in all the obvious places. And I took the book with me, to an island in Thailand. I thought I'd help you out a bit, Monica.' She didn't like how he used her name in such a familiar fashion, as if he knew her. 'Then, while I was there, I checked out every unattached bloke I met to see if he might make a good boyfriend. You know, for you . . .'

He tailed off. He must have seen how utterly mortified she was. It had all become horribly clear.

'And you turned up on this island, did you, Riley?' she said, hardly able to look at him. He said nothing, just nodded miserably. *Coward. Traitor.*

Monica turned the new reality over in her head. Riley hadn't appeared at the art class by happy accident. He'd been sent by Hazard to shag the sad old spinster back home. He hadn't snogged her because she was gorgeous and he couldn't help himself. Of course he hadn't. Stupid, arrogant girl. He'd read her story and felt sorry for her. Or thought she was desperate. Or both. Had they been laughing about her behind her back? Was she some form of bet? *I'll give you fifty quid if you can get the uptight café owner into bed.* Had Hazard deliberately targeted her after colliding into her that evening and, if so, why? What had she done to him? Was Julian in on the whole thing too?

Suddenly she felt utterly exhausted. The wine and the food she'd eaten with such gusto churned around in her stomach. She thought she was going to be sick, to vomit all over her beautifully laid table. Gold-sprayed rose petals mixed with chunks of reconstituted carrot. All her new visions of the future, the ridiculously optimistic happy ending that had been gradually forming in her mind, had to be rewound, deleted and overlaid with the bland, featureless plot she'd been used to.

'I think you'd all better get out,' she said. 'You've eaten my food. You've drunk my wine. Now FUCK OFF out of my café.'

Monica never swore.

Riley

How had everything gone so wrong? One minute he was contemplating Christmas pudding and sex, his only worry being how much he could eat of the former without ruining the latter. Then, the next minute, Monica was throwing him out. And it was all Hazard's fault.

'I'm really sorry, Monica,' said Hazard, 'I was only trying to help.'

'You were playing a game, Hazard. With my *life*, like we're on some sort of reality TV show. I'm not your charity case, or your social experiment,' Monica spat back at him.

What on earth could Riley say to make her understand?

'Monica, I might have *met* you because of Hazard, but that's not why I've stayed with you. I really care about you. You have to believe me,' he said, suspecting that his words were falling on stony ground. Monica pivoted on a heel to glare at him. He wished he'd stayed silent.

'I don't *have* to believe anything you say, Riley. You've

been lying to me all this time. I trusted you. I thought you were *real*.'

'I never lied to you. I didn't tell you the whole truth, I admit, but I never lied.'

'Bloody semantics, and you know it!' Semantics? What were they? 'You were only with me because of the book. And I thought it was fate. Serendipity. How could I have been so stupid?' She looked as if she might be about to cry, which Riley found way more alarming than her anger.

'Well, that's kind of true,' he said, trying to convey his sincerity with his tone, 'in that you seem so incredibly strong, but I knew from the book that, inside, you're really . . .' he grasped for the right word, finding it in the nick of time '. . . vulnerable. I think that's what's made me love you.' He realized that he'd never used the word 'love' with Monica before, and now it was too late.

For just a second, Riley thought that his words might have cut through. Then Monica picked up the Christmas pudding, which was mercifully no longer alight, but did still have a very prickly piece of holly sticking out of it, and threw it, overarm, like a shotput. He wasn't sure if she intended to hit him or Hazard, or both of them. He stepped sideways, and it landed in a sticky heap on the floor.

'Get out!' she yelled.

'Riley,' said Hazard under his breath, 'I think it's best if we do what the lady says, and wait for things to calm down a bit, don't you?'

'Ah, so I'm *the lady* now, not *stupid bitch*? Patronizing *arsehole*!' said Monica. Riley wondered what on earth she was talking about. Had she completely lost it?

They backed out of the door, lest Monica throw anything else in their direction. Riley saw Julian a couple of blocks ahead of them. He called after him, but Julian didn't hear. From the back, he looked like a much older man than the one Riley knew. He was hunched over and shuffling, as if he were trying to have as little impact on his surroundings as possible. A taxi drove past, splashing water from a puddle over Julian's bare legs. Julian didn't seem to notice.

'This is all your fault, Hazard,' said Riley, realizing, but not caring, that he sounded like a petulant child.

'Hey! That's not fair. I didn't know you weren't going to tell her about The Authenticity Project. That was totally your decision, and a rather stupid one, if you don't mind me saying. You should know that withholding a key piece of information never ends well,' Hazard protested. Riley did mind him saying, actually. Monica was right, Hazard was a patronizing arsehole.

'Look, the bar's open. Let's get a drink,' said Hazard, tugging Riley across the road by the arm.

Riley was torn. He wasn't sure that he really wanted to spend any time with Hazard right now, if ever, but he did want to talk to somebody about Monica, and he wasn't in the mood to deal with the drunken revelries of his flatmates. In the end, his need to talk won out and he followed Hazard into the bar.

'This is where I found Julian's book,' Hazard told him, 'on that table, right there. It feels like an awfully long time ago. What are you having to drink?'

'I'll have a Coke, please,' said Riley, who'd had more than enough booze for one day.

'One Coke and a double whiskey,' said Hazard to the barman, who was wearing a pair of flashing antlers with rather bad grace. Riley stepped in front of him.

'Actually, mate, can you make that two Cokes please?' He turned to Hazard. 'You forget, I've read your story. You do *not* want to do that.'

'I really do, you know. Anyhow, what do you care if I choose to hit the self-destruct button? I'm not exactly your favourite person right now, am I?'

'You're right there, but even so, I'm not letting you screw up your life on my watch. You've done so brilliantly. I had you down as a total health nut when I met you on Koh Panam.'

'How about I just have one? That can't do any harm, can it? And it is Christmas Day, after all.' Hazard looked at Riley, like a child who knows he's pushing his luck, but is giving it a go in any case.

'Yeah, right. And in ten minutes' time you'll be telling me that one more won't really matter, and by midnight I'll be wondering how on earth I'm going to get you home. You've caused me enough trouble already, frankly.' Riley's words caused Hazard to deflate.

'Ah bollocks. I know you're right. I would have hated myself in the morning. It's been eighty-four days since I had a drink or a drug, you know. Not that I'm counting or anything,' said Hazard, taking a Coca-Cola, rather unenthusiastically, from the barman. He walked over to the table he'd pointed out to Riley earlier, and sat on the banquette.

'Isn't it strange thinking that last time we had a drink together, we were on the other side of the world on the world's most perfect beach?' he said to Riley.

'Yup. It was a hell of a lot easier there,' Riley replied, and sighed.

'I know, but, believe me, after two months of that you start to realize it's all totally shallow. All those temporary friendships get really boring. I was desperate to get back to some real friends. The problem is, I'm not sure I've got any left. I replaced them years ago with anyone I could find who liked a party as much as I did. And even if I wanted to see those party friends, they'd be pushing booze and drugs on me before I'd taken off my coat. There's nothing an addict likes less than a sober person. I should know.' Hazard stared into his glass of Coke so mournfully that Riley was finding it difficult to stay angry with him.

'There's nothing wrong with shallow, mate,' said Riley. 'It's all this *depth* that causes the problems. What on earth do I say to Monica? She thinks the two of us were playing some kind of *game*. I know she didn't look it just now, but she's actually quite insecure underneath it all. She'll be gutted.'

'Look, I'm not the world's expert on what goes on inside the heads of women, as you may have guessed, but I'm pretty sure that as soon as Monica calms down she'll see that she's totally overreacted. By the way, impressive reaction speed. I thought she'd got you with that figgy pudding,' said Hazard with a grin.

'She was aiming at you, not me! She must be really angry. One thing Monica hates is food on the floor, even tiny little crumbs, invisible to the naked eye,' said Riley, wryly.

'So, how much do you like her?' asked Hazard. 'Was I right, or was I right?'

'It hardly matters now, does it?' Riley said. Then, worried that he was sounding a bit harsh, he added, 'It was all a bit confusing, to be honest, because of that bloody book. It made me feel like I really understood her. But it scared me a bit too. I mean, I'm only here for a while, and she's looking for all that *commitment*. Perhaps this is all for the best.' As he said it, Riley realized he didn't think that at all.

'Look, give her a day or two, then talk to her. Tell you what, try being *authentic*, ha ha,' said Hazard. 'I'm sure she'll forgive you.'

But what did Hazard know? He and Monica were not exactly on the same wavelength. In fact, the only comfort that Riley could find in the situation was that if Monica didn't like him right now, she really, *really* didn't like Hazard.

Alice

Lunch had been a disaster. Max had opened the champagne when his parents had arrived at 11 a.m. Alice had drunk two glasses on an empty stomach. Then she'd downed a glass of the red wine she'd set aside for the gravy while she was doing the cooking. The combination of no sleep, nerves and too much booze meant that she got completely muddled with all her timings. The turkey was dry, the sprouts were mush and the roast potatoes as hard as bullets. And she'd forgotten the gravy altogether.

Max's mother had made all the right complimentary noises about the meal, but – in her usual way – dressed up criticism as praise. 'How *clever* of you to use shop-bought stuffing. I always make my own. So silly, as it takes me absolutely ages to get it *just right*.' Alice knew exactly what she was doing, but Max hadn't a clue.

Alice wished she was at her mother's house, with her siblings and their families, squashed happily into the cramped front room. Over the years, carpets, curtains and furnishings, chosen by her mother for their availability and price rather than beauty, had combined to create a contrasting, clashing, riot of pattern and colour. They'd all be wearing gaudy festive jumpers and paper hats, bickering and taking the mickey out of each other.

Alice's Fulham house was painted just the right shade of Farrow & Ball, the furniture was coordinated and unobtrusive, with the occasional pop of the latest statement colour. Everything was open plan, and a lighting consultant had spent hours, and a large proportion of Max's bonus, making sure that the right mood could be created for any occasion. Utterly tasteful. Completely soulless. Nothing to dislike, nor anything to love.

After lunch, Alice helped Bunty unwrap more of her presents. Alice realized that she'd gone totally over the top and was sure a shrink would say it was a reaction to her own childhood Christmases, where the majority of the gifts had been hand-made and hand-me-downs. She still remembered the scorn with which she'd greeted the lovingly crafted sewing box her mother had made for her when she was ten, stocked with needles and a rainbow of threads, buttons and fabrics. She'd wanted a CD player. How could she have been so ungrateful?

Alice dragged herself back to the moment and uploaded a cute picture of Bunty chewing the wrapping of one of her presents to Instagram, with all the usual hashtags. Completely out of the blue, Max snatched her phone from her.

'Why can't you actually live your bloody life, rather than photographing it all the time?' he hissed, throwing her mobile into the corner of the room, where it landed in a box of building bricks, tipping them over like a wrecking ball.

There was a stunned silence.

Alice waited for someone to stand up for her, to tell Max that he was out of order and couldn't speak to his wife like that.

'Alice, dear. When is Bunty due to have her nap?' Max's mother asked instead, as if the previous few minutes hadn't happened.

'She – she doesn't have a set nap time,' replied Alice, trying not to cry. Her mother-in-law pursed her lips in disapproval. Alice braced herself for the familiar lecture on the importance of *routine* and how Max had been the perfect baby, sleeping through the night from the minute he came back from the hospital.

'Well, why don't you and Max take the sweet thing out for a little walk, Alice, and I'll tidy the place up for you? It'll do you good to get some fresh air.'

Alice saw this for what it was: a veiled criticism of her housework masquerading as kindness, but she wasn't going to argue. She couldn't wait to get away from it all for a while, despite knowing that the minute she walked out of the door her in-laws would be talking about her many inadequacies. Without humiliating herself further by scrabbling in the toy box for her mobile, she picked up Bunty and her shoulder bag and left the room, followed by Max who looked as if he didn't want to spend time with her any more than she did with him.

As soon as the front door closed, she turned to him.

'How dare you humiliate me like that in front of your parents, Max? We're supposed to be *a team*,' she said, and waited for the apology.

'Well, it doesn't feel much like a team to me, Alice. Every moment you're not with Bunty, you're playing around on bloody social media. I have needs too, you know!'

'Bloody hell, Max! Are you jealous of a *baby*? *Your* baby? I'm sorry if I'm not spending as much time pandering to you' – she wasn't, actually – 'but Bunty needs me rather more than you do. You could perhaps try helping a bit more.'

'It's not just that, Alice,' Max said, suddenly looking sad rather than angry. 'You've changed. *We've* changed. I'm just trying to get to grips with it all.'

'Of *course* we've changed! We're parents now! I've just had to push a melon through a keyhole, I've turned into a mobile milk bar overnight and I haven't slept for more than three hours at a stretch for weeks. I'm obviously going to be a bit different from the carefree PR girl you married. What were you expecting?'

'I'm not sure,' he said quietly. 'You know, I remember on our wedding day, looking at you walking down the aisle and thinking that I was the luckiest man in the world. I thought our lives were blessed.'

'I felt the same, Max. And we *are* blessed. It's bound to be hard right now. Everyone finds the first few months with a new baby difficult, don't they?' She waited for Max to respond, but he didn't.

'Look, you go back and talk to your parents,' said Alice. 'I don't want to row any more. I'm too exhausted. I'll be back in time for Bunty's bath.'

She had the feeling that another brick had been removed from the badly constructed foundations of her marriage.

*

Alice sat on the bench in the deserted playground. She was pushing Bunty's Bugaboo backwards and forwards with her foot to encourage her to go to sleep. She could see her daughter's eyelids getting heavier and heavier as she chewed her fist with her gums, drooling all over her reindeer print romper suit (@minimes).

Alice felt bereft without her mobile. She kept checking her pocket, then remembering that it was at home. She didn't want to go back to the house, but she was *antsy* without anything to like, post or comment on. She needed a distraction so she didn't have to think about the row with Max. It was too depressing. What did she *do* with unfilled time before she got into social media? She couldn't remember.

Alice opened her bag, just in case she'd left a copy of *Grazia* in there. No such luck. But she did find the green exercise book that she'd picked up in the playground a few days ago, and completely forgotten about. For want of anything else to do, she took it out and began to read.

Everyone lies about their lives. Well, ain't that the truth! @aliceinwonderland's hundred thousand followers certainly didn't see the miserable reality of Alice's existence. She thought of all the posts showing her and Max gazing lovingly at each other and at their baby. What *was* this book? Had it been left deliberately for her?

What would happen if you shared the truth instead? Does anyone want to know the truth? Really? The truth often isn't pretty. It's not aspirational. It doesn't fit neatly into a little square on Instagram. Alice presented a version of the truth; the one that people wanted to see pop up on their feed. Anything *too* real and she'd lose followers in droves. No one wanted to know about her less-than-perfect marriage, her stretch marks, or Bunty's conjunctivitis and cradle cap.

Alice read Julian's story. He sounded *wonderful*, but so sad. She wondered what he was doing today. Did he have anyone to share Christmas lunch with? Was he all on his own in Chelsea Studios? Did he still lay a table setting for his dead wife?

She started to read Monica's story. She knew the café well. She was pretty sure she'd tagged it in a number of posts recently. You know the kind of thing – look at my coffee, with a heart shape drawn into the frothy milk, and my healthy bowl of fruit, yoghurt and granola; look at me supporting local businesses. In fact, she could picture Monica bustling around the café being efficient: ten years older than her, but still pretty, in an intense, uptight sort of way.

Then Alice realized, with a shock, that the woman she'd become obsessed by, the one dancing with such carefree abandon the other night, was *Monica*. She hadn't put two and two together at the time, as the vision she'd been watching seemed so very different from the woman she was used to seeing in daylight hours.

She read about Monica's baby hunger. *Be careful what you wish for*, thought Alice, darkly, as Bunty started to stir, looking as if she might be working up to a screaming session. Had she been that desperate for a baby at some point? She couldn't remember being so, but she supposed she must have been.

How extraordinary that she had been envying Monica's life, when all the time all Monica wanted was what she took most for granted. She felt an invisible, but unbreakable, thread of connection between her and this strong but sad woman she'd never properly met. She looked down at Bunty, at her gorgeous plump cheeks and bottomless blue eyes, and felt a tidal wave of love she vowed never to let herself forget.

Hazard. Now, there was a name for a romantic hero. She really hoped he was gorgeous. It would be such a waste to be called *Hazard* and be all skinny with an overly pronounced Adam's apple and acne. She pictured him riding, bareback and bare-chested, along a Cornish cliff path. Oh God, it must be the hormones.

Alice was vehemently anti-drugs but, reading Hazard's story, she had an uncomfortable feeling that her relationship with alcohol was not dissimilar to his with cocaine. She wasn't just drinking to let her hair down at parties, she was drinking to get through the day. She pushed that irritating thought to one side. She deserved her glass of wine (or three) in the evening. And everyone else was doing it too. Her social media was filled with memes about 'wine o'clock' and 'Mummy's little helper'. It made her feel adult, like she still had a life. It was her 'me time', and – frankly – she deserved some of that.

Alice read to the end of Hazard's story and realized what he'd done. OMG! It was like being right in the middle of a Danielle Steel novel! Hazard had found the man of Monica's dreams, Riley, and sent him back to London to save her from miserable spinsterhood. How romantic! And it had worked! Surely Riley was the man he'd seen her with in Monica's Café, gazing into her eyes with such adoration?

Alice was dying to read the next story, which she assumed

was Riley's. She could see it scrawled in an obviously masculine hand, over the next three pages of the book, but she needed to get back for Bunty's bath time. Maybe she could spare an extra few minutes to do a *tiny* detour past Monica's Café, and just have a quick peek in through the window. It would keep her mind off that terrible row with Max for a little longer. She was pretty sure it would be closed on Christmas Day, but it wouldn't do any harm to trundle past. Bunty would enjoy the extra walk.

Alice turned left out of the park on to the Fulham Road, right by the Chinese restaurant. It had been there for as long as she could remember, but she'd never been in. She was more avocado and crab maki roll than chicken chow mein. The pavements were pretty deserted as most of Fulham seemed to have evacuated to the country for the duration of the holiday, which is why the two men standing outside the restaurant caught her attention. They were an unlikely-looking pair. One of them looked Chinese. He was tiny, and very cross, emitting an energy totally out of kilter with his stature. The other man was a tall, well-honed redhead who she was sure she recognized from somewhere. He looked as if he were *crying*. What on earth was that all about? Perhaps she wasn't the only one having a tricky day. She felt a little guilty about how much that thought cheered her.

As Alice walked towards the café, she realized it was the first thing she'd done for ages with a sense of excitement rather than just out of duty. The last few months had been one mundane chore after the other – feeding, wiping, cleaning, changing, cooking, ironing, washing, and repeat, ad infinitum. It was a novelty, not knowing exactly what would happen next. Life with a small baby was so terribly predictable. Then Alice chastised herself for the thought, reminding herself how lucky she was.

As she approached the café, it looked as if the lights were on. That didn't necessarily mean it was open. Many of the local businesses seemed to keep their lights on twenty-four seven. It made her rather cross – @aliceinwonderland was all about being kind to the planet. She'd stopped using disposable coffee cups and plastic bags well before it became trendy. She'd even tried reusable nappies for a while, but that hadn't ended well.

Alice peered in through the window. There, sitting by herself at a table which had been laid for several people, was Monica. Crying. Properly crying. Big, snotty, blotchy-faced crying, not the photogenic sort. Monica was definitely the sort of woman who'd be wise not to cry in public. Perhaps, if they became friends, Alice could let her know. That would be a kindness.

Alice felt her buoyant mood deflate. She'd so wanted to believe in the happily ever after. What on earth could be wrong? How could the perfectly romantic scene of just a few days ago have morphed into this one of solitary misery?

Alice was a huge believer in female solidarity. Women had to look after each other. She also lived by the motto 'in a world where you can be anything, be kind'. She had it printed on a t-shirt. She couldn't just walk on past leaving a fellow female *weeping* like that. Apart from anything else, she didn't feel like Monica was a stranger. She felt like she knew her, at least a little bit. Better than most of her 'besties', if truth be told.

Alice took the book out of her bag, by way of introduction, stood up tall, put a friendly, but concerned, smile on her face and walked in, carefully stepping over a malevolent-looking brown mass on the floor. What on earth was that?

Monica looked up, mascara running down her face.

'Hi, I'm Alice,' said Alice. 'I found The Authenticity Project. Are you OK? Can I help?'

'I wish I'd never set eyes on that damn book, and I certainly don't want to see it ever again,' Monica replied, delivering each word like machine-gun fire, making Alice physically recoil. 'I really don't mean to be rude, and I'm sure you – like everybody else – think you know me, having read the story I should never have written, but you don't. And I sure as hell don't know you. Nor do I want to. So please, just bugger off and leave me alone.'

Alice did.

Monica

Monica didn't come down from her flat until the evening of Boxing Day. The café looked like a theatre set, abandoned mid-play. There was the table, still set for pudding, glasses half full. There was the Christmas tree, with presents sitting underneath, unopened. And there, on the floor, like a giant, fruity cowpat, a sprig of holly still sticking jauntily out of its centre, was the figgy pudding.

Monica filled a bucket with hot, soapy water, pulled on a pair of Marigolds, and got to work. She had always found cleaning therapeutic, too much so, if she was honest. Her five-star hygiene rating, prominently displayed in the café window, was one of her proudest achievements. Even the language around it helped. A clean sweep. A clean sheet of paper. Wash that man right out of my hair.

Now that she'd had some time to calm down, Monica realized that it was unlikely that Hazard and Riley had deliberately set her up. She believed Riley when he said that he'd genuinely liked her (she didn't think those kisses could have been fake), but she still felt *humiliated*. She hated the fact that all this time Riley had been lying to her. She hated the idea of Hazard and Riley pitying her. She loathed the thought of them talking about her, planning how to rectify her sad old life. And she felt *stupid*. She wasn't used to feeling stupid. She'd won the Keynes prize for A level Economics, for goodness' sake.

She'd just started to believe that good things could happen, totally out of the blue, and that she was worthy of being loved by someone as amazing as Riley. Now it turned out it was all engineered. Her mother had always told her that if something looked too good to be true, it probably was. And Riley had definitely looked too good to be true.

Over the last few weeks, she'd felt herself unwinding. She'd started 'going with the flow' and stopped the worst of her obsessive planning. She'd felt happier and more carefree. But look what a mess it got her into.

Monica had no idea what to think any more.

What she did know was that she didn't want to see any of them, at least not for a while. She wanted everything to go back to how it was before she found that stupid book in her café, before she'd written her story and before she'd become unwittingly entangled in someone else's masterplan. That world was bland and featureless, but at least it was safe and predictable.

She realized, with a start, that she hadn't cancelled that week's art class. She picked up her phone and went on to the class WhatsApp group she'd set up. *No art classes until further notice*, she typed. She didn't feel the need to apologize or explain. Why should she?

Monica walked over to The Library. The beautiful portrait Julian had painted of her was lying, face up, on the coffee table. A different Monica stared up at her – one who didn't know her life was based on a lie.

She reached under the tree and took out the present labelled *To Monica, With love from Riley xxx*. She considered throwing it away without looking inside, that would be the proud thing to do, but her curiosity got the better of her.

Carefully, she peeled back the wrapping paper. Inside was a beautiful turquoise-blue notebook which she immediately recognized as Smythson. Had she told Riley it was her all-time favourite brand? It must have cost him a fortune. On the front, in gold lettering, the words *HOPES AND DREAMS* were embossed. She brought it up to her nose and inhaled the smell of leather. Then she opened it and read the writing on the inside cover: *Merry Christmas, Monica! I know how much you love good stationery, I know how much you love lists, and I know how much you deserve all your hopes and dreams to come true. Love, Riley xxx*

It was the perfect gift. It was only when she saw the words Riley had written start to blur that she realized she was crying, marring the perfection of the book cover with salty blotches. And that made her cry even more.

She cried for what might have been, for the version of a perfect future that had, for a while, shimmered in front of her, that she had just started to believe might become a reality. She cried for her lost belief in herself; she'd considered herself so strong and clever but she'd turned out to be gullible and stupid. But most of all, she cried for the girl she'd thought she was becoming; one who was impulsive, spontaneous and fun-loving, who did things on a whim, without worrying about the consequences. The girl who wrote secrets in note-books and scattered them to the wind. The girl who fell carelessly in love with handsome strangers.

She was gone.

Alice

It was 11 p.m., and Alice was sitting in the nursery rocking chair, in the dim glow of the Beatrix Potter nightlight, feeding Bunty. She was still feeling battered after her argument with Max yesterday, which hadn't been mentioned since. And being yelled at by Monica hadn't helped. So much for the sisterhood. She reached into her bag and pulled out the book, turning the light up one notch so it was bright enough to read, but not so bright that Bunty would wake up and not be able to settle again. She turned to the page where the handwriting changed from Hazard's to Riley's, feeling a tingle of anticipation. What secrets could a gorgeous man like that be hiding?

My name is Riley Stevenson. I'm thirty years old and I'm a gardener from Perth – the one in Australia. Apparently there's one in Scotland too. To answer Julian's questions, I know the names of all my neighbours back home, and they know me. They have done since I was tiny. It can be a bit stifling after a while, to be honest. That's part of the reason I left.

Blimey, how on earth is he coping with London? Talk about from one extreme to another. Alice shifted Bunty over slightly, so she could turn the page.

I guess my truth is that I'm pissed off with everyone assuming that, just because I'm not as messed up as so many of these Brits, I'm some kind of smiley idiot. I'm not being paranoid, you know. They really do.
Surely being happy and straightforward should be a good thing, not some kind of character defect? Uncomplicated doesn't mean simple, does it?

Oh bless, thought Alice, what a sweet boy.

Sometimes I see Monica or Julian looking at me as if I'm a kid, and they're thinking, 'Oh bless, isn't he sweet?'

Yikes. Was this book reading her mind?

You know, I don't actually like this book at all. It's made me some great friends, but since I found it my life has become less authentic, not more. My relationship with Monica is based on a lie. I haven't told her yet that this book is how we met, and I can't even remember why not.
Living in this city, with no sun, no plants, no soil, is

changing me. I feel like I have to get back to my roots. Even what I've written here doesn't feel like me. I don't do all this self-analysis stuff. I'm a 'what you see is what you get' type of bloke. At least I used to be.

And you know what? The book doesn't tell the truth about anyone else either.

Reading Julian's story, you'd imagine a sad, invisible old man. But the Julian I know is the most amazing human being ever. He makes life feel more colourful. He makes you want to see new places and experience new things.

As for Hazard, if I'd not met him, I'd think he was an arrogant, self-obsessed arsehole. But the man I talked to in Thailand was quiet and gentle and a bit sad.

Then there's Monica, who thinks she's unlovable. Yet she's warm and generous and kind. She brings people together and nurtures them. In that way she's a natural gardener, like me, and she'll make a great mum. If she'd just chill out a bit, I know she'd find everything she wants.

I'm going to tell Monica the truth. After that, I'm not sure what will happen. But at least our roots will be planted in proper soil, not in sand, so we'll stand a chance.

What will you do now? I hope this book brings you more luck than it has me.

Alice felt incredibly melancholy. Judging by her encounter with Monica yesterday, things had not gone as well as Riley had hoped. Monica hadn't appeared warm or generous or kind at all, nor had she made Alice feel nurtured. She'd been a bit mean, frankly.

Lovely Riley. A gardener without a garden.

And that's when she came up with a plan.

Julian

Julian was comfortable wrapped in his cocoon. He was vaguely aware of a buzzer sounding somewhere in the distance, but he couldn't do anything about it, even if he wanted to. He felt a very long way away from anything.

'Julian! It's time to get up. You can't stay in bed all day,' said Mary.

'Leave me be,' he protested. 'I was up most of the night painting. Check out the studio – you'll see. I've nearly finished.'

'I've seen it, it's brilliant, as always. *You're* brilliant. But it's nearly lunch time.' Then, because she knew it was his weakness, 'I'll make you eggs Benedict.'

Julian stretched out one leg to see if he could feel Keith lying at the end of his bed. He wasn't there.

He opened one eye. Mary wasn't there either. She hadn't been there for a very long time. He closed the eye again.

There was only one thing stopping him from drifting off entirely, keeping him tethered precariously to the ground. He knew there was *something* he had to do. He had a feeling that people were depending on him. He had a responsibility.

He heard a pinging noise. This time it was right by his ear. He reached over and picked up the mobile phone he'd forgotten he owned. There was a message on the screen: *No art classes until further notice.* That was it, the thing he'd been grasping for. Now he could let it go. Perhaps he could just stay here, under his covers, until he was eventually cleared away by the bulldozers and replaced with a corporate entertaining complex.

LOW BATTERY, it said on the screen. He put the phone down without attaching the charger and pulled the bedspread back over his head, breathing in its musty, comforting smell.

Hazard

Hazard was back in town, having spent the last four days in Oxfordshire with his parents. Incredibly, they didn't seem to bear him many grudges, they just appeared relieved to see him looking well and relatively happy, although Hazard's mum had seemed rather surprised to see him at breakfast every morning, as if she'd expected him to abscond overnight and go on a bender. To be fair, that's exactly what he would have done in the old days. He wondered how long it would take before she'd trust him again. Perhaps she never would.

Hazard would have stayed longer, but his parents were hosting a New Year's Eve party for the Rotary Club, and he thought it would be safer if he spent the evening alone. He planned to be in bed well before midnight, thanking his lucky stars that, for the first time in as long as he could remember, he'd start the New Year in his own bed, without a hangover or anyone whose name he couldn't remember.

Hazard picked up his phone to check the time. It was a basic pay-as-you-go model. It had never rung, as no one had the number (apart from, as of this morning, his mum). He realized he didn't even know what ringtone it was set to. Hazard had always been gregarious, sociable and hard-working, so was finding it difficult to adjust to this world with no friends and no employment. He knew he couldn't avoid life for ever.

It was 4.30 p.m. He put on his coat, locked up the flat, and walked towards the cemetery. He was sure that by now the fallout from the incendiary device he had accidentally triggered on Christmas Day would have diffused, and he'd find Monica, Julian and Riley all friends again. Given that his old social circle was currently off-limits, he was rather hoping he could join theirs.

He walked past Monica's Café. It was dark. A notice on the door read CLOSED UNTIL 2 JANUARY.

Sat on the Admiral's tombstone, Hazard was so busy looking out for Julian or Monica approaching from the south side of the cemetery that he didn't notice Riley coming from the north until he was just a few feet away. Perhaps Riley would like his phone number? How could he ask without looking a bit sad or desperate?

'No sign of them, then?' said Riley. 'I've been waiting all week for Friday 5 p.m, hoping they'd show.'

'Nope. I've been here for fifteen minutes. Only me and the ravens. How are things with you and Monica?' Hazard asked, suspecting from the defeated droop of Riley's shoulders that he knew the answer.

'She's not answering my calls, and the café's all closed up.

I'm worried about Julian too. His phone's gone dead and I've rung his bell every day since Christmas, but there's no answer. Julian usually only goes out between 10 a.m. and 11 a.m., and he didn't say he was going away. Do you think we should call the police?'

'Let's go round there now and give it another go,' said Hazard. 'Apart from anything else, if I sit here much longer, my bum may freeze to the Admiral's tombstone.'

The name alongside Julian's buzzer read J&M JESSOP, despite the fact that M hadn't been there for nearly fifteen years. Hazard found that unbearably sad. The new Hazard was, he'd noticed, becoming rather sentimental. Despite buzzing repeatedly for five minutes or so, there was still no answer.

'OK, let's check with Monica whether she knows where he is and, if not, we'll call the police,' said Hazard.

'She won't talk to me,' said Riley, 'so you'll have to give it a go. Although she's not your biggest fan either.' Riley sounded rather relieved that he wasn't the only one in the firing line.

'Does she live near by?' asked Hazard.

'Yes, over the café,' Riley replied.

'Great, let's go find her.'

The shared mission created a bond between the two, like soldiers on special ops, and they marched in companionable, purposeful silence towards the café. Riley pointed out the door, painted buttercup yellow, leading up to Monica's flat, and they rang the bell. No answer. They banged on the door of the café. Still no answer. Hazard stepped back off the edge of the pavement, causing a passing black cab to swerve and hoot, and craned his neck to look up at Monica's window.

'You've spent too long living on an island with only one road, mate!' said Riley.

'You can't take Class-A narcotics for a decade unless you have a healthy disrespect for death,' replied Hazard. 'Although it would be ironic, after all I've been through, to be killed by a taxi on the Fulham Road. Look, there's a light on up there,' he said. 'MONICA! WE NEED TO TALK TO YOU! MONICA! MONICA, HAVE YOU SEEN JULIAN? WE NEED YOUR HELP!'

Just as he was about to give up, the sash window was pushed up and Monica's head appeared.

'For God's sake, what will the neighbours think?' she whispered angrily, sounding scarily like Hazard's mother. 'Wait. I'll come down.'

A few minutes later, the door opened. Monica's hair was in a messy bun, skewered with a pencil, and she was wearing a large, shapeless t-shirt and sweatpants, neither of which were items of clothing Hazard would have expected her to own. She ushered, rather than welcomed, them into the café.

'Monica, I've been desperate to speak to you,' said Riley.

'Riley, let's just stick to the matter in hand for the moment, hey?' said Hazard, before Riley could get all intense and derail the whole thing. 'You can do that bit later. The important question is: have you heard anything from Julian recently? Since Christmas Day?'

Monica frowned. 'No. Oh God, I feel awful. I've been so wrapped up in myself that I haven't even thought about him. What kind of a friend am I? You've tried his cottage, I take it, and his mobile?'

'Loads of times,' replied Riley. 'I wish I knew his land-line. It's ex-directory.'

'Fulham 3276,' said Monica.

'Wow,' said Riley, 'how did you remember that?'

'Photographic memory. How do you think I became a City lawyer?' Monica replied, not falling for Riley's flattery. 'I think this area of Fulham is 385, so his number would be 0207 385 3276.' She typed the number into her phone and put it on speaker. It rang and rang until eventually it reverted to the dialling tone.

They were concentrating so hard on Monica's phone that it took them a while to notice the banging on the café door. It was Baz, wearing John Lennon-style glasses, a black leather jacket and a harassed expression. Monica unlocked the door and let him in.

'Hi guys. I really, really need to speak to Benji. Do you know where he is?' he said, slightly out of breath. 'I want to say sorry. I flew off the handle a bit.'

'It's a little late for that now,' said Monica, tersely. 'He's gone up to Scotland for Hogmanay. He's been desperate to talk to you for days. Baz, this is Hazard,' she said without once looking at him. She delivered his name as if it were a swear word.

'Hi,' said Baz, barely pausing to look at Hazard. 'D'you have a landline for him? His phone's turned off, or out of signal.'

'No, sorry. There's a bit of a theme here,' said Monica. 'We're trying to get hold of Julian. No one's heard from him since Christmas.' There was an uncomfortable pause after the mention of the word 'Christmas', as everyone thought back to that day.

'That's not good. Let's go find Granny. She usually sees him every morning for tai chi. She'll know what's going on.'

The four of them set off back towards the Broadway, hostilities pushed aside for the greater cause.

Betty shook her head vigorously. 'I came usual time for tai chi, but no answer Monday, Tuesday, Wednesday, Thursday, Friday,' she said, counting the days off on her fingers. 'I assume he with his family.'

'He doesn't have any family in the UK,' said Monica. 'Let's go over there, see if we can get in.'

The five of them walked past the Broadway and on to Chelsea Studios. By this point, they weren't feeling too optimistic about getting an answer at the front gate. And there was none.

'We find neighbour,' said Mrs Wu, pressing every buzzer above and below Julian's with aggressively pointed index fingers, in a random order, as if she were conducting an experimental piece with a full orchestra.

'Remember, Granny got out of communist China in the 1970s,' whispered Baz to Riley and Hazard. 'She and my dad swam across the bay to Hong Kong, with their most precious belongings strapped to their backs, like turtles. You don't mess with Betty Wu.'

Eventually, a tinny voice came over the intercom, sounding more than a bit cross.

'If you're trying to sell me dishcloths, or talk to me about eternal salvation, I'm not interested,' it said.

'Please let us in. We are worried about friend. Not seen him for days,' said Mrs Wu.

They heard an unmistakeable groan, then, a few minutes later, a well-coiffed platinum-blonde lady of a certain age opened the gate. Her face was waxy smooth, but she had a turkey-like neck, swathed in an Hermès scarf. She looked like the sort of woman who, when her husband was driving her somewhere, would sit in the back seat.

'Who are you looking for?' she asked, without any introduction.

'Julian Jessop,' answered Monica, who wasn't going to be intimidated by anyone.

'Well, good luck with that one. We've lived here for nearly six years and I can count the number of times I've seen him on two hands.' She waved her manicured talons at them. 'Maybe one hand, come to think of it. He's not turned up to any of the Residents' Association meetings.' She narrowed her eyes at them, as if holding them personally responsible for Julian's lack of participation. 'I'm chair,' she added, information that was both unnecessary and unsurprising. 'I suppose you'd better come in. Good God, how many of you are there?'

They walked past her, nodding their thanks as they did so, and headed towards the door of Julian's cottage.

'If you find him, tell him that Patricia Arbuckle needs to see him urgently!' she shouted after them. 'If I don't hear from him soon, I'm instructing my lawyers!'

Riley knocked hard on the door. Hazard's palms sweated as he waited for an answer. And he didn't even know Julian, although he rather felt as if he did.

'JULIAN!' shouted Mrs Wu, in a voice several times larger than her body. Monica and Riley peered in through the front windows, which, thanks to Monica, were no longer totally opaque.

'I can't see anything out of order, although it's a bit difficult to tell, to be honest,' said Monica. 'He's let it all get in a mess again.' She pushed the sash window up and it opened about twelve inches. What they really needed, thought Hazard, was a small child.

'I go through window!' said Mrs Wu, who was, he noted, the size of a small child. 'Biming! Hold feet! You, big boy, hold body!' Hazard took a few seconds to realize she was addressing him. Although it obviously wasn't the first time he'd been called 'big boy'.

Mrs Wu raised her hands above her head and he held her by the torso as Baz and Riley grabbed her legs. Her face was facing the ground. 'Right! Forward! Through window!' she shouted at them like a military commander, and they posted her through, like a parcel into a letterbox. There were a couple of minutes' pause while Mrs Wu lowered herself to the floor, then stood up.

'Open the door, Granny!' said Baz. A few minutes later, they were in.

Julian's cottage smelled unloved. The curtains were closed, it was freezing cold and the spiders' webs were back with a vengeance. Riley, who knew his way around better than anyone else, was doing a reconnaissance of the ground floor.

'No sign of him down here, let's check his bedroom. It's up there,' he said, pointing at the wrought-iron spiral staircase which led to the mezzanine floor. Monica led the way up the staircase with Riley and Mrs Wu following behind.

Hazard heard Monica shout, 'Julian!' They must have found him. Hazard held his breath, fearing the worst. Finally, Monica reappeared from the bedroom upstairs.

'He's OK, just very cold and confused,' she said. Hazard could see his breath form clouds as he exhaled slowly. 'God knows when he last ate. Baz, can you turn on the heating? Mrs Wu, can you bring round some of your magical healing soup? Julian's adamant that he doesn't want to go to the hospital, so I'm going to see if I can find a doctor who can come round and check him over. Riley, if there are any shops still open, can you try and find some Angel Delight? Butterscotch flavour, obviously.'

Why obviously? Hazard wondered. He felt like putting his hand up and asking if she had a job for him too, but thought she might just throw something at him again. He went to find a kettle. His mother always swore by a nice cuppa in a crisis.

Monica

He didn't look like the Julian Monica knew. He'd been curled up in bed, like an apostrophe, so thin and shrivelled that his body barely made a hump under the blankets. Three empty tins of baked beans, one with a fork sticking out of it, sat on the floor by the bed, along with his mobile phone. The tartan kilt and jacket he'd been wearing last time she saw him lay in a heap by the door, as if the person who'd been wearing them had simply evaporated, or spontaneously combusted, like the witch in *The Wizard of Oz*.

For a terrible moment, which felt like an hour, Monica had thought he was dead. He was so still and, when she'd touched his hand, his skin felt cold and clammy. But when she'd shouted his name, his eyelids had flickered and he'd made a groaning noise.

Now, he was sitting in an armchair by a roaring fire. Baz, after some time spent searching for the boiler, had realized that Julian didn't have central heating, just a few free-standing electric radiators, none of which was on. He was now wrapped in several blankets and sipping from a mug of Betty's chicken sweetcorn soup.

One of the GPs from the local surgery had come by and prescribed warmth, food and fluids, along with some anti-biotics for bed sores. He'd muttered darkly about how 'each of these episodes' was putting more strain on Julian's already weak heart, so Monica assumed this wasn't the first time something like this had happened. But at least now, some colour was slowly seeping back to his cheeks and he looked a little less cadaverous.

Monica was sure that Julian's decline was related to the arguments on Christmas Day, so she was going out of her way to be friendly to Riley in front of him. Riley, mean-while, appeared to be doing everything he could to get back into her good books. She'd pushed this, out of interest, to see how hard he'd try, by telling him that Julian's down-stairs loo needed a good clean. He'd trotted off with a bucket, some bleach and a scrubbing brush like an obedient puppy. There was no way she was going to get romantically entangled with him again, but they could be friends, she supposed, for Julian's sake.

As for Hazard, she didn't think she'd ever be able to like someone who played so carelessly with people's lives. What was he doing here? Who invited him to insert himself into their circle anyway? She'd come across his type before, so used to being admired and getting his own way that they didn't even question their right to be included.

Everything about him annoyed her, from his too-perfect Hollywood smile and stupid hipster beard right down to his preppy loafers. When she was sixteen, not long after her mother died, her dad had persuaded her, against her better judgement, to go to the school prom. She'd been kissed by a boy who'd looked just like a younger Hazard, and had begun to think that maybe, just maybe, things would start to get better. Then she'd found out he'd done it for a dare. *See if you can get the class swot to put out.* She'd stopped going to school for several months after that.

And what kind of name was Hazard, anyhow? Although it did suit him. He was the sort of guy who needed to come with a warning sign.

As if he could sense her thinking about him, Hazard turned to her.

'Hey, Monica. Did you manage to persuade Julian to teach an art class at the café?' he asked.

'Yes,' she replied, making a mental note to reinstate the art classes as soon as possible, for Julian's sake, if nothing else. Hazard ploughed on, despite Monica's terse reply.

'Can I join in? I haven't done any art at all since uni. I'd love to give it a go again.'

Monica pictured Hazard at university, hosting black-tie dinner parties and licking gelato off the razor-sharp hip bones of girls called Davina who'd gone to Roedean.

'I don't think there's enough room,' she said. Then added, 'Sorry,' as a churlish afterthought.

Unfortunately, despite his grand age, Julian had the hearing of a bat.

'Of *course* there's room, old chap. We'll just pull up an extra chair!'

'Would you like my new mobile number?' Hazard asked her, waving a surprisingly old-fashioned phone at her.

'Why on earth would I want that?' she snapped. Did he think every woman was interested in him?

'Er, so you can call me about the art class?' Hazard replied, looking a little taken aback.

'Oh, I see. No need, just turn up. Mondays at 7 p.m.' Thinking she may have been a little too aggressive, Monica decided to hold out the tiniest leaf of an olive branch. 'What were you doing out in Thailand, Hazard?' she asked, forcing her tone to sound more friendly.

'Umm. I was on a detox,' Hazard replied. Monica had to stop herself from rolling her eyes. She knew exactly the sort of thing. Celebs were pictured doing it all the time in the gossip magazines people left in her café, and she pretended not to read. He'd been in some luxury spa, drinking organic smoothies and being massaged and colonically irrigated several times a day, so he could drop a few pounds before the party season. She'd bet it was paid for by a trust fund set up by Mummy and Daddy.

'Lucky you, getting so much time off work,' she said, testing out her theory.

'Oh, I'm actually between jobs at the minute,' he said. That was posh-boy code for not needing to work. Hazard, she knew, had never had to worry about getting the right exam results or selling enough flat whites to cover the rent; he'd just call on a network of godparents and school friends to find him a fashionable occupation that wouldn't interfere with his social life, holidays or 'detoxes'.

Baz had gone back to the restaurant to help his parents, as they were fully booked for New Year's Eve (he'd been grinning like the Cheshire Cat having finally had a call from

Benji in Scotland). The others didn't want to leave Julian. Monica was worried that as soon as he was left alone he'd hibernate again. Betty had brought steamed dumplings and spring rolls for them all and, on Julian's instruction, Riley had fetched some champagne up from the cellar to toast in the New Year. He'd emerged looking pale and shaky. She hadn't had a chance to ask him what was down there.

'Mrs Wu,' said Julian, his voice still rather croaky.

'Betty!' she shouted.

'I'm sorry I upset you, talking about Baz and Benji.'

'Biming!' she shouted.

'Benji is a really nice boy, you know, and he makes Biming very happy. Isn't that all that matters?' he said gently. Monica looked at Betty who was frowning so hard that her eyebrows knitted together, like a giant grey millipede. She wondered whether Julian really did have a death wish.

Betty sighed. 'Of course, I want him to be happy. I love that boy. He is my only grandchild. I'm sure this Benji is nice man. But he cannot be wife for Biming! He cannot have baby Wus. He cannot cook Chinese food in restaurant.'

'That's not true, you know. They could adopt. Lots of gay men do these days,' said Julian.

'Adopt baby girl from China?' said Betty, almost thoughtfully.

'And Benji is a brilliant cook,' added Monica. 'He does most of the cooking in the café. He's much better than me.'

'Harrumph,' said Betty, crossing her arms. But Monica thought she detected just a little softening of her stance.

'Biming tells me he shouted at you,' said Betty to Julian. 'I tell him I am ashamed. He should show respect to elders.'

'Don't worry, Mrs Wu. He apologized just now, although there really was no need,' Julian replied.

Monica smiled at this. She'd overheard Baz's apology, which hadn't been entirely abject. He'd said sorry for calling the cottage a rubbish dump, and that it looked much better since Monica had had a go at it. Which gave her an idea.

'Julian,' Monica said. 'Why don't we start the New Year with another spring clean? I can drop round next week, if you like?'

'Hey, could you do my place while you're at it, Monica?' said Hazard.

That was it: the final straw.

'Why? Because you're too bloody lazy to clean it yourself, Hazard? Or because you think that cleaning is *women's work* and you're too *masculine* for that kind of thing?'

'Chill out, Monica! I was only kidding!' said Hazard, looking rather taken aback. 'You need to lighten up sometimes, you know. Have some fun. It's New Year's Eve, after all.'

Monica glared at him. He glared back. She still loathed him, but at least he stood up to her. As a lawyer, she'd hated it when an adversary settled too quickly.

'Five minutes till midnight!' said Riley. 'Everyone got a glass of champagne?'

'I've got a peppermint tea,' replied Hazard. 'Tea is the new champagne. Everyone's drinking it.'

'Starting your New Year's resolutions early, Hazard?' asked Monica, who loved resolutions so much that she spread hers out throughout the year. Why just confine them to January?

'Something like that,' he replied.

Monica thought about asking Hazard if he'd checked the

use-by date on the peppermint tea, but didn't. It was unlikely to kill him, more's the pity.

Then the skies over Fulham and Chelsea lit up and the sound of fireworks reverberated off the nearby buildings. Monica turned to the floor-to-ceiling windows of Julian's studio, which were filled with a riot of colour.

It was a brand-new year.

Riley

Riley was relieved to see Julian walking towards the Admiral the next Friday. On Monica's instruction, he'd been round to the cottage every day since New Year's Eve – ostensibly to sort through more of Julian's clutter, but also to check that he was getting up, staying warm and eating. He did seem, if not back to his old self, at least to be on the mend. This evening he looked positively buoyant.

'Riley! Glad you're here! Guess what?'

'What?' replied Riley.

'Monica's booked the Eurostar tickets for the art class field trip! I've spent all afternoon planning our gallery visits!'

'Awesome!' said Riley, who'd been longing to visit Paris ever since watching Nicole Kidman in *Moulin Rouge* as a teenager. He waited for Julian to notice what he'd brought with him.

'Who's your friend, Riley?' Julian asked, eyeing the wagging tail.

'I'm hoping he'll be your friend, actually. The builders

found him living in the empty house next door. We think he used to belong to the old lady who died recently. They've been feeding him on their sandwiches and Greggs sausage rolls, but he needs a proper home,' said Riley. The truth was, he thought Julian needed someone to look after even more. That way he'd have a good reason not to give up on life again.

'What is it?' asked Julian.

'It's a dog,' said Riley.

'No, I mean what *breed* of dog.'

'God knows. I think there must have been a fair amount of free loving going down. He's a bit of a mutt. Mainly terrier, I guess,' replied Riley.

'There's definitely some Jack Russell there somewhere,' said Julian. He and the dog looked at each other, quietly taking in their matching rheumy eyes, grey whiskers, arthritic joints and world-weariness.

'What's his name?' asked Julian.

'We don't know. The builders call him Wojciech.'

'Good grief,' said Julian.

'They're Polish.'

'I shall call him Keith,' said Julian. 'Keith is the perfect name for a dog.'

'Does that mean you'll take him on?' said Riley.

'I guess so. We can be two miserable old codgers together, hey Keith?'

'Full disclosure – he can be a bit *windy*,' said Riley.

'Well, that seals it. Another thing we have in common,' said Julian. 'It'll give me someone to blame when I have guests. Do you think he'd enjoy Paris?' he added, looking down at his new pet. Then, without waiting for an answer, he ploughed on, 'And is it overly ambitious to try to cover Modern Art and the Renaissance in one day? But how can one choose, Riley? I've never been terribly good at narrowing down my options. Mary was always telling me that.'

Riley shrugged. He was slightly out of his comfort zone. 'Make sure you leave enough time for us to go up the Eiffel Tower!' he said.

'Dear boy, this is a day of cultural enrichment, not a visit to all the tourist traps. But, I suppose if we have to do one of the clichés, it might as well be *la Tour Eiffel*.'

Riley was distracted by a woman walking towards them, pushing a pushchair, vigorously, as if it were a piece of gym equipment. She was definitely what you'd describe as a 'yummy mummy'. Posh, born with a silver spoon in her mouth, no doubt. She was in her mid-twenties, perfectly styled hair with the sort of highlights you'd pay a fortune for in London, but the Australian sun gives you for free. She looked like a well-groomed palomino pony on her way to a dressage competition. Her hand, clutching a water bottle (reusable), was beautifully manicured. Mothers didn't come like that in Perth. They tended to have tousled hair and wear crumpled sun dresses and flip-flops. Riley waited for her to walk past. But she didn't.

'Hello,' she said. 'You have to be Julian, and you must be Riley?'

'Yes,' he said, confused.

'I knew it. And the Aussie accent is a dead giveaway! I'm Alice!' She thrust out a hand, which they shook. 'And this is Bunty!' She waved at the pushchair. 'Who's this?' she asked, looking at the dog now sitting on the Admiral, next to Julian.

'Keith,' replied Julian and Riley in perfect synchronicity.

'How do you know our names?' asked Riley. Was she some kind of stalker?

'I found The Authenticity Project. In the playground,' she replied.

Riley had spent so much time thinking about what damage that stupid book had done in the past that he'd not considered at all what it might have been up to since he'd left it in the children's play area tucked between his flat and the café, a small patch of green where he often sat to clear his head.

'Oh, my goodness!' said Julian. 'My little book is still doing the rounds! How do you do? Charmed, I'm sure.' Riley rolled his eyes a little. Julian was a sucker for a pretty face.

'OMG! Julian, that jacket is amazing! It has to be Versace. Am I right? 1980s?'

Riley had become so immune to Julian's dress sense that he'd barely raised an eyebrow at the elaborately patterned silk jacket he was sporting under his overcoat, but it was giving Alice paroxysms of excitement.

'Oh, at last!' said Julian. 'Another fashionista! I'd begun to give up hope, surrounded by all these frumps. You're right, of course. The wonderful Gianni. Such a tragic loss to the world. I've never quite got over it.'

Frumps? Riley bristled. Had no one noticed he was wearing the limited-edition Nikes he'd found on eBay? He watched Julian dabbing at his eyes with a silk handkerchief.

He was really hamming it up for his audience. Surely Alice could see through him?

'Please can you take your coat off for a minute, so I can take a photo?' asked Alice. Was she for real? Julian appeared to be happy to take his coat off on one of the coldest days of the year when he'd just nearly died from hypothermia. He even started posing.

'The cowboy boots?' he said, in response to another of her inane fashion enquiries. 'They're from R.Soles on the King's Road. Great name, isn't it? It's probably closed now, of course. It'll be a Pret A Manger, or something similarly ghastly.' He looked wistful. 'Isn't this fun? Reminds me of the times I spent with my great friend, David Bailey.'

Riley thought Alice might faint. Where, he wondered, were all these 'great friends' when Julian was living like a hermit for fifteen years?

'Shall I just leave you two to it?' he asked, realizing as he said it that he was sounding a bit like a jealous child. Alice turned to him.

'Actually, Riley, you were the person I wanted to see, much as I'm *loving* your friend Julian.' Julian actually simpered. Monica, thought Riley, would never stoop to such obvious flirtation. 'I have a proposition for you.' She handed him a piece of paper. 'Can you meet me at this address, tomorrow at 10 a.m.? Julian, you could come, too! You'll love it. I promise! My number's on there in case you have to back out, but I know you won't! You won't, will you? Now, I have to get Bunty to Monkey Music. Laters!'

Laters???

'Gosh. Isn't she just *marvellous*,' said Julian. 'I can't wait to find out what that's all about. Can you? We simply must introduce her to Monica, she'll *love* her.'

Monica, thought Riley, was worth a hundred Alices. He really didn't want to keep this mystery appointment, but he could tell that Julian wasn't going to let it go.

Alice

Alice was super excited about her appointment with Julian and Riley. Since Bunty's arrival, her days tended to blend into onc, all similarly filled with baby-focused activities – baby swim, baby massage, baby yoga, and endless conversations with other mothers about developmental milestones, sleep routines, teething and weaning. Alice could feel her identity slipping away from her, to the point where she was just an appendage – either Bunty's mother or Max's wife. Except online. Online, she was still @aliceinwonderland.

She watched Julian and Riley approaching. Riley had a walk that was more suited to strolling along a beach than a London pavement. He was too exuberant and sunny to be caged up in a city. Or perhaps she just thought that because she'd read his story. It was strange knowing more about someone than you should. Julian, meanwhile, was *spectacular*. Like a bird of paradise, he could never be caged.

'Julian! You're even better dressed today than yesterday!' she said.

'You are too, too kind, dear girl,' he replied, and he actually picked up her hand and kissed it. She thought that only happened in movies. 'This is the exact silk Nehru jacket worn by Sean Connery in *Dr No*. 1962. It goes particularly well with these crocodile brogues, don't you think?'

'Was Sean a *great friend* of yours too?' asked Riley. A little tetchily, Alice thought.

'No, no. Just a passing acquaintance. I bought it in a charity auction,' Julian replied.

'Please, please can I take some photos?' she asked. Julian seemed delighted, leaning against a lamppost, looking suave. He even pulled some Ray-Ban Aviators out of his inside jacket pocket and put them on. Keith sat next to him, looking equally dapper in a bow tie.

'Much as I hate to break up the fashion show,' said Riley, who wasn't getting into the swing of things at all, 'can you tell us why we're here?'

'Well,' she said, 'you probably don't know, but I am an *influencer.*'

'A what?' said both Julian and Riley, in harmony.

'I have over a hundred thousand followers.' Julian looked around, as if expecting to see a crowd of people tailing after her. 'On *Instagram*,' she clarified. This was going to be hard work. Did she have to start her explanation with the invention of the world wide web? 'You must do Insta, Riley?'

'Nah. Instagram's all pointless pictures of skinny people doing yoga poses at sunset, isn't it?'

'Well, there is some of that, admittedly, but there's *a lot* more to it than that,' replied Alice, trying not to be offended. 'For example, this house' – she waved at the large, Victorian terraced house in front of them – 'was left to a local charity when its owner died. It's been turned into a free crèche for the children of local women who are doing rehab for drug and alcohol addiction. Women often refuse to seek help because they worry their children will be taken into care. This house will help them keep custody while they sort themselves out. And the volunteers make sure the children are being properly looked after – fed, clothed, washed and, crucially, played with. It's called Mummy's Little Helper.'

'That's so cool,' said Riley. 'So, do you work here?'

'Well, not exactly,' said Alice. 'They're throwing a few fundraising events, and I've been promoting them on @aliceinwonderland.' Noticing their blank expressions, she added, 'My Instagram account. You see, one post from me can lead to thousands of pounds of donations. So, it's not all downward dogs at dawn.' She realized she was sounding a little petulant.

'Why are we here?' asked Riley, for the second time. 'D'you need a hand with a bake sale?'

'Ha! No. We have lots of local mums on hand for that kind of thing. And actually, I don't need Julian at all – he's just here to pretty the place up. It's you I need, Riley. Come in and I'll show you.' Riley rather enjoyed the sensation of being needed. Julian rather enjoyed the sensation of being pretty. Alice rang the bell and a matronly-looking lady with a bosom like a car bumper opened the door. 'Lizzie, this is Riley and Julian,' said Alice.

'Oh yes, come in! I've been expecting you. Please ignore the mess. And the noise. And the smell! I was in the middle of a nappy change.' This was rather too much information for Julian, who had gone a little green and avoided shaking her hand. 'Oh sorry,' said Lizzie, 'I'm afraid you can't bring a dog in here.'

'Keith is not a dog,' said Julian. Lizzie gave him a look that could silence a whole room of rowdy toddlers. 'He's my carer,' he continued, undeterred. 'Tell you what, I'll carry him, then he won't even touch the floor.' Without even waiting for an answer, Julian popped Keith under his arm and walked in. Alice wondered if the fart Keith delivered on his way past Lizzie was deliberately timed. She wouldn't be surprised. That dog was more malevolent than he looked.

The walls of the hallway were covered with children's paintings, 'Old MacDonald' was playing in the next-door room and there was a cacophony of singing, banging and wailing. There was an extraordinary odour of Play-Doh, mixed with poster paint, cleaning products and the offending nappy.

'Come right through,' said Alice, taking them into the kitchen at the back. 'This is why you're here.' She gestured at the French doors into the garden. The garden was a jungle. The grass was a foot high and the flower beds were so overgrown with giant weeds that it was difficult to see if there were any actual shrubs or flowers there at all. A rambling rose had rambled amok, creating a wall of thorns like the one protecting Sleeping Beauty.

'Wow,' said Riley, which was exactly the reaction Alice had hoped for. 'I'm a gardener, y'know.'

'Durrrr. I've read *the book* remember. I *know* you're a

gardener. Like I said, that's why you're here,' replied Alice. 'We can't even let the children out there at the moment – health and safety nightmare.'

'You should talk to Monica about that,' said Riley. 'Health and safety is, like, her *thing*.'

'Riley's right,' said Julian, as if he were competing to show who knew grumpy Monica the best. 'If Monica were on *Mastermind*, it would definitely be her specialist subject.'

Good grief. How on earth can health and safety regulations be anyone's *thing*? Alice decided not to comment. They were obviously both very fond of Monica.

'Most of our children don't have any outside space at home, and it would be amazing if we could turn this into a proper garden, maybe with a Wendy house and a sandpit. What do you think?'

'I can't wait to get started!' said Riley, who was flexing his hands as if imagining digging the beds already.

'I'm afraid we can't pay you,' she said, 'and it's going to take a while, because we don't have much in the way of funds for gardening equipment and plants. The local gardening centre might give us some for free, with a bit of luck.'

'This is where I can help!' said Julian, who'd obviously been feeling a little left out. 'Riley, I am happy to donate all my share of the proceeds from our eBay project to the garden budget!' He looked rather pleased with himself, like a benevolent uncle dispensing boiled sweets at a birthday party.

'You can't do that!' protested Riley. 'You're a pensioner! You need that cash.'

'Don't be silly, dear chap. I'm not surviving on the state pension. I made a lot of money back in the day. I have investments that provide more than enough for me to live on. It would be my pleasure.' He beamed at them. And they beamed back.

'Old MacDonald had a farm!' came the cry from the front room.

'E-I-E-I-O,' chorused Riley.

Julian

Julian checked his pockets for the seventh time. He didn't need his ticket, because Monica was looking after them all. He suspected she didn't totally trust them. Euros – check, passport – check, schedule – check, guidebooks – check. Only two weeks ago, Riley had asked him if he had a valid passport, and he'd realized that, as he hadn't left the country for more than fifteen years (he'd barely left Fulham), his current one was out of date. Monica had helped him get a new one in super quick time.

He'd thought that she might lose her temper when he'd insisted on a pet passport for Keith as well. He'd had to issue a bit of an ultimatum. Either they both went, or neither of them were going. He knew it was a little melodramatic, but Keith was getting on a bit, and everyone should visit Paris at least once before they die.

Anyhow, Monica, being the most efficient person he'd ever met, made it happen. If only she'd been around in the sixties when he'd barely been able to work out what day it was, let alone where he was supposed to be. What would Mary have made of Monica?

They were all meeting at the café and Riley had persuaded the minibus driver from Mummy's Little Helper to take them to the Eurostar. Julian hadn't been so excited since he'd been asked to paint Princess Diana. Thinking about it, he wasn't sure if he actually *had* been asked to paint Diana. He'd certainly never done her portrait, so perhaps he'd never been asked. Sometimes he got a bit confused about what was true and what was a story. If you told a story enough times, it became the truth – or near enough.

Julian paused a few metres away from the café, waiting for the assembled group to notice him and Keith before they made the final approach. They were greeted, as he'd hoped, by a volley of exclamations.

'Julian! Keith! Flying the flag for England, I see!' said Riley.

'I'm not sure why I'm surprised,' said Monica, looking them up and down. He was wearing a Sex Pistols t-shirt with 'God Save The Queen' written on it, Doc Marten boots and a Vivienne Westwood Union Jack bomber jacket. Keith was wearing a matching Union Jack waistcoat, with all the confidence and nonchalance of a catwalk model. One with arthritic hips.

Monica had roped in a couple of her temporary staff to cover at the café, so she and Benji could both go on the trip. Sophie and Caroline, both working mothers, had been unable to take the time off, so Julian had invited Hazard and Alice to make up the numbers. Baz couldn't make it, as the restaurant was short-staffed, but he'd insisted that his granny go. Mrs Wu had never been to Paris.

Monica, who Julian thought (not for the first time) would make a great primary school teacher, was counting heads as they piled into the minibus.

'Five, plus me, that's six plus a dog. Who are we missing? It's your friend, isn't it, Julian?'

'Yes. Look, there she is!' he replied as he saw Alice walking towards them, carrying Bunty in a papoose. She had a giant bag over her shoulder that he recognized immediately as Anya Hindmarch. 'Monica, this is Alice. You're going to *love* her.'

Monica and Alice came together like two magnets of matching poles. There was definite *bristling* involved. Julian couldn't understand it at all.

'Oh yes. We've met already,' said Monica.

'We have indeed. You told me to *bugger off* out of your café, if I remember correctly. How do you do? I'm Alice and this is Bunty,' replied Alice, proffering a hand which Monica shook.

'I'm sorry,' said Monica. 'I wasn't having a very good day. Can we start again?'

'Sure,' Alice replied, as Julian noticed her face flitting from surprise to a momentary reluctance, before settling on a warm grin which revealed the product of years of expensive orthodontics.

'Right, everybody on board! Watch your heads!' Monica said this a little too late for Hazard, who at well over six foot tall, had managed to bang his forehead trying to get through the minibus doors. If Julian didn't know her better he'd have thought Monica was smirking. 'Don't forget your seat belts! Safety first!'

'We're just like the A-Team! Although I bet they never wore seat belts,' said Julian. 'Bagsy I be Mr T.' Then, seeing their blank faces, 'Oh, God, are you all too young to remember *The A-Team*?'

'Not all of us were born in the Bronze Age, you know, Julian,' replied Riley. 'This is just like being back at school. Remember how everyone fought to bag the back seats?'

'I always liked sitting at the front,' replied Monica, who was sitting at the front, next to the driver, clasping her travel bag, which was perched on her knee, with both hands.

'I have fortune cookies from restaurant for journey!' said Mrs Wu, delving into her bag and handing round cookies, individually wrapped in plastic. Hazard, who'd clearly never been good at resisting his impulses, opened his straight away, broke the cookie in half and removed the little piece of paper inside.

'What does it say?' asked Julian, who was sitting next to him.

'Oh my God! It says, *Help! I'm being held captive in a cookie factory!*' replied Hazard. 'No, seriously, it says, *You will die alone and badly dressed*. That's not exactly cheerful, is it?'

'At least that's one thing that could never be said of me,' remarked Julian. 'I may well die alone, but I am never badly dressed.'

'Maybe never badly dressed, but certainly always *over-dressed*,' replied Riley from just behind him. Julian swatted at his head with his hand, but Riley ducked, so Julian ended up hitting Alice who was in the next seat.

'So sorry, dear girl!' he exclaimed, as Bunty, in her baby seat, started to howl.

'The wheels on the bus go round and round!' sang Alice to Bunty, trying to mollify her.

'The geriatric on the bus goes, "I'm wearing Westwood,"' muttered Benji to Monica.

'I heard that!' said Julian, who had better hearing than Benji had counted on.

'Guess what my fortune says,' said Benji, quickly changing the subject. '*You are going on a journey!* Wow. They really do work!'

Julian spotted Mrs Wu giving her grandson's boyfriend a hard stare worthy of Paddington Bear, but nothing could ruin today. It was going to be *fabulous*.

Hazard

Julian wove his way down the train aisle on his way back from the buffet car, bouncing off the seats on either side, with Keith clutched under one arm like a fender on the side of a boat. Hazard winced, having visions of having to get Julian stretchered off the train with a fractured hip.

'As suspected, the wine selection on the train is appalling. Just as well I came prepared,' he said, as he pulled out a bottle of champagne from his bag. Hazard wondered how long it would take Monica to protest.

'Julian, it's *breakfast time*,' she said. Not long, as predicted.

'But, dear girl, we're on holiday! Anyhow, there's only enough for a small glass each. You'll join me, won't you, Mrs Wu? And you, Alice?'

Hazard wondered if Julian had any idea how much he'd love to wrestle that bottle off him and drink the lot. No need to bother with a glass. He caught several of their fellow passengers looking at them askance. They must look like a rather unlikely group, with over fifty years' age range from

Julian down to Benji and Alice – actually, seventy-nine years if you counted little Bunty. Was Mrs Wu older or younger than Julian? No one had dared ask.

Julian sat down happily with his champagne and his sketch book. He was drawing Keith, who was sitting in the seat opposite, staring out at the sheep in the Kent fields. He'd probably never seen a sheep before. A conductor approached, looking authoritarian and disapproving.

'Excuse me. No dogs on seats. He'll have to sit on the floor,' he said to Julian.

'He's not a dog,' said Julian.

'What *is* he then?' asked the conductor.

'He's my muse.'

'No muses on seats either,' replied the conductor.

'I'm sorry, my good man,' said Julian, who obviously wasn't, 'but where in your rule book does it say *no muses on seats*?'

'Julian!' said Monica. 'Do what you're told. Keith! Down!' Keith jumped down immediately. He knew not to mess with Monica, even if Julian hadn't caught on.

Monica carried on laying waste to a book of sudoku puzzles. Whenever she got stuck (which wasn't often), she would tap the side of her head with the end of her pencil, like a magician trying to magic a rabbit out of a hat. Bunty had her little face squashed up against the train window, which she was banging with her fists, while Alice took pictures of her with her iPhone. Riley was watching surfing videos on You-Tube and handing round a huge bag of M&Ms. Betty had covered the entire table in front of her with a tangle of wool, and was doing some knitting.

Hazard had been thrilled when Julian had asked him to join their trip to Paris. He was hoping that this eclectic bunch might welcome him in and replace his old friends.

One thing that was slightly taking the edge off his enjoyment of the day was Monica, who was definitely giving him the cold shoulder. Hazard wasn't used to being ignored by women. It seemed rather unfair, since he'd spent *weeks* on Koh Panam trying to help her out. He'd even sent her a postcard! Not even his parents had got a postcard, as his mother had pointed out more than once. There's gratitude for you. He tried again.

'Monica?'

She peered at him suspiciously over the top of her sudoku book.

'Thanks so much for inviting me along today. I really appreciate it.'

'It's Julian you should thank, not me. It was his idea,' she said. A bit gracelessly, he thought. Trying to get near Monica was like trying to cuddle a hedgehog.

Hazard had never been bothered about other people's opinions of him before, but since getting sober he found himself wishing that, just once in a while, someone would tell him he was doing a really good job, and that he wasn't a terrible person. But he knew that someone was unlikely to be Monica.

He steeled himself, conjuring up Tom Cruise in *Top Gun*. *Goose, we're going in again.*

'I really admire you, you know,' he said, realizing, as he did so, how true it was. Usually the way he admired women was almost entirely carnal, so this completely *wholesome* admiration was a new experience. Monica looked up. Ha! Got her attention! *Lock and load.*

'Oh, really?' she asked, a little suspiciously. *Stay on target!*

'Well, look how you've brought this motley, but rather cool, group of people together!' he said.

'It was Julian's book that did that,' Monica protested, although she was looking a little less prickly.

'Sure, the book kicked it off,' Hazard replied, 'but it's you, and your café, that has pulled it all together.'

Monica actually smiled. Not *at* him, as such, but in his general direction. *It's a hit! Back to base. We live to fight another day.*

Hazard turned his attention to Alice. An entirely different kettle of fish from Monica. Actually, he realized, that was a totally inappropriate expression, as nothing about Alice resembled either a kettle, or any type of fish. Maybe a sleek, photogenic dolphin, but they were mammals. She was far friendlier and more relaxed than Monica, and, Hazard had discovered, she was @aliceinwonderland! One of his ex-girlfriends had been obsessed by her and had shrieked every time Alice liked one of her Instagram posts. It had driven Hazard mad, but he was secretly impressed that Alice had managed to amass such a dedicated following. He took out his phone, glad that he'd finally upgraded the ancient Nokia, and surreptitiously opened up Alice's Instagram page.

There, as Hazard had expected, were lots of pictures of Alice wearing the right clothes, in the right places with the right people. But there were also, not at all as he'd expected, two pictures of Julian! One was obviously taken in the cemetery, near the Admiral, and in the other he was leaning against a lamppost on a London street with Keith at his feet. If anything, he looked even more eccentric and incredible on Instagram than he did in real life.

'Alice,' he said, forgetting to act cool, 'you've posted Julian on your Instagram page!'

'Doesn't he look marvellous?' she replied. 'How many likes does he have now?'

'This last one has more than *ten thousand*,' said Hazard.

'The dog helps,' said Alice. 'There's no such thing as too much dog on Insta.'

'And he's had loads of comments. They all want to know how to follow him. We have to make him a page,' said Hazard. 'Julian, can I borrow your phone?'

Hazard moved to sit next to Alice, and they bent their heads over Julian's phone.

'What shall we call him?' Hazard asked her.

'How about @fabulousat80?'

'I'm only seventy-nine! I was born on the day war was declared, so no one paid me the blindest bit of notice. I've been fighting for my share of the attention ever since,' shouted Julian from two rows ahead, causing several of their fellow passengers to lower their newspapers and stare over at them.

'You can't be *only* seventy-nine, that's a total contradiction in terms,' said Alice. 'Anyhow, it's near enough to eighty. Right, let's upload the two shots I've got, tag all the designers he's wearing and add all the fashion blogger hashtags. Then I'll let my followers know where to find him. He's going to be a sensation.'

Watching Alice work her way around social media was incredible. After ten minutes of furrowed brows and furiously flying fingers, she put Julian's phone down in a way that signalled satisfaction with a job well done. 'That should do it,' she said.

'I'm not sure what you're up to, you two, but I hope it's *legal*,' said Julian. 'I haven't been arrested since that night with Joan Collins in 1987.'

No one was going to give Julian the satisfaction of asking him to elaborate.

Monica

The view from the top of the Eiffel Tower was worth all the queuing, but Monica was exhausted. Not just with all the criss-crossing Paris by metro and walking around the museums, but with the effort of constantly counting heads and trying to keep everyone together. She'd tried holding up an umbrella, so that everyone could see her through the crowd and follow her easily, but Hazard had taken the mickey out of her, so she'd folded it up and put it back in her bag. If they lost anyone it would be entirely his fault. She could imagine only too clearly having to tell Baz that they'd mislaid his granny, last seen eating a fortune cookie near the pyramid at the Louvre.

Keith was an added complication. The museums all had no-dog policies. Julian had tried to persuade the authorities at the Pompidou that he was a guide dog. They'd pointed out, not unreasonably, that if Julian was blind, he wouldn't be bothered about not seeing the art exhibition. Eventually, Julian bought a large canvas bag from a gift shop with MY

PARENTS WENT TO PARIS AND ALL THEY BOUGHT ME WAS THIS LOUSY BAG written on the side. He used it to smuggle Keith past security, which had given Monica paroxysms of anxiety. Julian insisted on playing with fire by pausing by his favourite paintings and hissing into the bag, 'Keith! You have to check out this one. A classic of its oeuvre.'

Julian's commentary on all the art was fascinating, although, she suspected, not always entirely accurate. He seemed to have an aversion to admitting that he didn't know the answer to any question, so instead (she realized from cross-referencing his stories with her guidebooks) he'd make something up. She wasn't sure that anyone else had noticed, but they were bound to soon; he was gaining in confidence and each of his tales became more wildly colourful and inaccurate than the last.

The Seine glittered in the pale, winter sunshine, reminding Monica of the romantic fantasies of river walks with Riley that she'd had when she was first planning the trip. She chided herself again for having been so foolish. Life just didn't work out like that.

Monica watched as Hazard and Alice took a photo of Julian, working it like a gnarled and grizzled Kate Moss, leaning against the guard rail, overlooking Paris. A small crowd had gathered around them, as if trying to figure out if they were celebrities of some sort. Betty was adding to the spectacle by doing some of her tai chi moves with a pigeon sitting on one of her hands (one of the many things she appeared to have packed in her giant carrier bag was birdseed). Wasn't she worried that one of them might *poo* on her? Just thinking about it made Monica feel nauseated.

She was trying really hard to like Alice, with her perfect face and figure and gorgeous baby. Hazard and Alice reminded her of the cool kids at school, the ones who seemed to fit in effortlessly, to do and say the right things and wear the right outfits – even when they'd turned up in something ridiculous no one would laugh, and they'd inadvertently start a trend. She'd made a big point of finding all that stuff beneath her. She was going to go to Cambridge and do something worthwhile with her life. Secretly, she'd been thrilled on the (very) few occasions she'd been invited to sit at their lunch table.

Usually, if she was feeling inadequate, Monica would put on a concerted front, making sure she looked as happy and successful as possible. But now, she couldn't do that because of that damn book. Hazard and Alice both knew exactly how dissatisfied she was with her life. Well, at least she wasn't horribly shallow and obsessed by the validation of strangers on social media, she thought as she watched them bend over Julian's phone, uploading his picture.

Monica's mother would not have approved of Alice. Monica remembered all the times she'd gone with her to help at the women's refuge for victims of domestic violence. 'Battered women' they were called back then, which always made Monica think of fish and chips. *Always make sure you have financial independence, Monica. Never let yourself, or your children, be reliant on a man for your basic needs. You never know what might happen. You need to be able to support yourself.* Surely Alice's Instagram *thing* wasn't a proper job? It was just a vanity project.

'I love your dress, Alice,' she called over, because she was making an effort, and wasn't that what you said to people like her?

'Oh, thanks Monica,' Alice replied, with a perfect smile dimpling her cheeks. 'Cheap as chips, but don't tell anyone!' Who on earth, thought Monica, would she tell?

She felt someone take her hand. It was Riley. She snatched it away, then chided herself for being churlish.

'Thanks for organizing today, Monica, it's been totally awesome,' he said, which just made Monica feel sad for what might have been. She wished she could recreate the relaxed, uncomplicated, happy relationship they'd had, but she couldn't. It was like trying to get the stain out of a carpet. You could scrub and steam and brush for as long as you liked, but there would always be a faint outline of what had spilled. Anyhow, even if she could turn back time, what would be the point? Riley would be heading off around Europe soon enough, then back to Australia, which was not exactly commuting distance. No, it was far wiser to keep the wall she'd erected around her emotions firmly in place.

'God, look at those three with their stupid Instagram fixation,' said Riley. 'Here they are, at the top of one of the world's most awesome monuments, overlooking the most awesome city, and all they're focused on is Julian's *clothes.*'

And in that moment, Monica very nearly forgave him everything. Except his constant use of the word *awesome*, which was driving her crazy.

It took Monica an age to get the group back to ground

level, since nobody apart from her seemed to be at all concerned about the imminent departure of their train back to London. She was at the back of the group, trying to usher them through the exit turnstile, like a farmer herding his sheep into a sheep-dip. Betty was at the front, having difficulty getting her huge bag through the narrow exit. Monica watched as a charming young man gestured to her to pass the bag to him, so he could help her get it over the barrier. Seconds later, he was running at top speed away from the tower, clutching all of Betty's belongings. Not so charming after all, it appeared.

Betty started yelling in Mandarin. Although Monica couldn't understand a word, she got the basic gist. Swearing was definitely involved. Benji, like something out of an action hero movie, pushed the crowd aside, vaulted on one hand over the turnstile and chased after the thief.

The assembled tourists shouted encouragement in a cacophony of different languages, like a crowd watching football's European Cup final. Benji caught up with the robber, grabbing him by the arm. The crowd cheered, wildly. Mrs Wu even punched the air. Then the man slipped off his jacket and, still clutching Mrs Wu's bag, ran off again, leaving Benji holding his clothing. The crowd groaned, and swore – mainly unintelligibly. Benji took chase again, this time bringing his quarry crashing to the ground with an impressive tackle.

'GOAL!' shouted Riley. The crowd went crazy as Benji sat on the thief, holding his hands behind his back. Betty's bag was lying on the ground, spewing out fortune cookies, birdseed and a tangle of wool. Monica called the police.

Betty aimed a deft kick at one of the man's shins.

'Don't fuck with me, mister,' she said.

He would rue the day he crossed Betty Wu, thought Monica. She just hoped Betty hadn't spotted Keith cocking a leg over her knitting.

Riley

The return train journey was rather more subdued than the way out, as everyone was exhausted after the heady combination of exercise, culture and high drama.

Riley watched with interest as Betty stood up and walked over to the empty seat next to Benji. Benji looked surprised and more than a little terrified. Far more terrified than he'd been apprehending the thief earlier. Riley pretended to be fascinated by his guidebook, while he was actually straining to hear what Betty would say.

'So, Monica tells me you good cook,' she said.

'Well, I love cooking, but I'm nowhere near as good as you are, Mrs Wu,' replied Benji, with what Riley thought was just the right amount of deference and ingratiation. He noticed that Betty didn't shout at him to *call me Betty!*

'Next week, you come to restaurant. I teach you to cook wonton soup.' It was definitely an order, not a suggestion. 'Recipe my mother taught me, her mother taught her. Not written down. In here.' And she tapped her head, with a finger as determined as a woodpecker's beak digging out bugs from a tree trunk. Without waiting for an answer, Betty stood up and went back to her own seat, leaving Benji looking a little stunned. Riley felt all warm inside. Perhaps the City of Love had woven its magic already. He loved a happy ending.

Alice sat down next to Julian and pulled up his new Instagram page.

'OMG, Julian! You have more than three thousand followers already!' she said. Julian looked bemused.

'Is that good?' he asked. 'How did they find me?'

'It's not just good, it's SPECTACULAR in just twelve hours. You are going to be a SENSATION. I posted some of your pics on my page and suggested my followers follow you, and they're heading over in droves. Look at all the comments! They LOVE you! Hang on, you've got some private messages, look.' Alice jabbed her fingers at Julian's phone a couple of times and squinted at the screen.

'I don't BELIEVE IT!' she shrieked, making Bunty start wailing, causing some very disapproving looks from their fellow passengers. 'There's a message from VIVIENNE WESTWOOD! The *real* one.' Who was Vivienne Westwood, wondered Riley. Why was she causing such excitement, and was there an unreal one as well? He wished Alice would stop talking in capital letters. It was giving him a headache. Riley hadn't imagined it was possible for anyone to make him feel tired and jaded, but Alice seemed to be doing just that.

'She says she's pleased you're still wearing her clothes – I tagged her, you see – and if you come to her HQ you can try on the latest collection.'

'Oh, darling Vivi. Always liked her,' said Julian, 'but I'm afraid I can't afford any of her clothes these days. I haven't sold a painting for over a decade.'

'But that's the AMAZING thing about Insta, Julian. Once you get enough followers, they'll give you all their clothes FOR FREE. You don't think I actually BOUGHT any of this stuff, do you?' she asked, gesturing at her clothes and bag.

'Golly,' said Julian. 'You'd better show me how to do it then. I'm not very good at this phone thing. My fingers are too fat and clumsy. It's like trying to type with a bunch of bananas.'

'Don't worry, I'll buy you a little pointy thing you can use,' said Alice. 'You'll love Insta. It's so pretty. It's like ART, only more modern. Right up your alley. If Picasso were alive now, he'd like totally be into Instagram.' Julian's eyes bulged a little at that suggestion.

Julian had managed to buy more champagne at Gare du Nord, so they could – he explained – celebrate Benji's hero-ism on the return journey. He'd arranged several plastic cups on the table in front of him and was carefully filling each one. It occurred to Riley that only he and Alice had read Hazard's story in the book. He looked over to Hazard who was sitting on his own, resting his head against the train window. He seemed as if he might be asleep, until you saw his hands which were clutched so tightly into fists that his knuckles had gone white. Riley walked over and sat in the seat next to him.

'Hazard, you're doing really brilliantly, you know. *You* are the real superhero around here,' he said.

Hazard turned to look at him. 'Thanks, mate,' he said, sounding genuinely grateful, but immensely weary.

'Are you still looking for a job? It's just that Alice has got me doing some gardening. I'd love the extra help if you could spare the time?'

'Sure. I'd really like that. I've been at a bit of a loss, to be honest. I don't want to go back into the City, but I'm not sure I'm qualified to do anything else. It's not good for me to have too much time on my hands,' replied Hazard. 'I've even found myself becoming obsessed by *Neighbours* and *Countdown*. Once an addict, always an addict. And I could really do with the money. I've nearly spent my last bonus, and if I don't find myself some sort of job soon, I'll have to sell my flat.'

'I'm afraid I can't help you there. This work's for a local charity. But are you still interested?' asked Riley.

'Definitely!' replied Hazard, with genuine enthusiasm. 'I'll work out my finances later. I'm sure something will crop up. By the way, don't worry about Monica. I bet she'll come round in the end.'

Riley realized that if they'd been girls they might have hugged at this point. But they weren't girls, so he gave Hazard a little punch on the arm, then walked back to his seat.

Bunty had had enough of the day and was red-faced and yelling, barely recognizable as @babybunty. Alice was carrying her up and down the aisle, as the only thing that seemed to settle her was constant movement. Riley wondered whether this was putting Monica off the whole procreation thing. It was certainly making him think twice, and he'd always loved the idea of a big family.

A few minutes later, Riley walked down the carriage to the toilet and pressed the button to open the door. It slid across to reveal Bunty, on her back in the sink, naked, legs waving in the air, and poo *everywhere*. All over the basin, the mirror, the *walls* even. Alice gaped at him, hands full of baby wipes, and said, 'Sorry, I thought I'd locked the door.' He just replied with a strangled 'AARRRGGHH' as he pressed the button to make the door close, and it all go away, but the image remained seared on to his retinas. He mumbled something as the door closed. He could hear Alice's muffled voice.

'Actually, Riley, I'd love some help here!'

'Sure!' he said. 'I'll go find Monica!' That was what she meant, wasn't it?

Monica

Riley came back from the toilet looking decidedly queasy.

'Are you OK, Riley?' Monica asked.

'Yup, totally fine. But I think Alice might need some help,' he said, sliding quickly into a seat and not looking back. Monica headed in the direction Riley had come from, rather alarmed. She hoped the day wasn't going to be ruined, when they were so nearly home and dry. The door to the toilet was locked. Monica knocked.

'Are you in there, Alice? It's Monica. Do you need a hand?' she asked.

'Hold on, Monica!' replied Alice. A minute or two later, the door opened and Alice thrust Bunty at her.

'Could you take Bunty for me, while I clean up in here? I had her on the changing mat, but every time the train takes a bend I worry she'll be catapulted on to the floor. I'll be out in a minute. Thanks so much!'

The door slid closed again. Since she was on her own, Monica leaned forward and breathed in Bunty's downy head. She smelled of Johnson & Johnson, freshly laundered cotton and that indefinable scent of brand-new human being that reminded Monica of everything she didn't have. The door slid open and Alice stepped out.

'She's really gorgeous, Alice,' said Monica as they walked back towards their seats. She was expecting one of the obvious responses from Alice, an *I know* or *Isn't she just?* Or perhaps a mock-humble *Not at 3 a.m., she isn't!* But instead Alice stopped and looked at her intently.

'You know, the baby doesn't make the happy ever after, Monica? And sometimes a marriage can be the loneliest place in the world. I should know.'

'I'm sure you're right, Alice,' Monica replied, wondering what the story was there. 'There are actually loads of advantages to being single.' And, for the first time, Monica really thought that might be true.

'I remember!' said Alice. 'Eating what you want, when you want, total control of the TV remote, not having to tell anyone where you're going or who with. Slobbing around in yoga pants and slippers. Regular sex, too – ha ha. Those were the days!' She paused and looked wistful.

'Monica, I read something on Instagram the other day. It said, *Mother is a verb, not a noun.* I think it means there are many ways to mother without actually being one. Look at you and your café. You nurture loads of people, every day.'

Monica couldn't quite believe that such a life-altering, if slightly patronizing, thought could come from a woman she'd dismissed so lightly at the beginning of the day, outside a train lavatory, and courtesy of a rather saccharine Instagram meme.

After walking Bunty up and down the aisle a few times to help her settle, Monica passed her back to Alice, with as much relief as regret, and sat down next to Riley.

Riley must have felt emboldened by Julian's champagne, because he had that look on his face that he got when he was about to say something significant. Monica prepared herself.

'Monica, I really am so sorry I didn't tell you about the book. I honestly didn't mean to keep you in the dark, it's just I couldn't tell you the night we met, with all those people around, and then I just kinda missed the moment. It got too late, and I didn't know how to fix it. You probably won't believe this, but I'd planned to tell you right after Christmas.' And he looked at her so earnestly that she did believe him, and while it couldn't totally fix things, it really did make them feel better. She took his hand and leaned her head on his shoulder.

Alice

Alice went straight to the fridge and poured herself a large glass of Chablis. She was aware that she'd drunk more than her fair share of champagne on the return journey (she hoped no one else had noticed), but it had still barely touched the sides. She sat down at the black granite counter, kicking her shoes off on to the polished concrete floor. Her minimalist kitchen with its perfect lines and edges had, as Max was fond of saying, 'wow factor', but it wasn't warm. Sometimes you didn't want a room to make a statement or to say anything about you, you just wanted it to shut up and be a room.

It had been a wonderful day. If it hadn't been for constantly having to stop Bunty from yelling, trying to feed her without shocking Julian by displaying too much boob, and changing her nappy in cramped train toilets, it would have been perfect.

She'd never forget Riley's face when he'd interrupted the nappy change. So much for being in touch with nature.

Even as he'd been closing the door, looking as if he was about to vomit, he'd said, 'Are you OK, Alice?' in a strangled voice, his revulsion and good manners fighting for supremacy. Sweet boy. And what about Benji, who she'd last seen sobbing outside a Chinese restaurant on Christmas Day, heroically rescuing Mrs Wu's bag? It was as good as a Netflix drama. She heard the front door bang. Max was back from work, late as usual.

'Hello, darling! What's Bunty still doing up? It's nine thirty. And what's for supper? I'm ravenous.'

Alice peered inside the fridge. The only non-alcoholic contents were half a lemon, a packet of butter, some tired-looking salad and a quarter of a quiche, which Max insisted real men didn't eat.

'I'm sorry, darling,' she said, trying to be sorry. 'I haven't prepared anything. I've been in Paris all day, remember? Just got back.'

'God, it's all very well for you, isn't it, swanning around having lunch in Paris while I work every hour God sends to keep Bunty in disposable nappies. I guess I'll have to call Deliveroo.'

Alice eyed the unopened chilled packet of butter, about the shape and size of a brick, and considered at what velocity it would need to be thrown to hurt, but not cause permanent damage. She resolved to accidentally wash his bright-white Calvin Klein underpants with some red socks. The conversation Alice had had with Monica about the advantages of being single came back to taunt her.

Bunty, probably as a result of spending so much time next to the chill of the open fridge, started to yell again.

Alice carried her past Max without saying a word, and upstairs to the nursery.

While she was feeding Bunty, with one hand supporting her downy soft head, her other hand was scrolling through Instagram. Lucy Yeomans, editor of *Porter* magazine, sixty thousand followers, had reposted Julian's Paris pic. He now had more than twenty thousand followers himself. You're far from invisible now, Julian, she thought. Which reminded her about the book. She reached down the side of the rocking chair where she'd left it, put Bunty, who was now, mercifully, looking a little sleepy, into her cot, took out a pen from her bag and began to write.

Alice loved her visits to Mummy's Little Helper. On the estate where she'd grown up, several of the mothers had drug or alcohol addiction issues, and Alice's mother had expanded her dinner lady responsibilities to encompass feeding any undernourished child in her vicinity. Along with many of her neighbours, she would take turns looking out for them. As well as making sure they had proper meals, they'd pass on clothes and toys that their own children had outgrown and provide a quiet space for homework or a sympathetic ear. That informal caring system didn't seem to exist in the anonymity of London, so this place filled the gap.

It was only now that Alice had started to realize how incredible her own mother was, bringing up four children on her own and finding a job that allowed her to support them financially and still be with them after school to cook their tea and help with their homework. Alice remembered how she used to pretend not to know her mum at school when she served Alice her lunch, calling her Mrs Campbell in a dismissive tone, like everyone else. How that must have hurt her. Alice shuddered.

Usually, the mums and other carers picking up their children from Mummy's Little Helper at the end of the day dashed in and out as quickly as possible. Certainly, none of them had ever shown any interest in the garden before. But today there was a whole gaggle of them, standing by the kitchen windows looking out at Riley, Hazard and Brett, Riley's Aussie flatmate, wrestling with some giant thistles and the wayward rambling rose. It must be hard work because, despite the cold, they were all stripped down to their t-shirts.

'They can come and do my garden any time,' said one, to which, judging by the giggling, there was a lewd response from one of the others, which Alice missed.

Alice helped the boys load bags of garden rubbish into the minibus to take to the local dump. She watched a stereotypical yummy mummy, who was passing by, halt in her tracks.

'Are you chaps gardeners?' she asked, in a voice that was part girls' boarding school, part porn movie, talking to Hazard, who she'd obviously earmarked as the boss.

'Er, I guess so,' replied Hazard, who'd clearly never thought of himself as a gardener before.

'Here's my card. Call me if you'd like to come and quote on my garden.'

Hazard took the card and stared at it thoughtfully. He looked, Alice thought, like a man with a plan.

It was later that night that Alice realized the book was missing. She was absolutely certain she'd put it in her bag, as she was so worried about Max – or anyone else – reading what she'd written that she didn't want to leave it lying around. She'd confessed to some things in the heat of the moment that she didn't want to admit, even to herself. There was no way she was sharing that, whatever Julian said about authenticity. She'd thought about shredding the whole thing that morning in Max's office, but it didn't seem right to destroy everyone else's stories, so she'd popped it in her bag until she had a moment to carefully tear out her pages without damaging the others, and give the book back to Julian.

And now it was gone.

Julian

Julian had persuaded Alice to join his art class. This week they were drawing Keith. He wasn't the ideal subject, as he was unlikely to stay still for long enough, but it was the only way Julian could think to get around Monica's ridiculous dog ban in the café. 'He's not a dog, Monica,' he'd said. 'He's a *model*.'

'Mobiles in the hat as usual, please!' he said, as his hat was passed from one person to the next. Alice looked horrified. She'd handed over Bunty to Caroline and Sophie with no qualms whatsoever, but was clinging to her phone like a toddler to her favourite doll.

'I *promise* I won't touch it. Scout's honour. Cross my heart and hope to die,' she said, 'I'll just keep it on the edge of the table so I can see if any crucial notifications come through.'

'Yes, imagine if you miss a life-and-death announcement of the new release of a statement handbag,' said Hazard, earning himself a glare from Alice, who finally and reluctantly handed Julian her phone.

'Did you know that the fashion industry contributes *fifty billion pounds* to the UK economy? It's not all just airy-fairy nonsense,' said Alice.

'Really? Is that the exact number?' asked Hazard, smirking.

'Well, to be honest, I can't remember the exact number, but I know it's like *really big,*' confessed Alice.

Caroline and Sophie (Julian was never sure which one was which, but didn't suppose it really mattered) took turns bouncing Bunty on their knees and exclaiming over her cuteness.

'Doesn't she make you feel broody?' one of them asked the other.

'Only because I can hand her back by the end of the class. I wouldn't want to go back to all those sleepless nights . . .' said the second.

'. . . or nappies. And cracked nipples. Urgh,' finished the first, as they laughed in a conspiratorial fashion.

Julian hoped they weren't upsetting dear Alice, who was obviously a natural mother and enjoying every moment with the delightful Bunty, as anyone could see from her Instagram feed.

'Right, class, I have an announcement,' announced Julian, in his best announcer voice, trying not to betray quite how excited he was. It was cooler to appear blasé about these things. 'We're going to be joined by a photographer from the *Evening Standard*, who are doing a profile on me and my Instagram following. Do please ignore them. They are not interested in you, only me. You are just there to provide background and context.'

'Oh my God, we've created a monster!' said Hazard to Alice, not quietly enough for Julian to miss. 'What were we thinking?' Julian channelled his best schoolmaster glare and trained it on them both.

Today, Julian was embracing *preppy*, an homage to one of the greats – Ralph Lauren. Had he met him? He was sure he must have done. As the photographer and crew arrived and started bustling around him, Julian realized how much his life had changed in the four months since he'd left The Authenticity Project in this very place, and in the two weeks since he started 'rocking the world of Instagram' (the *Standard*'s words, not his, you understand).

None of this was new to Julian. He had the strangest sense of having come full circle, back to where he was always meant to be – in the limelight. The fifteen years of invisibility almost felt like they'd happened to someone else. He had a rather uncomfortable sensation that he only really existed in the eye of the beholder, that when he stopped being noticed, he actually stopped *being*. Did that make him horribly shallow? And if so, did it matter? All the people wanting to interview him and sending him invitations to parties and previews and catwalks didn't seem to think so. They thought he was rather marvellous. He was, wasn't he?

What would Mary think if she could see him now? Would she be thrilled to see him back to his old self? If he was totally honest, he suspected not. He could see her, rolling her eyes and giving him a lecture on what was real and authentic, and what was merely puffery. It was the memory of one of those lectures that had inspired the title on his book. The book that had changed everything.

He sat on the edge of one of the tables, legs crossed and leaning back casually, as requested by the photographer. He gazed off into the distance, as if he were thinking of things far more erudite and artistic than mere mortals. It was one of his signature looks. He'd worried that he might have forgotten how to do all this, but it turned out it was like riding a bicycle. Had he ever ridden a bicycle? Surely he had? Stylishly, of course.

'Julian?' said Riley. 'I know we're only here for *background and context*' – he sounded a little tetchy – 'but do you think you could give me a bit of a hand with my perspective?'

'Julian's lost his perspective, I'm afraid, Riley,' said Hazard. Julian laughed along with the class. It was important to be seen to laugh at oneself. His friends had never had to live life in the public eye. They didn't understand the pressure.

As the class, and the photographer, wound up, Benji called over from the kitchen.

'There's wonton soup for anyone staying for supper. And prawn dumplings. All made by my fair hand,' said the man whose large, freckly hands, with their chewed fingernails, had never been described as fair before.

'Don't worry. Is safe to eat. He's taught by me,' added Mrs Wu.

Hazard

Hazard loved working at Mummy's Little Helper. The more he chatted to the mothers about their various addictions – to heroin, crack cocaine, crystal meth – the more he realized how similar they were to him. They exchanged tips on how to deal with cravings and competed to tell the most shocking tales of the 'dark days'.

'Good job gang! Fin, Zac, Queenie, bag up!' said Hazard to today's gang of 'helpers', aged between four and eight, who'd been following him around, waiting for him to issue instructions. Digging holes here, planting seeds there, bagging leaves everywhere. He handed round rubbish bags for all the weeds they'd pulled up from the flower bed. Six eyes stared up at him, as if he were a person worth looking up to and emulating. While this made him feel a great deal better about himself, it also terrified him. He couldn't let them down. They'd been let down enough.

'Fin, buddy. Over here!' said Hazard, crouching down to the same level as the little boy who ran over, red-cheeked and grubby. 'Don't tell Queenie I ratted on her, but check your coat pockets for slugs before you go home.'

Hazard had even plundered his diminishing savings to buy a couple of tiny wheelbarrows and some rakes and trowels designed for small hands. He'd never spent much time with kids. He certainly hadn't been the kind of person who had babies thrust at him to hold, or who was ever asked to babysit, but he was amazed how much he enjoyed it. He'd forgotten how to appreciate the everyday highs, like a glass of orange squash after hours of hard digging, or the fun of making worm farms and racing snails.

Hazard was exhausted after the day's gardening. But it was a *good* tired. An honest tired. His muscles ached after hours of hard exercise and his body yearned for a long, uncomplicated sleep. It was nothing like the tiredness of old – toxic, tetchy and frazzled after thirty-six hours of non-stop partying, being kept awake by a cocktail of chemicals.

He loved the feeling of being connected to nature. It was the first job in his life that actually felt *real*. He was making something, growing, improving and doing some good. He couldn't, however, keep on working for free or he'd be homeless. If only he hadn't shoved so much of the fortune he'd earned in the City up his nose. Still, at least he'd quit while he still had a septum. One of his City friends had sneezed into a tissue in a meeting, and half of his nose had ended up in his hands. He'd ignored the shock on the faces of his clients and carried on presenting. At the time, Hazard had thought that pure class.

He took out the business card he'd been given by the

woman on the street last week. Hazard wasn't unaware of the stir that he and his Australian workmates were causing at Mummy's Little Helper. He knew that it wasn't just their physiques that were proving popular, but also the sunny, exuberant, straightforward nature of the Australian boys, whose very accents brought to mind beaches, wide open plains and *koala bears*, and were such a welcome antidote to the complex ennui of London.

Hazard had spent the afternoon grilling Riley and Brett about the Australian community in London. It turned out that London was full of Australian boys who, because of their Commonwealth links, were travelling on a Working Holiday Visa. They could work, legally, for up to two years in the UK – presuming they could find work to do.

What if, Hazard thought, he and Riley trained some of them up in the garden of Mummy's Little Helper, then they could take on paid work in the gardens of Fulham, Putney and Chelsea? There were many gardening companies in London already, he knew, but his would have a unique selling point, a raison d'être. He'd call it *Aussie Gardeners*.

He'd have to advertise, of course. What he really needed was someone with the ability to reach thousands of women, preferably in the local area, with a fair amount of money. And he had one of those, right under his nose – *Alice*. Just one or two Instagram posts from her showing him, Riley and Brett toiling in a garden, and giving their contact details, and he had no doubt they'd be inundated. He was sure that Alice would appreciate the sense of karma – they'd helped her out (and would continue to do so), now she could help them back. What goes around comes around.

Perhaps Julian would design a flier for them that they could post through all the local letterboxes. Although Julian didn't seem to have very much time for them any more, ever since he'd been sucked back into the black hole that was the world of fashion. What had possessed them, making him that Instagram page?

The more he thought about it, the more the idea of having his own business excited him. He could be like Monica! *What would Monica do?* had become his new mantra, in his bid to become more thoughtful, more sensible, more dependable. He had rather a long way to go.

Hazard opened the door to his apartment building, wiping his feet vigorously on the mat so he wouldn't tread soil all over the gleaming entrance hall. The modern, glass-plated block of flats in landscaped gardens and with twenty-four-hour concierge service, screamed 'successful City trader', not so much 'gardener'. One evening he'd left a bag of his gardening things in the entrance hall for a couple of hours. He'd come back to find a note taped to it saying WORKMEN: DO NOT LEAVE TOOLS HERE! REMOVE OR THEY WILL BE CONFISCATED!

He glanced over at the pigeonholes on the wall that held the residents' mail. In his, along with the usual fliers and bills, was a letter that his mother would describe as 'a stiffy' (which had always made him and his father smirk, while she'd pretend not to understand why): a good quality envelope containing a hefty piece of card. An invitation.

Hazard opened it as he climbed the stairs. In beautiful, engraved writing it said:

Daphne Corsander and Rita Morris

invite you to

celebrate their marriage

on Saturday, 23 February 2019, 11 a.m.

at All Saints Church, Hambledore

and afterwards at the Old Vicarage

RSVP

In the top left-hand corner, *Mr Hazard Ford plus guest* was written in fountain pen.

So, Daphne and Rita were coming out with a bang. Good on them. He wondered how Roderick was taking the news. He did hope he wasn't stressing about his father turning in his grave. They weren't wasting any time, either. The twenty-third of February was only three weeks away. He supposed that at their age it was sensible not to hang around.

Hazard was conflicted. On the one hand, he desperately wanted to celebrate with his old friends from the island, but, on the other, he hadn't yet been to a party sober, let alone *a wedding*, with their tradition of all-day drinking. But he'd been clean for four whole months now. Surely he was safe? He could trust himself. None of his old crowd were likely to be at Daphne and Rita's wedding.

He looked again at the writing in the corner. *Plus guest*. Who on earth could he ask? Any of his old girlfriends would pull him off the wagon quicker than you could say 'Cheers!' But he didn't think it was a good idea to go alone. He needed to take someone who would keep him on the straight and narrow.

Hazard sat down on his cream leather sofa, pulling off his boots and stretching out his toes, wrinkling his nose at the unmistakeable smell of feet that had worked up a good sweat. He'd picked up a copy of the *Evening Standard* on the way home, so he could read the article about Julian. There was a picture of him in the centre of the page, gazing into the distance looking wistful, and not at all like the Julian he knew. The interview was extremely gushy, covering Julian's life from losing his virginity in Shepherd Market at the age of sixteen to a prostitute, paid for by his father as a birthday present, to becoming a social media star at seventy-nine. It included a long-winded story about Julian's great friendship with Ralph Lauren, who – it transpired – had based a whole collection on Julian's eccentric English style, after the two of them did a road trip around the village greens, pubs and cricket pitches of Dorset. You learned something new about Julian every day.

Riley

When Riley arrived at the Admiral, only Monica was there.

'Where is everyone?' he asked her. 'I know Hazard's finishing up a garden on Flood Street, but I thought the others would be here.'

Monica looked at her watch.

'It's twenty past five. Perhaps no one else is coming. How strange. I've never known Julian to miss a Friday, except on New Year's Eve. Even when he was barely leaving his cottage he said he still came here every week. I hope he's OK.'

Riley took out his phone and pulled up Julian's Instagram page. 'Don't worry. He's more than OK. Look.'

'Bloody hell, you know that's Kate Moss he's with? And a bunch of self-satisfied fashion types, drinking mojitos at Soho Farmhouse. He might have mentioned that he was going out of town,' said Monica, sounding a bit like a sulky child. Julian was a grown-up, after all. He didn't have to get permission from them to go and hang out with celebrities for the weekend. 'Hey, talking of Julian, I realized that we have an art class on the fourth of March, which is the fifteenth anniversary of Mary's death. I figured that Julian might find it a bit hard, so I thought we could throw a sort of surprise memorial party for him. What do you think?'

'I think you are one of the most thoughtful people I've ever met,' replied Riley, who'd never been one for holding back or playing games. 'And clever. How do you remember dates like that? I can barely remember my own birthday.'

Monica blushed, which made her look less scary, and really rather cute. And now there were no secrets between them, Riley felt lighter and more like his old self. So, he leaned over and kissed her.

She kissed him back. Tentatively, but it was a start.

'I feel a bit awkward about kissing in a graveyard, don't you?' she asked him. But she was smiling.

'Something tells me the Admiral's seen a lot worse over the years,' replied Riley, shuffling closer towards her and putting his arm around her shoulders. 'Don't you think Julian and Mary would have, you know' – he waggled his eyebrows suggestively – 'at some point over the years. Back in the swinging sixties, perhaps?'

'Eew no!' said Monica. 'Mary would never have done that! Not in a cemetery!'

'You didn't know her, Monica. She was a midwife, not a saint. Perhaps she had a naughty side. You'd have to, married to Julian, surely?'

He leaned in towards Monica, muscle memory melding their bodies back into the familiar jigsaw. He tried to kiss her again, but she pushed him away, gently, but firmly.

'Riley, I'm not angry any more,' she said. 'I'm really glad

we're friends. But, honestly, what would be the point? You'll be leaving soon, so it really makes no sense to start this up again, does it?'

'Monica, why does everything have to have a *point*? Why does it all have to be part of a plan? Sometimes it's best to let things just grow naturally, like wild flowers.' He was quite pleased with that one. He was sounding positively poetic.

By way of illustration, Riley gestured over to a group of perfect white snowdrops, pushing their way up through the frozen February soil.

'Riley, that's beautiful,' she said. 'But I don't want to get hurt again by becoming embroiled in a relationship that has a natural end point. Life isn't as simple as *gardening*!'

'Isn't it though?' asked Riley, who was getting frustrated, and was a little put out by his profession being described as 'simple'. It all seemed so obvious to him. He liked her. She liked him. What was the problem? 'Why not just see where it goes? Fly by the seat of your pants. If you don't want to say goodbye in June, then you could always come with me.' As soon as he said it, he realized what a brilliant idea it was. They'd make perfect travel buddies (with benefits, he hoped). He could be in charge of fun, and she could do culture.

'I couldn't go with you, Riley,' she said. 'I have responsibilities here. I have my business. Employees, friends, family. What about Julian? Look what happened last time we left him alone for a few days – he nearly died of hypothermia.'

'It's *easy*, Monica,' said Riley, who really thought it was. After all, he'd left his whole life on the other side of the world with hardly a backward glance. 'You find someone else to manage the café for you for a few months. Your friends and family will miss you, but will be thrilled that you're having an adventure, and as for Julian – he seems to have picked up hundreds of thousands of new "friends" recently. I don't think we have to worry about him.'

Monica tried to interject, but he cut her off. 'When did you last see anything of the world beyond Fulham and Chelsea? Have you ever sat on a train just to see where you'd end up? Or ordered a weird-sounding dish off a menu, for the fun of eating something you weren't expecting? Have you ever had sex just because you *wanted to*, and not as part of some sort of life plan?'

Monica was silent. Perhaps he'd got through to her.

'Will you just think about it, Monica?' he asked her.

'Yes. Yes, I will. I promise.'

They walked together towards the cemetery exit. Monica paused next to a gravestone on her left, bowed her head and muttered something under her breath. It must be the grave of a relative. He read the inscription.

'Who's Emmeline Pankhurst?' he asked her.

She gave him one of her looks. The type he didn't like. But said nothing.

So often with Monica, he felt like he was failing an exam he hadn't realized he was taking.

Monica

Monica *had* been thinking about it. A lot. She'd rather liked the picture Riley had painted, and wondered if she *could* be that girl. Was it too late for her to live her life with an entirely different set of rules? Or, indeed, no rules at all?

She'd never taken a gap year travelling around Europe. She'd been too keen to get to Cambridge. There were so many cities she'd love to visit. And then there was Riley – the most gorgeous man she'd ever been out with, or met, even. And he was so thoughtful and cheerful. Going anywhere with Riley was like wearing rose-tinted glasses – everything looked so much better.

Did it really matter that he'd never heard of Emmeline Pankhurst?

She'd not wanted to continue the conversation, to explain that Emmeline was the most famous of all the suffragettes, in case it became clear that Riley had never heard of the suffragettes either. That would be a bit of a deal-breaker.

But he was *Australian*, she reminded herself. Perhaps

feminist history was not a thing in Australia. They'd given the vote to women way back in 1902.

She spotted Hazard, sitting at a large table in The Library which was covered in papers.

'Are you working here again, Hazard?' she asked him.

'Oh, hi Monica! Yup. Hope you don't mind me taking up so much room. I find it a bit lonely working at home. I miss the buzz of an office. Anyhow, the coffee here is better.'

'You're welcome. Although I'm just closing. You can stay here for a bit longer though, while I clean up and do the till.'

Monica craned her neck to see what Hazard was up to.

'Can I show you what I've been doing?' he asked her. 'I'd love your opinion.' Monica pulled up a chair. She loved giving an opinion.

'I designed these leaflets, look, for Aussie Gardeners. We posted them through pretty much every letterbox in Chelsea and Fulham. Took us days.'

'They're great, Hazard,' she said, genuinely impressed. 'Did you get a good response?'

'Yup. And Alice posted some pics of our work on Insta, which got loads of interest.'

Monica wondered if it was the workers, rather than the work, that had caused the interest, then ticked herself off, sternly. Sexual objectification worked both ways.

'I've got enough work to keep me, Riley, and the five Aussie guys Riley's helped me train up, busy for the next two months at least. And, if we do a good job, word of mouth should keep the projects coming in beyond that.'

'And have you done your projected income and outgoings?' Monica asked. 'Do you have a target profit margin in mind?'

'Yes, of course. Would you like to see my business plan?' Hazard asked her. And she did, actually. There were few things Monica liked better than a good business plan. And Hazard's was, even to Monica's critical eye, a good one. She did suggest a few tweaks and improvements, obviously.

'Don't forget that once your turnover is over eighty-five thousand pounds you'll need to get a VAT number,' said Monica. 'And have you registered with Companies House yet?'

'Nope. Is it difficult to do that?' he asked.

'Not at all. Don't worry, I'll show you.' Monica realized that she was actually starting to like Hazard. Could she have misjudged him? She was usually so good at reading people.

'Hey, Monica, I have to tell you, I don't think I've *ever* had a conversation like this with an attractive woman. You know, about business, with no flirting,' said Hazard.

An attractive woman? Monica felt like she should get on her feminist high horse, but she couldn't be bothered. Did enjoying those words make her terribly shallow?

'Talking of social events,' said Hazard, which was odd, because they hadn't been. They'd been talking about Excel spreadsheets. Monica had been explaining the many merits of colour-coding. 'I got an invitation to a wedding last week. It's a great love story – Rita and Daphne who I met in Thailand. Both in their sixties and both, as far as I know, totally new to the whole lesbian thing.'

'Ah, that's lovely. A new start in life. Is Riley going too?' Monica wondered if Riley might invite her.

'No. He was only on Panam for two or three days, so didn't really get to know them. Er, I don't suppose you'd like to come with me, would you?' he said, taking her completely by surprise, so much so that she was at a total loss for words. Why her?

'You see,' he continued, as if he'd read her mind, 'I feel like I owe you. Not just for the business advice, but for keeping me distracted back on Koh Panam.'

Monica felt the familiar irritation building. She'd started to forget about how she'd been a little game for Hazard when he'd got bored between massages and guided meditation sessions at his health spa. Now she remembered. Much as she loved a good wedding, Monica couldn't help thinking that spending too much time with Hazard might put an awful lot of pressure on their rather fragile new friendship.

'Tell you what,' said Hazard, before she could politely decline, 'do you play backgammon? We could play for it. If I win, you come as my guest to the wedding, if you win, you don't have to. Unless you want to, obviously.'

'OK,' said Monica. 'You're on.' Nobody ever beat her at backgammon, and it would save her having to make a decision, either way, for the time being.

Monica's Café had a games shelf for customers, with a choice of chess, draughts, Trivial Pursuit, Scrabble and, of course, backgammon, as well as some classic favourites for the kids.

'I've been trying to teach Riley to play,' said Monica, as they set up the board, 'but he prefers Monopoly.' She thought for a minute that Hazard was sniggering, but it turned out to be a cough.

Monica threw the starting roll. A six and a one. This was one of her favourite openers. There was only one reasonable way to play it – blocking your bar point. Which she did.

'I'm so glad you did that,' said Hazard, almost under his breath.

'Why?' she asked. 'It's a good move. The only move for that throw, in my opinion.'

'I know,' he replied. 'It just reminded me of the last time I played. With a Swede in Thailand. He was not a good opponent.'

They played on, in silent concentration, evenly matched, equally determined. They were in the final straight, when Monica rolled a combination which she saw immediately would allow her to send one of Hazard's pieces to the bar. It was the deciding throw. He'd not recover from that.

Before she'd really analysed what she was doing, Monica moved a different piece.

'Ha!' said Hazard. 'You missed an opportunity to take me there, Monica!'

'Oh no, how could I have been so stupid,' Monica replied, hitting her forehead with her palm. Hazard threw a double six.

Looked like she'd have to go to the wedding after all . . .

Alice

Alice had just got Bunty changed into a gorgeous, hand-smocked pink and white dress by @vintagestylebaby, ready for the day's photoshoot, when she did a poo so explosive that it escaped the confines of her nappy and covered her back, almost up to her neck.

Alice nearly cried. She considered taking the shots anyway. She could angle Bunty so the mustard-coloured poo stains weren't on show. No one would know. But Bunty was starting to object to sitting in a dirty nappy, and was howling like a banshee. Again.

Alice was exhausted. She'd been up every three hours in the night. Every time she'd managed to nod off again, Bunty would give her just enough time to claw her way into deep sleep and then – as if she knew – she'd yell for more service, like an overly entitled, disgruntled customer at The Savoy.

She changed Bunty, picked her up and started carrying her down to the kitchen. Maybe caffeine would help?

Every time Alice walked down the stairs carrying her baby

she had the same vision. She imagined herself tripping, and tumbling down the seagrass-clad steps. In version one, she kept Bunty hugged into her chest, then landed at the bottom, accidentally crushing the life out of her. In version two, she released Bunty as she fell, then watched as Bunty's head hit the wall and she collapsed to the floor in a lifeless heap.

Did other mothers spend their whole time imagining the various ways in which they might accidentally kill their own babies? Falling asleep while feeding them and smothering them to death? Driving while exhausted and crashing into a lamppost, crumpling the back of the car containing the baby seat like a concertina? Not noticing that they'd swallowed a two-penny piece, carelessly dropped on the floor, and were blue in the face?

She wasn't grown up or responsible enough to keep another human being alive. How could they have just let her walk out of the hospital carrying a real-life baby without even giving her an instruction manual? How stupidly irresponsible was that? Of course, there were millions of instructions all over the internet, but they all contradicted each other.

Alice had, until recently, been rather successful. She'd been an account director for a large PR company, before leaving when she was six months pregnant to be a full-time mum and social media influencer. She had run meetings, given presentations to hundreds of people and planned global campaigns. Yet she was struggling to cope with one small baby.

And she was *bored*. The endless repetition of feeding baby, changing baby, loading dishwasher, hanging up washing, cleaning surfaces, reading stories and pushing swings was doing her head in. But she couldn't tell anyone. How could @aliceinwonderland, with her perfect, enviable, aspirational life, confess that, even though she loved her more than life itself, she often didn't like @babybunty very much? Actually, she didn't like life itself that much. She was pretty sure that Bunty didn't like her a great deal either. And who could blame her?

Alice pushed a stack of magazines off the armchair in the corner of her kitchen, making space for Bunty to sit while she put the kettle on and went to retrieve the milk from the fridge.

She heard a terrible scream. Bunty had managed to pitch herself, head first, off the armchair and had landed on the hard, tiled kitchen floor. Alice rushed over to pick her up, checking her for any obvious damage. Luckily, her head had landed on a copy of *Parenting Magazine*, which had cushioned the fall. At least parenting magazines were good for something.

Bunty glared at her, communicating even more clearly by using no words: *what kind of a useless mother are you? Can I please swap you for another one? I didn't ask to be cared for by such an imbecile.*

The doorbell rang. Alice walked over to the front door like an automaton, an avatar of the woman formerly known as Alice, leaving Bunty still yelling on the kitchen floor. She stared, silently, at her visitor. She couldn't work out what she was doing here. Had she forgotten some arrangement? It was Lizzie, one of the volunteers from Mummy's Little Helper.

'Come here, you poor duck. Give me a hug,' she said. 'I know exactly how you're feeling, so I've come to help you with Bunty.' Before she even had a chance to wonder *how* Lizzie knew exactly how she was feeling, she was smothered in a giant, pillow-like bosom.

Alice, for the first time since she'd brought Bunty home, wept and wept, until Lizzie's floral blouse was drenched in tears.

Lizzie

Lizzie loved her part-time job at Mummy's Little Helper, even if it only paid her expenses. She was sixty-five last year, and officially retired, but sitting at home was just making her fat and slow, and Jack, her husband, was driving her crazy, so her two days here were her favourite of the week.

Lizzie had looked after children all her life – first as the oldest of six siblings, then as a nanny, a mother to her own brood of five, and, most recently, as a maternity nurse where she was passed, by word of mouth, from one posh, over-privileged, Chelsea or Kensington new mother to another. 'Lizzie is an absolute darling! Total godsend!' they would say. 'Salt of the earth!' as if that actually *meant* anything other than *she's not like us you know, but you can probably trust her not to nick the silver.*

She'd just handed all the children back to their various carers, including little Elsa, with the constantly dripping nose and dirty fingernails, whose mother was, as usual, more than half an hour late. Rather confusingly, there were three Elsas currently registered. That film, *Frozen*, had a lot to answer for.

Lizzie went to take her coat off the peg in the hall and noticed, on the floor, directly beneath it, a pale-green exercise book, like the ones her kids had done their sums in. It must have dropped out of someone's coat or bag. She picked it up. On the front was written *The Arithmetic Project*. She popped it in her handbag. Someone was bound to ask after it tomorrow.

It was a few days before Lizzie thought about the maths book again. She'd asked some of the mums if one of their children was missing it, and had been carrying it around with her, waiting for someone to claim it, but no one had. So, since she was having a well-earned break with a cuppa, she took it out and looked at it. It didn't say 'arithmetic' at all; she hadn't been wearing her reading glasses, so she'd misread it. It said *The Authenticity Project*. What on earth did that mean? She flicked through the pages. There were none of the sums she'd been expecting to see, instead several different people had written in it.

Lizzie felt a wonderful tingle of anticipation. She had always been nosey. It was one of the best things about being a nanny or a maternity nurse – you could learn all sorts of things about a person by having a good old snoop in their knicker drawer. You'd think people would be a little more inventive with their hiding places. And this book looked as if it might hold *secrets*. Like a diary, maybe. She never did anything with the information she collected. She prided herself on being honourable and decent. She just found other people fascinating, is all. She sat back and started to read.

How well do you know the people who live near you? How well do they know you? Do you even know the names of your neighbours? Ha! Actually, Lizzie knew all her neighbours. She knew their names, their children's names and the names of their cats. She knew who didn't sort their recycling properly, she knew who had the most marital arguments, who was having an affair and who was spending too much time at the bookies. She knew far more about everyone than they'd want her to know. She was, she was aware, renowned for being a curtain-twitcher. But at least she was popular with the Neighbourhood Watch.

Julian Jessop.

Sometimes she would hear a name and the walls would fall away, like a set change at the theatre, and she'd be transported right back to another time, and now she was in 1970, on the King's Road with her friend Mandy. They'd spent so much time together back then that they were known as 'Lizandmandy'. They were fifteen years old, and had dressed up specially in mini-skirts, with their hair backcombed and eyes ringed in jet-black kohl.

They were looking through the window of the fabulous Mary Quant studio when a group of people, in their late twenties or early thirties, walked towards them. They were *impossibly* glamorous. The three men were wearing the latest flared trousers, and the girl a mini-dress, hem several inches higher up the thigh than theirs, a fur coat and *bare feet*. In public! Her hair tumbled down in messy curls to her waist, as if she'd just got out of bed. Lizzie was sure that if

she got close enough to her, she'd smell of sex. Not that
Lizzie knew what sex smelled like back then, but she imagined it would be a bit like *tinned sardines*. One of the men
had an actual parrot sitting on his shoulder.

Lizzie had been aware that her mouth was wide open.

'Blimey, Lizzie, do you know who that was?' said Mandy.
Then, not waiting for an answer, 'That was David Bailey,
the photographer, and Julian Jessop, the artist. Weren't they
gorgeous? Did you see Julian wink at me? He did, I swear
he did.'

Until that day, Lizzie had never heard of Julian (although
she'd not let on to Mandy, obviously; she didn't want to
give Mandy any more reason to think herself the cooler of
the two), but she'd seen his name several times in the years
that followed, in the gossip columns usually. She'd not
heard it for decades, though. If she'd thought about him at
all, she'd have assumed he was dead, from something tragic
but faintly glamorous, like a drug overdose or a venereal
disease. Yet here he was, living just down the road still,
writing in a little book which someone had dropped right
into her lap.

Monica. Lizzie knew her too – she'd been in her café and
had a cup of tea and a slice of cake once or twice when she
was feeling flush. She'd liked Monica, because although she
was obviously busy, she'd generously stopped what she was
doing for a chat. They'd discussed the local library, if she
remembered correctly, and what a godsend it was to the
community.

She knew exactly what Monica's problem was. Young
women today were just too fussy. In her day, they'd

understood the need to settle. You found a young man, about the right age, usually one whose parents your family knew and lived near by, and you got married. He might well pick his nose when he was driving, or squander too much of the housekeeping down the pub, or have no idea where to find a clitoris, but you realized that you probably weren't perfect either, and an averagely good husband was better than no husband at all. The problem with all this new technology was people had so much choice that they just couldn't make a decision. They carried on looking and looking until one day they realized all their eggs had hard boiled. Monica should stop fannying around and get on with it.

Bugger. Her tea break was over. She was dying to read more, but it would have to wait.

'What are you reading there, Liz?' asked Jack. It came out a bit mumbled as he was still trying to get a bit of chicken out of one of his back molars with an index finger. No wonder she'd not kissed him on the mouth for years. These days she tended to just give him a peck on the top of his head, where there was a large bald spot, like a helicopter landing pad, as she passed by.

'Just a book from work,' she replied, being deliberately vague. She was reading Hazard's story. She knew him, too. Presumably there couldn't be two young men from Fulham with the name Hazard, in which case he'd come back from Thailand and was working in the garden at Mummy's Little Helper. He was quite dishy, despite the beard. Lizzie generally had no truck with men in beards. I mean, what did they have to hide? Apart from the chin.

She didn't judge him for the whole addiction thing. She knew how these things could sneak up on you. She'd gone through a phase of being rather too fond of the cooking sherry herself, not to mention the scratch cards, and Jack still smoked twenty John Player Specials a day, at vast expense, ignoring the ghastly photos of blackened lungs plastered all over the packets.

Riley sounded like a sweetheart, the poor confused lad. She knew him as well. He was one of the lovely young Australians working with Hazard. She was dying to find out if Hazard was still on the wagon, if Julian was teaching the art class, and if Riley had sorted things out with Monica. This was better than *EastEnders*.

There was one story left to read. Who was it next? She'd save it for her break tomorrow.

Lizzie was settling in for the perfect tea break in the staff room: PG Tips, two Jammie Dodgers, *Steve Wright in the Afternoon* on Radio 2 and a book containing someone else's secrets. As her kids would say, what's not to like? She made herself comfortable in her favourite armchair and began to read.

My name is Alice Campbell. You might know me as @aliceinwonderland.

BINGO! Lizzie had a full house. She knew everyone in the book. What's more, she knew exactly how the book had come to be here. Alice was the pretty blonde who helped them with their fundraising. She remembered Archie, one of the toddlers, playing with the shoulder bag Alice had left in the hall, under the coats. He must have taken out the book, and left it on the floor.

Lizzie worried slightly whenever Alice turned up at Mummy's Little Helper that she might make the other mothers feel inadequate. She was always so perfectly dressed, so obviously in control, so different from the mums they helped, who were usually chaotic and invariably struggling. Although Lizzie did wonder how much of Alice was a front. Sometimes her carefully modulated, uptight accent slipped just a little, revealing shades of a much more colourful and accessible one. She carried on reading.

Although, if you follow me, you don't actually know me at all, because my real life and the perfect one you see are diverging further and further apart. The messier my life becomes, the more I crave the likes on social media to convince me that it's all OK.

I used to be Alice, the successful PR girl. Now I'm Max's wife, or Bunty's mum, or @aliceinwonderland. It feels like everyone has a piece of me except for myself.

I'm really tired. I'm tired of the sleepless nights, the feeding, the nappy changing, the cleaning and the washing. I'm tired of spending hours documenting the life I wish I had, and replying to messages from strangers who think they know me.

I love my baby more than I ever thought possible, but every day I'm letting her down. She deserves a mother who feels constantly grateful for the life they share, not one who's always trying to run away, into a virtual world that's much prettier and more manageable than the real one.

I wish I could tell someone how I feel, that sometimes I sit in the circle at Monkey Music and just want to punch my fist through the stupid pink tambourine. Just yesterday, at Water Babies, I felt an almost uncontrollable urge to sink to the bottom of the pool and take a deep breath in. But how can I confess that @aliceinwonderland is just a sham?

And if I'm not her, then who am I?

Oh, Alice. Even before post-natal depression was officially 'a thing', the women in Lizzie's family and social circle knew the signs. Back in the days when Lizzie had her first baby, all the grandparents, aunts, uncles, godparents and friends would rally round a new mum. They'd offer babysitting, bring casseroles and help with the housework, which helped ease the physical, emotional and hormonal shock of giving birth.

And there was Alice, feeling she had to do it all alone, and desperately trying to make it look perfect.

As soon as her shift finished, Lizzie looked up Alice's address in the contacts book. What little Alice needed was a *professional*.

Hazard

Hazard had borrowed the minibus from Mummy's Little Helper for the day. Monica had, he'd discovered, never learned to drive, having spent her life in London with its plethora of public transport options, and the village was miles away from any train station, so he was playing chauffeur. One of the mums had stuck a big sign on the back saying DRIVER HAZARD, which was hilarious. Not.

He pulled up on the double yellow lines outside Monica's Café and hooted.

'Is that you with your hazards on, Hazard?' said Monica. He hadn't heard *that* one before either. He did a slow wolf whistle.

'Monica, you look like a buttercup! A particularly *sexy* buttercup!' he said, as she climbed into the passenger seat wearing a bright-yellow shift dress and matching wide-brimmed hat. 'I don't think I've seen you wearing anything other than black, white or navy before.'

'Well, I do like to make an effort sometimes,' she replied,

looking rather chuffed, he thought. 'And look at you, all dandy in a morning suit. You've even trimmed that beard, if I'm not mistaken.' She said 'beard' in a way that implied ironic air quotes. 'Here, I've got takeaway coffee for the journey. Yours is a large latte, full-fat milk. I know I'm right,' she said, gesturing at the brown paper bag she was holding.

'Bang on, thank you,' he said, oddly thrilled that she'd remembered his coffee order. 'And I have Rowntree's Fruit Gums. Help yourself. Don't hold back – I bought a family pack, the ones shaped like little fruits. Always liked those.'

As they motored down the M3, they relaxed into an easy banter.

'Are you excited?' he asked.

'Not really. I find weddings rather depressing. Marriage – it's only a piece of paper, and the divorce statistics are shocking. Waste of time and money, frankly.'

'Really?' he asked, surprised.

'No, of course not really! You've read my story, haven't you? Nothing I like better than a happy ending and a good old wedding.'

Then, apropos of nothing, Monica piped up with, 'Hazard. I'm sorry I gave you such a hard time when you arrived. I was embarrassed. And I thought you were just some lazy, trust fund kid who liked meddling around in other people's lives, feeling superior.'

'Ouch. No wonder you hated me,' Hazard said. 'I've always earned my own money, actually. My parents are solidly middle class, but spent every penny of their savings sending me to a posh private school where I was teased mercilessly for being the only boy whose house had a number, not a name and who turned right on an aeroplane, instead of left.'

'So, what did you do before the gardening business?' asked Monica.

'I was in the City. Trading. I suspect now that I chose that career because I was fed up with always being the least rich person in the room. I guess you didn't read my story in the book, did you? Riley didn't tell you?'

'No, he's quite sensitive like that, Riley. He'd leave it to you to tell me. So, what *did* you write, if you don't mind me asking? You have read *my* story after all.'

'Er, I wrote about how I was done with the City, was taking some time off to get my head together, and wanted to find a career that was more rewarding and fulfilling,' he said, which was the absolute truth, but definitely not the *whole* truth. There was a huge great elephant in the minibus, sitting between them and crushing the gear stick. Monica was, however, the last person in the world he wanted to discuss his addiction with. She was so decent and clean and shiny, and talking about it all was so grubby. Monica made him feel like a better person, and he didn't want to remind himself that he wasn't. He suspected that she'd never so much as taken a toke on a joint. And good for her.

'And now you have! I swear that book works magic. Look at Julian, with all his hundreds of new friends, and you with a successful new business. I'm so impressed with how you've built it up so quickly. You've done a great job.'

Hazard glowed with pride. He wasn't used to feeling good about himself, or other people complimenting him.

'Well, I've been trying to do things properly, for once. Like you do. You're a really good business person – creative, hard-working, and a great boss. Plus, you have principles.' Was he laying it on a bit thick? Hazard always found himself trying a bit too hard with Monica. He wasn't sure why; it wasn't like him at all.

'How do you mean?' asked Monica.

'Well, for example, if a customer really, really pisses you off, do you ever spit in their food? Just to get them back?' asked Hazard. Monica looked horrified.

'Of course not! That would be horribly unhygienic and, most probably, illegal. If it isn't illegal, it bloody well should be.'

'And if you drop some food on the floor in the kitchen, but it lands the right way up, do you just put it back on the plate, or would you throw it away?'

'You can't put food that's been on the floor back on the plate! Think of the bacteria,' said Monica.

'You see. You have standards.'

'Don't you?' she asked.

'Oh yes, of course I do. But they're *low*. Barely off the ground.'

'Hazard,' Monica said, glaring at the dashboard, 'you're going well over the speed limit.'

'Oops, sorry,' he replied, giving the brake pedal a token squeeze. 'I'm afraid I have a tiny problem with *rules*. You show me a rule, I want to break it. I have never stayed within the speed limit – literally or metaphorically.'

'We really are total opposites, aren't we?' said Monica. 'I love a good rule, me.'

'Yellow car,' said Hazard, as he overtook a garish Peugeot 205. Monica stared at him, nonplussed.

'Didn't your family ever play "yellow car"?' he asked her.

'Er, no. How do you play?'

'Well, whenever you see a yellow car, you say "yellow car",' Hazard explained.

'And how do you win?' asked Monica.

'No one ever really wins,' he said, 'because the game never ends. It just goes on for ever.'

'It's not exactly intellectually stimulating, is it?' said Monica.

'Well how did you keep yourself amused on family car journeys then?' asked Hazard.

'I had a notebook and I'd write down the number plates of cars as we passed them,' she said.

'Why?' asked Hazard.

'In case I saw the same one again.'

'And did you?'

'No,' she said.

'Well, I think I'll stick with yellow car, thanks. So, has The Authenticity Project worked its magic for you, too?'

'Well, yes,' she replied. 'In a way, it's saved my business. Setting up the art class led to lots of other weekly evening events, and then Alice and Julian keep featuring the café on Instagram and bringing in loads of new customers. I might even have to hire an extra barista. Before I found the book, I thought by now the bank would have pulled the plug and I'd have lost the café, and my life savings with it.'

'That's amazing,' he said. Then, more tentatively, 'And did the book sort out your love life too? Is everything good now with you and Riley?' He hoped she didn't think him too nosey.

'Well, we're just playing it by ear. Going with the flow. Seeing what happens,' she said.

'Don't take this the wrong way,' said Hazard, 'but I'd never have associated any of those expressions with you.'

'I know, right?' she said with a grin. 'I'm trying to be more easy-going. I have to say, it's a bit of a challenge.'

'But Riley's leaving in a few months, isn't he?' said Hazard. 'Early June?'

'Yes, but he's asked me to go with him,' she said.

'And are you going?' Hazard asked.

'You know, at the moment I have absolutely no idea, which is a most unusual situation to find myself in,' she replied.

'It must be so easy to be Riley,' said Hazard.

'Why?'

'You know, walking through life in such a happy-go-lucky way, seeing everything so simply and two-dimensionally,' said Hazard. 'Yellow car.'

'I know you don't mean to, but you make him sound like an imbecile,' said Monica. And he didn't mean to, of course he didn't.

Monica slipped off her high heels and rested her narrow feet on the dashboard. Just that one casual movement showed Hazard how much she'd changed.

'I've changed quite a lot since I met Riley,' she said, as if she'd read his mind.

'Well, don't change too much, will you?' said Hazard. Monica said nothing.

They drove for another hour, the roads becoming narrower and less busy, and concrete giving way to nature.

'Hey, according to Google Maps we have reached our destination!' said Monica, as they drove into the kind of perfectly formed village that would give a Hollywood location scout paroxysms of excitement. Bells were ringing joyfully from the honey-coloured stone church. 'I didn't think the Church did gay weddings yet.'

'They don't, but they did the legal marriage yesterday at the town hall, and this is a blessing. I imagine it'll look just like a traditional wedding, just slightly different words,' he replied.

They parked the minibus and followed the well-dressed crowd towards the church entrance.

Monica

Monica stopped in at the Portaloos on the way into the reception, to check that she didn't have mascara running down her face. She'd blubbed just a little bit in the church, at the sight of the two brides, both dressed in floor-length white. Weddings always did that to her, even those of people she didn't know. It was mainly happiness for the couple, of course, but she was uncomfortably aware that it was mixed in with a tiny bit of envy and regret.

Hazard was waiting for her as she came out, and they walked together into the marquee. The entrance was decked with white roses, and on either side a waiter stood holding a silver platter bearing glasses of champagne. Monica and Hazard took one each.

'I thought Riley said you'd quit drinking while you were in Thailand,' said Monica. Or had Alice told her that? She was sure someone had, anyhow.

'Oh yes, I did,' replied Hazard. 'I was drinking *way* too much. But it's not as if I'm an *alcoholic* or anything. I can have just one or two drinks, on special occasions. Like this one. I'm all about moderation, these days.'

'Quite right,' replied Monica, who thought staying in control an underrated art form. She was liking Hazard more and more. 'Don't forget you're driving us home, will you?'

'Of course not,' said Hazard. 'But it's several hours before we'll be leaving, and it'd be rude not to join in, don't you think?' And he raised his glass at her and took a large gulp. 'What do you reckon's on the dinner menu? Chicken or fish?'

'Judging by the crowd, I'd opt for fish. Poached salmon,' she replied.

Monica was really enjoying herself. Hazard kept up a hysterical running commentary on all the other guests, despite the fact that – with the exception of Roderick and the brides – he knew none of them. They shared stories of weddings they'd attended in the past, both the wonderfully romantic and the totally disastrous.

It was so much more relaxing being on a date with someone she wasn't dating. At every previous wedding she'd attended, she'd found her imagination fast-forwarding the relationship she was in. She'd make mental notes of how her wedding would differ, which of her relatives might make photogenic (but not too photogenic) bridesmaids and who he might choose as best man. She'd give him sidelong glances during the service, to see if he were overcome with emotion and having the same thoughts as her.

With Hazard, it was just – fun. She was really glad she'd come.

They were on the same table for dinner, although it was huge and round with a giant floral display in the middle, so

Monica couldn't talk to Hazard and could only see him if she craned her neck around the flowers. There was a dinner menu in the centre. Poached salmon. She did love being right. She caught his eye, pointed at the menu and gave him a wink.

The meal seemed to go on for ever, as each course was interspersed with speeches. Monica was doing her best with the men sitting on either side of her, but was rapidly running out of small talk. They'd done how they each knew the happy couple, wasn't the service lovely, and weren't house prices in London astronomical, and then ground to a halt.

She was getting increasingly worried about Hazard, because she was pretty sure that he'd accepted a glass of white wine from a waiter, and then a glass of red, and it looked as if they were topping both glasses up regularly. She tried to catch his eye, to give him a meaningful stare and remind him about the drive home, but he seemed to be deliberately avoiding her gaze. The girls on either side of him kept tipping their heads back and laughing uproariously. One looked as if she had a hand resting on his thigh. He was obviously being *hilarious*. But it wasn't hilarious. It was irresponsible and selfish.

As the meal, finally, drew to a close, and people started wandering away from the table, Monica went and sat down in an empty seat near Hazard, clutching her glass of sparkling water, as if to prove a point.

'*Hazard*,' she hissed at him, 'you're meant to be driving us home, not getting *drunk*.'

'Oh Monica, don't be such a killjoy. It's a *wedding*. You're supposed to get drunk. That's what weddings are *for*. Let your hair down for once. Live a little,' he said, draining another glass of wine. 'Monica, this is . . .' he said, waving in the direction of the blonde sitting next to him. Her lips had definitely had something artificial pumped into them, and she obviously hadn't heard the sartorial advice about only displaying legs *or* cleavage.

'Annabel,' she finished for him. 'Hi.' How was it possible to draw out a two-letter word for so long? She waved at Monica with only the tips of her fingers, as if Monica didn't deserve a whole hand. 'Hazard? I've got some Charlie in my bag if you fancy a quick snifter?' she said, not even bothering to hide the conversation from Monica, or to include her. Did she think Monica was too square to take drugs? Well, she was, but that wasn't the point.

'Now you're talking, gorgeous,' said Hazard, pushing back his chair and standing up, rather unsteadily. 'I'll follow you – apart from anything else, it'll give me more opportunity to check out your gorgeous arse.'

'Hazard!' shouted Monica. '*You're* the arse. Don't be such a bloody idiot!'

'Oh, for fuck's sake, Monica, stop being such a bore. Why don't you go and de-stress in a haberdashery? You are not my mother, or my wife, or even my girlfriend. And thank fuck for small mercies.' He left, weaving through the crowd after Annabel's capacious backside, like a rat following the Pied Piper. Annabel shot Monica a look over her shoulder, tossed her head and brayed, her lips peeling back to reveal overly large teeth.

Monica felt as if she'd been slapped. Who the hell was that? He certainly wasn't the Hazard she'd thought she knew? Then she remembered. He may not be the Hazard she'd got to know recently, but he was one she'd seen before, the one who had barged into her in the street and called her *stupid bitch*. The one who'd meddled with her life, then crashed her Christmas lunch expecting a round of applause. And how *dare* he bring up her haberdashery obsession? She'd totally forgotten about writing that in the book. That was a low blow. She didn't want to be here any longer. She just wanted to go home. Monica took her mobile out of her bag, found a quiet corner of the marquee and called Riley.

Please answer, Riley, please answer.

'Monica! You guys having fun?' he said in his wonderfully upbeat voice.

'Not really, no. At least I'm not. Hazard's having rather too much fun, actually. He's completely plastered. And not slowing down either. I don't know how to get home. Hazard's too drunk to drive, and I don't know how to. I can't leave the minibus here. They need it first thing tomorrow for an outing. What am I going to do?' Monica hated asking for help, and particularly hated acting like a damsel in distress. It went against all her feminist principles. Her mother would be turning in her grave. If she ever managed to get herself out of this damn marquee she was going to book a course of driving lessons.

'Don't worry, Monica. You stay there, I'll jump on the train and come and get you. I can drive you and the bus home. Just text me your address and I'll get a taxi from the station. It'll take me a couple of hours, but the wedding will go on for a while longer, won't it?'

'Riley, I don't know what I'd do without you. Thank you. I have no idea what's got into Hazard. I've never seen him like this,' she said.

'I guess that's the problem if you're an addict. Once you start, you just can't stop. He was doing so brilliantly, too. Nearly five months, totally sober,' said Riley. Monica's stomach lurched. She was such an idiot.

'Riley, I had no idea. He told me he could handle it. I should have stopped him,' she said.

'It's not your fault, Monica. I'm sure he deliberately misled you. And himself probably. If it's anyone's fault, it's mine. I should have warned you to keep an eye on him. Still, at least he's not hoovering up the cocaine again,' said Riley. Monica said nothing. There didn't seem to be any point. 'Look, the sooner I leave, the sooner I'll get there. Hold tight.' And he hung up.

Sometimes, there is nothing lonelier than a room full of people. Monica felt like a child, with her nose pressed against a window, looking in at a party she wasn't party to. Hazard was dancing, showily, in the centre of the dance-floor, with women sticking to him like those flies on Julian's ghastly fly paper. She felt a tap on her shoulder.

'Might I request the next dance?' It was Roderick, Daphne's son. Hazard had introduced them in the church.

Monica, who'd always felt it impolite to turn down anyone who plucked up the courage to ask you to dance, nodded mutely, and allowed herself to be led up to the floor where Roderick, ignoring all the conventions of modern dance moves, threw her around in a clumsily energetic version of 1950s rock and roll. This gave him plenty of opportunities to rest a clammy hand on her back, shoulder or buttock. She felt like a show pony at a dressage competition.

Hazard, who was obviously finding her predicament

hilarious, gave her an exaggerated thumbs-up through the crowd. Roderick leant over and whispered in her ear, his breath hot and sticky, smelling of whiskey mixed with strawberry pavlova.

'So, are you and Hazard *an item?*' he asked.

'God, no,' replied Monica. Roderick took her obvious strength of feeling as a green light, and clutched her bum even more enthusiastically.

Riley picked his way carefully through the thinning crowd, a sure-footed interloper amongst an unpredictably lurching mass. Monica was the only person sitting at a large, round table, like the sole survivor of a shipwreck, stranded on a desert island. Hazard was circling the tables like a shark, picking up abandoned wine glasses and draining them.

'Riley!' Monica shouted over at him, causing everyone in the vicinity to turn and stare at the newcomer. Riley smiled, and it was like the sun bursting through the storm clouds.

'I can't tell you how pleased I am to see you,' said Monica.

Hazard

It was like coming home. Hazard had forgotten how much he liked this feeling. From that very first sip of champagne, he'd felt his jaw unclench, his shoulders relax and all the edges fall away. After months of dealing with every emotion with the focus on sharp and the definition high, the booze overlaid everything with a fuzzy filter that made it all softer, kinder and more manageable. He was wrapped in a feather-down duvet of lassitude.

By the time he'd drained the first glass he really couldn't remember why he'd fought this sensation for so long. Why had he thought the booze was his enemy, when it was his very best friend?

The minute he'd discovered in the minibus that Monica was unaware of the extent of his addiction issues, the thought had been planted: *maybe, just for today, since it's a special occasion, I could have a drink. Just one. Two, tops. After all, it's been months. I'm better now. I know better. I can be sensible. It won't be like before. I'm a different person.*

All through the wedding ceremony those thoughts had gone around and around his head on a loop. So, as soon as they'd walked into the marquee, and a waiter had been stood there with glasses of champagne on a silver platter, he'd just taken one. Just like everyone else. How he loved the thought that he was just like everyone else. He'd told Monica that he wasn't 'an alcoholic' and was really good at moderation, and as he'd said it aloud he'd started to believe it. After all, alcoholics slept on park benches, smelled of wee and drank methylated spirits, and he wasn't like that at all, was he?

He'd drunk way more than he'd been meaning to, but it didn't really matter. It was just for today. He could go back to being good again tomorrow. What was that expression his mother had always used? *Might as well be hanged for a sheep as a lamb.* Although she'd been referring to an extra slice of Battenberg cake.

On that basis, the cocaine had seemed like a blessed opportunity, and a few lines had thrown a buzz and a wave of confidence and invulnerability into the mix. He was a superhero. He noted that he hadn't lost any of his pulling power either. He was on fire. This was the first wedding he'd been to where he hadn't already slept with at least two of the congregation. Perhaps he should rectify that.

Hazard spotted a familiar figure. He blinked and rubbed his eyes, thinking his mind was playing tricks on him. That was far more likely than Riley actually being here. After all, he'd got Monica confused with his mother earlier. Hazard sniggered to himself. But it *was* Riley. Why the fuck had he shown up, raining on Hazard's parade?

'Hazard, mate, it's time to go home,' he said.

'Don't "mate" me, Riley. What the fuck are you doing here?'

'I'm the cavalry. Come to take you home.'

'Well, you can get back on your bloody horse and ride the hell off. I'm having fun with my *new friends*.' And he waved over at what's-her-name and the other one.

'Well, I'm taking Monica home. And the minibus. And this party's winding up, so unless you want to spend the night with your *new friends*, I suggest you come with us. Your call, *mate*.' Riley was sounding a bit pissed off. Riley was never pissed off. Monica, however, was *always* pissed off, and she was standing next to Riley like the bloody vicar's bloody wife, looking at him like he was a choirboy who'd pilfered all the communion wine. He was really fed up with all this bloody disapproval.

Hazard did a quick mental calculation. Or as quick as his mental capacities would allow after what he'd put them through over the previous few hours. If he stayed here he would have to bank on the blonde taking him home with her. Not only was he having problems remembering her name (Amanda? Arabella? Amelia?), but he knew that her main attraction was the drugs she had in her handbag, and he was pretty sure they were, by now, all but gone. He had better, much as it pained him, do what he was told. So, he followed his goody-goody friends, as meekly as a superhero on cocaine could manage.

An hour into the journey, and the effect of the last line of coke that he'd snorted, a couple of hours previously, was starting to wear off, leaving him feeling twitchy and anxious. And now he wasn't able to maintain the delicate balance of upper and downer, all the booze he'd drunk was making him feel woozy and drowsy, although he knew from experience that sleep would elude him for hours.

He lay down across three of the seats in the back of the bus, and watched the dementors approaching. He remembered this feeling too. What goes up must come down. Every light has a shadow, every force a counter-force. This was payback time.

He felt someone, Monica, throwing something over him – a blanket? A coat?

'I think I love you, Monica,' he said. He was pretty sure he'd been really horrible to her. He was a truly evil person who didn't deserve any friends.

'Sure, Hazard. The only person you love is yourself,' she replied, which wasn't true at all. The only person he'd never been able to love was himself. He'd spent months building up his self-esteem brick by brick, learning to respect himself again, and in one day it had all come tumbling down.

'I'm so sorry,' he said, 'I thought I could just have one.' And that was the problem. He always thought he could just have one. After all, other people seemed to manage it. But he never could. It was all or nothing with Hazard. Not just with the booze and the drugs, with everything. If he found something – anything – he liked, he always wanted *more*. It was what had made him such a successful trader, a popular friend and a terrible addict.

He could hear Monica and Riley chatting in the front. He could remember when he used to be able to chat like that, about the weather, the traffic, the news of mutual acquaintances, but right now he couldn't imagine how. An unwelcome thought muscled its way in amongst all the other unwelcome thoughts. *Where were his keys?* He checked his pockets. He knew they'd be empty.

'Monica,' he said, trying not to slur. 'I can't find my keys. I must have dropped them in the placebo.'

'Gazebo,' corrected Monica.

'Don't be such a peasant,' he replied.

'Pedant,' she said.

He heard her sigh. It was the sort of noise his mother would make when he was little and had forgotten his homework or ripped his trousers.

'Don't worry, Hazard. You can sleep on my sofa. At least that way I can keep an eye on you.' For a while everything was silent, except for the rhythmic scraping of the windscreen wipers and the gentle hum of the tyres on the tarmac.

'Yellow car,' Hazard heard Monica say from the front of the bus.

'What?' asked Riley.

'Nothing,' she replied.

Hazard would have smiled, but his cheek was stuck to the plastic of the seat he was lying on.

Monica

Before Monica even opened her eyes, she knew something was different. Her flat, which usually smelled of coffee, Jo Malone, Cif Lemon Fresh and, occasionally, Riley, reeked of dank, stale booze. And Hazard.

She got out of bed, threw on a baggy sweatshirt over her pyjamas – she was *not* going to make an effort – and tied her hair up in a messy bun. She went into the bathroom, splashed her face with water, then doubled back and added a lick of mascara and some lip gloss. She wasn't trying to impress, obviously, just making sure that Hazard didn't have any excuse to sneer at her again.

Monica opened the door into her living room rather cautiously. She tiptoed in, trying not to wake him. He wasn't there. The sofa she'd left him on was empty, her spare duvet folded up neatly. The washing-up bowl she'd left on the floor, in case he needed to vomit (again), had been put back in her kitchenette. The curtains had been drawn and the windows opened to air the room. There was no note.

Monica had no desire to see Hazard, particularly not at this time in the morning and after yesterday's events, but – even so – it was a little rude of him to do a runner like that. How could she have expected any different?

The front door opened behind her, making her jump. A huge bunch of pale-yellow roses walked in, followed by Hazard. 'I hope you don't mind, I borrowed your keys,' he said, placing them on the table with a hand that was shaking.

Monica had seen Hazard in many guises – the brash bully who'd called her a bitch, the Christmas Day returning hero who wasn't, the hard-working and determined gardener and businessman, and the irresponsible, rude bore of yesterday – but in all those guises, Hazard had been so sure of himself. He'd always occupied far more space in any room than even his six-foot-three frame required.

This Hazard was different. He looked awful, for a start, tired and saggy and grey, still dressed in a crumpled morning suit, but, more disconcertingly, he looked *uncertain*. All the bombast and self-confidence of the night before had ebbed away, leaving him diminished. Sad. The light behind his eyes had dimmed.

'Thank you,' she said, taking the roses and filling the kitchen sink with water to stop them wilting. These things needed to be done instantly. Hazard sat down heavily on the sofa.

'Monica, I don't know what to say,' he said. 'I was inexcusably horrible to you yesterday. I'm so, so sorry. That man was not me. At least, I guess he is a part of me, but one I've tried to keep locked away. I hate the man I become when I'm drunk, and I really liked the man I've been turning into these last few months. And now I've ruined it all.'

He sat with his head in his hands, his hair, matted and sweaty, falling forwards.

'You were awful,' said Monica. 'Indescribably awful.' But she realized that, for the first time, she was seeing the authentic Hazard. The imperfect, insecure and vulnerable boy who must have been there all along, hidden beneath the bluster. And it didn't seem fair to stay angry with him. He was obviously doing that job pretty well himself. She sighed, and shelved the speech she'd rehearsed in her head during the journey home last night.

'Let's just start again from today, hey? You wait here. I'll go downstairs, get us some coffees and arrange for Benji to mind the café.'

Monica and Hazard sat at either end of the sofa, sharing a large duvet and a bucket of popcorn, and watching back-to-back Netflix. As Hazard reached over for the popcorn, Monica spotted his fingernails, bitten right down to the quick, the skin around them red and sore. It reminded her vividly of her own hands after her mother died, inflamed, cracked and bleeding from the endless washing. She wasn't sure if she was trying to help Hazard, or heal herself, but she had to tell the story.

'You know, I do understand about compulsions, about that overwhelming need to do something, even when you know you shouldn't,' she said, looking straight ahead rather than directly at Hazard. He said nothing, but she could sense him listening, so she carried on.

'My mother died when I was sixteen, just before Christmas, in my GCSE year. She wanted to die at home, so we had the sitting room converted into a hospital room. Because her immune system had been completely shot by the chemo, the Macmillan nurse told me to keep her room disinfected at all times. It was the one thing I could control. I couldn't stop my mother dying, but I could kill all the bugs. So, I cleaned and cleaned, and I washed my hands every hour, several times. And even when she died, I didn't stop. Even when all the skin started peeling off my hands, I didn't stop. Even when the kids at school started whispering about me behind my back, then calling me a nutter to my face, I couldn't stop. So, I do know.'

'Monica, I'm so sorry. That's a terrible age to lose your mother,' said Hazard.

'I didn't *lose her*, Hazard. I bloody hate that expression. It makes it sound as if we went to the shops and I just left her behind. And she didn't *pass over* or *slip away*. It was nothing as gentle or peaceful as that. It was raw and ugly and smelly and *fucking unfair*.' The words scratched at her throat.

Hazard took her hand, unclenched it, and held it in his. 'What about your dad? Couldn't he help you?'

'He was struggling too. He's an author. Did you ever read those children's books set in a fantasy world called Dragonlia?' She saw Hazard nod, out of the corner of her eye. 'Well, he wrote those. So, he would disappear into his office and bury himself in a fairer world where good always triumphed and evil was defeated. That first Christmas, we were like two shipwrecked sailors, both trying to stay afloat, but clutching on to separate pieces of wreckage.'

'How did you get better, Monica?' Hazard asked, gently.

'I got worse before I got better. I dropped out of school

for a while, and stopped even leaving the house. I just buried myself in my books. And I cleaned, obviously. Dad used a huge chunk of his royalties to pay for lots of therapy, and, by the time I'd finished my A levels, I was much better. I'm still a little bit over-zealous on the hygiene front, but other than that, totally normal!' she said, with a trace of irony.

'And I thought you were the most sane person I knew. Just goes to show, doesn't it?' said Hazard.

'Well, I thought you were the most sober person I knew, until yesterday,' Monica replied, grinning at him.

They turned to watch the screen as a new episode loaded automatically.

Hazard took a handful of popcorn and flicked a kernel across the room. Monica had no idea where it had landed. Then he did it again. *Three times.*

'Hazard!' Monica said sharply. 'What the hell do you think you're *doing*?'

'Call it aversion therapy,' said Hazard, flicking another kernel across the room. 'Just try and watch a whole episode without worrying about the popcorn.'

Monica could do that. Of *course* she could do that. How long were these bloody episodes, anyhow? She sat for fifteen minutes which felt like hours, trying not to think about the rogue kernels, nestled into cracks and crevices and lurking under her furniture.

Enough was enough. She went to get the dustbuster.

'You did really great, Monica,' said Hazard, once they'd tracked down and sucked up every last kernel and sat down again.

'You have no idea how hard that is for me, Hazard,' she said.

'That's where you're wrong,' he replied. 'I know exactly how hard it is. It's the same way I feel every time I walk past a pub. You know, we all try to escape life somehow – me with drugs, Julian by becoming a hermit, Alice with social media. But you don't. You're much braver than any of us. You meet life head on and try and fight it and control it. Just a little too much, sometimes.'

'We all need to be a bit more like Riley, don't we?' said Monica. 'That's why he's so good for me.'

'Mmmm,' replied Hazard.

They sat in silence for a while. They'd started off at opposite sides of the sofa, but now they met in the middle, head to head, legs dangling over the arms at either end.

'You know, that's the story you should have written in the book, Monica,' said Hazard. 'Dealing with your mother's death and coming out the other side, *that's* your truth, not all that marriage and baby stuff.'

She knew he was right.

'Just out of interest,' said Hazard, 'do all the tins in your cupboards face outwards?'

'Of course,' she replied. 'How on earth could you read the labels otherwise?'

He reached over and carefully disentangled a kernel of popcorn from her hair, and put it down on the coffee table. Just for a moment, she thought he was going to kiss her. But of course, he wasn't.

'Hazard?' she said. He turned and looked at her intently.

'Could you put that piece of popcorn in the bin?'

Riley

The English, Riley decided, were much like their weather. They were changeable and unpredictable. Complicated. It would look like it was going to be fine, then a squall would appear from nowhere and hailstones could rain from the sky, bouncing off the pavement and car bonnets. However diligently you checked the cloud formations and the forecast, you could never be quite sure what was coming next.

Hazard had not been himself since the disastrous wedding. Riley was sure he wasn't still drinking, or doing drugs. He was incredibly contrite, and seemed to have learned a hard lesson, but he'd drooped.

Monica, meanwhile, had bloomed a little. They were spending lots of time together, and had shared rather steamy sessions on her sofa, but she was like a prickly rose – beautiful, fragrant, lots of promise, but if you got too close, there were thorns.

Although he'd stayed the night a couple of times, they'd still not had sex. This confused Riley. Sex, for him, was one of life's simple pleasures – like surfing, freshly baked pastries and a good hike at sunrise. He didn't see the point in holding back, now there were no secrets lurking between them. And yet Monica seemed to load it with so much significance and approach it with such caution. Like it was an unexploded bomb.

And she still hadn't told him if she was coming travelling with him. Not that it affected his plans. He didn't need plans. He'd just pack his rucksack, make his way to the station, and see what happened next. But he *would* like to know, just so when he imagined himself on the steps of the Colosseum, he'd know whether to imagine Monica sitting next to him. Or not.

Riley pulled a small weed from the herbaceous border that had been pretty immaculate before he'd even started work. Mrs Ponsonby was the sort of lady who liked everything to be perfect. No stray weeds, pubic hairs or husbands for her. And no fun either, he suspected. She'd made him and Brett a cup of tea – the type that had pretensions and tasted slightly of flowers. He preferred regular tea. The sort that knew what it was.

As Mrs Ponsonby had passed Riley his mug, she'd brushed up against his arm, and held his gaze for rather too long.

'Do let me know if you need anything else, Riley,' she'd said, 'anything at all,' like the script from a bad 1970s porn movie. What was it with these Chelsea housewives? Was it boredom? Were they just looking for a workout that would be more fun than their regular Pilates, or was it the thrill of the risk they'd be taking that attracted them? Perhaps he was just imagining it, and all Mrs Ponsonby was offering was an organic chocolate-chip cookie.

As soon as Riley was finished here, he was going over to Mummy's Little Helper, where he'd been growing pots of daffodils for Monica's Café. The idea was to fill the place with flowers for the art class on the fourth of March, for Mary's fifteen-year anniversary. Monica was baking a cake. Lizzie, Alice's new friend from the nursery, had lived in the area back in Mary's day, so she'd offered to try to find some photos of her from the internet that they could mount on to cardstock.

Alice had changed a bit since Lizzie got involved in her life. She seemed a lot less tired and frazzled, as Bunty was sleeping properly since Lizzie had 'got her into a proper routine'. Riley didn't know what this really meant, but Alice had announced it as if Lizzie had split the genome. Riley didn't really know what a genome was either, but that was beside the point. Since Lizzie was doing lots of babysitting for her, Alice no longer had Bunty permanently welded to her hip. She'd also stopped staring at her phone so much. Apparently, 'Lizzie said' she needed to cut down on the whole social media thing. The way Alice kept starting every sentence with 'Lizzie says' was a bit annoying, to be honest.

Julian still had no idea that the party was happening. He probably wasn't even aware that Monica had made a mental note of the date he'd mentioned so casually, a while ago. Even Alice had managed to keep it secret. It was going to be a great surprise.

Lizzie

Lizzie had, so far, resisted the urge to poke through Alice's drawers. It seemed a little disloyal. She had no such loyalty towards Max, however, so she had a good rummage through his. She hadn't come across any indication that Max was playing around – no dubious receipts in pockets, lipstick on collars or hidden mementos. Lizzie was an expert at sniffing out infidelity – like a pig rooting for truffles. She was relieved. Alice, despite being a flibbertigibbet, had a good heart and did not deserve to be messed around. She wasn't letting Max off the hook entirely, however. If it wasn't a woman keeping him away from home so much, it was neglect and disinterest in his exhausted wife and young baby.

Lizzie had also been keeping an eye on the recycling. Alice and Max were getting through a rather large number of wine bottles, and she suspected that Alice was drinking the lion's share. But, on the upside, she was rather pleased to note the number of bottles decreasing since she'd managed to get Bunty settled into a more predictable and manageable routine.

Finally, she'd had a quick poke in the bathroom bin. Always interesting. And this one did not disappoint. She found an empty pack of sleeping pills (no wonder Max was no use with the night-time feeds) and one used pregnancy test. It was negative, thank the Lord. That might have just tipped Alice over the edge. And at least she and Max were still having sex.

Now she was having a great deal of fun doing Google searches on Alice's laptop, looking for photos of Julian's dead wife. She loved rummaging around the internet. It was like one giant knicker drawer, just waiting to spill all its secrets. She'd had a quick check on the browsing history. Max had, predictably, been looking at some porn, but nothing too distasteful or illegal.

She'd searched under Mary and Julian Jessop, and had found a wonderful photo of them on their wedding day, standing on the steps of Chelsea Town Hall. She was wearing a white mini-dress and white high-heeled boots, and he was dressed in an extremely dapper white suit, with flared trousers and a purple silk shirt. They were both laughing uproariously. She sent the picture off to Alice's printer. Under the wedding photo she found a mention of Mary's maiden name: Sandilands. She opened the Google search engine again, and this time typed in Mary Sandilands. Now that was even more interesting.

Lizzie heard the key in the lock and quickly closed down the page she was on.

'Hi Lizzie! Is everything OK?' asked Alice.

'All fine and dandy. I gave Bunty some baby rice and apple puree and she went out like a light, bang on time. I doubt you'll hear a peep from her until 6 a.m.'

'You are an angel,' Alice said, as she took off her cashmere coat and hung it on the hook by the door, shook off her vertiginous heels, and sat down at the kitchen table next to Lizzie. Max had gone straight upstairs. She heard the door of his study closing.

'How was date night?' Lizzie asked her.

'Fine, thank you,' replied Alice, not entirely enthusiastically, Lizzie thought. 'Fabulous new restaurant, just down the road. Super trendy. Hazard was there too, with a *girl*. Stunning one. How did you do with the photos?'

'Great. I've got some lovely ones. Mary was a knockout. Reminds me a bit of Audrey Hepburn. All wide-eyed and innocent-looking, like Bambi. Have a look.'

She was sitting in bed listening to Jack snore. Sometimes, the noise would stop for what seemed like ages, and she'd wonder if he'd died, and if so, how much she'd care. Then, like a car engine firing violently into life, he'd start up again.

She scratched her head. Damn. She was pretty sure that one of those little buggers at the nursery had given her head lice again. Should she sleep in the spare room until she'd napalmed them? She looked at Jack's nearly bald head. The likelihood of a stray louse finding anywhere to hide there was remote. She didn't want to have another parasite discussion with him. It had taken him weeks to get over the threadworm incident.

She reached into her own knicker drawer – chuckling to herself at the irony – and pulled out the notebook she'd picked up at the nursery. It was her turn to write in it now, and she knew exactly what to say.

Hazard

It was six days after *the wedding*, and Hazard felt, finally, that things were back on track. He'd recovered physically from his bender, and he felt more resolved than ever. Throwing himself off the wagon so spectacularly had reminded him why life was so much better on it. He'd also learned that 'just the one' was a mirage he was never going to be able to touch.

Hazard's business was growing nicely and he was, for the first time in as long as he could remember, feeling happy and *peaceful*. There was only one area of his life that he was concerned about. Apart from his new art-class friends, Hazard had no social life. Since he'd gotten sober, he'd become a bit of a recluse, and that state of affairs could not continue for ever. Hazard was also still a bit shaken about the fact that he'd very nearly kissed *Monica*. Not only was she absolutely not his type, but she was Riley's girlfriend, and Hazard didn't mess around with other blokes' girls. At least, not any longer.

The problem was, Hazard couldn't remember what his type actually *was*.

Hazard was trying to get a comb through the tangle of his hair, when he spotted, half hidden on his chest of drawers, like a message in a bottle, thrown into the sea of his ancient history and cast up on today's shore, a note. It read HER NAME IS BLANCHE, in his rather drunken handwriting. Then, underneath, in another, girlish hand, it said AND HER NUMBER IS 07746 385412. CALL HER.

Hazard smiled. Most women would have been furious if they'd found that note. Maybe there was more to Blanche than he'd remembered. He had been off his face, after all. And she was undoubtedly his type – stunning, blonde, confident and up for anything. He should call her. There was a new restaurant, super trendy, exactly the sort of place he loved, just down the road. They could go tonight, if she was free.

Hazard was right about the restaurant. It was exactly his kind of place – minimalist, industrial style, and filled with the beautiful people and the hubbub of gossip and one-upmanship. It was ghastly. He couldn't help thinking of his table at Monica's Café, and his old leather armchair under a standard lamp, surrounded by books. He looked over at his date, trying to see behind the wide blue eyes, but all he could see was his own face reflected back at him.

Blanche was pushing the endive and beetroot salad she'd ordered around her plate in a desultory fashion. She couldn't have eaten more than a few mouthfuls. Hazard, meanwhile, was *starving* and had polished off the tiny portions of food he'd been given with gusto. This was a new sensation for him. Hazard hadn't actually *eaten* in a fancy restaurant for years. He'd spent most of his time going backwards and forwards to the toilets to snort coke, then having to feign enthusiasm for food that tasted like cardboard.

'Don't you just *love* this place?' said Blanche, for the third time, shouting to be heard above the noise.

'Yup,' lied Hazard. Then, trying to make a bit more effort with the conversation, 'I wonder what my friend Julian would make of the artwork. He's an artist.' He gestured to the pointless, ugly installations hanging from the ceiling like children's mobiles designed by someone on acid.

'Ooh, an artist! Do I know him?' yelled Blanche.

'I doubt it. He's seventy-nine,' said Hazard. Blanche looked a lot less interested.

'Hazard, you're just *too sweet*, looking after a *geriatric*!' she tittered. 'You know, when I was at school we had to go and have tea with *old people* once a week as part of our community service. We called it "granny bashing".' She wiggled two sets of two fingers in the air. 'Not that we did bash anyone, obviously. We just sat, in rooms smelling of wee, listening to endless boring drivel about the olden days and counting the minutes before we could escape for a ciggie with our mates before going back to school.' She giggled, then looked thoughtful. 'Hey, do you think he'll leave you a *massive* bequest in his will?'

Hazard stared at her. He kept thinking about Monica, and how much more fun he'd be having if she were here. Which was weird, because 'fun' and 'Monica' were not words that you'd usually put together. Anyhow, they wouldn't be here. No way Monica would book a table at this place. He forced his concentration back to the mindless chit-chat about mutual acquaintances, soulless places and pointless status symbols.

It was quite clear to Hazard that he couldn't just slot into his old life again. He was a different shape now, and he didn't fit. And he just couldn't shake the thought, however hard he tried, that maybe where he did fit was with Monica. Monica, the strongest, and most vulnerable, woman he knew.

As soon as he could, Hazard paid the bill, wincing at the exorbitant price of the salad that Blanche hadn't eaten, and left her with some friends she'd spotted at the bar. Over the other side of the restaurant he could see Alice and her husband having dinner. How wonderful that, even after marriage and children, you could still share a romantic dinner like that, and be so comfortable in each other's company that you didn't even have to talk.

Hazard walked out on to the Fulham Road and past Monica's Café. A light was on in her flat above. She was probably up there with Riley having wild, Australian sex.

He walked on towards his empty, quiet, safe home.

Alice

Alice was still feeling a bit *meh* after her 'date night' with Max. In a burst of determination to bring back the romance in her relationship, after the conversation she'd had with Monica on the train, she'd booked a table for two at the new restaurant down the road. She'd made the mistake of telling Max, as they'd arrived, that they were both banned from talking about anything to do with Bunty. The problem was, neither of them seemed to be able to remember what they'd talked about before Bunty had blessed their lives. They'd had several awkward periods of prolonged silence, and Alice realized, to her horror, that they'd morphed into one of those couples they'd derided when they first got together, who sat in a restaurant with *absolutely nothing to say to each other.*

Alice took a photo and loaded it to her Instagram page. It was the first she'd posted for three days. She was trying to rein it all in. This photo she couldn't resist, though, because Monica's Café looked beautiful. They'd lit loads of tea light candles, and the tables were filled with daffodils. On the centre table were several gorgeous pictures of Julian and Mary, a lemon drizzle cake (Julian's favourite) and some bottles of Baileys.

'I'm starting to fret now,' said Monica. 'Do you think it's all a bit morbid, having a party for someone who's *dead*? Should we clear it all away quickly before Julian gets here?'

'No, it's lovely,' said Hazard. 'It's really important to celebrate the lives of people we've loved. And, anyway, isn't that what Julian's been doing every Friday at 5 p.m. for the last fifteen years? Only now he has friends to celebrate with him.'

Alice was surprised at Hazard. She hadn't thought him such a softie. That man was a mass of contradictions. If it weren't for Max, she'd be the teeniest bit in love with him by now. As she looked at him, she saw him frown. She followed his gaze over to where Riley was giving Monica a hug. Interesting. The things you noticed when you weren't looking through an iPhone screen. Who knew?

Everything was ready, and it was past seven o'clock. The whole class was assembled, waiting expectantly. The only thing missing was Julian.

'Julian's never late for the art class,' said Monica, rather ignoring the evidence to the contrary. 'The only thing he takes incredibly seriously is his class. Oh, and fashion, obviously. And that scruffy dog.'

'He's not a dog, darling,' said Riley in an uncanny impression of Julian. 'He's a *masterpiece*. Do you think we might get stuck into the Baileys anyway? He can catch up.'

'Sure,' said Monica, looking over towards the door again.

By half past seven, the mood was starting to fall a little

flat. They kept trying to distract Monica, but it wasn't working. Alice picked up her phone and loaded up Julian's Instagram page.

'Monica, I've tracked down our star guest,' she said. 'He's just posted a photo of himself with the cast of some reality TV show in Sloane Square.'

'Bloody hell. What a total *wanker*,' said Monica. Alice hadn't heard her sound so cross since the time she'd thrown her out of this very café on Christmas Day. 'And he's not answering my calls.'

'I'll message him via Insta,' said Alice. 'I bet he's checking that.'

JULIAN. GET YOUR BONY ARSE DOWN TO MONICA'S RIGHT NOW OR SHE WILL EXPLODE. LOVE ALICE, she typed as she watched Monica pacing up and down, winding herself tighter with every step.

It was eight o'clock before Julian finally showed up, looking way less apologetic than Alice imagined Monica was expecting. He was going to need to start grovelling pretty smartish. Alice knew how it felt to be in Monica's bad books, and it was not fun.

'So sorry, everybody! I hope you started without me! You'll never guess what happened . . . Goodness, what's all this about?'

'Well, we've thrown you a surprise party. We imagined that you might be feeling a bit *low* today, since it's the fifteenth anniversary of Mary's death, so we thought we'd help you remember her,' said Monica, in a voice that was pure steel. 'You'd forgotten the anniversary, hadn't you?'

'No, of course not!' said Julian, who obviously had. 'And

thank you all *so* much for all of this. I can't tell you how much it means to me.' Alice looked over at Monica, to see if Julian had succeeded in calming her down. Not a bit of it.

'What happened to *authenticity*, Julian? What happened to *sharing the truth*? Do you even know what the truth is any more?' she said. Everyone else had fallen silent, their gazes switching from Julian to Monica and back like a crowd watching a tense final at Wimbledon.

'OK, OK, Monica, I'm just a foolish old man, I'm sorry,' he said, not sounding entirely convincing, putting his hands up in front of him, as if to ward off an attack. Monica hadn't finished.

'Why are you spending all your time with your Instagram "friends"' – she put aggressive little air quotes around the word 'friends' – 'with shallow, B-list celebrities, for Christ's sake, rather than with the people who really care about you? You have no idea what friendship means.'

Alice was rather relieved when the door opened, thinking that a new arrival might help break the tension. And it did seem to stop Monica in her tracks.

She turned away from Julian, and stared towards the door, at the well-dressed, white-haired stranger who looked strangely familiar.

'This is a private party,' she said. 'Can I help you?'

'You must be Monica,' the newcomer replied, looking composed, despite the obvious tension in the room. 'I'm Mary. Julian's wife.'

Mary

Mary hadn't had a chance to open the post until the evening. Gus and William, Anthony's sons, had both been round for lunch with their wives and children. They had five children between them, whom she loved as if they were her own grand-children. Whenever their mothers weren't looking she slipped them pound coins, chocolate bars and cheesy Wotsits.

She'd adored playing the matriarch today. She'd watched them tucking into her roast lunch from her position at the head of the large, scrubbed-oak kitchen table, Anthony, her partner, at the other end. But, at seventy-five, she also found days like today rather exhausting.

The pile of post was, on the whole, unexciting. It usually was these days. Surprises were for the young. An electricity bill, the Boden catalogue, and a thank-you letter from a lady she'd had round for lunch the previous week. But there was also a slim package, hand-addressed, in writing she didn't recognize. The name on the front was Mary Jessop, a name she hadn't used for fifteen years. As soon as she'd left Chelsea Studios, she'd gone back to Mary Sandilands, which had been like rediscovering the girl she used to be.

She'd not just left her married name behind fifteen years ago, she'd left everything. She'd written a note explaining that, after years of putting up with the humiliation and pain of all the other women, she'd finally had enough. She'd also left a whole load of instructions, like how to work the washing machine, written on little pieces of paper and hidden around the cottage. She'd looked after Julian for so long that she knew he'd find it difficult to manage without her. Perhaps every time he found one of her messages he'd be reminded of how much she'd done for him. That thought had comforted her a little, until she'd realized that he'd probably moved in one of the models as soon as he'd cleared the cupboards of her clothes.

Some instinct told her to sit down before she opened the package, so she made herself comfortable in the kitchen armchair, put on her reading glasses and carefully cut open the tightly taped envelope with the kitchen scissors. Inside was an exercise book, covered in clear sticky-backed plastic, on the front cover of which were the words: *The Authenticity Project*. How strange. Why on earth had someone sent this to her? She opened the book to the first page.

She recognized the handwriting immediately. She remembered the first time she'd seen it. It had formed the words: *Dear Mary, I would be most honoured if you would join me at The Ivy for dinner on Saturday, 9 p.m. Sincerely, Julian Jessop.*

She'd thought everything about that writing glamorous and exciting. *The Ivy*, which she'd heard so much about, but never been to, not eating until 9 *p.m.*, and, most of all, the author of the words – Julian Jessop, the artist. She'd turned over the paper the words were written on, and on the other side was a sketch – just a few bold pencil strokes but, even so, unmistakeably her face.

Why her? She had absolutely no idea, but she was unbelievably grateful. And she remained grateful for almost forty years, until, one day, she discovered that her gratitude had left. And, not long afterwards, she followed.

She started to read.

I AM LONELY.

Julian? The sun around which they had all rotated, held in place by his gravitational pull. How could Julian be *lonely*? *Invisible*?

Then she read the next words: *Mary . . . died at the relatively young age of sixty.* The bastard. He'd bumped her off. How dare he?

She supposed she shouldn't be entirely surprised. Julian had always had a rather flexible and creative relationship with the truth. It was his ability to rewrite events in his head to suit his requirements that had allowed him to lie to Mary for so long. All those artist's models who he'd *only painted, never anything more, how could she even suggest such a thing?* She was *deluded, paranoid, jealous.* And yet, the smell of sex, mixed with paint, had hung in the air with the dust motes. She'd never been able to smell oil paints since without being reminded of betrayal.

She'd spent years, decades, avoiding reading the gossip columns and ignoring the way chattering groups fell silent when she entered the room, before subjects were rapidly changed. She tried not to notice the pitying looks from some women, and the hostile glances from others.

Then, swiftly following on from Julian's latest great untruth, a simple truth: *I had to be the most loved . . . I took Mary for granted.*

And that, she realized, was why she had stayed for so long: he had made her feel less than him, as if he were so much better than her in every single way, that she should feel happy just to be allowed to share his life, to hang in his firmament.

It was a relatively small event that had tipped the balance.

She'd come home early, still dressed in her midwife's uniform, after an expected delivery had turned out to be Braxton Hicks contractions. Julian was sprawled across the sofa, wearing nothing but an artist's smock and smoking a Gauloises. Delphine, the latest of his models, was standing next to the fire, naked apart from a pair of stilettos, and playing Mary's viola, badly.

Other women had played with her husband for years, but nobody played her viola. She threw Delphine out, ignoring Julian's standard protestations about *art* and *muse* and her *overactive imagination* and *it's only a bloody viola.*

Mary had spent years thinking that Julian would eventually *grow out* of all the womanizing, that one day he'd just discover he didn't have the desire, or the energy, or that he'd lost his allure. But the only thing that changed was the age gap between herself and Julian's girls. The latest one, she estimated, must be thirty years younger than she was. The next day, while Julian was painting the

Countess of Denbigh in Warwickshire, she left her little household notes and him.

She'd never looked back.

A year later, she'd met Anthony. He'd adored her. Still did. He told her constantly how lucky he was to have found her. He made her feel special, loved and secure. He'd never made her feel grateful, but she was – every single day.

She'd tried calling Julian about a divorce, and had written to him several times, but she'd not had any response, so she'd eventually given up. She didn't need an official piece of paper to feel safe with Anthony, and marriage hadn't worked out terribly well for her the first time.

Sometimes she'd wondered if Julian were dead. She'd not heard anything about him for so long. But pride stopped her from Googling him, or seeking out anyone who might know where he was or what he was up to. Anyhow, as his official next of kin, surely she'd have been informed if he'd died?

She read through the stories following Julian's in the book pretty quickly, unable to concentrate properly, trying – but failing – to not make snap judgements:

Monica – try to relax a little more.

Hazard – brave man, confronting your demons.

Riley – sweet child, hope you get your girl.

Alice – you have no idea how lucky you are having that baby.

There was only one story left. A short one. It must have been written by whoever had posted her the book. The writing was unashamedly large and loopy, and there was a smiley face in the 'o' of 'love'.

Dear Mary,

My name is Lizzie Green. Here is my truth: I am extremely curious. Some might say nosey. I love people – their quirks, their strengths and their secrets. Which is how I found you. Not dead at all, but living in Lewes.

Another thing you should know about me is that I hate deceit. I will defend anyone to the hilt, so long as they are honest, with me and with themselves. And Julian, as you know, has not been honest.

If there is one thing The Authenticity Project should achieve, it's making its creator be more authentic.

So, that's why I've sent you this book, and that's why I'm telling you that Julian teaches an art class at Monica's Café every Monday evening at 7 p.m.

With love,
Lizzie

Julian

How was it possible to feel so horrified that she was here, and yet so thrilled to see her simultaneously? The conflicting emotions churned together like the two colours in a lava lamp. She was different, of course she was – it had been fifteen years. Her face had – drooped – a little. But she was as straight, tall and strong as a silver birch, luminous.

Had she always been like that, and he'd just failed to notice, or had she only become like that since she left? And then, an uncomfortable realization: perhaps it was he who'd destroyed it – that luminescence. It was what had drawn him to Mary in the first place, and then he had snuffed it out.

He remembered the first time he'd seen her, in the cafeteria at St Stephen's Hospital. He'd broken his toe climbing over the wall to the studios, having lost his keys. He'd heard one of the other midwives call her name – *Mary*. He'd not been able to stop looking at her, so he drew her portrait on a page of the sketch book he always carried with him, wrote an invitation to dinner on the other side, tore it out and placed it on her tray as he hobbled past.

'Hello, Mary,' he said now, 'I've missed you.' Three words that couldn't even begin to describe fifteen years of regret and loneliness.

'You killed me,' she replied.

'Your leaving killed *me*,' he said, clutching on to the nearest chair for support.

'Why did you lie, Julian?' asked Monica. Gently, this time. Mary answered before he could.

'He just wanted you to like him. All he's ever wanted is for people to like him. You see . . .' She paused, searching for the right words. The only sound in the café was from the traffic, still trundling up and down the Fulham Road. 'If the truth wasn't how he wanted to see himself, he'd change it. Like adding more colour to a painting to cover over the imperfections. Isn't that right, Julian?'

'Yes, although it wasn't just that, Mary,' he said, then stopped, looking like a fish gasping for air.

'Carry on, Julian,' said Monica.

'I guess I found it easier to believe you were dead than to constantly remind myself that I'd driven you away. All the women, all the lies. I'm sorry. I'm so, so sorry,' he said.

'You know, it wasn't just the women, Julian. I was used to that. It was the way you made me feel so *insignificant*. You have such energy. You're like the sun. When you're interested in someone, you turn your rays towards them and they luxuriate in your warmth. But then you turn somewhere else, leaving them in the shadow, and they spend all their energy trying to recreate the memory of the light.'

Julian hardly dared to look at Monica, his new friend who he'd let down, just as he'd let down so many others over the years.

'I didn't mean to hurt you, Mary. I loved you. I still do,' he said. 'When you left, my world fell apart.'

'That's why I'm here. I read your story, in the book.' He noticed, for the first time, that she was holding The Authenticity Project in her hand. How on earth had she got hold of that? 'I'd thought you'd barely notice my absence, that one of the many girls would slot into my place. I had no idea you'd found it so hard. I was angry with you, but I never wanted you to suffer.'

She walked over to him, put the book down on the table and took both his hands in hers. 'Sit down, you old fool,' she said. And they both sat at the table. Monica brought them over a bottle of the Baileys and some glasses.

'You know, I never drink this stuff any more,' Mary said. 'Too many memories. Anyhow, it tastes ghastly. I don't suppose you have any red wine do you, my dear?'

'Don't worry, Monica, I got the Baileys on sale or return,' Julian heard Riley say, as if it mattered.

'Julian, we're going to go now, to give you some space,' said Hazard. Julian nodded at him and waved absent-mindedly at his students, as Hazard ushered them out. Only Monica and Riley stayed behind, clearing up the detritus of the party.

'Are you happy, Mary?' he asked, realizing that he really wanted her to be.

'Very,' she replied. 'After I left, I learned to be my own sun. I found a lovely man, a widower, Anthony. We live in

Sussex.' OK, of course he wanted her to be happy, but not *too* happy.

'And you look happy too,' she said, 'with all these new friends. Just remember to treat them well, and don't get side-tracked by all that *nonsense* again.'

Monica came over with a bottle of red wine and two wine glasses.

'Maybe it's just too late for me to change,' said Julian, feeling rather sorry for himself.

'It's never too late, Julian,' said Monica. 'After all, you're only seventy-nine. You've got loads of time left to finally get it right.'

'Seventy-nine?' said Mary. 'Monica, he's eighty-four!'

Monica

The Authenticity Project was based on lies. Monica's friendship with Julian, which had grown to take up so much of her life of late, was not what it seemed. What else had Julian lied about? And she'd just spent hours planning and executing a memorial for someone who wasn't dead.

It was nearly midnight by the time Julian and Mary left the café.

Mary had hugged her as she'd gone. 'Thank you, for looking after my Julian,' she'd whispered in Monica's ear. Her breath was like the memory of a summer breeze. She'd squeezed Monica's hand, her skin rendered so soft and fragile by the passing of the years. Then the door closed behind Mary and Julian, the bell announcing their departure with a desultory chime. And with them went half a century of love, passion, anger, regret and sadness, leaving the air behind them feeling thinner.

Monica felt terrible about the assumptions she'd made; that Mary was insipid, a doormat, and far less interesting than her husband. The Mary she'd met that evening was wonderful – she radiated warmth, and yet her softness covered a core strength, strength that had enabled her to walk away from nearly forty years of marriage and start all over again.

Riley followed Monica up to her flat.

'Blimey. What an evening. That was all a bit *intense*, don't you think?' he said. Monica bristled at the way he'd distilled an evening of such high emotion so casually. 'Who d'you think sent Mary the book?'

'It must have been Lizzie,' said Monica. 'She found the notebook at the nursery after it fell out of Alice's bag. That's how she ended up helping with Bunty.'

'Do you think it was a bit *mean* of her to land Julian in it like that?' Riley asked.

'Actually, I think she did him a favour, forcing him to confront his lies. He was different by the time he left this evening, wasn't he? Less bluster and show, more real. I think he'll be a much nicer, and happier, person from now on. And maybe he and Mary can be friends.'

'I guess. Although I always rather liked him as he was. Do you have anything to eat? I'm ravenous.'

Monica opened her kitchen cupboard which was embarrassingly bare.

'I've got some cooking chocolate, if you'd like some,' she said, breaking off a square and putting it in her mouth, feeling her energy returning with the infusion of sweetness. Now the tension had dropped she realized how hungry and exhausted she was.

'Monica, *stop*!' said Riley. 'You can't eat that. It's poisonous.'

'What on earth are you talking about?' asked Monica, her mouth full of chocolate.

'Cooking chocolate. It's poisonous until it's cooked.'

'Riley, did your mother tell you that when you were little?'

'Yes!' he replied. She watched the penny drop. 'She lied to me, didn't she? To stop me stealing the chocolate.'

'That's one of the things I love so much about you. You always assume that people are good and telling the truth, because that's how you are. You always think that things will turn out well and, because of that, they generally do. By the way, did she tell you that when the ice-cream van played music it meant they'd run out of ice cream?'

'Yes, she did actually,' he replied. 'I do have a dark side, you know. Everybody thinks I'm so bloody nice, but I have as many evil thoughts as the next man. Honestly.'

'No, you don't, Riley,' she said, sitting down next to him on the sofa. 'There's so much I love about you,' she said, passing him a few squares of chocolate, 'but I don't love you.'

Monica remembered what she'd overheard Mary saying, about learning to be her own sun. She remembered the conversation with Alice on the train. *There are advantages to being single.* She didn't need anyone else to orbit around. She didn't need a baby either. *A baby doesn't make the happy ever after.* She knew what she had to say.

'I can't come travelling with you, Riley. I'm sorry. I need to be here, with my friends, and the café.'

'I was kind of expecting you to say that,' Riley said, looking uncharacteristically defeated. He placed the chocolate down on the coffee table like an unwanted consolation prize. 'I understand, Monica. I'd originally planned to go alone, in any case. I'll be OK.' And she knew he would. Riley would always be OK. 'And if you decide you've made a terrible mistake, you can always come and find me in Perth.'

'We can still be friends until you go, can't we?' she asked him, wondering if she had, indeed, made a terrible mistake. Surely this was what she'd always wanted, and now she was just throwing it away.

'Sure,' he replied, as he stood up and walked to the door.

She kissed him. It was a kiss that said much more than goodbye. It said sorry, and thank you, and I very nearly love you. But not quite.

And she didn't want to live with not quite.

Riley left, taking all her daydreams with him. The two of them standing on the Bridge of Sighs in Venice, swimming in a secluded cove on a perfect Greek island, kissing in a bar in Berlin while a band played. Riley teaching their children to surf. Monica taking them back to Fulham to show them the café where it all started.

Monica sat down on the sofa, feeling very, very tired. She looked over at the photo of her mum on the mantelpiece, laughing into the camera. She remembered when she'd taken it – on a family holiday in Cornwall, just weeks before the diagnosis.

I know I don't need a man, Mum. I know I shouldn't compromise. I can look after myself, of course I can.

But sometimes I just wish I didn't have to.

Hazard

It was a week since Hazard's disastrous date with Blanche, and his realization about Monica.

He'd thrown himself into his work, taking on all the most back-breaking gardening jobs himself, as a form of distraction. He'd stopped using the café as an office, and was shocked how much he missed his working sessions and games of backgammon with Monica.

It was ironic that, after all those weeks of matchmaking, the only person he really wanted her to be with was him.

But he'd blown it.

His memory of the wedding was patchy at best, but one scene stayed with him, in startling clarity, replaying over and over in his head: *Get a fucking life, Monica, and stop being such a bore. You are not my mother, or my wife, or even my girlfriend, and thank fuck for that.* Or something along those dreadful lines.

She'd been lovely to him the day after, and perfectly friendly ever since. She didn't seem to bear a grudge, but

350

there was no way she'd ever consider going out with him now she'd seen him at his worst.

Anyhow, she was going travelling with Riley. Good old Riley, who was the complete opposite from him – trustworthy, honest, uncomplicated, kind and generous.

If he really cared about Monica, he should be happy for them. Riley was obviously the right man to choose. But Hazard wasn't that nice, that was part of the problem. He was damaged and selfish. And he really, really wanted Monica for himself.

Everything about Riley was annoying him, from the stupid Australian accent, to the way he whistled as he worked. *Snap out of it, Hazard. It's not his fault. Riley's done nothing wrong.*

He turned to Riley, whistling happily alongside him. 'So, where are you and Monica going to visit first?' he asked, despite knowing that this conversation was going to hurt.

'Actually, mate, she's not coming with me after all,' Riley replied. 'She says she's got too much going on here, so I'm going on my own, unless I can persuade Brett to tag along.'

Hazard tried really hard not to look at Riley, or to give away any clue as to quite how much this casually uttered sentence meant to him. He was aware that he should reply to Riley or run the risk of seeming rather uncaring, but he knew if he did, he'd give himself away.

Was it at all possible that Monica was staying in London because of him? He very much doubted it, but perhaps it was *a sign*. It was certainly an *opportunity*, and one he couldn't let just slip through his hands. He had to at least talk to her, before he drove himself crazy.

As Hazard pulled giant thistles from the overgrown flower bed, he thought about what he might say.

I know I'm a rude, egotistical bloke with addiction issues who was unforgivably horrible to you recently, but I think you're wonderful, and we'd be really good together, if you'd just give me a chance? Not exactly selling himself.

Monica, I love everything about you, from your strength, ambition and principles, to the way you care so much about your friends and your obsession with your food standards hygiene rating. If you'll just give me the opportunity, I'll do everything I can to be worthy of you? A bit too needy, perhaps.

Monica, all those things you wrote about – wanting a family and children and the whole fairy-tale – well, maybe I could want that too. Mmmm. The truth was, he was still trying to get his head around that one, and he was determined to be honest. Was he ever going to be grown up and responsible enough to be a father? Besides, he wasn't sure that bringing up what she'd written in the book was a good idea; she was rather sensitive about it, as he and Riley had both discovered.

Maybe he should just turn up at her flat and play it by ear. After all, what did he have to lose?

Hazard drove to Mummy's Little Helper on autopilot. He had to drop off the gardening tools they'd been using. It was, however, impossible to get in and out of the place quickly, since he was always mobbed by his gardening buddies.

'Hey, Fin,' he said to the small, skinny boy helping him stack the tools in the shed, 'are you any good with girls?'

'Me? I'm the best!' said Fin, puffing out his chest. 'I have FIVE girlfriends. That's more even than Leo. And he has a PlayStation 4.'

'Wow. What's your secret? How do you let them know you really like them?'

'That's easy. I give them one of my Haribos. And you know what I do if I really, really like them?'

'What?' asked Hazard, leaning down to Fin's height.

Fin whispered, his breath hot in Hazard's ear, 'I give them the one shaped like a heart.'

Alice

'I wasn't sure you'd be here, Julian, what with Mary not being dead and everything,' said Alice, as she reached the Admiral's grave. 'Hi Keith,' she said, bending down to pat the dog's head. Keith looked rather put out, as if patting were an affront to his dignity.

'Mary, it turns out, hasn't been dead for the last fifteen years, dear girl,' said Julian, as if this were news to him, 'but I still came here. Not just to remember her, but to keep a link with the past – so much of which I'd left behind. I've brought this, instead of the Baileys though,' he said, pulling a bottle of red wine, some plastic glasses and a corkscrew out of his bag. 'I never really liked Baileys, and it turns out that even Mary doesn't drink it any more, so I don't think we need to.'

Alice, who'd secretly been emptying her glasses of Baileys into the undergrowth for the past few months, was rather relieved. She sat down on the marble, next to Julian, taking the glass of wine he handed her. The graveyard was filled with bluebells, and blossom was falling from the trees like

354

snow. Spring, a time for new beginnings. She took Bunty out of her pushchair, and sat her on her knee. Bunty reached out for one of the flowers, clutching it in her fat fist.

'Alice, dear, can I tell you about my new idea?' he said. She nodded, a little nervously. You never knew quite what Julian was going to come up with next. 'I've been thinking about The Authenticity Project, about why I started it, how lonely I was. And I know there are so many people out there feeling just the same, spending whole days without talking to anyone, and eating every meal by themselves.' Alice nodded. 'Then I remembered Hazard talking about his stay in Thailand and how, although he was on his own, the place he was staying at had a communal table and everyone ate together every night.'

'Yes, I remember that,' said Alice. 'It's a great idea. Think of all the different people you'd meet, the conversations you'd have.'

'Exactly,' said Julian. 'So, I thought, why don't we do that once a week at Monica's? We could invite anyone who has no one to eat with, for dinner around one big table. We could charge ten pounds a head, bring your own bottle. And I thought we could ask anyone who can afford it to pay twenty pounds, so anyone who *can't* afford it can eat for free. What do you think?'

'I think it's brilliant!' said Alice, clapping her hands. Bunty laughed, and clapped her hands too. 'What does Monica say?'

'I haven't asked her yet,' replied Julian. 'Do you think she'll go for it?'

'I'm sure she will! What will you call it?'

'I thought maybe *Julian's Supper Club.*'

'Of course you did. Look, there's Riley.'

'Riley, my boy, sit down,' said Julian, handing him a glass of wine. 'I've been wanting to talk to you,' said Julian. 'It's my birthday on the thirty-first of May, just a few days before you leave. I thought I'd throw a party, a send-off for you, and a thank you to all of you for putting up with me. What do you say?'

'That would be awesome!' said Riley. 'You're going to be *eighty*. Wow.'

'But Julian,' said Alice, 'you said you were born on the day we declared war on Germany, and I know for a fact that was in September, not May.' Alice had won the history prize at school. It had been her greatest (and only) academic achievement.

Julian coughed, and looked a little bashful. 'You do know your history, don't you, my dear? Yes, I might have miscalculated the month slightly. And the year, in fact. I'm not going to be eighty, more like eighty-five. The day after war was declared was actually my first day at primary school. I was furious that no one wanted to hear how it went. Anyhow,' he said, moving swiftly on, 'I thought we could have a party in Kensington Gardens, between the bandstand and the Round Pond. I always used to have my birthday parties there. We'd gather up all the nearby deckchairs and fill large buckets with Pimm's, lemonade, fruit and ice, then anyone with an instrument would play, and we'd stay until it got dark and the Parks Police threw us out.'

'That sounds like a totally perfect way to say goodbye to London,' said Riley. 'Thank you.'

'It's an absolute pleasure,' said Julian, beaming. 'I'll get Monica organizing.'

Julian

Julian couldn't quite believe that Mary was sitting *in his cottage*, next to the fire, drinking tea. He scrunched his eyes up really small, to make his vision go blurry, and it was just like they were back in the nineties, before everything had gone wrong. Keith wasn't quite as happy about the situation though; Mary was sitting in his chair.

Mary had come round to collect some of her things. She'd taken very little, saying it wasn't good to immerse yourself too much in the past. This was a new concept for Julian. He steeled himself to have the conversation he knew was necessary. If he didn't do it now, she'd be gone, and he may never find the right moment again.

'I'm sorry about the whole *death thing*, Mary,' he said, not sure if that had come out quite right. 'I honestly didn't see it as lying. I'd spent so many years imagining you dead, that I'd started to think it was actually true.'

'I believe you, Julian. But why? Why kill me off in the first place?'

'It was easier than facing up to the truth, I suppose. What I should have done, obviously, is spend every hour of the day trying to track you down and make amends. But that would have meant facing up to how awful I'd been, and risking more rejection, so I . . . didn't,' he said, staring into his cup of tea.

'Out of interest,' said Mary, with a slight smile, 'how did I die?'

'Oh, I toyed with a few different versions over the years. For a while, you'd been hit by the number 14 bus, when on your way home from buying groceries at the market on the North End Road. The road outside the studios had been strewn with apricots and cherries.'

'Dramatic!' said Mary. 'Although not terribly fair on the bus driver. What else?'

'A particularly rare, but aggressive, form of cancer. I nursed you heroically through your final months, but there'd been nothing I could do to save you,' he said.

'Mmm. Unlikely. You'd make the most terrible nurse. You've never been good with illness.'

'Fair point. I'm quite proud of my latest version, actually. You were caught up in a shoot-out between rival drug gangs. You'd been trying to help a young man who'd been stabbed and was bleeding out on the pavement, but had been killed for your kindness.'

'Ooh, I like that one best. It makes me sound like a real heroine. Just make sure I was shot right through the heart. I don't want a slow, painful end,' she said. 'By the way, Julian.' Julian didn't like it when Mary started sentences with *by the way*. Whatever followed was never casual. 'On my way here I bumped into one of your neighbours. Patricia, I think she was called. She told me about the freehold, about wanting to sell up.'

Julian sighed. He felt like he used to in the old days, when Mary caught him out doing something unsavoury.

'Oh God, they've been badgering me about that for months, Mary. But how can I sell? Where would I go? What about all this?' He gestured expansively at all the possessions crowded into his living room.

'It's just *stuff*, Julian. You might find that, without it, you'll feel liberated! It'd be a new start, a new life. That's how it felt for me, leaving all this behind.' Julian tried not to bristle at the thought of Mary feeling 'liberated' from him.

'But there are so many memories, Mary. My old friends are all here. *You're here*,' he said.

'But I'm not here, Julian. I'm in Lewes. And I'm very happy. And you're welcome to come and visit us, any time you like. All these *things*, all these memories, they're just suffocating you, keeping you stuck in the past. You have new friends now, and home is wherever they are. You could buy a new flat and start afresh. Imagine that,' she said, staring at him intently.

Julian pictured himself in an apartment like the one Hazard lived in, where he'd gone for tea the week before. All those big windows, clean lines and clear surfaces. *Under-floor heating*. Pots filled with white orchids. Dimmer switches. The thought of himself somewhere like that was totally bizarre yet also strangely thrilling. Did he have the courage to clamber out of his rut at the age of seventy-nine? Or eighty-four. Whatever.

'Anyhow,' Mary continued, 'selling would be the right thing to do. It's not fair on your neighbours to hold out. You're messing up a lot of lives. Isn't it time you thought about other people, Julian, and did the honourable thing?'

Julian knew she was right. Mary was always right.

'Listen, I have someone else I need to see, so I'm going to leave you to think about it. Promise me you'll do that?' said Mary as she leaned forward to give him a hug, and planted a dry kiss on his cheek.

'OK, Mary,' he said. And he meant it.

Julian knocked on the door of number four. The door swung open to reveal an imposing woman with her hands on her hips and an inquisitive, but not friendly, expression.

They both waited for someone else to speak. Julian cracked first. He loathed an unfilled silence.

'Mrs Arbuckle,' he said, 'I believe you've been wanting to speak to me.'

'Well, yes,' she replied, 'for the last *eight months*. Why are you here now?' She spanned the word 'now' out for several beats.

'I've decided to sell,' he said. Patricia Arbuckle unfolded her arms and let out a long breath, like an airbag deflating.

'Well, I never,' she said. 'You'd better come in. What changed your mind?'

'Well, it's important to do the right thing,' said Julian, thinking that saying his new mantra aloud might help him to stick with his resolutions, 'and selling is doing the right thing. The rest of you have years ahead of you, and I can't be the one to rob you of your nest eggs. I'm sorry it's taken me so long to accept it.'

'It's never too late, Mr Jessop. Julian,' said Patricia, looking positively cheerful.

'You're not the first person to say that to me recently,' said Julian.

Monica

Monica put Julian's poster up in the window in exactly the same spot she'd posted her advertisement for an art teacher six months previously. She placed the tape carefully over the marks left by the last one, which she'd not been able to totally remove.

ARE YOU FED UP WITH EATING ALONE?

Join the communal table at

Julian's Supper Club,
Monica's Cafe

every Thursday, 7 p.m.
Bring Your Own Bottle
£10 per head, £20 if you're feeling flush
If you can't afford it, <u>you eat for free</u>

She remembered how Hazard had stolen her poster and photocopied it. She should ask him to copy this one and distribute it around Fulham by way of penance. She was just turning the sign on the door to CLOSED when a customer arrived. Monica was about to tell her that she was too late, when she realized that it was Mary.

'Hi, Monica,' she said. 'I've just been visiting Julian, so I thought I'd drop in so I could give you this.' She put her hand into her bag and pulled out the book that had been left in the café six months before. 'I tried to give it to Julian, but he said it only reminded him how *inauthentic* he'd been, and that you should have it.'

'Thanks, Mary,' said Monica, taking the book. 'Would you like a cup of tea? And cake? I think this calls for cake.'

Mary sat at the counter as Monica made up a pot of tea. 'I'm sorry I gave you all such a shock, turning up here like that,' she said. 'I'd thought I'd sneak quietly into the back of an art class, and talk to Julian privately. I hadn't expected to gatecrash a memorial service. Certainly not my own.'

'Honestly, please don't apologize!' said Monica, pouring the tea. 'How on earth were you to know? I'm just glad I got the opportunity to meet you.'

'Me too. I've realized that The Authenticity Project actually did me a bit of a favour. You see, I left the cottage without any explanations, or goodbyes, and I left a bit of myself behind too. All that history. And Julian, who is deeply flawed but, as you know, extraordinary. Seeing him again has helped me put some things to rest.'

'I'm glad,' said Monica.

'By the way, I hope you don't mind me asking, but have you sorted things out with that man who's so passionately in love with you?' Mary asked.

'Riley?' said Monica, thinking that 'passionately in love' was overdoing it somewhat. 'I'm afraid not. Quite the reverse, in fact.'

'No, no,' said Mary, 'not the sweet Australian boy, the other one. The one who was sitting right there' – she gestured over to the corner – 'like a brooding Mr Darcy, looking at Riley as if he'd stolen something that he desperately wanted back.'

'*Hazard?*' said Monica, astonished.

'Ah, so that was Hazard,' Mary replied. 'That figures. I've read his story in the book.'

'You're wrong about Hazard, Mary. He's not in love with me. We're total opposites, in fact.'

'Monica, I've spent a lifetime as an observer. I'm very quick to see things. And I know what I saw. He looked like a man who's a bit complex and damaged, and I know all about those.'

'Even if you were right, Mary,' said Monica, 'isn't that a very good reason to steer well clear?'

'Oh, but you're so much stronger than I was, Monica. You'd never let anyone treat you the way I let Julian treat me. And, you know, despite everything, I don't regret one single day I spent with that man. Not one. Now, I must get going.'

Mary leant over the bar and kissed Monica on both cheeks, and then she was gone, leaving Monica feeling strangely *elated*.

Hazard? Why was that thought not making her snort with derision? It was purely vanity. She was just enjoying the fact that Mary thought she was the kind of woman who inspired passion. Pull yourself together, Monica.

Monica picked up the exercise book, which had come full circle, from the counter. It occurred to her that almost everyone had read her story, but she'd read none of theirs, apart from Julian's. That hardly seemed fair. She poured herself another cup of tea and started to read.

Hazard

Hazard rang Monica's doorbell. It was nearly ten o'clock, rather later than he'd meant to turn up, but he'd twice changed his mind about coming. He still wasn't sure if he was doing the right thing, but one thing he wasn't was a coward. A tinny voice came through the intercom.

'Who is it?' Too late to back out now.

'Er, it's Hazard,' he said, feeling like a modern-day Romeo, trying to declare his love for Juliet. If only she had a balcony rather than an intercom.

'Oh. It's you. What on earth do you want?' It was hardly Shakespeare. Or the welcome he'd been hoping for.

'I really need to talk to you, Monica. Can I come up?' he said.

'I can't think why, but if you must.' She buzzed the front door and he pushed it open, then walked up the stairs to her flat.

He only had a hazy recollection of Monica's flat from the day he'd spent there after the disastrous wedding. He took in all the details, this time with a clear head. It was just as anyone who knew Monica at all would expect – neat as a pin and relatively conformist, with pale-grey walls, minimalist furniture and polished oak floorboards. There were, however, a few items showing unexpected flair, much like Monica herself – a lamp in the shape of a flamingo, an antique mannequin used as a coat stand, and a wall dominated by a fabulous painting of David Bowie. The faint smell of coffee beans seeped through the floorboards from below.

Monica was not looking at all happy to see him. This was obviously not good timing for his grand declaration. Backtrack! What other reason could he possibly give for turning up here so late? *Think*, Hazard.

It was no good, he'd just have to go for it.

'Well?' she said.

'Er. Monica, I wanted to tell you how I feel about you,' he said, pacing up and down, since he was too nervous to sit down, and she hadn't offered him a seat in any case.

'I know exactly what you think of me, Hazard,' she replied.

'You do?' he said, confused. Perhaps this was going to be easier than he thought.

'Uh huh. *She has an intensity to her that I find off-putting to the point of terrifying*. Does that ring any bells?' Only then did he see what she was holding. The book. She was reading his story.

'Or how about this? *She makes me feel that I must be doing something wrong. She's the sort of person who arranges all the tins in her cupboards so they're facing outwards, and puts all the books on her shelves in alphabetical*

367

order. I wondered why you asked me about my bloody *tins* the other day!'

'Monica, stop. Listen to me,' Hazard said, as he watched his dreams explode in a slow-motion car crash.

'Oh, I can't stop before the best bit! *She has an air of desperation that I might be exaggerating in my imagination because I've read her story, but it makes me want to run for the hills.*' And then she threw the book at him.

'That's the second time you've thrown something at my head. Last time it was a figgy pudding,' he said as he ducked. This wasn't going well, but God she was gorgeous when she was angry, a fireball of energy and righteous indignation. He had to make her listen.

'Go on, Hazard. Run for the fucking hills, why don't you? I'm not stopping you!'

'When I wrote all that, I didn't know you.'

'I know you didn't know me. So why did you feel qualified to make judgements about my kitchen cupboards, for fuck's sake?'

'I was wrong. Totally and utterly wrong. Not about the cupboards it turns out, but about everything else.' She glared at him. Humour wasn't going to work, obviously. 'You are one of the most incredible people I've ever met. Listen, what I *should* have written was this . . .'

He took a deep breath, and continued. 'I went to Monica's Café so I could return Julian's book. I had no intention of playing his stupid game. But, when I realized who she was – the woman I'd barged into a few nights before – I lost my nerve. I held on to the notebook and took it with me all the way to Thailand. I couldn't forget her story, so I decided to find the perfect man for her and send him in her direction. But then I started to realize that the perfect man was actually me. Not that I'm perfect, obviously, far from it.' He laughed. It sounded hollow. Monica didn't join in. 'I totally realize I don't deserve her, but I love her. Every last bit of her.'

'I *trusted* you, Hazard! I told you things about my life that I'd told no one – not even Riley. I thought you, of all people, would understand, not mock me,' said Monica, as if she'd not heard a word he'd said.

'Monica, I *do* understand. More than that, I love you *more* because of what you've been through. After all, it's the cracks that let the light in.'

'Don't misquote bloody Leonard Cohen at me, Hazard. Just get out. And don't come back,' she said.

Hazard realized that he wasn't going to get through to Monica today, if ever.

'OK, I'm going,' he said, backing towards the door, 'but I'll be at the Admiral, next Thursday at 7 p.m. Please, please, just think about what I said, and if you change your mind, meet me there.'

Hazard was walking the long way home, through Eel Brook Common. He couldn't face going back to his empty flat just yet. A man was sitting on a bench just ahead of him, lit up by a streetlamp and looking as miserable as Hazard felt. Hazard was sure he recognized him from somewhere. Probably the City. He was wearing the regulation bespoke suit, Church's brogues and a heavy Rolex watch.

'Hi,' said Hazard, then felt stupid. He probably didn't know this guy at all.

'Hi,' replied the man, shuffling along the bench so Hazard could sit down. 'You OK?'

Hazard sighed. 'Not really,' he said. 'Girl trouble. You know.' What was he doing? All this *sharing*. First Fin, and now some random bloke on a bench.

'Tell me about it,' replied the guy. 'I'm avoiding going home. You married?'

'No,' said Hazard. 'Right now I'm single.'

'Well, take my advice, mate, and stay that way. Once you get married, they rewrite all the rules. One minute you've got it made – sex on tap, the stunning wife who keeps your house looking beautiful and your friends entertained, then they change. Before you know it, they've got stretch marks, their boobs *leak*, the house is filled with garishly coloured plastic toys, and all their attention goes on the baby. And you're just the mug who's expected to pay for the whole shebang.'

'I hear what you're saying,' said Hazard, who'd decided that he didn't like his new confidant very much, 'and I'm sure marriage isn't easy, but the problem with me is when someone tells me what to do, I have a habit of doing the opposite.'

Hazard said an awkward goodbye. He felt rather sorry for the man's wife. Was he so perfect himself? What happened to 'for better for worse, in sickness and in health'? What an *arse*, frankly.

Then he remembered where he knew the guy from. He'd seen him not that long ago, in that terrible restaurant he'd gone to with Blanche. He'd been having dinner with Alice.

Riley

Riley had assumed that his life would go back to normal: simple, uncomplicated and easy. But it hadn't been like that. He'd been unable to forget about Monica. He felt like a tornado had whisked him off for a few months to a technicolour land, where everything was a little strange and *intense*, where he had no idea what lay around the next bend in the yellow brick road, and now he was back in Kansas feeling strangely . . . deflated.

Why had he given up so easily? Why hadn't he tried harder to convince Monica to come with him? Why had he not offered to stay here? He could travel around Europe, as planned, but then come back to London and pick up where he'd left off. Suddenly, it all seemed so obvious.

Riley shook off the lethargy that had plagued him for the last few days, and with a surge of energy, purpose and passion, left his flat and walked towards the Fulham Road. It was late, so the cemetery was locked up, but he barely noticed the extra distance he had to travel, he was so fired up with determination. Riley felt like he had joined the ranks of romantic heroes who would do anything to win their fair princess. He was Mr Darcy, he was Rhett Butler, he was Shrek. Maybe not Shrek.

As Riley neared Monica's flat, he could tell she was still awake. Her curtains were open, and the light from her sitting room shone out like a homing beacon. Riley crossed the road, and craned his neck, to see if he could see her.

He couldn't. But he could see Hazard. What was Hazard doing in Monica's flat so late at night?

Suddenly he felt very stupid. All those excuses about her responsibilities and her business, when the truth was that Monica was seeing someone else. All the times he and Hazard, his *friend*, had been gardening and Hazard kept bringing the conversation round to Monica. Now it made sense.

Was that why Hazard had invited Monica to the wedding? He'd thought it was a bit strange, but Riley had trusted him. Trusted them both. He shouldn't be surprised. Hazard with his rugged, dangerous good looks, his quick wit and his brilliant business acumen was the obvious choice.

How could he have been so naive? No wonder Monica couldn't love him.

Riley felt a wave of exhaustion engulf him. Since he'd first turned up here, at this café, he'd found a perfect Riley-sized space, in this wonderful city, amongst these extraordinary people. But now that space had closed up and he'd been spat out. An unwanted intruder, a foreign body. It was time to move on.

Riley turned back towards Earl's Court, a different man entirely from the one who'd left there barely half an hour ago. People thought that because Riley was so cheerful and sunny he didn't *feel*. But they were wrong. They were very wrong.

Monica

Monica looked at the long queue outside the café. Lizzie had done a brilliant job finding many of tonight's guests. She'd told Monica that the advantage of knowing the business of all of her neighbours was she knew exactly who lived alone and didn't get visitors, so she'd knocked on their doors and invited them along. Then, she'd gone to her GP and given her some fliers to hand out, then done the same with the librarian at Fulham Library and her friend Sue, who was a local social worker.

Monica opened the doors and welcomed everyone in. The café tables were arranged into a large square, with seats for around forty people. Mrs Wu and Benji were doing the cooking, Monica and Lizzie were waitressing, and Julian was playing host with Keith, the only dog who was now officially allowed in the café. Keith was sitting at his feet under the table, farting noxiously. Or maybe that was Julian.

Before long, the café was buzzing with conversation and laughter. The average age of the guests was around sixty, and, encouraged by Julian, everyone was sharing stories about the neighbourhood over the years.

'Who remembers the Fulham public baths and wash house?' asked Julian.

'Oh, I do, like it was yesterday!' said Mrs Brooks, who was possibly even older than Julian. Lizzie was giving Monica a running commentary on who was who. Mrs Brooks, apparently, lived just down the road from Lizzie, at number sixty-seven. Her husband had left her after 'that unfortunate incident with the gas man', and she'd been on her own ever since. 'We used to fill our prams and pushchairs with sheets, towels and bedspreads, and wheel them all down to the North End Road. It was a great excuse for a gossip, was wash day. We'd chat for hours, scrubbing away until our hands looked like prunes. I missed it when we finally got our own twin tub. It's a dance studio now, you know. I go there every week to practise my pliés.'

'Really?' asked Monica.

'No, of course not really!' said Mrs Brooks, with a cackle. 'I can barely walk. If I did a plié, I'd never get back up!'

'Who saw Johnny Haynes play at Craven Cottage?' asked Bert from number forty-three, somewhat predictably. Bert was a regular at the café, and every conversation Monica had had with him over the years was about Fulham Football Club. 'Did you know Pelé described him as the best passer of the ball he'd ever seen? Our Johnny Haynes.' He looked almost tearful, then took a large glug of Special Brew and seemed to rally.

'I used to drink with George Best, you know,' said Julian.

'That hardly makes you special. George drank with every-one!' replied Bert.

Mrs Wu beamed as her food was exclaimed over and ordered Benji around like a benevolent dictator. Monica wondered if he rued the day he'd been pulled into the bosom of the Wu family.

Monica recognized one of the men, tucking enthusiastic-ally into the sweet and sour chicken, as a local rough sleeper. Whenever they had leftovers at the café, she'd take them down to the towpath, under Putney Bridge, where she'd usually find him. She'd tucked Julian's leaflet into his last delivery.

'This is the best meal I've eaten in years,' he said to Julian.

'Me too,' said Julian. 'What's your name?'

'Jim,' he replied. 'Pleased to meet you. And thank you for my dinner. I wish I could pay you.'

'No need, dear chap,' said Julian, waving a hand dismis-sively. 'One day, when you're feeling wealthy, you can pay for your dinner and someone else's too. Now, you look like a man who appreciates good clothes. I don't usually let anyone near my collection, but if you pop by my cottage tomorrow, you can choose a new outfit. So long as it's not a Westwood. My generosity only goes so far.'

Monica sat down next to Julian and clapped her hands to quiet the room. No one paid her any attention.

'Everyone shut up!' barked Mrs Wu, creating an instant, shocked silence.

'Thank you all for coming,' said Monica. 'And a huge thank you to Betty and Benji for this delicious food, and, of course, to our wonderful host, the creator of this supper club, Julian.'

Monica looked at Julian, tipped back in his seat, smiling

broadly and enjoying the applause, cheers and whistles. Once everyone had resumed their own conversations, he turned to Monica.

'Where's Hazard?' he asked her.

'I have no idea,' she replied, although she did. She couldn't help herself checking her watch. 7.45 p.m. Maybe he was still waiting in the cemetery.

'Monica, Mary told me her theory. I'm such a fool, not seeing it. I'm always too wrapped up in myself. Riley is the most lovely boy, but that's what he is: just a boy, for whom life is easy. He's never had to deal with adversity. Hazard is more complicated. He's stood on the edge of the preci-pice and looked into the void. I know, because I've been there too. But he survived, and he came back stronger. He'd be good for you. You'd be good together.' He took her hand in his. She stared at his skin, lined by age and experience.

'But we're so very different, Hazard and I,' said Monica.

'And that's a good thing. You'll learn from each other. You don't want to spend the rest of your life just looking into a mirror. Believe me, I've tried it!' said Julian.

Monica absent-mindedly shredded the fortune cookie sit-ting in front of her into small crumbs, then, noticing what she'd done, swept them neatly on to a side plate.

'Julian,' she said, 'do you mind if I leave you to it? I have something I need to do.'

'Sure,' he said. 'We can manage. Can't we, Mrs Wu?'

'Yes! You go!' said Mrs Wu, waving both hands in front of her as if she were shooing a chicken off its nest.

*

377

Monica ran out on to the street, just as a number 14 bus was pulling away from the bus stop. She chased after it, banging on the door, and mouthing *please* at the driver, despite knowing that that never worked.

It worked. The bus driver stopped, and opened the doors to let her on.

'Thank you!' she said, and sank into the nearest seat. She checked her watch. 8 p.m. Surely Hazard wouldn't have waited a whole hour? And didn't the cemetery close at 8 p.m. anyhow? This was going to be a wasted journey.

Why hadn't Hazard just given her his mobile number and told her to call him? It would be easy enough to find his number, or his address, but now it felt as if destiny were somehow involved. If she missed this meeting then, quite simply, it wasn't meant to be. Monica knew this was entirely illogical and totally unlike her, but she seemed to have changed a lot over the past few months. The old Monica would never have considered getting romantically entangled with a *drug addict*, for a start. Where did *that* fit on her list of criteria?

Monica could see, as soon as she jumped off at the cemetery, that the wrought-iron gates were locked with a giant chain and padlock. She ought to be just a little bit relieved that she was too late. But she wasn't.

There were crowds of Chelsea football fans on the streets after a recent game, eating burgers from the temporary vans that had set up on the side streets. One very large, rather drunk man, dressed in head-to-toe Chelsea memorabilia, stopped and stared at Monica. This was all she needed.

'Smile, love!' he said, predictably. 'It might never happen, you know!'

'It won't ever happen if I can't get into that cemetery,' snapped Monica.

'What's in there? Apart from the obvious! I bet it's love. Is it love, love?' he asked her, guffawing at himself, and slapping his friend on the back, who spat a mouthful of beer all over the pavement.

'You know, I think it might be,' said Monica, wondering why on earth she was saying this to strangers when she hadn't even admitted it to herself.

'We'll get you over that wall, won't we, Kevin?' said her new friend. 'Hold on to this.' He passed Monica a half-eaten burger, oozing ketchup and mustard. She tried not to think of the grease on her fingers. In her rush to leave the café, she'd left her anti-bacterial hand gel behind. He picked Monica up as if she weighed nothing, and lifted her on to his shoulders. 'Can you reach the top of the wall from there?' he asked her.

'Yes!' she said, hauling herself on to the wall, so she sat with a leg on either side.

'Can you get down all right?'

Monica looked down. There was less of a drop on the cemetery side, and a pile of leaf mulch would soften her fall.

'Yes, I can! Thank you! Here, this is yours.' She passed him back his burger.

'If it all comes good, you can name your first child after me,' said the football fan.

'What's your name?' asked Monica, purely out of interest.

'Alan!' he replied.

Monica wondered how Hazard would feel about a son or daughter called Alan.

She took a deep breath and jumped.

Hazard and Monica

Hazard looked at his watch. Again. It was 8 p.m. and getting dark. He could hear the low thrum of an engine, as a car drove slowly down the central aisle. The only cars allowed in the cemetery were the Parks Police. They were closing up, and checking for stragglers. His time was up.

Hazard knew that he had to leave. He had to accept that Monica wasn't coming. She was never going to come. It was all just a ridiculous fantasy. Why had he thought this was a good idea? He could have just left her his mobile number and said, *Call me if you ever change your mind.* Why had he blurted out that stupid instruction to meet him, in a *graveyard* of all places? He'd obviously watched too many Hollywood movies.

And now, here he was, hiding from the police behind a gravestone, which was a bloody stupid thing to do, because now they'd be locking the gates. Monica wouldn't be able to get in anyway, even if she'd wanted to, and he'd be stuck here for the night, freezing his arse off amongst the ghosts.

Hazard pulled his overcoat around him and sat on the cold ground, leaning against the Admiral's tombstone, hidden from view. Yet he had absolutely no idea what he was going to do next. Then, he heard something:

'Oh, for fuck's sake. Of course he's not bloody here. Stupid woman.'

Hazard peered around the tombstone, and there she was, all cross and beautiful, and absolutely, unmistakeably, Monica.

'Monica!' he said.

'Oh, you are still here then,' she said.

'Yup. I was hoping you'd turn up.' Oh God, Hazard, the breaker of so many hearts over the years, the ultimate womanizer, had no idea at all what to say. 'I don't suppose you'd like a Haribo?' This was possibly the most important moment of his life and he was taking the advice of an eight-year-old. He was a total idiot.

'Hazard, are you a complete idiot? Do you think I just broke into a locked cemetery, breaking the law for the first time in my entire life, because I was looking for a bloody *Haribo*?'

Then she walked over to him and kissed him. Hard. Like she meant business.

They kissed until it was completely dark, until their lips were swollen, until they couldn't remember why they'd never done this before, until they couldn't tell where one of them stopped and the other one started. Hazard had spent nearly two decades chasing the ultimate high, the most efficient way of making his brain fizz and his heart pump harder. And here it was. Monica.

'Hazard?' Monica said.

'Monica?' he replied, just for the thrill of saying her name.

'How are we going to get out of here?'

'I guess we'll have to call the Parks Police and make up some reason why we're stuck in the cemetery,' he replied.

'Hazard, it's only been an hour, and you've already got me lying to the police. Where will it end?' she said.

'I don't know,' said Hazard, 'but I can't wait to find out.' He kissed her again, until she didn't care who she had to lie to, just so long as he didn't stop.

Monica knew that she wasn't at home. She could tell, even through her closed eyelids, that this room was brighter than hers, bathed in sunlight. It was quieter too – no noise from traffic on the Fulham Road or her ancient central heating system. And it smelled different – of sandalwood, peppermint and musk. And sex.

And that's when she started to remember, scenes from the night before playing out in her mind. In the back of the police car, Hazard's hand on her thigh. Hazard fumbling for his keys, which he'd dropped in his urgency to unlock the front door. Their clothes abandoned in a heap on the bedroom floor. Had she remembered to fold them before she went to sleep? She remembered frantic, breathless, urgent sex, followed by slower sex that didn't stop until the sun started coming up.

Hazard. She reached her foot across the wide expanse of Hazard's bed, searching for him. He wasn't there. Had he gone? Run off without even leaving a note? Surely she couldn't have got it all so terribly wrong?

She opened her eyes. And there he was, sitting in nothing but a pair of boxer shorts, emptying things from a drawer into a pile on the floor next to him.

'Hazard,' she said. 'What are you doing?'

'Oh, morning, sleepyhead,' he replied. 'I'm just making some space. For you. In case, you know, you have anything you want to keep here. In your own drawer.'

'Oh wow,' she said, laughing. 'Are you sure you're ready for that level of commitment?'

'You may jest,' said Hazard, crawling back into bed and kissing her gently on the mouth, 'but I've never given anyone a drawer before. I think I'm finally ready to take that leap.' He put his arm around her and she rested her head on his shoulder, breathing in the smell of him.

'Well, I'm truly flattered,' she said. And she was. 'And I think I'm ready to just go with the flow. You know, to take life as it comes.'

'Really?' said Hazard, raising a sceptical eyebrow.

'Well, I'm ready to *try*,' said Monica, grinning back at him. And, for the first time, she really wasn't worried about what happened next, because she knew, she just *knew*, with every fibre of her being, that this was where she belonged.

'OK, let's take it one drawer at a time,' said Hazard.

Alice

Alice had been waiting for the perfect moment to talk to Max, calmly and rationally, about the state of their marriage. Then, of course, she picked the very worst one.

Max had come back late, as usual, from the office. Alice had, for once, managed to prepare an evening meal, *from scratch*, but now it was overcooked and dried out. Bunty was teething, and had taken an age to settle, and Alice was exhausted.

They'd sat at the kitchen table, exchanging the sort of news of their respective days that you'd share with strangers. Max picked up his (unfinished) plate, took it over to the dishwasher, and left it on top of the counter.

'MAX!' yelled Alice. 'There is plenty of room IN the dishwasher. Why don't you EVER put anything IN the dishwasher?'

'Alice, there's no need to start shouting like a bloody fishwife. You've had too much to drink again, haven't you?' Max replied.

'No, I haven't had too much to BLOODY DRINK,' said Alice, who probably had, 'I've had TOO MUCH OF BLOODY YOU! I'm fed up of being the only one who ever loads the sodding dishwasher, the only one who ever picks up your wet towels off the floor, the only one who gets up in the night when Bunty wakes up, the only one who does any tidying, cleaning . . .' The list was so long that she ended it by waving her arms and going 'AAARRGGGHHHH!' like a proper grown-up.

'Do you even know how to use the washing machine?' Alice asked, glaring at her husband.

'Well no, but it can't be that difficult,' said Max.

'It's not DIFFICULT, Max!' yelled Alice. 'It's just mind-blowingly BORING. And I do it twice EVERY DAY!'

'But Alice, I have a *job*,' said Max, looking at her as if he had no idea who she was.

'AND WHAT DO YOU THINK THIS IS, MAX?' yelled Alice. 'I'M NOT EXACTLY SITTING AROUND ALL DAY HAVING MY NAILS PAINTED!' As she said it, she remembered she had, actually, had a manicure the day before while Lizzie looked after Bunty. But it was the first time in *months*. She clenched her fists to hide her nails. Then, somewhat to her alarm, she found herself crying. She sat down at the table, and put her head in her hands, forgetting about her nails.

'I'm sorry, Max,' she said between sobs. 'It's just I'm not sure if I can do this any more.'

'Do what, Alice?' he said, sitting down opposite her. 'Being a mother?'

'No,' she replied. 'Us. I'm not sure I can do us any more.'

'Why? Because I didn't put my plate in the dishwasher?'

'No, it has nothing to do with the fucking dishwasher, or at least not much, it's just I feel so alone. We're both parents to Bunty, and we live in the same house, but it's like we're strangers. I'm lonely, Max,' she said.

Max sighed. 'Oh, Alice. I'm sorry. But it's not just you who's found all this hard, you know. Frankly, this is not the way I saw my life either. I love Bunty, obviously I do, but I miss our perfect world. The weekends away in fancy hotels, the pristine house and my gorgeous, happy wife.'

'But I'm still here, Max,' said Alice.

'Yes, but you're cross and tired all the time. And, to tell the truth' – he paused for a few beats, as if weighing up whether or not to continue, then made the wrong decision – 'you've rather let yourself go.'

'LET MYSELF GO?' shouted Alice, who felt like she'd been punched. 'This is not the bloody 1950s, Max! You can't expect me to ping back into shape within months of giving birth to *your child*. That just doesn't happen in the real world.'

'And I feel left out,' said Max, who'd obviously realized that moving swiftly on was the only possible tactic. 'You know exactly how to deal with Bunty, what to do when, and how to do it. I feel useless. Surplus to requirements. So, I end up staying in the office for longer and longer, because there I know exactly what's expected of me, and people do what I say. They *respect* me. Everything happens on schedule. I'm in control.'

'I'm doing my best, Max, but I'm fed up with feeling like I'm not meeting expectations. Not yours, not your mother's, not Bunty's, not even my own. Marriage and family are all about compromise, surely? You have to work at it. It's not perfect and easy and beautiful, it's messy and exhausting and bloody difficult a lot of the time,' said Alice, waiting for Max to tell her he loved her, that he'd help more, that they could make it work.

'Maybe we could hire a nanny, Alice. For a few days each week. What do you think?' said Max.

'We can't afford that, Max, and even if we could, I don't want to pay someone else to look after my child just so I can spend more time keeping up the pretence of being your ideal wife in your ideal life,' said Alice, trying not to cry.

'Well, I don't know what the answer is, Alice. I just know that you're not happy and neither am I.' And he walked up the stairs to his office and closed the door, just like he always did.

Alice felt unbearably sad. She picked up her phone and scrolled through her Instagram page, looking at all the photos of her flawless world with the gorgeous husband and cute baby. Could she give up the mirage? Could she and Bunty cope on their own?

She thought of Mary, walking out on Julian after forty years, and looking so luminously happy. She thought of Monica, who, she'd learned yesterday, had dumped Riley, despite the fact that she was *nearly forty*. She thought of all her new friends, with their lives that didn't look beautiful on an Instagram square, yet who were so much deeper, stronger and more interesting than that.

She could be like that too. Couldn't she?

Surely it would be better to live a messy, flawed, sometimes not very pretty life that was real and honest, than to constantly try to live up to a life of perfection that was actually a sham?

Alice looked at her page again: @aliceinwonderland. *Real life fashion for real life mums and their babies. Smiley face.* Maybe she could show what real-life mums *really* looked like. She could post about the mess, the exhaustion, the stretch marks, the bulging tummy and the disintegrating marriage. She could ditch that irritating smiley face emoji too. What had she been thinking? Surely she couldn't be the only mother in the world who was fed up with trying to be perfect all the time?

The thought of ending the pretence was such a relief, like peeling off the control underwear at the end of the day.

I'm doing a great job. Or, at least, the best job I can, she told herself, since no one else was going to. *And if that's not good enough for Max, or for my Instagram followers, then they can go find someone else to stick on a sodding pedestal, because I can't stay up here any longer.*

Alice shifted Bunty on to her hip with one hand, and rang the doorbell with the other. Lizzie opened the door, revealing a warm, happily chaotic and cluttered home, just like the one Alice had grown up in. Max would sneer at it, thought Alice, which reminded her why she was here.

'Lizzie, I'm so sorry to bother you so late,' she said, 'but could Bunty and I possibly stay for a few days? Just until we work out what to do?'

Alice really hoped Lizzie wouldn't ask her any questions, because she hadn't yet worked out any of the answers. All she knew was that she needed some space to think, away from Max. Away from all the expectations and recrimin-ations. Lizzie must have understood this, because, for once, she kept her curiosity at bay. Alice was sure that wouldn't last for long.

'Of course you can, duck,' she said, ushering Alice in and closing the door firmly behind her.

Monica

Monica sat, holding a glass of Pimm's, her back against a tree in Kensington Gardens. She saw a couple standing on the edge of their group. They were holding hands and looked entirely self-contained.

'Julian. I'm so pleased you invited Mary!' she said.

'Yes. And her boyfriend. Can you call someone a boyfriend when they're nearly eighty? It sounds like a contradiction in terms.'

'He's definitely what you'd describe as a silver fox, isn't he?' said Monica. 'As are you, of course,' she added quickly, knowing that Julian's pride would be hurt otherwise.

'He seems like a nice enough chap, if you like that kind of thing,' said Julian. 'A little bland, but hey ho. I'd better introduce him to everyone.'

Julian walked over towards Mary and Anthony, followed by Keith. Both of them looking a little stilted and arthritic. 'Keith's not a dog,' she heard him say to Anthony, 'he's my personal trainer.' Benji came over and sat next to Monica.

'Monica, I wanted to tell you something,' he said. 'I don't want to steal Julian and Riley's thunder, but I can't keep it secret from you any longer.' She suspected she knew what he was going to say.

'Baz and I are getting married.' Yay! Just as she'd hoped. The next sentence was, however, a surprise. 'And we'd very much like you to be our best man. Or best woman. Best person. Whatever. Will you? Please say yes!'

'Oh Benji, I'm so thrilled for you,' she said, throwing her arms around him. 'I'd be totally honoured.'

'Hurrah! I can't wait to tell Baz! Betty thinks the wedding is all her idea, obviously. She's already planning the menu for the reception. We're getting hitched at Chelsea Town Hall – like Julian and Mary, but with a happier ending, I hope. Then we're having a party at Betty's restaurant.'

'So Betty's completely relaxed about the whole thing now?' Monica asked.

'She seems to be,' Benji replied. 'Although, she's got herself completely worked up about gay rights in China. Did you know that homosexuality was only legalized there in 1997? But the thing that really upsets her is that China won't allow gay couples, there or abroad, to adopt Chinese babies.'

'Well, if anyone can persuade the People's Republic of China to change their policy, I'm sure it's Mrs Wu. Oh, it's all so wonderful,' said Monica, realizing that, possibly for the first time, she was nothing but genuinely pleased to hear news of another wedding. She waited to feel the familiar gnawing sense of envy, but it didn't come. Hazard came over and sat down on her other side.

'You look happy,' he said.

'I am,' she replied, wishing she could share the news, but Monica prided herself on being good with secrets. 'It feels like everything's coming together.'

'You know, this is the first party I've been to since I was a child when I haven't felt the need to get off my face. Even back then I'd overdose on Smarties and Coca-Cola. Isn't that amazing?'

'It is, Hazard. *You* are amazing. Oh, I have something I need to give to Riley. I'll be right back.'

She walked over to Riley, who was surrounded by a group of his Australian friends, including Brett, who was going with him to Amsterdam in a few days' time.

'Riley, can I have a quick chat?' she asked. Riley immediately disentangled himself from the crowd and followed her to a quiet spot, on the edge of the party.

'I've been wanting to say thank you. For what you wrote in the book about me. About how I'd make a great mother. I can't tell you how much that means to me, even if I never get the opportunity to see if you were right.'

'I'd forgotten I'd written that, even though it's absolutely true,' he said, with a smile.

'I have something for you,' she said, reaching into her bag and pulling out an oddly shaped parcel, wrapped in paper dotted with holly and ivy. 'I bought this for you at Christmas, but with all the excitement of Hazard's arrival and the flying figgy pudding, I never gave it to you. Today feels like the right time for you to have it.'

Riley took the parcel and tore it open, with all the genuine excitement of a five-year-old.

'Monica, it's beautiful!' he said, turning it over in his hands. It was a perfectly engineered trowel, with *Riley* engraved on the handle.

'It's so you can garden wherever you are,' she said.

'Thank you. I love it. I'll think of you, *all* of you,' he corrected, quickly, 'whenever I use it. Please can we stay in touch? In any case, I want to find out what happens with you and Hazard,' he said.

'Is it that obvious?' asked Monica, secretly rather thrilled that it was. 'Do you mind?'

'You know, I did at first. Just a bit,' replied Riley, 'but I love you both, so now that I've come round to the idea I couldn't be happier.' Monica wondered how Riley could be so generous. In his place, she'd have been seething and sticking pins into wax effigies. And he did look just a little sad, behind the effusive smiles. Or perhaps she was imagining it.

'Riley, you really are one of the nicest people I've ever met,' she said, giving him a hug that he held for just a beat too long. 'I'll miss you. We all will.'

'Hazard will make a great dad too, you know,' said Riley.

'Do you think so? He's not so sure. He doesn't entirely trust himself yet,' said Monica, realizing as she said it how little it mattered to her now.

'Well, just get him to ask the kids at Mummy's Little Helper if he'd make a good father. They'll convince him!' said Riley.

'You know, I might just do that,' said Monica.

'Everyone, I have an announcement to make,' said Julian, using a ladle to bang on the side of the bin filled with Pimm's. 'When Mary left, she left behind something very special. No, I don't mean me.' He paused for the laughter, like a West End performer working his audience. 'She left her viola. I'm hoping she'll play it for us now. Mary?' And he handed her the viola, which he must have hidden in one of his bags.

'Gosh, I haven't played for years. Hello, my old friend. I'll give it a go,' said Mary, turning the instrument over in her hands, getting used to the feel and weight of it again. Carefully, she tuned each of the strings, then she started to play, slowly and cautiously at first, then exuberantly, playing a wild Irish jig. A crowd formed around them. Families, on their way home after feeding the swans, stopping to see who was making music with such flair and passion.

Monica walked over to Julian, and sat down on the grass next to his deckchair, scratching Keith, his ever-present shadow, behind the ears.

'I've been wanting to tell you, Monica, that I'm so pleased about you and Hazard,' said Julian. 'I'd like to take just a little bit of credit for that, if you don't mind?'

'Of course you can, Julian. After all, if it wasn't for your notebook, I'd never have talked to him again after the first time we bumped into each other. Literally,' said Monica.

'Don't let it go, will you, Monica? Don't make the mistakes I did.' He looked over at Mary and Anthony, with an expression that managed to flit between happiness and sorrow.

'You don't think Hazard's just a little too much like you, Julian, do you?' asked Monica tentatively, hoping he wouldn't take offence. Julian laughed.

'Oh no, don't worry. Hazard's far nicer, and less stupid, than me. And you're far stronger than Mary was back then. Yours is going to be a very different love story, with a very different ending. Anyhow, don't you worry, I've had a little chat with him. A sort of fatherly *pep talk*.' Monica was both horrified and intrigued by this thought. How she wished she'd been a fly on the wall for that one.

'I have something for you, Julian,' she said.

'Darling girl, you've given me a present already,' he replied, gesturing to the paisley silk cravat he had tied jauntily around his neck.

'It's not another present, it's just something coming home,' she said, passing him a pale-green notebook with three words on the front cover: *The Authenticity Project*. It was looking a little battered after all its travels. 'I know you told Mary you couldn't keep it, because you hadn't been *authentic*, but now you are, and you should have it. You're where it started, and you should be where it ends.'

'Ah, my notebook. Welcome back. What an adventure you've been on,' he said, placing the book gently in his lap and stroking it, like a cat. 'Who gave it this smart, plastic cover?' he asked. Then, seeing Monica grin, 'Oh, how silly of me. I shouldn't have to ask.'

Mary was playing a Simon and Garfunkel song that everyone was singing along to. Bunty, who was sitting with Alice and Lizzie, stood up and clapped, then, noticing that she wasn't holding on to anything, looked shocked and fell over. Where was Max? Monica wondered.

It was getting darker. The sunbathers and dog walkers had all gone, and the midges had come out to feed. Monica had hailed some black cabs to help them take the picnic remains, glasses and rugs back to the café. Julian watched them pack everything up and start walking over towards the road.

'Come on, Julian!' said Monica.

'You folks go ahead,' said Julian. 'I'd just like five minutes by myself. I'll follow on.'

'Are you sure?' Monica asked him, not wanting to leave him alone. Julian was, she realized, suddenly looking every day of his real age. Perhaps that was just the effect of the falling dusk, the dark filling in all of his creases.

'Yes, honestly. I'd like some time to reflect,' he said.

Hazard held his hand out from the back of the taxi, helping Monica to climb in. In that gesture, Monica realized, was everything she wanted in life. She looked back at Julian, sitting in his deckchair, Keith's head resting on his lap. He gave her a wave, still holding the book in his hand. For all his idiosyncrasies and imperfections, he really was the most extraordinary person Monica had ever met.

Of all the cafés in all the world, she was terribly grateful he'd chosen hers.

Julian

Julian watched the taxis disappear with a sense of contentment. He realized that, for the first time in as long as he could remember, he liked himself. It was a good feeling. He reached down and patted Keith's head.

'It's just you and me now, old boy,' he said.

But it wasn't just them. He watched as several people approached, from different directions, carrying deckchairs, picnic blankets, musical instruments. Didn't they know the party was over?

Julian thought about standing up, walking over and telling them it was time to go home, but he couldn't make his muscles cooperate. He was very tired.

The light was so low now that it took him a while to make out any of the faces of the new revellers, but as they got closer he saw that they weren't strangers at all, but old friends. His fine art teacher from the Slade. The owner of the gallery in Conduit Street. Even a friend from school he'd not seen since they were teenagers, middle-aged now, but with the same unmistakeable red hair and cheeky grin.

Julian smiled over at them all. Then he saw, skirting around the Round Pond, his brother. No crutches, no wheelchair, but walking. His brother waved to him, in a fluid, controlled motion that Julian had not seen him use since he was in his twenties.

As the outlines of his friends and family become more distinct, the details around them – the trees, the grass, the pond and the bandstand – fell away.

Julian felt a pang of nostalgia so deep that it was like a knife in his chest.

He waited for the pain to subside, but it didn't. It spread out, working its way to the tips of his fingers and soles of his feet, until Julian couldn't feel his body at all, just the sensation of pain. The pain morphed into light – bright and blinding, then into the taste of iron, then into sound. A piercing shriek, which muted into a buzz, and then nothing. Nothing at all.

Epilogue

Dave

Dave was rather sad his working day was coming to an end. Usually he was desperate to lock up the park and get to the pub, but today he'd been sharing his shift with Salima, one of the new trainees, and time had passed too quickly as he'd spent the whole shift trying to pluck up the courage to ask her to go to the movies with him. It was nearly dark. He was running out of opportunity.

'Dave, stop!' said Salima, making him jump. 'Isn't that someone sitting in a deck chair over there?' He looked over at where she was pointing, towards the bandstand.

'I think you're right. You'll discover there's always one! You wait here, I'll go over and turf them out. Don't want anyone getting locked in for the night. Watch how I do it – polite but firm, that's the trick.' He pulled the car over into a parking bay and turned off the engine. 'Won't be long.'

He walked over towards the man sitting in the deckchair, trying to stride in a way that looked strong and manly, as he was aware of Salima's eyes on his back. As he approached, he realized that his renegade was rather old. And asleep. An ancient, scruffy terrier sat beside him like a sentry, his eyes unblinking, and misty with cataracts. Perhaps it would be a good idea to offer him and his dog a lift home, presuming he lived close by. That would give him more time with Salima, and make him look kind – which he was, obviously.

The man was smiling in his sleep. Dave wondered what he was dreaming about. Something nice, by the look of things.

'Hello!' he said. 'Sorry to wake you up, but it's time to go home.' He put his hand on the man's arm and shook it a little, to rouse him. Something didn't feel right. The man's head dropped to one side in a way that looked – lifeless.

Dave picked up his cold hand and felt his wrist for a pulse. Nothing. And no sign of any breathing. Dave had never seen a dead body before, let alone touched one. He took out his phone with slightly shaking hands and began to dial 999.

Then he noticed that the man was holding something in his other hand. A notebook. Cautiously, Dave prised it out of his fingers. Maybe it was important. His next of kin would want it. He looked down at the cover. On it were three words, written in beautiful italics: *The Authenticity Project*. Dave put it carefully in his inside jacket pocket.

ACKNOWLEDGEMENTS

The Authenticity Project is a very personal story for me. Five years ago, I was – like Alice – living a seemingly perfect life, and yet the truth was very different. Like Hazard, I was an addict. My addiction was high-priced, good-quality wine (because if the bottle costs enough, you're a connoisseur, not a lush, right?). After many failed attempts to quit, I decided – like Julian – to tell my truth to the world, and started writing a blog about my battle to quit booze, which turned into a book: *The Sober Diaries.*

What I discovered is that telling the truth about your life really can work magic, and change the lives of many other people for the better. So, my first thank you is to all the people who read my blog and my memoir and took the time to contact me and tell me what a difference that honesty made to them. This novel was inspired by you.

I was rather terrified about moving from non-fiction to fiction, and not at all sure that I could do it, so I enrolled on the Curtis Brown Creative three-month novel-writing course. I recently looked back at my application, and the three-thousand-word excerpt of *The Book That Changed Lives* (as it was called back then). It was truly dreadful, so I have a huge amount to thank my course tutor, Charlotte Mendelson, for, as well as Anna Davis and Norah Perkins.

One of the best things about the CBC course was the fabulous group of writers I met there. After the course ended we formed 'Write Club', and we still meet regularly to share each other's work over beers (for them, and water for me), and to laugh and cry about the rollercoaster that is the life of a writer. Thank you to all of you – Alex, Clive, Emilie, Emily, Jenny, Jenni, Geoffrey, Natasha, Kate, Kiare, Maggie and Richard. And a special thanks to Max Dunne and Zoe Miller, who were the first two people to read my terrible first draft.

Thanks also to my other first readers: Lucy Schoonhoven, who advised me on Australians and gardening, and has a mean eye for a typo or a repetition; Rosie Copeland, for her invaluable advice about art and artists; Louise Keller for her knowledge of mental health issues; and Diana Gardner-Brown for her perceptiveness.

My two dog-walking buddies – Caroline Firth and Annabel Abbs – kept me sane and provided a sounding board through the last few years of writing, submitting and editing. I remember when I first met Annabel, rather nervously telling her that I wanted to write a book. She replied that she was writing one herself, *The Joyce Girl*. I still can't quite believe that we've now both been published. I've loved travelling this road with you, my friend.

My next thank you goes to my wonderful agent – Hayley Steed – for loving my book from the beginning, for helping to make it so much better and for being a wonderful friend and mentor through the publishing process. Monica owes her obsession with colour-coding Excel spreadsheets to Hayley. A huge thanks to the phenomenon that is Madeleine Milburn for her sage advice and guiding hand, and to the amazing Alice Sutherland-Hawes for managing simultaneous auctions in multiple territories, and selling *The Authenticity Project* to a whopping twenty-eight markets in the fortnight leading up to the Frankfurt Book Fair. The Madeleine Milburn Agency is an extraordinary power-house, but it's also a family, and everyone has made me feel so welcome and has helped make this book as good as it can be. Thanks to you all.

And next, Sally Williamson, my brilliant editor. I have the huge honour of being Sally's first signing at Transworld. She has championed this book from the very beginning, and has a huge talent for pinpointing exactly what needed to be done to make it better. Thank you so much Sally, for seeing the things I couldn't see, and for being so supportive through the editing process. Working with you has been a masterclass, and I am hugely grateful.

Thanks also to Vicky Palmer and Becky Short, my fabulous marketing and PR duo. If you heard about this book before stumbling across it in a book store, that will be down to their genius.

I've saved the best until last – my family. My husband John, for always believing in me, even when I didn't believe in myself, and for being so insightful and honest about my writing, even when it led to me throwing a manuscript at his head. My wonderful parents, who couldn't be more proud or supportive. This book is dedicated to my dad, who is the best writer I know, and whose column in the parish magazine is legendary. Dad read not just my first draft, but each one of the following nine, providing detailed feedback at every stage. Just to warn you, if you're planning to leave a less than favourable review on Amazon, he will be responding! And to my three children – Eliza, Charlie and Matilda – my biggest fans and my inspiration, every day.

One thing I've been amazed by since working with the publishing industry is how many people it takes to publish a book. Not just all the people I've mentioned above, but so many others, who have added their talent, their enthusiasm, their wisdom, their time and their energy into getting this book into your hands. The cover designers, the copy editor, the proofreaders, the sales people, and many more. The reason I chose Transworld as a publisher – apart from their unparalleled reputation and the fact that they publish Jilly Cooper and employ Sally Williamson – was because from the moment I walked in, everyone from the receptionist to the CEO made me feel like one of their family. So here is a full credit list, of all of those people who have helped bring my story to you.

Thank you to all at Transworld who worked on the publication of *The Authenticity Project*.

Editorial
Sally Williamson
Katrina Whone
Viv Thompson
Josh Benn

Copy editor
Bella Bosworth

Proofreaders
Clare Hubbard
Nancy Webber

Marketing
Vicky Palmer
Lilly Cox
Shafah Hanif
Marie Goodwin
Leon Dufour

Sales
Tom Chicken
Deirdre O'Connell
Emily Harvey
Gary Harley
Hannah Welsh
Chris Wyatt
Bethan Moore
Natasha Photiou

Publicity
Becky Short

Production
Cat Hillerton
Phil Evans

Audio
Alice Twomey

Design
Jo Thomson
Beci Kelly

Operations
Mariana De Barros Van
   Hombeeck

Finance
Christine Coorey
Anshu Kochar

Contracts
Rebecca Smith
Kiranjit Halaith

Reception
Kathy Webb
Jean Kriek

ABOUT THE AUTHOR

Clare Pooley graduated from Newnham College, Cambridge, and spent twenty years in the heady world of advertising before becoming a full-time mum. Her blog *Mummy was a Secret Drinker*, written under the pseudonym Sober Mummy, has had over two million hits. Her memoir, *The Sober Diaries*, was published in 2017 to critical acclaim and she recently gave a TEDx talk entitled 'Making Sober Less Shameful'.

The Authenticity Project is Clare's debut novel and is inspired by her time in advertising, a world where the line between authenticity and fiction is constantly blurred, and by her own experience of exposing the rather grubby truth about her seemingly perfect life in her memoir.

Clare writes from her kitchen table in Fulham, London, where she lives with her long-suffering husband, three children, dog and African pygmy hedgehog.